THE CO

Elizabeth Harring... ...Wight in 1957. At ...London where she worked for a magazine editor before moving into public relations work.

She now lives with her family in Herefordshire where she is concentrating on her writing career. *The Corporate Wife* is her first novel.

'A fast-paced, warm-hearted romantic thriller: the sex and skulduggery will keep you racing from start to finish.' SALLY BEAUMAN

ELIZABETH HARRINGTON

The Corporate Wife

Fontana
An Imprint of HarperCollins*Publishers*

Fontana
An Imprint of HarperCollins*Publishers*
77–85 Fulham Palace Road,
Hammersmith, London W6 8JB

A Fontana Original 1992
9 8 7 6 5 4 3 2 1

A catalogue record for this book
is available from the British Library

ISBN 0 00 647121 8

Set in Palatino

Printed in Great Britain by
HarperCollins*Manufacturing* Glasgow

Prologue

The carousel started to move. The rubber webbing clicked along the rickety mechanism, pulling all the baggage through the plastic slatted curtain. Most of the passengers rushed to the edge, waiting impatiently for their suitcases to materialize. Others, cooler than the rest, knew that it was just as easy to see what was coming through, from a rear viewpoint, as to hang awkwardly over the conveyors, and that nothing could be done to speed it along.

A man stood browsing through a copy of *Newsweek*, seemingly oblivious to those around him. He had a shock of thick, russet-coloured hair which, together with his height, made him more prominent than he would have liked. While perusing the headlines, occasionally he would lift his deep copper eyes and glance surreptitiously at the back of one of the other passengers.

The first of two red Samsonite suitcases appeared through the hole in the wall and rattled on to the conveyor belt. The man in the light raincoat, whom the redhead had been watching, took a half-step forward and craned his neck towards the case. Both men were now focusing hard on the single suitcase, trying to see a small piece of airline tape, placed strategically on one of the sides. From its upright position it was hard to see but then another piece of luggage fell against it, causing it to topple forward. There was no tape visible.

The man turned and looked around agitatedly. It had been a long and arduous trip from Karachi and he'd be bloody glad when it was all over. Suddenly an identical case tumbled on to the belt. Immediately the man in the mac picked it off and without so much as a glance at the redhead walked off in the direction of the Green Channel – 'Nothing to Declare'.

So far so good, but the tall man still didn't feel too happy about something. He looked around, shifting his weight, casting eyes around the vast baggage reclaim area. The first of the two suitcases was on its way through the Green Channel together with the man in the raincoat. The man's ticket said he had joined the flight in Paris, and that's what mattered. For when he carried through the case that had come all the way from Karachi the customs men would assume his luggage had also come from Paris. The real beauty of the scam was that should he be stopped, and the stuff found, he could just say he had picked up the wrong case and prove it by showing his tickets didn't match with those on the suitcase.

Unbeknown to them both, higher up, from where the galleried balcony skirted the top of the luggage hall, two more men had been watching the same suitcases. They wore dark sombre suits, and grim faces. As soon as the first suitcase had been lifted, one of them spoke quickly into a small radio. Then he spoke to his colleague and walked briskly away.

Just as they separated the redhead caught sight of them. Something was definitely wrong. It just didn't feel right. His stomach felt raw with nerves and fatigue. Getting through JFK was always a bloody nightmare. He swallowed hard, trying to wet his dry tongue. These runs never got any easier. Experience didn't ease the tension, it just shortened the odds against getting caught.

Then he saw something that made him want to choke with fear. The man who had picked up the first Samsonite walked back to the luggage carousel, relief breaking his frown when he saw the remaining suitcase. He turned to the three uniformed men who shadowed him and smiled. They shook their heads and said

6

something to him, but it was too far away to catch. They collected the second suitcase.

The tall red-haired man had seen enough. He turned on his heel and marched quickly through the Green Channel, carrying only the copy of *Newsweek* with him. Out of the corner of his eye he saw the first suitcase already opened, a small cut made in the inside of the lid. He increased his pace, striding through the seemingly endless length of the customs hall, gulping down air, already wondering just what the hell he was going to tell his so-called friends about the latest consignment. Three million dollars' worth of stuff sitting on a trestle table, while his partner picked up a suitcase full of clothes. Three million dollars which had suddenly become State property, found in an unclaimed suitcase.

Chapter One

The light of the fading September sun cast soft shadows around Charlotte's bedroom. A large square of luminous warmth fell across the carpet and rose to cover half the bed. Charlotte lay stretched out, luxuriating in the sun-heat on her naked body. She curled her toes and sighed. A feline contentment. What a pity she had to move. She turned on to her side, resting her head on the crook of her arm. The taxi was coming in half an hour and she must start getting ready. She wanted to do the evening, and William, justice.

She rolled out of the sunlight and her skin chilled. She pulled the huge white towel around her with a well-practised twisting of the fabric to hold it in place and went to her dressing table. She felt oddly guilty about the amount of time she was able to spend getting herself ready for William's important dinners. But that was just what he had wanted – a wife who didn't always arrive an hour or so late for one of his important client functions; a wife who hadn't just thrown on some party frock in a ladies' loo, and a wife who didn't have a tendency to detach herself mentally from those around her when she should have been making polite conversation because she was too preoccupied with her own deadlines. He wanted one hundred per cent support from his woman.

Charlotte grimaced at the girl facing her. The girl grimaced back. She stared into her own eyes. Green saucers with dancing blue flecks watched her critically. Dark lashes framed narrowing eyes considering the contours of their owner's face, a face made shiny, squeaky clean from a long hot bath. There was a splattering of freckles over a smallish nose. Two fine furrows travelled down to an even mouth which a more objective critic would say was not overly generous, but sensuous, and good natured – with tell-tale laughter lines deepening at the corners. A firm chin formed the base of the oval and carried her gaze back along a straight jawline to perfectly pink ears, on up to a wide, smooth brow. The only imperfection was a small white scar, running pencil thin from the edge of her left brow to her temple. The sun played tricks in her hair, changing the light in the tawny mass: hazy copper switched to honey blonde, honey to ash, and brown to auburn. It fell in an untamed wildness to her shoulders.

Charlotte began her 'face' routine. The subtle mask kept in tempting tubes and bottles with gilt lettering quickly transformed the scrubbed beach girl into a sultry, city sophisticate. The golden storm of hair was captured in a grown-up knot with concealed pins and silvered combs making her appear much older, and much more worldly, than she felt inwardly. Role playing she knew well: dressing up in mother's dresses and high heels; best suits for interviews, best dresses for best behaviour. Well, she certainly intended to play the game for William tonight!

She stood back from her cheval-glass to survey the effect. A familiar stranger pirouetted and posed in the mirror, a grown-up woman with the world at her feet. William was certainly in for a surprise. The hair seemed to give a kind of arrogance, a haughtiness alien to Charlotte's nature. But the dress . . . should she *really* not wear anything under it? The girl in the shop had sneered at the very thought of underwear. Charlotte just hoped to God that she didn't get her period or suddenly find herself incontinent due to the strain of the evening ahead. But sophisticated knickerless ladies don't worry about things like that!

Five more minutes . . . just time for a quick gulp of

Dutch courage. The wine tasted good and cold. Condensation formed wet circles on her fingertips as she hurriedly knocked it back. The doorbell. 'OK Charlie,' she said encouragingly to herself, 'Give 'em all you've got.'

The black cab rumbled its bronchial rattle. The driver, elbow on the window, already back in his seat, drummed his fingers on the wheel. Sliding the privacy window across he shouted back to her: 'Where to, lady?'

'Langan's, please,' Charlotte answered. She grinned into his rearview mirror and leaned forward, sliding the glass back into place. She heard him sniff. No doubt he had been looking forward to a moan – about the weather, or the traffic . . . He might think her unfriendly but that was too bad. She needed time for her own thoughts. The dinner was very important to William. A celebration, the culmination of months of negotiation. He had 'made it', as they say. He was merging with one of the 'big boys'. Never again would he have to worry about searching for blue-chip PR accounts or sweat over whether the existing ones would renew their annual contracts. From now on clients would be knocking on his door and he'd be free to choose which ones could enter, and which ones could turn away. For the last few months he had eaten, slept, talked agencies, clients, fees, budgets, offices. He had uttered streams of incomprehensible initials – ABM, JWT, CDP, Y & R, O & M. Charlotte was lucky that she at least had some knowledge of the industry. She knew the jargon. She understood the psychology behind it. After all, she too was a media person. But she found the public relations/advertising associates that William dallied with to be almost without exception self-absorbed, egocentric, acquisitive and intolerant of anyone not bleeding off the same mega-buck host as themselves.

Still William had every reason to celebrate. After all, nearly fifteen years of his life had been spent building up the business so that just such a merger, or takeover, would eventually happen. And William was 'going to bed' with one of the hottest of the lot. The legendary Daniel Cornwallis.

Charlotte glanced back at the disappearing sight of their home, a sort of temple to middle-class yuppiedom. The four-storeyed façade sat tastefully amongst a terrace of similarly appointed pastel-rendered houses. The row climbed to the summit of Richmond Hill. From the top floors you could see over the tree-tops to where the Thames cut its way through the flat meadows of its plain towards Twickenham and beyond.

The merger would not make them immediately wealthier – they were already seriously well-off – but it would add considerably to William's own private sense of esteem. He had built up his company from nothing, starting with just one, tenuous, client and now, fifteen years later, he had more than a hundred.

William liked to make money. Loads of it. His first signs of acumen had appeared when he was a mere sixteen-year-old. When the scandal of the house master's little black book broke through the school, the parents, governors and staff decided it was politic to hush up the whole issue. William, with ice-cold audacity, picked up the phone to the gutter press and told them with relish how a certain member of this illustrious establishment kept a log of beatings meted out to unfortunate boys. Details included such perversities as position, number of strokes and reaction. The revelations did nothing to help the reputation of his school, but they did plenty for William's future ambitions. Publicly his father admonished him; privately he'd been excessively proud of his son's entrepreneurialism. William had the nose for a story.

Journalism beckoned for a short while; with a spell on a trade magazine, followed by an even shorter stint on the *Mail* diary – a seemingly natural position for him, with his polished upper-middle-class manners and aspirations;

11

and his clean good looks which gave him an entrée to all the best parties. It was just that he realized he was not going to keep himself in the style he'd like to be accustomed to through a lowly journalist's pay.

A number of public relations people had brushed shoulders with him during his time in Fleet Street and William observed that this was an easier way of making money and, more importantly, bigger money. Using his grand social contacts he started off promoting exclusive holidays to the extremely well heeled and then graduated to promoting a glossy champagne label and a French perfumier. Within five years he had built up a fee income of £1 million, with a staff of twenty-five housed in prestigious offices in Berkeley Square. And six years later he met Charlotte. Back in those halcyon days when she too had a career. Back in the days when it never occurred to her that she could lose her identity . . .

He had swept into her life with the subtlety of an express train. They had been the classic perfect couple. A match made in heaven. Oh, she'd certainly given him a run for his money at the beginning. After all, she had serious career commitments to think about. But William had been desperate to have her and bit by bit he had worn down the edges of her hesitance to make her realize she could no longer live without him.

She laughed at herself, almost bitterly. Here she was three years later – such a short time – dressed up to the nines, determined that tonight William would remember he still had a reason to go home other than to collect a clean shirt.

'It won't do, Charlotte, really it won't!' She could still hear William's voice, cold and angry and bitter. 'You knew how important this was to me . . .' Her mind drifted back to that terrible quarrel. They had been standing in the rear of one of the private boxes at the Royal Albert Hall, hired by William to entertain one of his most prestigious clients. The remnants of the delicious cold buffet were being cleared away for the show had already begun. Charlotte had just arrived. She stood quietly, squaring up to William while he ranted on in his vicious whisper. 'It's really no good at all. I simply must have a wife that I can rely on. I mean to say, Charlotte, the whole point of this evening was that the wives could all meet. Don't you understand how stupid you make me feel? Haven't you any sensitivity?'

'But William, the magazine . . . we had to put it to bed today, and the woman the main article was about just dropped dead. I had to write another piece myself. I had no alternative – there'd have been no next issue if I hadn't stayed on.'

He had regarded her as if she'd gone stark raving bonkers. 'Look, Charlotte, I'm sorry to have to spell this out to you, but important as I know your job is to you, there has to be a clear definition of whose career is to take primary place. And I'm surprised to have to remind you that it's mine!' As they joined the others he was managing to smile, in order not to spoil the evening for his precious clients. But Charlotte sat reeling from the vehemence of his words.

Was that really how it was – all the time she had spent as editor of *Today's Woman?* Even though she had fulfilled her brief of turning an anachronistic thirty-year-old knitting companion into a best-selling glossy monthly magazine her career should still come second?

The stupid thing was that she had wanted to be what he wanted, simply because she was in love with him. It didn't please her that she always arrived late to everything, or that William ended up on a diet of Marks & Spencer's ready-meals instead of lovingly prepared food. It didn't please her that she seemed to spend her whole life feeling so bloody tired. And what's more she couldn't seem to please anybody else. She always seemed to be making excuses for herself, either to the magazine staff, or to William.

The magazine wanted a fully dedicated, high-flying leader, prepared to sweat blood. William wanted a cook, laundress, and housekeeper – oh, and whore on occasions – to look after him and perform the wifely duties. Charlotte, of course, wanted to be best at both worlds, and the reality was that it was just plain impossible. And this was before they had children . . .

Children. Now there was the nub of the matter. Not that she was paranoid or anything, but a whole year of giving up work to please William and hoping that the wifely role might pull the motherly trigger hadn't amounted to anything at all. Still no baby had arrived with which to justify her domestic existence, and on top of all that William seemed to find her about as stimulating as a pair of old socks.

She felt she had turned into a kind of staging post. More often than not when she cooked for William he had already eaten. He came home when he needed a bath. And of course to sleep.

As the deal with Cornwallis approached they'd given up seeing friends at weekends. He always had a meeting. Evenings at the theatre were replaced by late nights in the office. Raucous Sunday lunches had become serious affairs spent poring over accounts, contracts, cash-flow projections, expense accounts. Charlotte felt almost as if she had died and no one had told her. Had her hair turned green William would not have been any the wiser.

She was tired of being an invisible shade. The deal was signed. The negotiations were final. Now it was time to show William that she was still a hot-blooded, sexy woman who needed a bit of attention every so often. And tonight was the night . . .

She delved into the iridescent purse bag she was carrying and found the small but expensive bottle of Eternity. She dabbed the perfume on to her pulse points and the gap in her dress that showed a glimpse of cleavage. She caught the cabbie grinning into his rearview mirror, winking his approval. Then they slowed to a halt outside the imposing glass doors of Langan's. She paid the driver.

'Have a nice evenin', love.'

'Thanks,' she smiled, and resolutely squared her shoulders as the doors swung open in front of her.

'Mrs de Sallis . . .' The manager rushed forward to greet her. He kissed her on both cheeks and then again on her left cheek, in the Parisian style reserved for those who merited an extra fondness. He collected her discarded jacket and held his hands out expressively. 'May I say . . . you look as beautiful as ever.'

'Thank you,' she smiled.

'Your husband is already in the bar with his guests.'

Charlotte took a deep breath and followed the directions of his glance into the softly lit brown and cream interior of Langan's Brasserie. Small, elegantly upholstered gilt chairs were arranged around gleaming mahogany tables. Concealed tiny downlights made the atmosphere intimate and relaxed. It was easy to feel yourself slowing down when you came here. You could spend a long time cosily hidden in one of the corners, talking and swapping gossip, often reluctant to move when it was time to eat.

At first she couldn't see them, her eyes unaccustomed to the gentle gloom. Then she heard a deep but unmistakably feminine laugh and a 'William . . . how could you!'

The woman tossed her burnished copper blanket of hair back, her slim crimson-tipped fingers tucking it behind ears adorned with ostentatiously large diamonds. Too large to be real, thought Charlotte fleetingly. She had heard about Daniel Cornwallis's plaything. Her name was Valentine. She was the latest thing to hit the most expensive lenses in town – the new face of the nineties. Superlatively beautiful and inordinately spoilt. Valentine glanced quickly at Charlotte and then turned her attention back to William, who was sitting with his back towards Charlotte. She gave no acknowledgement of having seen her.

The third member of the party, on the other hand, gave every impression that he had noted her arrival. He looked at Charlotte steadily, with an obvious, almost impudent appraisal. Charlotte's tall, lithe body had somehow been poured into the silver sheath which clung to every mound and curve like a second skin. Her graceful tanned shoulders were bare above two arcs which rose over her breasts. The effect was simple but stunning and she saw that he knew the only thing between her and the dress was flesh. His eyes below raised brows mirrored the amusement which flickered across his lips. Daniel Cornwallis looked like a man who had found exactly what he wanted on the menu and was relishing the forthcoming feast. Charlotte bristled.

He stood up. William turned and his mouth dropped open when he saw his wife. Daniel was speaking. 'My, my, William. No wonder you've kept us apart for so long. You must be Charlotte. I'm delighted to meet you.' He reached for her hand and pulled it to his mouth. His lips were warm against her cool flesh. His eyes, a deep, deep blue, burned into her own. She felt a strange sensation akin to a kick in her belly as his brazen masculinity assaulted her senses. He was wearing an immaculately tailored city suit, but it did nothing to camouflage the animal sexuality that was threatening to overturn her equilibrium. His fingers pressed into her hand and she felt herself pull away, retreating towards the safety of William's familiar embrace.

William looked as if he had had cold water poured over him. He seemed torn between the desire to take off his jacket and cover his wife's body and the wish to sit back and enjoy the view. Charlotte threw him a look, almost daring him to say anything about her appearance. But then he saw Daniel's appreciative appraisal of his wife

16

and his look changed to one of pride. She was worth coveting, Charlotte thought. And with the competitiveness born of an English public school education, that meant she was worth having.

William embraced her more thoroughly than he had done in several months. Then he turned back to the redhead. 'Charlotte, let me introduce you to Valentine.'

The lovely Valentine was clearly unamused at no longer being the centre of attention, however temporarily. Her petulant mouth twitched into a full and charming smile, bordered with an unmistakable edge of coolness. 'Hello Charlotte,' she drawled. 'I've been dying to meet you. William has told me so much about you . . .' Her voice was deep and husky. 'I already know him so well.' She touched William's arm lightly. Childishly possessive.

'I've been dying to meet you too, Valentine. Your photographs hardly do you justice. You're even prettier in the flesh.' The spoiled child-woman's face twisted into a smugly satisfied beam. Valentine's position was affirmed. Her beauty reinforced. To her this was a victory over Charlotte.

As William poured her a dry martini from the jug already on the table, Charlotte pondered how Valentine had had the opportunity to get to know her husband 'so well'. Maybe his business meetings had breaks for a little light relief occasionally. Charlotte took two or three surreptitious gulps of the bitter icy liquid, feeling its paradoxical warmth beginning to seep into her blood. Valentine's strange copper eyes met her own. They seemed to be lit by an orange flame-light, tilting, cat-like, under the soft shadows of the room, almost pagan. Her gaze didn't falter as Charlotte studied her. They were two adversaries assessing the competition. Finally Charlotte tore her eyes away. William was talking to her.

'Now that everything's settled, we're discussing the move. As you know, Charlotte, de Sallis will be moving into Dan's offices. There's quite a bit of administration to tie up. It's going to be chaos of course. Office moves always are . . . But we're going to try and do it by the beginning of November, otherwise we'll be hitting Christmas. Luckily you've got the space, Dan, or we'd find everything much more awkward. Presumably you've given that design company their marching orders?'

'They'll be out, don't you worry. I bought them. As our design team were getting more and more overloaded we were putting so much work their way it seemed the only practical thing to do. I'm moving them to Gray's Inn Road and if they keep expanding the way they are at the moment we might give them another branch to play with. That three thousand square feet should easily be enough for your twenty-five staff. Naturally you'll be up with me in the fifth-floor executive suite.'

He was interrupted by the arrival of the menus. Charlotte studied the three-page gastronome's dream before her. She'd eaten nothing bar a tub of Greek yoghurt all day, but, strangely, her appetite was dwindling. She scanned the printed hand-scrawl searching for something light, deciding on the cucumber mousse and the salmon with hollandaise sauce.

Valentine looked up from her menu. 'Spinach soufflé for me, and I think the plain sole with acres of green salad.'

Charlotte felt almost sorry for her. It was all very well being a top model, but all the good things in life had to be put aside. She knew only too well how an extra pound could ruin a whole day's shoot. If the clothes didn't fit perfectly, they sure as hell wouldn't photograph perfectly. Valentine had to be an exact size eight or she was out of a job. And if one little spot should rear its ugly head on her immaculate visage she was done for.

Suddenly Valentine leapt to her feet. 'Cassie!' she cried. Then, as an afterthought, 'Excuse me . . .' Long, black, witch-like legs stepped over Charlotte's as Charlotte came face to bumper with Valentine's rear. Fine black jersey stretched over her stick-thin body as she clambered off to make 'darling . . .' noises with her crony.

'Now all the legal side of it's tied up we'll have to start thinking about what sort of a splash to make with the announcement, won't we, William?' Daniel continued. 'I'd say that's probably more your speciality than mine – statements to the rags and general PR. Have you got any thoughts yet?'

'Well, a few,' William said reticently, 'though I must admit I haven't had time to give much attention to it. There'll be no problem getting *Campaign* and *Marketing Week* and the other main industry mags to cover it. There'll be more of a problem stopping them spilling the news before the main announcement. I'll probably offer them a company profile to keep them happy and to keep them to an embargo. We should be able to get a nice piece in the *FT* and maybe some of the other quality dailies.'

'I was thinking we ought to throw some kind of do,' Daniel interrupted. 'After all, William, I need to score a hit with your clients as much as you do with mine. Let's throw a big party at the agency and get them all well oiled so they'll go away patting themselves on the back for having involved themselves with such a nice pair of guys.' He took a satisfied gulp of martini.

William laughed. 'I wish getting business was as easy as that. But yes, it's a nice idea. Though if we do it, we'll have to get moving quickly. We need at least six to eight weeks which will bring us to . . . let's see . . .' he calculated, 'the end of October/beginning of November. And we need an organizer. Someone with a lot of flair for this sort of thing. Normally I'd put Anna Goodman on to it, but she's tied up with preparing the in-house magazine for Lejeune's. I could ask Kate, my secretary, but she'd probably resign on the spot if I heaped any

19

more on her plate right now.' He shook his head doubtfully, then he grinned over at Charlotte who was busy tracing lines on the outside of her glass. 'Darling,' he said, 'why don't you do it?' She raised her eyebrows at him, then narrowed her eyes, a silent signal for him to shut up. 'You'd be perfect, I know. You said how bored you've been lately, how you need something to get your teeth into. And it would be a tremendous help.'

'No, William,' she said firmly. 'I couldn't possibly. Apart from anything else I don't want to tread on anyone's toes in the agency. Daniel, you must know someone who'd be willing to do it?' She couldn't for the life of her have explained why, but she had a very strong intuition that getting involved, however loosely, with Daniel Cornwallis was not a very bright thing to do. She also had a nasty suspicion he was damned well aware of her discomfort.

He grinned at her as he spoke. 'William. That, if I may say so, is one of your better ideas. Of course Charlotte shall organize it. Say "yes", Charlotte. You can have lots of fun spending our money. I just know you'll handle things beautifully. And just think, I'll have an opportunity to get to know you better.'

Charlotte was seething. How dare he assume that she'd be willing to just jump in and work for the pair of them? She wanted to wipe the stupid smirk off his face. And how dare William drop her in it? But she was too angry to speak. She'd have to deal with the matter later, privately, with him. She certainly did not intend to let Daniel see how cross she was. She gritted her teeth and smiled.

William said: 'That's settled then. Good. We'll talk about it later.'

You bet, thought Charlotte.

The waiter arrived to tell them their table was ready and Daniel stood to help Charlotte out of her chair. They collected Valentine on the way, and she linked her arm through William's and strode forward, leaving Charlotte following with Daniel's hand pressed firmly into the small of her back. She lengthened her stride and gave him a snarl of a smile. Why was this man getting to her so much?

The restaurant was buzzing. Voices engaged in lively conversations rose and fell, mixed with different shades of laughter. Glasses chinked and knives slid over embossed china. A few diners raised their eyes in well-bred, slightly veiled curiosity. The immaculate pale pink damask-covered table was half-hidden in an alcove. William followed Valentine to the far side, leaving Charlotte all too close to Daniel on the other. Valentine bounced down into her chair. The girl seemed to live life at speed, Charlotte thought. Her every move seemed exaggerated. She didn't just get up, or sit down, it was as if she was always making some sort of statement that she didn't want anyone to miss.

'I was so glad to see Cassie. We did this amazing shoot together.' She looked at Charlotte. 'I suppose you've heard of Miles Trent, the new photographer?' Charlotte nodded. 'What an imagination that guy has.' Valentine paused to light a very long cigarette and exhaled slowly through perfectly glossed scarlet lips. The smoke hit Charlotte full face and she waved at it conspicuously.

'He had us wearing skin-tight rubber. Masses of zips and chains. Then he made Cassie and I writhe all over each other. It was really quite a turn-on. God knows what the editor will say. But the fashion editor seemed to be quite happy with it. I hope they realize it's art, not smut . . . ' She took another drag on her cigarette and went on. 'Anyhow, Cassie and I got to know each other pretty well. Dan, you should have been there. Of course, if you're really nice to me I could ask for some proofs . . . hmmm, darling?'

Daniel looked as if he was only half-listening. 'No thanks, love. Rubber's really not my scene. Don't

21

worry though, I'm sure someone will appreciate it.'

Charlotte watched and listened with interest. She was learning a lot about this couple – not least the fact that they were hardly a couple. Next Valentine turned to William. 'How about you, William?' She lowered her voice so that it was huskier still. 'I bet you've got a secret fantasy somewhere. All men have at least one, in my experience.'

Charlotte felt sympathy for William. Valentine was obviously trying to wind him up in order to annoy Daniel.

'Well, Valentine, I'm really a man of simple tastes,' he laughed. 'As for wild fantasies, we Englishmen have them torn from us at a very early age. It's something to do with potty training, I believe.'

Charlotte giggled but Daniel roared with laughter. 'Well done, William. Though I'd hardly class our beautiful Charlotte as a "simple" taste.'

Valentine glowered at Charlotte and stubbed her cigarette out viciously. Oh dear, thought Charlotte. Here I am making an enemy of Valentine before I've hardly said two words to the girl. But she does ask for it. Her better nature was fighting against the rising temptation to put Valentine even more in her place. As usual manners won over menace. 'Tell me, Valentine,' Charlotte smiled charmingly, 'how did you two meet?'

Valentine looked up at Charlotte sullenly. Daniel interrupted, 'I was the poor defenceless fee-payer on a shoot I had no wish to be at – she made this huge play for me and I was putty in her hands . . .'

'Oh shut up, Dan,' Valentine said. 'You know very well it was absolutely the reverse. You begged me to have dinner with you and luckily for you I said yes. Must be at least four months ago, darling. A bit of a record for us both, isn't it?'

'You shouldn't have reminded me. Can you imagine – the tongues will have us married off soon. I'll have to

22

start playing the field again . . .' Valentine's orange eyes blazed at him. She moved her chair a fraction closer to William's. William looked embarrassed.

What a bastard!, Charlotte thought. Whatever Valentine's behaviour, Daniel had no right to be so poisonous to her. And he seemed to be oblivious, or just plain uncaring, about the effect he was having on her.

His thigh touched her own; she could feel the hard warmth of his body through her thin dress. She could not have said whether it was contrived or not, but suspected it probably was. Now he was studying her. His voice was low and intimate. 'What about you, Charlotte? William's been pretty reticent. What do you do when he's not hiding you away? Do you have some dark secret life . . . ?' His taunting, insinuating tone irritated her.

'I was a journalist,' she almost snapped the words out. 'Still am, actually. Just a bit of freelance stuff here and there.'

'Did you work on anything I'd have heard of?'

Valentine interrupted. 'Of course, Daniel. Didn't you know? Charlotte was editor of *Today's Woman* for three years. She was the bright spark who trebled its circulation . . . She made media history by relaunching the old title . . . In fact you're quite a star, aren't you, Charlotte?' Her voice was thick with sarcasm. Charlotte was silent.

'Really,' Daniel said, with considerable interest. 'I had no idea. Why didn't you tell me, William, you were closeting such a clever girl?'

William shrugged and smiled proudly. Valentine continued. 'Yes, Charlotte was queen of the editors while I was still touting my portfolio around the streets. Of course *Today's Woman* wouldn't use me. I hadn't got the right look for them.'

Charlotte groaned inwardly. So that was why Valentine carried the knife between her teeth. She'd been turned down. But it was hardly surprising. She was much too sexy for a magazine aimed at more mature women. Valentine was more *Cosmopolitan*'s style, all come-to-bed and watch me smoulder. Charlotte's readers didn't need sex to sell them merchandise. They were more interested in quality. But all she said was, 'Well, I'm relieved that it obviously hasn't had too detrimental an effect on your career, Valentine. You must be Europe's top model now, aren't you?'

'Oh yes. I think that's probably true.'

Daniel continued to gaze at her. Charlotte felt extremely unsettled by them both. And William seemed utterly unaware of Daniel's attentions. 'So why did you retire? If the magazine was going so well, it seems a strange thing to do, Charlotte,' Daniel persisted.

'I'd just had enough of it. It was taking over my life. I rarely saw William and the day I decided I wasn't enjoying myself any more was the day I decided to quit. That was a year ago. I keep my hand in, as I said, by doing the odd freelance article. That's enough for now.'

'Don't you find it awfully tedious, just sitting at home all day? I know I'd find it dreadfully boring. I have to be busy all the time.' Valentine heaved an exaggerated sigh. 'I suppose you'll soon be producing children? That's the natural progression, isn't it? I can just imagine you with a couple of little ones hanging round your legs. Though I'm not sure I can imagine William as a father. He's much too ambitious to be tied down, don't you think?'

Charlotte almost choked on her salmon as hot anger rose like bile in her throat. How dare this empty-headed overgrown beanpole speak to her like that? She looked over at William whose eyes were seemingly riveted to the duck on his plate, as he studiously and determinedly stripped the pink flesh.

Daniel, on the other hand, was clearly finding it all very entertaining and was waiting with interest for Charlotte's reply. 'Valentine, as I've just said, I do work, and I choose how to fill my time. Now that's a luxury that working girls like you are sadly unable to do.' She laid

24

heavy emphasis on the words. 'And yes, William is very ambitious. That's one of the things that first attracted me to him. There are an awful lot of successful family men who seem more than capable of combining their roles without feeling "tied down" by their children. I would imagine it's more a case of the mothers being tied down in any event, wouldn't you?' She was fighting to keep her cool. Unwittingly, Valentine had successfully hit right on her Achilles heel. She wanted more than anything to be pregnant. The house was ready, she was ready, but in two years of trying nothing had happened. She'd been for tests and time after time they came back the same: negative. There was simply nothing wrong with her reproductive system. But when she asked William to take the next logical course of action and get himself checked out he had flatly refused. Now looking across the table at Valentine she had the delicious urge to slit her throat.

At last William decided to come to her rescue. Pushing his duck reluctantly aside he said: 'Dan, why don't you tell us how you got to be chairman of Cornwallis? I know the story backwards, but I'm sure Charlotte would love to hear it.'

Daniel raised his hand in protest. 'Absolutely not, William. It's a very tedious story and I've no wish to bore the girls . . .'

Charlotte leaped at the chance of a change of subject. 'Oh, I would like to hear it very much, Daniel. Seriously.'

Daniel looked pleased and considered the matter as the table was cleared. 'Well, like most things,' he began, 'it was just a combination of luck, struggle and a degree of ability . . . it really wasn't that difficult. I happened to be in the right place at the right time. You see I left school early – straight after O-levels at sixteen. In our family further education was something for the rest. As soon as you were old enough, you got out and earned your keep. Schooling was soft . . . for the likes of people like you, William,' he chided good-humouredly. 'I knew a bit

25

about advertising – well, mostly I knew that whoever went into it seemed to make a lot of money, and you didn't always need a long list of paper qualifications to do it. I joined MacArthur's and worked in the post room licking stamps, photocopying, that sort of thing . . .' he paused to take a sip of the fine Chablis, 'which as I'm sure you can imagine was not exactly taxing. I may not have had a degree in marketing, but I knew how to sell. With a father who graduated from a second-hand furniture warehouse to a chain of smart antique shops I had to pick up a few tips on the way.'

Valentine's nose curled in distaste. 'You never told me that, Daniel . . . that your father worked in a second-hand furniture shop.'

'You never asked, Valentine. And besides I had no reason to mention him. He's dead. So's my mother.' He drained his glass and turned back to Charlotte, focusing his cool dark eyes directly on her. 'Eventually someone must have spotted my budding talents for I was pulled out of the post room and created assistant to one of the least inspiring account directors. He was so pedestrian that I realized I'd have to do something radical in order to get noticed in his department.'

Here he paused and laughed quietly. 'God . . . sometimes I still wonder how I had the gall to do it,' he said, almost to himself. He looked back up at Charlotte. 'My boss was told to go to this huge potential client for a briefing. At least I was supposed to give him the message to go a couple of days earlier than he was planning. I went to the meeting in his stead. The client gave me the brief. I talked to them and came up with a couple of ideas which they loved, and by the end of the meeting I had a ten million pound account in my pocket.' He leaned back into his chair. 'I could have been fired on the spot – instead they fired my boss, eventually. You see they couldn't afford to lose me because the client was willing to give them fifteen per cent of £10 million for the

26

privilege of having me working on the account. It was just a question of having the balls to take a risk. Lots of people sit back complacently, expecting the opportunities to pile up in front of them. You have to make those opportunities yourself. The trick is to have the ability to recognize them and the conviction to act on them. Kids should be taught that. It's all very well being brilliant at writing, or drawing pictures, or whatever the talent, but there's a hell of a lot of competition and it's the tough nuts who push who make it in the end.'

His voice had an almost hypnotic quality, a compelling softness. More effective than a loud assaulting boom. It quietly and subtly demanded attention. Charlotte pictured him in a boardroom. No need to call attention, no need for endless labouring of important points. If you missed what he said first time round then you were in the wrong place.

Warming to his subject, Daniel continued: 'You must also have principles and you must always be straight with a client. If they come to you expecting you to sell a crap product, you tell them it's crap. But you also tell them why. Then maybe you can work on it. Maybe you'll end up with a successful campaign. The client may have to spend a lot of money, but if you get it right his sales will scrape the sky. There's a hell of a lot of cowboys out there, yes-men who take the money, produce shit and give advertising its bad name. Cornwallis is different. That's why we're successful.'

'And William works on the same lines. I'm not saying that we're a moralizing godly lot who only do what's right for altruistic motives. We're in it to make money. And the only way to do that is to give a good service. We know the competition out there. New agencies starting up; young talent. Each commercial, believe it or not, is a mini movie taking the same creative input and planning as a major movie. Big money is spent, and if the

27

commercial is wrongly aimed, you've wasted that money and you'll lose the client . . .'

'With a PR division under the same umbrella,' William broke in, 'we can provide a full service. We're going to have a marvellous opportunity for cross-fertilization; both Dan's clients and mine want a co-ordinated strategy. There's often infighting and bitchery when separate ad and PR companies are used. Everyone's busy watching their backs, and if a campaign doesn't work each one blames the opposite side. Managing creative teams together has got to be a more attractive proposition for the client. We can work a total plan right across the board from below-the-line sales promotion to the biggest TV spend with little outside help. It saves the client having to waste valuable time liaising with up to three separate agencies.' He paused to refill his coffee cup. 'Anyway, Dan, we're in danger of boring the girls. That's the trouble with the pair of us at the moment. Because we've lived, breathed and slept this deal for so long we're becoming obsessive.'

'Not at all, not in the least . . .' smiled Charlotte. Despite herself she had been fired by their enthusiasm. 'It's nice to hear about it properly. I'm very excited too. I'm just nervous for all those poor little agencies about to go bust when you two get together.' She laughed.

'Don't you worry about that, lovey, there'll be plenty left over for them – the ones that have survived the recession, that is. We're only after the really big fish! So, seeing as the night is young, and so am I, let's go dancing. I'm dying to see you move, Charlotte. What do you say, William? Valentine?'

William groaned. 'Well, OK, I'm not so hot at dancing, but seeing as tonight's special – if you'd like to go, darling . . .'

The last thing Charlotte wanted to encourage was Daniel's attentions on the dance floor but Valentine interrupted: 'Of course we're going, you know I love the opportunity to wriggle around the floor.'

Charlotte resisted the sneaking temptation to make some comment about snakes.

Dan's sleek BMW drew up outside the canopied entrance to Hustlers. A green-liveried doorman leapt to open the door for Charlotte and Valentine. Dan stepped out of the car and handed him the keys. 'Thanks, Harry.'

Harry said: 'Evenin', Mr Cornwallis,' and climbed into the driving seat to take the car to the private car park behind the nightclub.

The two girls behind the reception desk stood preening themselves as Dan said: 'Hi Maggie . . . Bella. Hope you've been behaving yourselves since I last saw you – and not done anything I couldn't.'

The taller of the two pancaked blondes grinned at him: 'Well, that would be hard, wouldn't it, Mr Cornwallis?'

Valentine threw her jacket in the general direction of the girls and without waiting for a cloakroom ticket said, 'Come on, William, let's go see the action.'

Daniel and Charlotte followed them through the dark corridor to the bar room which, as usual, was crammed to bursting point with steamy bodies. The bar itself was, in places, three deep with people trying to get a drink. For a moment they stood, but only for a moment. From nowhere a waiter appeared at Daniel's elbow. 'Mr Cornwallis, your table is ready . . . if you'd like to follow me.'

Incredibly, an empty table seemed to have been conjured up out of the thick air. All around the dance floor, as far as one could tell, all the tables were full. Charlotte saw Daniel slip a twenty-pound note into the grateful waiter's hand. She was curious to know what had happened to the table's previous occupants. Maybe the waiter had slipped them some money to leave!

The heavy bass notes drove into her. A mass of waving

29

and jerking bodies gyrated around a too-small dance floor. The lights flashed loud colours in time with the music, now and then interspersed with ultraviolet which turned faces deep brown and collars livid blue-white, picking out dandruff on dark blazers like psychedelic salt.

A silver ice bucket appeared on the table, together with four fluted champagne tulips. Daniel reached into his wallet once more and handed the smiling waiter another large note. Then he reached across Charlotte and picked up the dripping bottle. He wrapped the linen napkin around its neck and then quietly, expertly, popped the cork. As he filled the glasses pale golden bubbles spilled white foam down the sides and on to the tray beneath. He handed them each a glass. 'Here's to a very successful and prosperous venture . . . to Cornwallis de Sallis.'

They raised their glasses and drank. The champagne was wonderfully icy and sent small shivers down Charlotte's naked back in spite of the heat. William laughed. 'That must be the fourth toast we've made this evening.'

'But we are celebrating, old chap. What the hell . . . ? Let's have another one – here's to us making lots and lots of money . . .'

'I'll certainly drink to that.'

Charlotte looked around at the people. A fascinating cross-section: mixed ages, mixed races, mixed stages of drunkenness. She herself was beginning to feel more than a little lightheaded. There were several people she recognized but none that she wanted to acknowledge. The music was almost unbearably loud. She saw, rather than heard, Valentine say something to William. William pulled a face. Valentine grabbed his arm and pulled him up towards the dance floor.

Daniel spoke. Charlotte shook her head at him. 'I'm sorry . . . what did you say?'

'I said I think we should sit this one out.' His lips were

close to her ear, he was almost shouting to make himself heard. She felt his breath warm against her cheek. 'Maybe we'll wait for something a bit slower.'

She smiled at him, took another sip of her champagne and then noticed her hand tremble. Dan watched her, that same amusement playing around his mouth. She twisted on the bench so that she could see the dance floor more clearly. She had the disturbing sensation of being slightly out of her depth with him. But that was ridiculous. Men didn't usually frighten her. And she'd been with some pretty tough cookies in her time in journalism. Still she'd be glad when the others came back . . .

She caught a glimpse of orange hair. The heaving mass parted slightly and Charlotte could see Valentine rocking her hips rhythmically to the music. Arms outstretched, lips pouting, she was giving William some semi-private performance of pelvic agility. He was watching her very appreciatively, wearing a kind of silly, inane grin as she sidled around him, now and then grasping at his shoulders and pulling at his hands.

My God, thought Charlotte, does the woman never stop? If I didn't know better I'd begin to think that William was actually enjoying it. Still, to give him his due he was dancing with the most beautiful woman in the place, which must be good for his ego.

The record came to a stop, or rather another broke into its final chords and took its place, giving no pause for the sweating bodies.

Daniel stood up. 'Come on, Charlotte, let's dance. Please. I'd really like to.' His voice was softer and his touch gentle when he led her across to the dance floor. His clasp felt firm and dry and her hand was lost in his, giving her an odd feeling of little-girlishness. She felt awkward, self-conscious almost, trotting along behind his tall form. Finding space to stand, let alone dance, was a problem in itself. They half pushed and half stumbled

31

in their jostle for position. She avoided his eyes, yet all the time their bodies were being pushed closer together, and she was aware of his animal grace. Without looking, she could feel his eyes burning her. Suddenly he reached for her, pulling her close, catching her off balance so that she almost fell forward towards his chest. Giving her no chance to escape, his arms closed around her. Warm flesh encircled by solid steel. His chin rested on the top of her head and he let a slow sigh escape through his teeth, having inhaled deeply on the warm, beautifully fragrant scent of her hair. He pulled his head back slightly, so that he could see into her eyes. Her head swam; a vague dizziness made her momentarily weak. His masculinity assaulted all her senses. She felt his body hard against her own.

She pushed him away. 'Excuse me . . .' Angry and confused she squeezed her way almost blindly through the other couples on the dance floor and headed straight for the cloakroom. It was deserted except for the kindly silver-haired woman who policed the lavatories. She looked up incuriously as Charlotte burst in. Charlotte smiled weakly at the woman and rushed to the first cubicle. Once safely inside she fought to regain her composure. Drawing deep breaths she cursed herself and Daniel Cornwallis.

She must have had far too much to drink. What with the dry martinis which were probably almost neat gin, all the wine at Langan's, and then champagne on top, it was hardly surprising she had felt dizzy. She laughed at herself for thinking it had been the effect Daniel was having on her. She flushed the loo, an automatic reflex, and stepped out into the bright lights of the cloakroom. Her reflection showed flushed cheeks, eyes bright from the alcohol. She splashed cold water on to her face and patted it dry with a soft white towel. Then she thanked the woman in the corner and braced herself for her return.

William was alone at the table. He moved up to make room for her and put his arm out towards her. 'You look lovely tonight, darling.' He smiled and kissed her cheek warmly.

'Thank you,' she said. 'I wasn't sure whether you might think it rather risqué for your new partner.'

'I did. I wanted to send you home again when I saw you. I thought Daniel might have you for his dinner.'

'I didn't think you'd noticed.'

'Well, I did. Anyway you look bloody sexy and I think it's time we went home. We'll wait until the others come back then I think we'll make our excuses. It's been a long day.'

'That's fine by me. I can feel my head already. If I have one more drink I'll probably fall over!'

Daniel and Valentine came back. Charlotte could have sworn that Daniel's eyes narrowed when he looked at her, and his grip tightened around Valentine's shoulders. William was speaking. 'Sorry to break up the party but I'm going to take Charlotte home. She's feeling a bit tired.'

Typical, thought Charlotte. Turn her into the party-pooper. As usual, she was William's scapegoat. As usual, she smiled supportively.

'Are you all right, Charlotte?' Daniel asked, in a manner suggestive of a shrink talking to a committed lunatic.

'Yes, fine. Just a headache. It's nothing . . . really.' She smiled at them both. 'It was so good to meet you both, a really great evening,' she lied sincerely. She left William to finish their farewells and went in search of her jacket.

William turned the key in the lock. 'Well done for tonight, Charlotte, I was proud of you. Dan obviously liked you . . . Valentine's great fun isn't she . . . ?' he drifted on. Charlotte only half listened, just grateful to be safe inside her own front hallway. William finished bolting the door, sliding the security chain into place. He turned to her and placed his hands around her waist, nuzzling her neck. 'Mmmmm . . .' he sighed. 'You smell delicious. Would you like a nightcap before bed?'

'Good God, no. I've had quite enough already. But you go ahead. I'll go on up.'

She undressed quickly and slipped between cool white cotton sheets. She closed her eyes, grateful the evening was behind them. Most of all she thought about William's new partner. A man of many contradictions it seemed. He was a womanizer, but she'd seen a spark of something more gentle. He was arrogant and a ruthless tycoon, but he talked of something akin to integrity. She couldn't say she liked him. She felt sure he'd be a great asset for William, but she felt uneasy. Somewhere, deep in the pit of her gut, she felt a small seed of anxiety. Something she couldn't quite put her finger on.

She heard William come into the room. Every move was catalogued in her mind. The wardrobe being opened. The coathanger being removed. The slide of fabric on to the wooden hanger. Shoes placed neatly on the shoe rack. Then into the bathroom. The whoosh of the basin tap followed by the familiar but irritating gargle as he finished brushing his teeth. Finally he joined her in bed. His body felt cold next to her own. He slid his arm under her and twisted her round so that she faced him. His fingers traced a line along her temple, over the small scar, triggering memory.

He crooked his leg proprietorially over hers and pushed his hips forward, tightening his body so that she could feel him hard against her thigh. His lips parted and his breath touched her hair. She opened her eyes and pushed away from him. She had worn the dress in order to seduce him. She had been determined to make him notice her tonight, to make him realize that she was not just a piece of furniture. Yet now she felt empty and tired. The thought of his body on hers was mildly repulsive.

She felt like the child who had been given too many good things and was now paying the price for over-indulgence. To make love now would seem a travesty after the fickle nature of the evening they had spent. They had all sat together and played their parts to perfection like the beautiful, successful people they were. Now she was at home with her husband and that husband wished to claim her body. Just as she had planned. It was another part of the game. But suddenly she wanted to be wanted for herself. Not for her ability to role play.

'William, please. I'm not really in the mood. It's been a long day. I've had too much to drink. Would you mind if we . . . ?'

'No, of course not. I understand.' He started to stroke her belly. She squirmed away, but he caught her with his other arm. He clearly had no intention of accepting excuses.

She sighed. Resigned. Turning to face him she dutifully slid her knees up and he climbed on top of her. Without further preliminaries he thrust his way inside her. She moaned, not with pleasure, but with the discomfort of being unprepared for him. William was oblivious. The alcohol had clearly clouded his sensitivity. He pushed deeper and deeper. She lay, supine, willing him to get it over with. After what seemed like an age he reached his climax, then he flopped on top of her, a dead weight. She struggled to free herself, so that she could breathe properly, and shifted his weight so that he wasn't crushing her abdomen quite so hard. Usually she felt empty, sometimes she felt angry. But tonight she was too tired to feel anything other than relief that it was over.

Their lovemaking hadn't always been so. In their early days together William had been an extremely passionate and attentive lover, and Charlotte herself certainly hadn't lacked in the experience department. She knew what pleasure could be achieved in a tender, loving

35

relationship. She knew how her body could respond with care and consideration from her partner. But lately their coupling had been almost mechanical. The combination of William's exhaustion from his demanding career, and Charlotte's obsession over ovulation charts seemed to have taken any passion out of it. All the spontaneity was missing.

Finally William rolled away from her, giving her a perfunctory kiss before falling on to his own side of the bed, his back towards her. She curled up into a foetal ball, feeling the sticky ooze dribble down her buttock. She felt a deep sense of violation. Valentine's sneering drawl still echoed in her ears. Her strange cat-like eyes gazed down at her. Charlotte turned over and squeezed her own eyes shut tighter. Another set of eyes swam before her. Deep, deep blue piercing eyes. She remembered the feel of his body. 'Damn you, Daniel Cornwallis . . .'

Chapter Two

Charlotte turned over in bed, her outstretched arm searching the space for another warm body. Her hand met nothing but empty bedclothes. Slowly she opened her eyes. All that was left of William's presence was a dent in the pillow and a ruffled duvet. She listened for tell-tale signs of movement, but the house was silent. The drawn curtains suffused bright daylight into the bedroom. Her head, in retribution for the night before, now pounded and throbbed. Her mouth felt dry and her skin burned. She tried to wet her mouth and her tongue rasped over her teeth. She felt utterly revolting. She pulled the duvet back over her head and burrowed deeper into the pillow.

Suddenly the shrill bleep of the phone assaulted her eardrums. She let it ring and ring, not wishing to speak to anyone. But whoever wanted her was certainly persistent. On about the tenth ring she tentatively reached over and plucked the handset from its cradle.

'Hello,' her voice croaked. It sounded as if it had been dragged up from the depths of her feet. Slow and sluggish, still drowsy and unoiled for speech.

A woman's voice reverberated around her head. 'Charlie? You're not still in bed, are you? Lazy cow!'

'Oh Claudia. Yes. What's the time?'

'Ten thirty. I've been in the office for two hours already. What's up with you? You're usually up and about at some ungodly hour pounding the park. I thought you'd have been on your tenth bowl of muesli by now. Are you all right?'

'Oh, nothing that a week in bed wouldn't put right, thanks very much.'

Claudia giggled. 'Now there's a thought. Question is . . . who with?'

'I was thinking by myself, actually, hussy! Anyway, did you ring just to wake me up, or is there some good reason for your untimely intrusion into my hangover?'

'Sounds as if it's lucky for you I did ring. It's no good hiding yourself away in that hole of yours. I've got a free slot at lunchtime. I've been through my Filofax. All the men are unavailable so I thought I'd ask you to lunch – on my expense account, of course! What are you up to, apart from dying?'

'Dying she says. Claudia, this is serious. I mean this is really worse than dying. Dying would be good compared to this. Ooh!' she exclaimed, touching her brow theatrically. 'I daren't open my eyes. They might just fall out. Just lead me to the drugs . . . You couldn't possibly expect me to face the outside world like this – I mean . . . uuggh!'

'I'll call you back in one hour. If you're not up and together by then I'll come round and drag you out myself.'

'No, Claudia. Go through your filothing again. Find a more entertaining date.'

'Nonsense. I want to see *you*. Come on, there's a good Charlie. Up you get now.' The line clicked dead.

Charlotte lay back for a moment and concentrated on the sledgehammer motion in her head. She'd once seen a church clock where a little man equipped with a large mallet came out hourly and beat the hell out of a brass gong. She now knew how the gong felt. She sat up very gingerly and then lowered her legs on to the floor. Clutching her head she made it to the bathroom door and then from there to the edge of the bath, where she took a well-earned rest.

She turned the taps and the water hissed, spluttered and gushed like a mini-Niagara. Why hadn't anyone invented silent water? A sort of gentle filling from underneath the tub, perhaps. Next she searched the bathroom cabinet. Eventually behind half-empty bottles of Collis Brown and Bergasol she found the paracetamol and frantically tore at the silver wrapping. This done, she filled the tooth mug with water from the basin tap and swallowed down the pills. Then she searched through the little pack of essential oils her mother had given her last Christmas and found one which read: 'to refresh and revitalize tired, aching limbs'. Well, she was certainly tired and aching. She emptied the entire bottle into the foaming water, which turned a kind of putrid green. She sank down into it, and heaved a sigh of achievement.

As the water lapped over her she could feel herself relaxing even though the almost overpowering smell of pine made her nose itch. She laid her head back against the cold enamel and closed her eyes. William had obviously decided not to disturb her when he left. Not that that was particularly unusual; she often woke to find him gone. Mostly he left so early that she was still deeply asleep, though sometimes she couldn't help feeling it would be nice if he just gave her a quick hug before he left. But the more involved he became with the business, the less romantically inclined he was.

It was a funny thing, how relationships sometimes seemed to turn themselves around completely. For a long time it had been she who paid the piper and called the tune. William had been desperate to have her, with his terrier-like tenacity he had worn her down. From the very beginning she hadn't wanted to meet him. Her position as editor made her the target of almost every public relations man in town. A journalist's legendary bête noir was the archetypal PR man who would try to wine and dine them in the hope of getting them to write a lengthy article singing the praises of whoever, or whatever, they represented. Equally, any journalist worth their salt would not, in general, rely on any information passed to them via a PR person. All information would be biased so heavily in the client's favour that any resulting coverage would be sycophantic advertorial – in other words an advertisement posing as an unpaid-for feature.

Of course there were always exceptions to the rule. She knew of a few excellent PRs who had the nose for a real story and wouldn't bother their precious media contacts with clearly unsuitable trash. Their methods allowed the setting up of independent interviews held direct with the client, or maybe help with research on articles, or arranging press trips on the writer's behalf. These people were worth their weight in gold and well known to Charlotte. She wasn't interested in the others.

So when her secretary told her that a William de Sallis was insistent on having a meeting with her to discuss his clients, she told Nicky to tell him she was busy. For a very long time. But he rang daily. He rang until Nicky was on the point of resignation. She was sick of giving Charlotte's excuses. And Charlotte just maintained she was too busy to go. She knew damn well that if he had anything newsy to sell, she'd know about it already. And if the news had to come through a PR man, chances were that at least ten other magazines would carry the same story.

Eventually, just to please Nicky, she agreed. Also, this man was becoming such a pest, and was so insistent, she had become rather curious.

Nicky had come into her office wearing a large smirk.

'Well?' Charlotte had asked.

'I just wanted to say that if you change your mind about lunch – with William de Sallis I mean – well, I'll go in your stead . . .'

'Why?'

She winked. 'See for yourself.'

When Charlotte finally came out of her office to meet

him she could see exactly what Nicky meant. He had the classic, clean-shaven good looks that all prospective mothers-in-law craved. Six feet of ex-Harrow schoolboy. Blond, blue-eyed, with a cut to his suit as immaculate as his jawline. Charlotte summed him up immediately: too dumb for the professions, too pretty for the army, but perfect for a career that demanded just the right degree of charm and well-rounded vowels. She put out her hand and he shook it correctly. Not limp, or overly firm, a no-nonsense sort of shake.

'At last. I'm delighted to meet you,' he said, smoothly. 'Thank you for finding the time to see me.' She thought she detected a small degree of amusement in the words, but chose to ignore it.

He had taken her out to Maxim's. Intimate little tables lit by miniature pink table-lamps and overlooked by murals of rampaging Rubenesque nudes. He had seemed more interested in finding out about her than telling her anything about his client list. The two hours went by surprisingly fast. It was only when he was settling the bill that she realized he still hadn't mentioned anything about his business.

'Don't you want to talk to me about anything . . . ? I mean, you must have brought me here to tell me about your business, surely.'

'What?' he said. 'Oh God, no. I wanted to meet this hot-shot lady that had got Fleet Street buzzing. Besides, I can easily tell you about my clients next time.'

'Oh really!' she laughed.

Two whole weeks passed before he called her again. This time she allowed Nicky to put him straight through.

'Hello, Charlotte,' he said smoothly. 'How do you feel about opera? I've got two tickets for tomorrow night and I wondered if you were free?'

'Well . . . I don't know.'

'*La Traviata*'s playing at the ENO. At least it's fairly

light – even if you can't stand opera. Come on. It'll be fun. Promise.'

'I'm sorry,' she said. 'I'm afraid I really can't. I've just checked with the diary, and I already have to be somewhere else.'

'Can't you change it?'

She laughed. 'No, I can't. It's important.' In truth all she had planned was a leg wax and a sunbed. Still, she didn't want to be too available to him. He was no doubt well used to getting 'yes' for an answer.

'Then how about lunch? Next week?'

'What day?'

'Monday.'

'Sorry.'

'Well, what about Tuesday?'

'Sorry, that's out too.'

'Wednesday?'

''Fraid not.'

'OK, Charlotte. When?'

She flicked through the pages of her diary. 'Looks like a week on Friday.'

'Right. I'll call you on the day to let you know where we're going. See you.'

And thus their courtship started. He pursued her relentlessly. He called her three times a day. She was, quite literally, swept off her feet. William never did get around to talking about his clients. They were much too busy on other things. About two months after their first meeting they became lovers, quite a long wait for both of them. Obviously William had been keen to take her to his bed, but Charlotte hadn't wanted to commit herself to the relationship in the same way as he did. After all, she had a great career, a nice flat, a busy social life. In fact a great life-style. At the age of twenty-five she was editor of a leading national magazine and one of the last things on her shopping list had been a man – for the moment, of course.

But life has a habit of not sticking to a particular plan. Slowly but surely she found herself falling in love with William. Six months later and with just a few friends present, they duly found themselves at Marylebone Registry Office, and Charlotte became Mrs William de Sallis.

Charlotte fiddled absently with the large cabuchon emerald on the third finger of her left hand. How times had changed. Here she was, hungover and sorely neglected, 'doing the odd bit of freelance stuff', while William built himself an empire. The high spot of her day was the prospect of lunch on Claudia's expense account.

She dragged herself out of the by now lukewarm water and towelled herself quickly, the sudden movements once more jarring her fragile head. She had just got dressed when the phone rang. Without waiting for the voice on the other end she said, 'OK Claudia, you win. Contrary to my earlier expectations, I am still alive. Just make sure you've got a very large Marguerita waiting for me!'

'You know, I had a feeling you'd pull through. I'll see you later – usual time, usual place.'

Joe Allen's was a popular rendezvous for media hacks, actors, publishers and, of course, tourists – though mercifully few of the latter as the place was tucked away in a side street. An unassuming arched doorway led to steps down into the basement restaurant; a discreet brass plaque set in the wall was the only announcement of its whereabouts.

Charlotte was shown to the table. Claudia, true to form, had not yet arrived. She ordered a Marguerita and squinted at the huge blackboard at the end of the restaurant. The statutory mixture of different salads, complemented by chopped liver, chilli, ribs and so on, and a tempting list of egg brunch dishes. The best eggs Benedict in town. Her mouth watered and her stomach

43

churned once more. The last remnants of hangover were dwindling. The bitter mix of tequila and lemon juice would sort it out for good.

From the desk by the door Claudia grinned and waved enthusiastically. 'Hi darling,' she cried as she approached the table. She bent to give Charlotte an enormous hug and a kiss on both cheeks. A lovely warm orange scent clung to her. She plumped herself into her chair. 'Sorry I'm late,' she breathed. 'Last-minute phone calls. Always happens. Just as I get to the door it bloody well rings. Anyhow, I'm really glad you came. Why are you looking at me like that, Charlotte? Close your mouth or you'll catch flies!'

'Your hair – I can't believe it, where's it all gone?'

'Oh that . . . yes . . . I suppose I'm used to it now. I keep forgetting. Anyway, how's the head?'

'Beating a retreat, thanks. Margueritas should be available on prescription. I'm feeling more human than I've felt for days. Yes, I'm glad I came too. To be honest I'm in a foul mood and you can tell me the worst gossip you can possibly think of. You can tell me about the nastiest people in your life, you can tell me all the gory details of your sex life and I'll lap it up.'

Claudia looked at her watch: 'Well, in that case I'd better call the office now and tell them I won't be back for a week.' She paused and lit a cigarette, holding it well away from Charlotte who grimaced at the acrid smoke, and wafted the air in front of her. 'Whoops . . . sorry!'

'It's about time you gave up, you know.'

'Yeah, yeah. I know. You stick to your Margueritas, I'll stick to my nicotine. Now it's you I'm worried about. What's up?'

'Later. I'll spill all after a couple of drinks. Let's talk about you first. Now, why don't we start with the hair. What happened?'

Claudia's long dark curls, which had previously fallen in a wayward mass to her shoulders, had been close-cropped to above her ears. The curls were still there but the previous Amazonian temptress had been transformed into a mischievous pixie. Her small, pert face was exposed and had a new air of elfin vulnerability.

'What do you think?'

'I love it. It makes you look almost innocent, God help the world!'

'I know,' laughed Claudia, 'but don't let looks fool you. I feel wicked! I've had a bloody awful morning. The phone hasn't stopped. The editor's been breathing down my neck about last week's shoot. The pictures are fantastic, so sexy they almost burn your fingers, but he thinks our dear old readership will be offended. In fact they probably will but that doesn't alter the fact that they're really amazing pictures. The trouble is, our readers are so conservative they'd be offended by a bare midriff.' She laughed. 'Do you remember that woman who used to send all the advertisements back, you know, the ones for men's underwear, and how she used to draw circles around all the rude bits.'

'God, yes. With little arrows saying "disgusting", "obscene", "filth" . . .' They both dissolved into fits of giggles.

Claudia continued: 'Can you imagine anyone actually going to the lengths of ripping them out and sending them off to us? That's what I call really perverted. Anyway, we have these photographs which are beautiful to behold. Sexy and tasteful. Lots of rubber and zips, but nicely done.' She laid ironic emphasis on the words. 'The editor wants a re-shoot. I tell you I'm mad as hell. No editorial freedom. So I had to tell the photographer who's now throwing an artistic tantrum. I've got to pacify him, reorganize the shoot and smile grimly through it all. If I had the guts I'd sell the pictures elsewhere. Trouble is, I need the job!'

'Did you say rubber?' Charlotte interrupted. 'You didn't use the voluptuous Valentine, did you?'

'How on earth did you know? I only got the transparencies myself yesterday.'

'I had the dubious pleasure of her company over dinner last night. What a nasty piece of work she is. Pity she's so good-looking.' Charlotte studied her nails, frowning. 'I haven't been able to tell you before. It's all been very hush hush and all that, but William is going into partnership with Daniel Cornwallis.'

'You're joking. Not the legendary Dan Cornwallis?' Charlotte nodded. Claudia's voice rose gleefully. 'Charlotte, you lucky cow. You mean that beautiful hunk is joining up with William? Why, that means you'll be practically related. When can I meet him? Rich . . . handsome . . . exciting . . . single,' she drifted on, eyes glazed in wanton fantasy. 'Did you meet him? What's he like? Come on. Blow by blow. I thought I'd heard he was going out with Valentine. How did they seem? Happy?'

Charlotte couldn't help laughing. 'No, and you can have him. He's boorish and boring. Rude, brash, arrogant, self-opinionated, conceited – shall I go on?' She surprised herself by the strength of her venom.

'You obviously liked him then?'

'No!' Claudia leaned forward conspiratorially. 'And as for Valentine.' Charlotte's scowl deepened. 'Do you know she had the cheek to insinuate that I was a boring little housewife tying my darling husband to my Liberty-print apron strings!'

'Well, she picked the wrong lady for that routine. No doubt you set her straight, darling.'

Charlotte nodded. 'Too right I did. Of course what really bugged her was the fact that I'd apparently vetoed using her for *Today's Woman* before she was discovered. I can't honestly say I remember her at all. Anyway, there wasn't much I could say to that really.'

'So this dinner explains the mystery around the sexy little number you were after. Was it a success?'

'Well, judging from William's expression I think it probably was. I really thought he was going to have a fit. And Daniel looked as though his eyes were about to pop out. I think I inadvertently made quite an enemy out of Valentine.'

Claudia rubbed her hands together. 'Ah ha, so the plot thickens. Daniel took a bit of a shine to you?' Claudia considered her friend critically. 'After all, Charlotte, you're looking pretty good these days. Maybe young Valentine was a little jealous. She certainly wouldn't appreciate any competition. God, what a coup. Daniel Cornwallis.'

'Oh come on, Claudia, you know he's the sort of man to chase after anything in knickers. As I said, I couldn't bear him.'

'But that's the point. He doesn't just chase after anything in knickers. He's pretty choosy so far as I can gather.'

'Well, whatever, I'd say that he and Valentine are a well-matched pair. I can just imagine them awarding each other gold stars every time they make it together. A sort of mutual self-admiration society!' Charlotte lowered her eyes and squirmed uncomfortably on the hard chair. She couldn't help remembering the feel of his body next to hers, his breath warm against her ear. She felt her cheeks colouring. She just hoped that Claudia's ultra-sensitive antennae didn't pick up her discomfort.

'If he's so awful why on earth is William going into partnership with him?'

'He's very clever. As far as business is concerned he's obviously very good, and very powerful. I have to admit that I was a bit impressed when I heard him talking about it. Oh God . . .' she put her hands up to her face. 'Claudia, I've just remembered . . . they've asked me to organize the bloody announcement party. William was babbling on last night about how they should have some sort of do to tell their clients about the merger, and the idiot went and suggested me. They've sort of taken it as a fait accompli that I'll do it. Frankly I can't think of anything worse than dealing with that man. Uggh!' She shivered dramatically.

'Well, if you need a hand . . . I certainly wouldn't kick him out of bed.'

'If you can elbow Valentine out of the way you're welcome to him. Anyway, what happened to Henry? Your honourable member for muchdoingit? Last I heard you were passionate about him – the real thing – well, for the fiftieth time – and all that. Don't tell me his performance didn't live up to his manifesto?'

'Oh shut up, Charlie. Really you've been so rude about him . . . '

'Well, he was wet. Self-confessed wet, as well.'

'Then you'll be pleased to know that he's history. He forgot to tell me about the wife and children deep in the heart of Sussex. Not that that in itself bothered me too much. It was the night he rang from the labour ward to let me know he couldn't make dinner that really cracked it for me . . . '

'What happened?'

'He'd told me that he hadn't slept with his wife for years. You know, the same old bullshit they usually spin to get you to lie back and die for them, and then, well, he rang to say that he wouldn't be seeing me as his wife had just given birth . . . '

'Oh dear.' Charlotte was fighting to keep a straight face. 'What did he have, boy or girl?'

'Twins actually.' Charlotte exploded. Claudia set her mouth firmly. 'A boy and a girl. He rang me straight after the delivery to let me know. I think he wanted me to congratulate him, he was so pleased with himself. So I did. I also told him I wasn't in the habit of being a postnatal exercise and put the phone down. I haven't heard from him since.' Charlotte was still laughing.

48

'Oh Claudia,' she spluttered between helpless convulsions. 'You do pick them.'

'So. I'm on the loose. No man is safe – except maybe William, of course. How is the boring old fart? Painful as ever?'

'I wish you wouldn't talk about him like that. But seeing as you ask, the answer is yes! I've hardly seen him in weeks he's been so busy money-spinning. And, well, to be perfectly honest, Claudia, this pregnancy business is really getting to me. It's been so long now. And I'm almost beginning to lose sight of why I actually wanted a baby in the first place. The rest of the bloody world seems to be able to manage it. Every time I turn around I see someone's fat stomach. And they always look so damned smug – and serene!'

'What about those tests you've been trying to get him to have. Is he still refusing to go?'

'Yes. Categorically and emphatically. What can I do? I think it's partly because he considers it some sort of attack on his precious manhood. Because I'm OK he knows there's the strong possibility there's something missing in him, and he just can't face the thought of finding out. You know how frail men's egos are. All his life he's been surrounded by women telling him how manly and important he is because he was born with a penis, and now the woman he shares his life with is threatening to cut it off, so to speak.' She paused to take a sip of the wine Claudia had poured for her. 'I can understand all that, but I feel he's not considering my feelings at all. He's just dismissing me completely. All it needs is a bit of courage and maturity. And I feel I've given him such a lot of support lately that it's the least he can do. Maybe I should buy a poodle or something, you know, some sort of child substitute. Isn't that what barren women usually do?'

Claudia smiled at Charlotte sympathetically and squeezed her hand. 'Well, you could. Though I can't imagine for one minute William allowing mucky little paws into that immaculate house of yours. If it so much as thought of widdling on the carpet you and it would be out! No, Charlotte, what you need is something far better than a poodle. You need to get out. You know, in a way William's right about you having something else to do. You're absolutely wasted at home.' She put her hands up as Charlotte was about to protest. 'Oh, I know you're doing freelance stuff, and all the reasons you have. But it's not getting you anywhere, is it? I mean, what will you do when you go home today? Brood I suppose?'

Charlotte just looked at her, rather dejectedly.

'I know I may sound hard, Charlie, but I'm really worried about you. It sounds to me as though William's got so used to neglecting you that it's become the norm. For God's sake, girl, claw back some of your old identity. Come back to work. Why don't you let me have a word with the editor? I'm sure he'd leap at the chance of having you back.'

'No. Not yet, anyway. Let me think about it, Claudia. I do hear what you say and I'm sure there's a lot of truth in it.'

'OK.' Claudia smiled. She felt she might be in danger of pushing her friend a little too far. She tried to lighten the mood. 'Of course you could always have an affair . . .'

'What?' Charlotte shrieked.

'An affair. I mean, it would certainly take your mind off things. I know, how about a sort of baby by donor? Just think, you could end up with a child that didn't turn out to be like William. Now there's a real incentive for you, Charlie.'

'You really are the end, you know. I suppose that's just the sort of thing you'd do.'

'Of course. It's called being in control of your own destiny. I mean, if William won't play ball, as it were, you'll just have to change studs.' She burst out laughing. 'Of course the choice is fairly important. I mean you have to consider the pedigree of potential donors. And taking into consideration things such as looks, health, and brains, I'd say that someone like Daniel Cornwallis would be a pretty good horse to back. Reading between the lines of what you say, he's clearly interested.'

Charlotte could feel her cheeks turning beetroot. Claudia examined her closely.

'Good grief. Have I hit a raw nerve? What exactly did happen last night? Are you being less than honest with Auntie Claude?'

'Don't be ridiculous,' Charlotte snapped a bit too vehemently. 'Of course there's nothing else to tell about last night. It's just that you do seem to be labouring the point a bit, Claudia. Just for the record I have no intention of having an affair with anyone – least of all Daniel Cornwallis. Just because your whole life revolves around sordid encounters doesn't mean we all have to follow your example . . .'

'Whew. Sorry, Charlie. I obviously have upset you. Look, forget it. I was just trying to cheer you up. I'll call you tomorrow to see how you are – OK, love? And try not to brood on smelly old William. Think about what I said. About the job I mean, not the affair!'

On the way back to Richmond Charlotte did brood on Claudia's teasing. She felt Claudia had sensed more than Charlotte would admit, even to herself. She knew Charlotte too well and had an unnerving ability almost to read her mind. They'd both been very close for a long time. Charlotte remembered when they'd first met, both of them fresh from college; editorial assistants on *Girl* magazine. Claudia had been to the London School of Fashion, following her father's ambition that she should step into the family business, a huge fashion house

51

designing ready-to-wear collections for the high street. The label was synonymous with style and high fashion at affordable prices. But Claudia had finally bucked the system. Much to her father's horror and disappointment she had thrown aside her honours degree in fashion design to go into journalism. He had cut off her extremely generous allowance while Claudia decided from then on to wage a personal vendetta against the label. She vowed never to mention it in any fashion page of her creation. Her own ambition, already powerful, was fired by a burning desire to prove she could be extremely successful without her father's help.

Together Charlotte and Claudia had thrown themselves into London life with the passion of two young people knowing exactly where they were headed and having a ball along the way. They'd had a succession of flats together, starting with a very humble studio flat in the backstreets of Pimlico where they had existed on a diet of cornflakes, boiled eggs and toast, in order to fund their tube fare to the office near Oxford Street, their insatiable appetite for clothes, and their wild social life. Photographers, artists and writers courted them. The buzzing magazine offices had a stream of men pouring in and out all day long. Most of their days had ended in the local wine bar and then on to dinner, and maybe a nightclub with various partners. They would fall into bed at 5 a.m. then be up for the office again at 7.30.

They were lucky in that, like most things creative, old blood makes way for the new, and they arrived at a particular time in journalism when publishers were becoming more sensitive to the fickle nature of style. What suited their young readers three years ago would now almost certainly be old hat and stale. The high turnover of editorial staff certainly reflected this awareness.

As the two girls worked their way up Claudia became

assistant to the fashion editor, and Charlotte got the grand title of features editor. Then after a three-year apprenticeship the real break came. *Today's Woman* was getting relaunched. It hadn't changed its image since the 1950s when it had been a staple for knitting, baking and all matters domestic. The title had seemed an anachronism for all that time. It was being taken over by a large publishing group and the first person they approached to consider editing the relaunch was Charlotte. She felt as though Christmas had come early that year. Here was the golden opportunity all young journalists dreamed of. Her own particular brand of style had been noted. Her reputation for producing snappy features and witty profiles was just what the publishers were seeking. And she was given more or less free rein to design and develop the new look for the thinking, career-orientated eighties woman.

It had been only natural to take her team-mate with her to run the fashion side of the magazine. The money still wasn't too great but it was enough for the pair of them to buy into a larger flat in a purpose-built block in Battersea. It was a mark of the strength of their friendship that they had managed to live and work together without feeling suffocated by the arrangement. They both loved their work so much that they were more than happy to bring it home with them.

But when William came on the scene Claudia took an instant dislike to him. Secretly nicknaming him 'Willy the Wally' she told Charlotte she thought he was arrogant, humourless and utterly tedious. But as the weeks went by and she saw her friend fall hopelessly for him, she thawed her teasing slightly. And when Charlotte announced they were to be married, Claudia had bitten her tongue. She sensed that Charlotte was making a huge mistake but she was grown up enough to know it was really not her business and that if Charlotte was happy she should be happy for her. She'd thrown her arms round them both and said how delighted she was. William knew she privately couldn't stand him, but a sort of uneasy truce existed between them. They had something in common. Both of them loved Charlotte. But a niggling resentment grew after the marriage. The two women still spent a lot of time together, and William, quite rightly, nursed the suspicion that perhaps Claudia had a slightly unsettling effect on his wife – that she was a subversive influence who occasionally incited Charlotte to riot.

Claudia herself seemed to be content with a stream of lovers, and had no wish to settle down with a husband. She'd seen her own mother become so insecure and shadowy during her father's meteoric rise that she never wanted to feel dependent, or secondary, to any man. Because of that she had a tendency to be over-sensitive to William's behaviour. She could see he was too weak to accept the challenge of an overly successful wife. He had a patronizing and indulgent attitude to Charlotte's talent which Claudia's shrewd intuition picked up immediately, and scented her nostrils for blood. She would do her utmost to rescue her friend from the familiar old trap. She was as fiercely protective of Charlotte as Charlotte was of her.

And now Claudia's comments about Daniel were hitting a very raw nerve. Charlotte had tried to dismiss him from her mind, but he had a tenacious habit of crawling back in there. She shrugged. It was because she'd found him so irritating the previous night.

Charlotte walked back up Richmond Hill. The sky was hung with bulbous black clouds which threw strange artificial, electric casts of light; the pressure of the threatened rain held in suspension. Great heavy drops finally splattered on to the pavement in front of her as she delved into her handbag for her keys.

The door slammed shut behind her, a pile of leaflets littered the floor. The house was oppressively silent, gloomy and chill. It was too early in the year for the heating to be switched on, yet too late for natural warmth to filter in through the thick walls. The house, a beautiful Georgian villa, was much too large for the pair of them. Bought at the time of their marriage, it had previously been divided into flats and shamefully neglected. Many people had considered taking on the renovation and balked at the amount of work involved before she and William had noticed it in the agent's window, a screaming bargain. If Charlotte could have foreseen the time and money to be eaten up by the old house she'd have turned tail and fled from the agent's offices.

They had lived in William's flat while most of the work was being done. It had taken over a year of juggling her hectic schedule to fit in trips to bathroom shops, tile warehouses and kitchen manufacturers, and she had leaned on her secretary to search London for out-of-stock taps on nine-week deliveries. In fact the magazine had carried more than a fair proportion of home improvement features while the project was under way. She had become a sort of pocket expert on architraves and the mysterious two by one that the builders bandied around all the time. She knew exactly what the electrician was talking about when he mentioned two-way three gang switches and ring mains. The whole thing had been a complete organizational nightmare.

Eventually they had closed the door on the builders and moved in to enjoy the 'impressive Georgian family home', as the agent had described it. Set over four floors, the basement contained the kitchen and dining room; the ground floor comprised a gracious drawing room with sweeping views down towards the Thames and Twickenham beyond, and a small study where she hid herself to write. On the first floor was a master bedroom leading to their own beautifully co-ordinated ensuite bathroom, and a separate guest room. And then there was the top floor. The nursery suite. Three rooms designed to accommodate babies and nanny, lovingly designed with feminine furnishings in pale pastels. Charlotte very rarely ventured up there now and they were just called spare rooms, cleaned once a week by Mrs Kelly, who whipped round with a Hoover on already clean carpets, dusted dust-free surfaces and scrubbed spot-free paint.

As Charlotte stood there brooding, a bunch of leaflets in hand, the phone rang. It was Kate, William's secretary. 'Hello, Mrs de Sallis,' she said brightly. 'William asked me to call you.'

'Hi, Kate, how are you?'

'Very well, thank you. William asked me to let you know that he won't be home till late. He said to say he's very sorry.'

'Thank you, Kate, for letting me know.'

The prospect of another long, lonely evening yawned ahead of her. She went down to the kitchen, took a bottle of wine out of the fridge, climbed the stairs back to the drawing room, and helped herself to a glass out of the cupboard at the side of the fireplace. She turned on the gas log fire and curled up on the enormous cream sofa. She watched the blue flames lap around the fake coals, slowly turning them a glowing red, and closed her eyes miserably.

Chapter Three

❦⟡❧

Charlotte was asleep when William came home that night. But she saw him in the morning. He kissed her and said, 'I won't be late tonight, Charlie . . . see you about eight.'

She checked her watch. It was 7.30 p.m. Her arrangements were well under way. Subterfuge was never something Charlotte liked using, but she felt she had reached the point where, if she achieved the right end, she would resort to any means, short of Claudia's suggestion of course. She couldn't help smiling to herself as she put the last of the chopped onion into the casserole, sniffing loudly as she did so. Maybe Valentine was right and she was turning into the little suburban housewife, using culinary skill to get to her man. There was a time when there had been plenty of other devices to soften him up. She'd have resorted to cookery last of all. She quickly threw in the sliced mushrooms and thin strips of fillet steak, half a bottle of good claret, and stirred. The smell was wonderful.

Satisfied that everything was well under control she removed her apron, smoothed down the tight little black skirt she was wearing and poured herself a glass of the remaining wine. She took one last look at the table, laid complete with starched linen napkins and two large white candles, then went up to the drawing room to wait for William. Whatever his mood tonight, she had resolved to tackle him over the fertility tests. She had put his needs first for long enough and she intended to make him listen to hers. She picked some music from their CD collection and sat back, letting Sade's sexy tones wash over her, closing her eyes. When she finally heard the front door slam shut at half past eight she was feeling pleasantly lightheaded and very relaxed.

'Hi, darling!' William shouted. She heard him rustling papers, leafing through the post. He came into the room and smiled down at her on the sofa. She returned his smile and stretched up, catching his head in her hands, pulling him down for a warm, inviting kiss.

'Mmmmm, that's nice,' he said. 'Sorry I'm late.' He picked up the bottle. 'Three-quarters of a bottle late!' He sat down beside her, yawning. 'What sort of a day have you had? God, I'm tired, aren't you? I've had a ghastly day.' He turned the volume of the music down. 'Sorry about last night, darling – there wasn't anything I could do about it. The Reiser Group crisis is going from bad to worse. Anyway, what did you do today?'

'Hmm? Oh not much really. I went to the gym this morning, apart from that I've been in the house all day.'

'Oh.' He sounded bored.

'I met Claudia for lunch yesterday,' she volunteered. 'In town. And we talked about my going back to work, maybe.'

'Oh.' His voice sounded flat and disapproving. Dismissal and lack of interest.

Charlotte continued doggedly. 'She said she'd have a word with Henry Phillips about it – you know, the new editor. As you pointed out the other night, I need something to get my teeth into.'

'But we both know a full-time job would be too much for you, don't we darling?' With that he stood and turned off the music completely and then pressed the button on the television set. It was the beginning of the Nine o'Clock News.

Charlotte bristled. But she wasn't giving up yet. Although he was, as usual, giving her the wayward child treatment, she had resolved not to be fazed by him. She continued smiling at him charmingly. 'Now, darling, I hope you haven't had lunch. I've got something extra special for you.'

He frowned, trying to remember. 'No, no. I just had a sandwich.'

'Would you like a drink before we eat?'

'I'd just like to watch the news first . . .'

'Supper has been ready for half an hour already. You did tell me you'd be home at 8 o'clock, darling.'

'Well, I don't mind waiting.'

'I do.' She had to stop herself from snapping. She forced herself to smile sweetly. 'Really. It's ready now. Come on, darling.'

He shrugged reluctantly and switched off the TV set. 'OK. Coming.' He followed her down the stairs to the dining room.

'Just sit down. You don't have to do a thing other than talk to me.' He looked at her curiously. Suspiciously. He was taking in the candles, the gleaming silver and the crystal which caught the flickering candlelight and cut it into shards.

'Um, have I forgotten something? It's not our anniversary, is it?'

'No, you haven't forgotten anything. I just decided that tonight we'd have a special supper together. I thought we could just talk. We seem to spend so little time talking.' She spooned the delicious-smelling casserole on to his plate. Settling herself down she reached over and stroked his hand tenderly. 'It's time we rekindled some fire . . .' she breathed suggestively.

William reached for his wine. 'I'm so shattered. God, what a day. I may have to go to Paris in the morning, so let's not have a late night, eh?'

Charlotte ignored this slap in the face. 'What's happening in Paris, sweetheart?' Her voice sounded calm and interested. Inside she was fighting rising resentment.

Between mouthfuls he began to explain. 'Remember I

told you about Reiser – the problem with the plant in Lyons?'

Charlotte nodded. 'What's happened? I thought it was an unfounded scare?'

'Well, that's what we hoped. Obviously as soon as the word poisoning was mentioned in connection with them, they had to close down the plant and check everything. No stocks of dried milk have left the factory for a week pending results. It seems that they may have traced the source of contamination to a faulty water cooler. Whatever happens, it's going to be a huge PR job to convince the press of Reiser's integrity. It's about as tasty as a nuclear plant leak. Especially when young babies are at risk.' He paused to take a sip of his wine. 'The batches are always thoroughly pre-tested before they leave the factory and this particular lot was obviously destroyed immediately. Head Office have to decide whether or not they need to issue announcements throughout Europe to stop anyone using the milk.'

'God, I see what you mean.' Charlotte knew the implications. Reiser was one of William's largest clients. As press spokesperson he would inevitably be a core part of any decisions taken. This was bloody typical. Every time she wanted to speak to him, something, or someone, stepped in the way.

'How long will you have to go for?' Already she sensed defeat.

'It depends on them. How they want to play it and what the press's reaction is. It could be a couple of days, till the weekend, it could be longer. It's impossible to say until I know more about it.'

She studied her husband as they ate. Small lines were beginning to etch themselves into the corners of his mouth and the laughter lines were deepening around his eyes. His boyish good looks were taking on a new earnestness though he still looked younger than his thirty-eight years. Clear light grey eyes which some-times had an unfortunate glint of coldness in them now observed her warmly.

'So, my darling. As I said, let's not be too late to bed as I've got a very heavy day ahead.'

Charlotte was caught in a bind once more. However strong her resolve was to tackle him about going for the tests, if she did so now she knew he would close up immediately. She was headed for sure failure. Out too went her resolution to tell him she had no intention of organizing a party with Daniel Cornwallis. If she mentioned it tonight, in the mood he was in, he probably wouldn't listen. So all her effort had been wasted. Admittedly he'd had a nice meal and was now smiling rather daftly at her, but she knew the minute she got up to clear the plates, he'd excuse himself to watch *Newsnight*, or whatever it was he 'had' to watch for his business.

'Now my love. Is there anything else you want to talk about, or can I be excused?'

She wanted to slug him, hard. She'd talked about bugger all. He'd talked to her about his wonderful business. She bit her lip and lowered her head so that he couldn't see her eyes as she lifted the casserole dish off the table. 'No William. That's OK. I'll see you upstairs.'

Later, when she slipped in between the bedsheets, sounds of the television drifting upstairs, she lay rigid with pent-up frustration. Everything seemed to be out of her control. William was running his life just the way he wanted it, and she was fitting in with him. He hadn't paid any heed to her talk about going back to work. Bitter tears of angry resentment spilled silently down her cheeks and on to the pillow. She screwed her eyes up tightly to stem the flow. Charlotte felt she was start-ing on a steep and dangerous slope which would eventu-ally lead to her becoming a very unhappy woman.

*

Next thing she knew William was bending over her. 'I'll be back late afternoon to pick up my case. See you later, darling,' he said.

Charlotte buried her head in the pillow, only surfacing after she heard the click of the bedroom door closing. She climbed out of bed, feeling hard knots of tension in her neck and shoulders. Although she had slept heavily, it was not a restful sleep. More the kind of semi-coma induced by deep unhappiness and defeat.

Pulling on her tracksuit she went down to the kitchen and set about clearing up the solidified mess from the night before, cursing William more and more as she slammed the plates into the gawping dishwasher. Thank God he was going to Paris. She couldn't stand him in the house a moment longer. And nor could she stand to be in the house any longer. A ten minutes' brisk walk brought her to the doorway of her health club. Polly, the girl on the reception desk, looked up in surprise.

'Hi, Charlotte. Twice in two days? Is this the start of a new regime?'

'Something like that, Polly.' She smiled. She followed the corridor down past the steam and sauna rooms, past the sunbeds and beyond the swimming pool to the vast gymnasium. Four white, half-mirrored walls housed thousands of pounds' worth of fitness machines. Strangely formed black leather and steel monsters sat patiently, waiting to attack every muscle.

Charlotte collected a towel from the pile at the gym manager's desk and hung it around her neck. There were only a couple of other people in the gym and the row of ten exercise bikes stood unused. She adjusted a saddle to hip-height and climbed on, programming in her exercise level and duration. The dial ticked away the seconds and small green dots marched across a window on the panel in front of her, between the cycle handlebars, showing flat stretches followed by hills which rapidly became mountainous inclines – turning her legs to jelly and her bum to concrete. Six minutes later a supposedly healthy light film of sweat moistened her forehead.

David, the gym manager, watched her as she slid down from the bike and staggered over to him. 'Charlotte, are you OK? You look very red. Don't overdo it, will you? You pushed yourself very hard yesterday. And you hadn't been in for a while before that. You're supposed to work yourself in gently. If you go at it like a bull at a gate, you'll end up pulling muscles and damaging yourself.'

She started to work through her routine. It was a kind of mental, as well as physical, therapy. As the repetitions got harder, she thought about William, her anger and frustration driving her on. What was she going to do about him? At this rate she'd be forty before she was pregnant. And in the meantime she was well and truly rotting away at home. She needed to do something – if only to preserve her sanity. Also he might take a bit more notice of her if she had more on her mind that his sperm count.

She could chase up Claudia's suggestion, but she had a funny feeling Henry Phillips would not be as keen as Claudia suggested to get her back on *Today's Woman's* staff. The last thing he would want was his predecessor back in the camp, especially as he had spent a year putting his own mark on the magazine. He'd probably think she was trying to steal his job or something. No, that would politically be much too difficult. She'd have to join another magazine – and that was certainly easier said than done. When you've been a successful editor it's very tricky going into someone else's domain as a humble staff writer. Everyone had a tendency to walk round backwards anyway, to prevent being stabbed in the back. Even though it was her last wish at the moment to take on another editorship, she knew whoever she worked with would be convinced she was after their job. And that didn't make for a satisfactory working relationship.

There was always the party. It would certainly keep her busy for a while and she might even do a damn good job with it. And that could kill two birds with one stone: something to keep her occupied, and something to make William notice her.

She strained to do the last eight reps on the quads machine, pushing the weighted bar with the full force of her bent legs. She let out her breath and mopped her damp neck with the white towel draped at the side of the machine.

Arranging the party might remind her husband that she could be quite a powerful force when she put her mind to it. She'd have preferred it if she didn't have to get involved with Daniel Cornwallis. But surely she'd have no problem handling him, even if he turned into a complete pest.

She had a quick shower, dressed, and with considerably more purpose than her outward journey had shown, strode home.

It was 4.30 p.m. when she heard the key turn in the front door. She was at her desk in the study, her pen poised over an article she was drafting on the psychological implications of artificial insemination by donor. William's voice called, 'Hello, darling. Charlotte . . . where are you?'

'Hi, darling,' she answered. She often privately wondered if they used the term simply because they couldn't remember each other's names. The sight of his ultra-slick dark grey suit, pencil-stripe shirt and essential spotted bow tie did nothing to warm her towards him. His face was firm and unemotional. Clearly he was having a heavy day. She waited for him to speak.

'I'm catching the 7 o'clock flight to Paris. I just need to

pack a few things.' His voice was clipped, precise, business-like. A still in the office sort of voice. She wanted to scream at him. She wanted to shake him. But she just watched him climb the stairs. She had not spoken.

He paused mid-way and turned to her. 'Charlotte, are you all right?'

'Of course I'm all right. Why should I not be?'

'You just seem a little, well, quiet I s'pose. Never mind, do I have enough shirts up here? And did you pick that stuff up from the cleaners for me?'

She nodded. 'Of course.'

Minutes later he was back, suit replaced by grey slacks, shirt and blazer. Over his arm he carried a suit holder emblazoned with red and green braid and a gold initial motif.

'Would you like me to take you?' she asked.

'No, no. There's a cab due any minute.'

'How long will you be gone?'

'It's still impossible to say. Hopefully I'll be back tomorrow night. But if things aren't sorted out by the weekend obviously I'll have to stay on. I'll call you as soon as I have some idea. Anyway, you'll be all right, won't you?'

'Oh. Of course I will. Don't worry about me.'

He smiled. 'I won't.'

The cab arrived and blew its horn. 'Bye then, sweetheart.' And then he was gone.

She returned to her study and leafed through the article she was working on, but somehow she couldn't get back into it. She felt very restless. And bored. She picked up the phone and punched out Claudia's direct line. She didn't expect to get through. Claudia was usually tied up in meetings, or out on location somewhere. So she was doubly pleased when she heard Claudia's snapped 'yes'.

'Hi. It's me. Are you in the middle of something?'

65

'Always. But I can make time to talk. How did it go? And I'm sorry I didn't get back to you yesterday. I was on my feet all day sorting out that shoot I was telling you about, then I didn't get in till about eleven. Did you talk to him?'

'No, I didn't. And now he's fucked off to Paris. What are you doing tonight? I feel like a night on the town. Want to join me?'

'Love to. But I don't think I can. I've got to go to a charity fashion show . . .' She thought for a moment. 'Tell you what, why don't you come with me? It starts at seven thirty. If you can meet me at the Intercontinental at seven fifteen . . .'

'Have you got a spare ticket?'

'Well, no. But I can have one rustled up by then. We gave them a nice big plug for it so I'm sure the organizers won't be too stingy. You might even enjoy it. You'd better dress up too. I think it's going to be quite a glitzy affair.'

'I wouldn't miss it for the world. I'll see you in the foyer.'

Charlotte quickly rang the cab company and booked a car, then raced upstairs three at a time. She threw open the wardrobe doors while kicking off her trainers. She'd have to really hurry to make it up to Park Lane in just over an hour. She pulled out a black dress. It had a high neck and long sleeves, and it was a very tight fit, finishing about two inches above her knees. She hoped she could still get into it comfortably. Then she found a pair of sheer black tights, and some high suede court shoes – a sort of poor-man's Kim Basinger. She swept her hair back and piled it up on to her head, leaving just a few ends spilling out, and then caught it with a black bow clip. A string of pearls and large teardrop pearl earrings finished the whole thing off. She threw her black blouson leather jacket over her shoulders and tripped precariously down the stairs, unpractised on her high stilettoes.

*

She eventually found Claudia amid a sea of glamour and glitterati. She was nodding and smiling at a very tasty-looking man. Tall, with chiselled features and slicked back dark hair, he could have been a model. Charlotte struggled through the crowd to get to them. She smiled at Claudia's companion and then kissed her on both cheeks. 'Hello, lovey,' Claudia said. 'This is Miles Trent. Miles, this is Charlotte de Sallis – Charlotte Grange, before her marriage.'

Miles put out his hand and shook hers warmly. 'Hello,' he said. 'I've heard a lot about you.'

'Likewise,' said Charlotte. 'I gather you're the one responsible for the sexy rubber that everyone's talking about.'

'Well, talking about is right. Whether anyone ever gets to actually see it is the point. God spare us from the narrow-minded. Anyway, I must go and find the people I'm supposed to be meeting. See you later. And it was good to meet you, Charlotte.'

'Cor blimey, he's a bit gorgeous, isn't he?'

'Yes, he is. He's also very gay.'

'What a shame. I suppose you have that on good authority?'

'Well, he told me himself, so I s'pose that's pretty good. That was after I made a rather unsubtle pass at him.'

'Oh dear. I hope he let you down gently.'

'He did. He's a lovely man. And a brilliant photographer. Now, let's see if we can find our seats.' They were ushered through the foyer and up to the giant ballroom on the first floor. The entire area had been 'tented' to resemble a sultan's palace. A central catwalk was lined each side with wooden stakes, six feet apart and a foot high. Each stake bore a platform on which were placed enormous bunches of green grapes, spilling down the sides, towards the raised dais. A faint, but slightly cloying scent of incense drifted across the room.

Charlotte followed Claudia down the rows of neatly laid out gilt chairs and was pleased to note they were in the front row – real grandstand seats. The seats were quickly filling up and Charlotte recognized many faces among the slickly polished assembly.

Claudia nudged her and Charlotte realized that her friend, true to form, had made suitable arrangements for their creature comforts during the show, and had commandeered their own bottle of Lanson champagne which she was now offering. 'Top up?'

'Thanks.' Charlotte grinned and held out her glass.

Claudia was busily turning her head to get a good look at all the other guests, most of whom had paid £150 for the privilege of being seen there. She gave Charlotte a kind of running commentary on who was who and who owned what. She pointed to a very exotic-looking young Indian boy – who looked no more than eighteen or nineteen – accompanied by Frankie Day, a blonde stunner and sometime page-three lady. 'That's Sonny Chattanee. His father left him about £75 million and most of New Delhi. I can't think the family will be very impressed by her pedigree. Still he's probably just in training for when he finds his nice Indian girl to settle down with. Judging from that necklace she's not doing too badly though!' Charlotte squinted at the twenty enormous diamonds sparkling against Frankie's smooth tanned skin, each one a hefty chunk of at least two carats. When Sonny grew bored, or was recalled to the fold, she could probably retire on the proceeds.

There were several mother and daughter teams from the English aristocracy – fresh-faced young debs whose sole purpose in life was to be seen in the right places so that eligible young men could eye the new bloodstock and make their purchases accordingly. The bank clerks must have worn quite a trench to their vaults this afternoon, Charlotte thought, as she glanced around at the fabulous display of priceless jewels worn like gaudy Christmas decorations. She touched the pearls at her neck self-consciously, pleased that she had chosen to wear them. This was certainly not the night to air cheap paste imitations.

Suddenly the lights dimmed and the previously unobtrusive background strains of gentle sitar music burst into an ear-splitting electronic cacophony of new wave sound. The cunningly draped silk at the rear of the stage slid back to reveal a tableau of long-limbed eastern goddesses, posing with legs apart, feet turned out at impossible angles, wrists bent over at forty-five degrees and chins artfully jutting. Their clothes were definitely Asian in style: rich brocades and satins in peacock shades of blues, purples and greens, rich drapes spangled with tiny mirrors and sequins. They moved slowly and perfectly in unison, bare feet sliding silently over the wooden platforms.

The audience were hushed in admiration as the models twisted and turned, manoeuvring around the catwalk, all the while their haughty pale faces set in arrogant condescension. When the last girl finally disappeared behind the curtain the applause was deafening.

The lights flashed again and the real show began. First of all Rifat Ozbek's beautifully simple off-the-shoulder white spangled dress and comfortable jogging pants. A white bomber jacket with curly yin and yang symbols. Then Bruce Oldfield's white jersey, deliciously draped in Grecian simplicity. Arabella Pollen's instantly recognizable tailored suits in beautifully fitted grosgrain. The audience held its breath and then applauded enthusiastically at each new showing on the platform.

Claudia kept whispering in Charlotte's ear, giving rundowns on the histories of the designers – and how much you'd have to pay for one of their numbers.

Charlotte could hear pencils furiously scribbling down numbers on the tasteful little marbled paper pads which had been hopefully laid out on every chair. Several thousands of pounds' worth of orders would no doubt be placed as a result of tonight's show. The price for each garment would vary enormously according to whether it was from the more accessible ready-to-wear collections, or from the four-figure couture range, hand fitted to cling like a second skin, flattering even the dullest figure.

Charlotte lost herself in the excitement. It was quite a while since she'd been to such a glitzy affair and the absence, she realized, bothered her more than she had known. She felt utterly at home people-watching. She loved the glamour, and even the artifice. It all added spice to the job of journalism, a welcome antidote to the drier side of the career. It was also fun to realize that Claudia was becoming quite a celebrity in her own right. A few people had glanced over at them, and then whispered to one another. Claudia was one of the new breed of style dictators. Not only could she pick out the best of the top-notch designers, but she could tell you exactly what was de rigueur down on the street. She looked relaxed and utterly at her ease, enjoying the show. The only evidence that she was anything other than a celebrity guest was her own slim notebook where she made a few discreet scribbles every now and then. She certainly didn't intend to labour the fact that she was 'working'.

Eventually the show came to an end. The star of the grand finale was on loan from London Zoo: a baby Indian elephant decked out in rich braids and giant sequins. He seemed to be rather bemused by the noise of the crowd, but stood peacefully centre stage. As the audience applauded even more, the show slowly disappeared behind the curtain, and the main lights came back on. Everyone began chattering simultaneously.

70

Claudia turned to Charlotte. 'Look, Charlie, I just want to catch Miles before he disappears. I won't be a second.'

As soon as Claudia left Charlotte felt a firm tap on her shoulder. She turned and found herself almost nose to nose with Daniel Cornwallis, his deep navy eyes gazing levelly into her own, his mouth still carrying that slightly amused twist. 'Charlotte,' he said, his voice silky warm with pleasure. 'How lovely to see you. You were clearly enjoying the show.'

She nodded and smiled back at him, determined not to let him know how off-balance she felt. 'Yes, did you?' she said weakly.

'Very much.' He turned to the pretty brunette at his side. 'Charlotte, this is Sarah Sanders. Sarah, this is Charlotte de Sallis.'

The girl smiled. 'You must be William's wife.'

Charlotte nodded. 'Yes. That's right. You know William, do you?'

The girl looked surprised. 'Oh yes, very well. Don't I, Daniel?'

She seemed very comfortable with him. Charlotte found herself wondering why he wasn't with Valentine. He certainly hadn't wasted any time finding a new escort. And why was Charlotte beginning to feel that the rest of the world seemed to know her husband a hell of a lot better than she did?

'Really,' Charlotte said, more than a little icily.

'Anyway, Charlotte, it was good to meet you but I have to go. Daniel, thanks so much for bringing me but I have to rush to catch that train.'

Daniel leaned down and kissed her cheek. 'Take care, love,' he said fondly. 'See you tomorrow.'

Charlotte's confusion must have been plain to see. Daniel grinned at her. 'Sarah's my secretary. Valentine's away on some blasted trip so Sarah agreed to come with me rather than waste the ticket.'

'Oh.' Charlotte laughed. 'I see.' For the life of her she couldn't understand why she was suddenly so relieved. They were left, the pair of them, standing uncertainly. Then Daniel said, 'I see your glass is empty. Shall I try and find you a refill?'

She looked down at the forgotten glass in her hand. 'Thanks. Actually I'm waiting for somebody. I suppose I should really go and see where they are . . . '

'Won't they come and find you?'

She thought for a moment. Here was her chance to escape. All she had to do was excuse herself and quickly find Claudia, then be gone. She smiled at him. 'Yes, I suppose they will.'

She followed him back across the rows of seats until they found a waiter carrying brimming glasses on a silver platter. On the way across the room she couldn't miss the many admiring glances cast in Daniel's direction by the other women in the room.

He handed her the glass. 'So. William should be in Paris by now. Sounds as if the Reiser business is going to keep him busy for a while.'

'That's what he said. He might have to stay over the weekend. Poor William,' she said, sounding a lot more supportive than she felt. 'He's working so hard at the moment. What with the merger and now this. Still, he does seem to thrive on it. I've never seen him look healthier.'

'It's the adrenalin. I've noticed that William only seems to be really content when he's crisis managing. He seems to enjoy the challenge. It's exhilarating to work alongside someone like that, but it can get a bit exhausting living with them, can't it?'

Charlotte wasn't sure what Daniel meant by that. He must have sensed, though God knew how, that underneath her supportive wife role she was sick to death of his over-commitment to his career.

She shrugged. 'You must be the same, Daniel. It's

72

that sort of business, isn't it? I mean you don't get to be a success in advertising without giving it everything you've got. Business must come first.'

He shook his head. 'No, Charlotte. Funnily enough that's not the way it is. I made the decision a long time ago that life was for living. I do get a lot of kicks from the business, but there's more to it than that. I learned the art of delegation a long time ago. I've been lucky with the team around me. I work hard, but I play even harder . . . '

'There you are, Charlie . . . I thought I'd lost you. I managed to find Miles and he says he's got some great pics . . . '

Claudia stopped mid-sentence as she realized just who Charlotte was deep in conversation with. 'Oh, er . . . hello,' she said, putting on her best smile. She threw her shoulders back ever so slightly to display her cleavage to best advantage. Charlotte recognized immediately Claudia's sexy temptress routine. 'Charlotte . . . ' Claudia's voice had lowered by at least half an octave. 'Aren't you going to introduce us?'

'Yes, of course. Claudia, this is Daniel Cornwallis. Daniel, this is Claudia Williams – a close friend of mine.'

Claudia held out her hand and Daniel raised it to his lips. 'Hello,' he drawled. She withdrew her hand prettily and preened visibly. 'Claudia, would you let me get you a drink? You're empty handed!'

'Thank you, Daniel. That would be nice.' She made it sound as though he'd just offered her a full body massage.

Charlotte narrowed her eyes as soon as he turned away. 'Really, Claudia. You're so bloody obvious. Why don't you just wear a badge saying "eat me"?'

'If I'm that obvious I don't need to, do I? What a hunk, Charlie. He's even better in the flesh. And after all, you've already told me you can't stand him. He's single and available. Anyway, where is Voluptuous Val tonight?'

'Away. He brought his secretary but she had to catch the train home.'

'Really . . . So he's all alone. How very interesting.'

'Claudia!' Charlotte snapped. 'Remember you're supposed to be with me tonight.'

'Killjoy!' Claudia hissed. 'Thank you, Daniel.' She turned quickly and smiled up at him over the rim of her glass, giving him the full benefit of her sable lashes. 'Charlotte and I were just saying how hungry we were, weren't we, Charlotte?'

Charlotte glared at her. 'I . . . er . . . were we?' She was almost choking, fighting an almost overpowering urge to kick Claudia.

Daniel jumped in, as if he'd just been given a prompt. 'Why don't you let me buy you both dinner? I can't think of anything I'd like more.'

In unison Charlotte said, 'No, absolutely not . . .' and Claudia said, 'What a delightful idea.'

Charlotte tried once more. 'That's very kind of you, Daniel, but we have plans already, don't we, Claudia?'

'Nothing that can't be changed, Charlie . . .'

Cow! thought Charlotte. Just you wait till I get you in the loo later. She smiled through gritted teeth.

Daniel and Claudia looked at each other triumphantly. 'That's settled then,' he said. 'Now, where shall we go? What do you fancy?'

Charlotte snapped her lips shut with the venom of a Venus flytrap. Claudia had got them into this and she could bloody well carry it through. She was tempted to plead a headache and leave them to it, but for some strange reason she didn't relish the thought of Daniel and Claudia getting it together. She'd come as a chaperone if nothing else.

They collected their jackets from the hall porter and went outside into the chill night air. Charlotte pulled her jacket tight and shivered, while Claudia strode purposefully ahead, keeping step with Daniel. Charlotte

74

felt ridiculously insecure on her stilettoes and concentrated on wobbling as little as possible over the
potholes laughingly described as a pavement. Daniel
flagged down a taxi and held the door open for them
both. She climbed in ahead of Claudia, and Daniel
squeezed into the gap between them on the seat.
Charlotte was painfully conscious of him. Yet again that
indefinable scent – a mixture of soap and warm musky
masculinity – pervaded her senses. She concentrated on
staring out of the window, saying nothing, while
Claudia made small talk. Why was it that Claudia was
irritating her so intensely?

A few minutes later they pulled up at the restaurant.
The Meridiana – Charlotte might have guessed he'd pick
that, you never knew who you might rub shoulders
with. Just as in the nightclub several nights before, a
table was magically available for them. This man
certainly had clout in the right places, yet he shrugged
off the attention casually, as if he hadn't noticed.
Charlotte picked up her menu and studied it, almost
petulantly, listening to Claudia's account of how they'd
first met. She could be wildly entertaining when she
wanted to be and Daniel was certainly amused.

'I've been trying to talk Charlie into coming back to
work, haven't I, Charlie?'

'Hmmm? Oh yes,' she said, noncommittally.

'But she's got a job already.'

'You mean her freelancing?'

'No, no. Charlotte's going to organize a great big
party for us, aren't you, Charlotte?'

Charlotte felt a bit like a patient at a teaching hospital
when the students are doing their rounds, being
discussed as if she wasn't there. 'Well, actually, Daniel,
I haven't decided. William left for Paris before I had a
chance to speak to him.' She paused and took a large
slug of wine. 'I'm thinking about it. I'll let you know
when I've decided.'

'Why not do it, Charlotte?' Claudia wheedled. 'At least it would get you out of the house. And isn't that just what we were talking about at lunch the other day? You can't sit there brooding all the time, can you?'

Charlotte was livid with Claudia. The last person she wanted to hear about her insecurities was Daniel smartypants Cornwallis. She wanted him to think of her as a ruthless editor not a hopeless waif. She sent silent messages across the table to Claudia, which, had Claudia been able to read them, would probably have made even her blush. Daniel in the meantime looked like the dog that had just dug up his neighbour's bone store. What an insight Claudia was giving him.

'OK, I'll do it,' Charlotte snapped.

Daniel raised his eyebrows. 'Really?'

'Yes. I've decided. Of course you're quite right, Claudia. And when I've finished that, I'll get back to work. OK?' She smiled, hiding her anger. There was no point in arguing. The more she fought her corner, the more they'd be assured she was trying to justify something that didn't exist. But as soon as she closed her mouth she began to wonder just what she had let herself in for.

Charlotte didn't eat very much, but watched Claudia stuffing down half a cow and enough chocolate mousse to make any self-respecting child throw up. As her friend attacked the petits fours, Charlotte looked at her watch rather obviously. 'I'm afraid I'm going to have to make a move.' She scrabbled in her handbag for her purse.

Daniel put his hand across hers. 'Good heavens, Charlotte, this is on me . . . I insist,' he said as she started to protest. 'Now, how are you going to get home?'

'Oh, I can easily get a cab.'

'Where are you going? Richmond?'

'Yes.'

'How about you, Claudia? Where do you live?'

'Battersea.'

'In that case you and I might as well share a cab. We're almost in the same direction.'

Charlotte could see Claudia glowing as she beamed at him. 'Oh, what a good idea. Now, Charlie, are you sure you'll be all right going back on your own?'

'Of course, darling,' Charlotte smiled through sugar-coated lips. 'Listen, I'll get a cab myself. Don't you two rush. I really don't want to break up the party . . .'

Daniel stood up. 'I'll find you one,' he said. He disappeared, leaving the two women alone.

'What's up, Charlie? You look as though you're about to knife me.'

'Can you blame me? I thought we were going for a girls' night out. The last thing I wanted was to get roped into spending more time with him,' Charlotte hissed.

'Charlotte, he's just gorgeous. Look, I know you can't stand him, though God knows why. You've been a prickly old bag all night. I've really enjoyed his company and I'm very sorry if you didn't. He *is* William's partner for Christ's sake. *And* you've agreed to work with him. Frankly I don't see the problem in my making a play for him! Unless there's something you don't want to tell me . . .'

'Oh, don't be so bloody ridiculous. What on earth would I not be telling you? No, Claudia, you really are welcome to him, I mean it. It's just that he's so damn smug and . . . and . . . well . . .' Actually she couldn't really think what he was. It was pretty irrational if you thought about it too hard. He was perfectly charming. Smooth. Successful. And as the tabloids said, devastatingly handsome. She just supposed it was one of those things, chemistry or something, that got her back up about Daniel.

'Charlotte, there's a cab outside. Thank you for having

dinner with me.' Daniel leaned forward and pecked her on the cheek.

She waved cheerily to Claudia. 'Bye, darling,' she called. 'Enjoy the rest of the night.'

For some unfathomable reason she felt as if her stomach had been shrunk in the tumble dryer. The thought of Claudia and Daniel presumably about to spend a wild night of passion – if she knew anything about Claudia, which she did – filled her with the most abject misery she could remember feeling in years.

'Liqueur, Claudia?'

Claudia almost purred with pleasure. 'Lovely idea,' she smouldered at him.

Daniel had to smile to himself. He knew Claudia's game only too well and under different circumstances he just might have succumbed to her more than obvious charms. It wasn't that he didn't like her. She was funny and easy to be with. It was Charlotte who was the problem. Ever since he had noticed her in the row in front at the fashion show he had been unable to take his eyes off her. She seemed to draw him like a magnet, though why she should do so remained a huge mystery to him. He was not in the habit of seducing colleagues' wives. Indeed, he wasn't into adultery at all. Life was complicated enough without screwing around with other men's women. And she'd hardly encouraged him. It was more than obvious that she'd only come along to dinner under pressure. But since she had left he felt deflated and oddly disappointed.

'I'm glad Charlotte is organizing the party for you. I really think it will do her a lot of good to get out of the house, and take her mind off that shit she's married to.' Claudia clapped her hand to her mouth. 'Whoops! Oh Daniel, I'm sorry. I don't think I should be saying things like that about your partner, should I?'

Daniel laughed quietly. 'Don't worry, Claudia. Being

in business with William is rather different from being married to him. So long as his private life doesn't affect the office, I don't really mind what he does.'

'He and I don't really get on,' Claudia confessed. 'Charlie knows I can't stand him. He can be such a selfish brute at times. She's given him so much support – even left her job for him – and he doesn't seem to appreciate anything she does, or take much notice of her. And between you and me I wouldn't be at all surprised if he were having a bit on the side.'

Daniel was beginning to wonder if Claudia was a bit the worse for the bottle, but he was finding this information about Charlotte's marriage really rather fascinating.

'And on top of all the baby business it's no wonder she's upset right now.' She paused and frowned. 'God knows why I'm telling you all this, Daniel . . . It's just that I can't help worrying about her.'

Daniel nodded solemnly. 'I know, I know,' he said quietly, using that age old tactic most men resort to when they don't know at all. He would have loved to ask what she meant by the baby business, but felt it might have been rather presumptuous of him. And anyway, Charlotte seemed to have been temporarily forgotten.

'Good grief!' Claudia whispered.

'What?'

Her eyes were fixed on a point somewhere behind Daniel's head. Daniel started to swivel round. 'Don't look now,' she warned. 'They'll think we're staring . . . What on earth is he doing over here, I thought he was still in the States.'

'Who, for God's sake?' Daniel's curiosity could stand it no longer. He turned to take a gander at whomever Claudia seemed so excited to see.

To his mind, the three men behind him looked as if they had just come back from a funeral, with their dark

79

grey suits and sombre black ties. They all had rather swarthy complexions. 'Looks like a bunch of spivs to me,' he said acidly.

'Nonsense, I think they look rather attractive. Sort of Mediterranean and exotic. Wait, he's coming over.'

'Who?'

But Claudia had started to grin over Daniel's right shoulder. 'Giles,' she simpered.

'Claudia, how lovely to see you,' a voice oozed oily charm.

'I had no idea you were over here,' she said. 'Giles, do you know Daniel Cornwallis? Daniel, this is Giles Ferguson. Giles is a publisher – about five hundred titles, isn't it?'

'Was,' Giles corrected. 'I've just sold out in the States. And I'm looking at projects over here.' He looked at Daniel. 'Aren't you something to do with Lester Advertising?'

Daniel nodded. 'Bob Lester's my partner in New York.'

Giles's eyes narrowed thoughtfully. 'Yes, well, I've had dealings with Bob in the past, and I've certainly heard very good things about the London end of Lester's.'

'Actually we're called Cornwallis on this side of the Atlantic,' Daniel said coolly. There was something about Ferguson he didn't quite take to.

Claudia broke in with an excited squeal. 'If you're thinking of setting up new magazines over here you will remember me, won't you?'

'And don't forget Charlotte, Claudia,' Daniel said. Whatever he thought of Ferguson it seemed a shame to miss an opportunity to help her.

'Well done, Daniel, how clever of you. Yes, you remember Charlotte Grange, don't you, Giles? She used to edit *Today's Woman*. I know she's looking for something to get her teeth into.'

'Is she now?' Giles said quietly. 'Now that is interesting. I tell you what, Claudia, why don't you give me your card, and I'll be in touch with you. I don't know Charlotte personally but do mention me to her. And Daniel, why don't you give me your card too? I might need an advertising agency over the next few months.'

When Daniel had paid the bill they left, Claudia pushing her arm proprietorially through his.

Chapter Four

Sarah put a fresh cup of coffee in front of Daniel.

'You're a doll. Thanks. Did you get home all right?'

'Hmmm, thanks. I really enjoyed the show. How much longer did you stay?'

'Oh, I ended up having dinner with William's wife and a friend of hers.'

Sarah raised her eyebrows and grinned. 'Rather attractive, isn't she? It's funny you know. I'd thought judging from the way William behaves he'd have some old frump at home.'

'What do you mean the way William behaves?'

'Oh you know what he's like, Dan. He's just one of those men who need to feel attractive. He's a flirt. And it seems so silly when he's got such a lovely wife.'

Daniel stared down at the report on his desk. 'Really? Can't say I'd particularly noticed,' he grunted. 'What's the diary look like today? What meetings have I got?'

'Only internal ones. A graduate interview at eleven. And John Graham wants you to look at a video this afternoon before he presents it to the client. Oh, and *Campaign* phoned up and asked to speak to you. They've probably got wind of the merger. I said you'd call them back.'

'OK. Give me a few minutes and then come in with your pad.'

He picked up the steaming coffee mug and sipped thoughtfully. So Claudia wasn't the only one who suspected William's fidelity. Daniel had no time for that kind of stuff. There was something unsavoury and underhand about it, almost cowardly. If you had to be devious in order to go to bed with someone, or do it at someone else's expense, however unknowing they might be, it could hardly be a fulfilling union – for him at any rate. God knows there were plenty of people who needed just that excitement to fire them.

He found his thoughts drifting back down the years to another blonde-haired temptress. The woman who had brought him so close to marriage. Until, that was, the night he had caught them at it: his so-called best friend, and his fiancée, hard at it in his own bed. The fiercely sharp pain of that memory had blunted considerably, but it still hurt. The foul-tasting bile of betrayal. It was hard to trust a woman and if you let them get close to you they could damn nearly destroy you. Which was why he chose to fill his life with the sort of transient good-time type of woman who was open and up-front about what she wanted. And didn't want, like marriage and settling down. Because there was no way Daniel intended to commit himself to either for a long time yet.

But what was it that kept pulling his thoughts back to those damned eyes of Charlotte's? If he wasn't such a cynic he'd say lesser men could almost drown in them. Soft green pools that invited. Soft warm water to bathe and comfort you!

Jesus Christ! He pulled himself up, out of his reverie. What was the matter with him? He must be feeling sorry for her, recognizing the bitterness of the cuckold. When it came to women William was a shit and she deserved better. But, as he'd told Claudia, it wasn't his affair how William chose to conduct his personal life. Business was different. In order to form a successful partnership it wasn't necessary to be best bosom buddies with your partner. In fact it paid to have some kind of professional distance so that when a problem came up you could take an unemotional look at it, without letting the loyalty of friendship get in the way. It wasn't a surprise to him to

83

know that his suspicions about William were probably true, and that hadn't bothered him up till now. Up until he'd met Charlotte, that was.

He looked at the date, 23rd September. They'd have to move quickly to get the merger and announcement co-ordinated by November. He buzzed through to Sarah. He'd have to talk to Charlotte about the party right away. 'What's William's home telephone number?'

'He's away in Paris.'

'Sarah, how many times do I have to tell you, you're not paid to think . . .'

She laughed. 'OK. I'll have a look. Would you like me to make the call?'

'No, thanks. Just give me the number.'

A short time later Charlotte was wondering just why her wardrobe, which yesterday had been perfectly adequate, had today somehow transformed itself into the dowdiest collection of garments ever to sully a coathanger. She was looking for something to wear to have lunch with Daniel!

As soon as she heard his voice on the end of the line she had known exactly who it was. She had politely thanked him for dinner and he had sounded a bit hesitant, almost as if he wasn't quite sure why he had called her. All she could feel was an intense and exceedingly irrational jealousy about him and Claudia the previous evening. She didn't want her best friend involved with him. And she didn't like the way he seemed to be quietly but surely insinuating himself into her own life.

'I'd like to discuss the party with you,' he'd said. The largest part of her had wanted to make an excuse and say that she had changed her mind and would not be helping him with the party after all. But there was a small, traitorous part of her that wanted to show him that she wasn't afraid of him, that he didn't affect her in any way whatsoever and she was a woman to be reckoned with. And it was that kind of woman who now dragged on the stiff navy suit and stared out at her reflection from behind serious-looking spectacles. She intended to be a statement in asexuality following what for him had no doubt been a night of unbridled passion. She knew she'd recognize the signs immediately. Several years spent meeting Claudia's shagged-out conquests in the bathroom the morning after had given her a head start. The red eyes, slowed speech, heavy limbs. She pulled her hair back into a severe pony tail, tied up in a blue velvet bow.

When she saw Daniel in the restaurant looking his normal clean, healthy, clear-eyed self, she knew she was either looking at a seasoned all-nighter or she had misjudged Claudia. She cursed the giant moths dipping and diving through her stomach. He stood up and took her hand and a small jolt, almost like an electric shock, pulsated through her arm as he touched her hand to his mouth. His fiercely blue eyes met her own. Once more, she felt off-balance and unsure, almost gauche.

'Hello,' he said cheerfully. 'So you got back all right last night?' He poured a glass of wine and handed it to her.

'Oh yes, all in one piece, thanks. Did you?' She smiled sweetly.

Daniel grinned back. 'Yes, I did. Tempting as it was I declined Claudia's offer of a nightcap. I was in bed by midnight.'

'Oh,' she said brightly, suddenly feeling considerably better than she had for several hours. 'Great, isn't she?' she added charitably.

'Oh yes.' She waited for him to elaborate. He didn't.

'We've known each other for years. We're very close . . .'

'Yes. I could tell.'

As she talked, she felt embarrassed and self-conscious at the way Daniel was just gazing at her. She crossed her legs, and leaned back in her seat away from him. If he thought she was going to be just another of his conquests he was very much mistaken.

'Now, about this launch,' she heard her voice, clipped and businesslike.

'Ah yes, that.'

'The reason we're here.'

'Yes, quite so, Charlotte.'

'What was it you wanted to talk about, then?'

'You certainly like to come straight to the point, don't you?' Daniel laughed quietly.

'It is the only point after all,' she said frostily, then wished that she hadn't sounded quite so prim.

'Well, I thought maybe we should hold it on Hallowe'en. What do you think? It might be interesting to give it a theme. And there's enough ghouls among the clients – they wouldn't even need fancy dress.'

She counted up mentally. 'But that only gives us five weeks,' she said, slightly horrified.

'Yes, but we're going to have to announce the merger then, Charlotte. I'll give you all the help I can. I think the best place to hold it would be in our executive suite. There's an enormous conference room with kitchen facilities and so on. The only thing that's pressing at the moment is the guest list and invitations.'

'All, he says,' she mimicked, for a moment forgetting her personal feelings towards him and getting caught up in the details. 'It could take two weeks just to get invitations sorted out.'

'No it won't. The rate we use printers we should get them set and printed within three days. I'll get the studio to put together some ideas and you finish off the guest lists. William's secretary was sorting out his lot with him, and I'll get my secretary to pass you ours. In fact once you've checked the lists over, Sarah can send the invitations out for you.'

'She's going to love me, isn't she.'

He grinned. 'How could she fail, my dear Charlotte?'

She felt herself blush. How could she have stepped right into that one?

'OK,' she said, her voice resuming its businesslike tone once more. 'I'll get on with that and Sarah and I can liaise over the numbers for the printers.'

'That's that all settled then.' He relaxed back and refilled their glasses. 'Heard from William?'

'No. Have you?'

'No, but then I'm not expecting to again . . .'

'Neither am I . . .' Charlotte lied.

'I've been thinking about some of the things Claudia said last night.'

'Oh yes?' Charlotte could feel her defences rising. 'Like what?'

'Like you needing something to occupy you, and like the support you've given William . . .'

Charlotte's eyes blazed at him. 'Look, Daniel, I don't mean to be rude but I rather wish Claudia hadn't been quite so frank last night. And I do think my relationship with William is really none of your business.'

Daniel felt as if he'd had cold water thrown in his face. 'Oh, please don't get the wrong idea, Charlotte. It's only because . . . well, I only wanted to help.' Charlotte watched with disbelief as he reached out and took her hand, giving it a small squeeze. She almost snatched it back, painfully conscious of the burning sensation his touch had left.

'Let's get one thing straight,' she almost hissed. 'I am William's wife and you are William's partner. I am very happily married and I have no wish to become just another one of Daniel Cornwallis's . . . well . . .' she fought for the right word – 'floozies.'

'Floozies?' he said, incredulously.

'Yes, floozies. You've got your pick of women, so don't just play with me – I have no wish whatsoever to be just one of your little games. We have to work together because I've agreed to take this party on. But please understand that there will never be anything other than that between us.'

'Charlotte, you're wrong.' Daniel was outraged. How could she possibly have thought that he . . . he of all people could possibly have been interested in fouling his own patch, as the saying went. All he'd done was try to offer some friendly advice. 'That wasn't why I wanted to see you or why I talked to you like that. I just hate to see William neglecting . . .'

Charlotte's eyes blazed. She was already standing. 'Thanks for lunch, Daniel.' And she was gone.

Charlotte quickly hailed a taxi and jumped into the back, her shoulders heaving with self-righteous indignation. That had told him in no uncertain terms. He wouldn't try and pick her up again after that little lecture she had given him. And fancy patronizing her like that and nosing about her marriage. How she loathed him.

She got out by the grand office building where 'de Sallis Communications' was emblazoned in silver letters, two feet high, across the front door. The receptionist looked up from *True Romance* in surprise.

'Hello, Mrs de Sallis. How are you?'

'Fine thanks.' Charlotte smiled. 'Is Kate in?'

The girl looked at her oddly. 'No. She's er, in Paris. With your husband. They both left yesterday.'

'Oh. Yes, of course. How silly of me. I forgot,' she said lamely. It was painfully clear that Sally was not fooled. She looked at Charlotte almost with pity. 'I'm sure I can help.'

'Yes. Of course.' For the minute Charlotte had completely forgotten what she had actually come here for. 'I er . . . the party! Kate was going to draw up a guest list for the party. Do you know anything about it, Sally?'

'Well, she asked me to type a whole load of names and addresses so I suppose those must be the ones. If you can hang on a while I'll copy them, and then you can take them away with you.'

While Charlotte waited for Sally to return she considered the news. Why the hell hadn't he said he was taking Kate? The very fact that he hadn't mentioned it made her mighty suspicious. Of course it was entirely possible that they were just working together – Charlotte knew that they operated as a close team. But Kate had always held the fort in the office. She looked after his clients in his absence because she knew his work inside out. The other account executives and directors would be so busy working on their own business that they wouldn't know what William was up to. No, it was definitely strange. She paced up and down restlessly, trying to remember if he had said anything about Kate, let slip anything more than a casual interest in her. He'd often said how capable and efficient she was, and how difficult his life would be without her. But Charlotte had certainly never had cause to think anything more about it. She wasn't his type to start with. She was a mouse, for God's sake. Charlotte almost laughed at the old cliché: 'Take off your glasses, Miss Smith.' How could she have been so blind? All that endless working till all hours of the night. His lack of interest in her. His 'business trips'. Her mouth set in a firm line of bitter outrage.

Sally reappeared with the duplicate lists. 'Is there anything else I can help with?'

'No, Sally, thanks very much. Those were all I needed.' And she left.

Once outside she breathed in great gulps of air, throwing her head back, eyes closed against the grey London sky. She stood for a moment, alone with her thoughts. An island of rejection, of betrayal, lonely and bitter amid the sea of London crowds.

Daniel arrived back at the office feeling as if he'd just stood trial for someone else's murder. He hardly noticed Sarah's cheery 'hello'. He just could not believe how Charlotte could have misread him so completely. Him – of all people, who had never made a pass at a married woman in his life. He hated that kind of thing. She had confused his caring and concern with a desire to take her to bed. Not that he could entirely deceive himself and say that he wouldn't want to under different circumstances, of course. She must have misunderstood his habitual flirtatiousness, the charming outer shell he assumed with women which they seemed almost to expect of him. No, she just couldn't have taken that seriously, surely? He was angry that she should be thinking he would stoop to betraying his partner and ruining their marriage.

He gazed out, almost unseeingly, as the panoramic views of London unfurled from his fifth-floor vantage point. It was a sight almost too compelling in its drama, and would sometimes draw his mind away from more important things. But not today. Nothing could distract him from the feelings of injustice that Charlotte's outburst aroused in him.

Charlotte wandered listlessly around the cold lifeless house, feeling unutterably lonely, as if she were the only person left on a long-vacated planet. She opened the curtains to reassure herself there was still life out there. It was a dismal rain-drenched night. People strode briskly past the window, heads down, collars turned up. She leaned her head against the cold glass, her breath clouding the already dim picture. She watched tiny water droplets merge into one another to trace rivers down the wet glass.

What kind of a fool was she becoming? William must be laughing all over his smug features. He had exactly what he wanted: safe little wife at home, successful business, and now a mistress to amuse himself with. No wonder he came home tired. And she'd been so high and mighty with Daniel. Already she was beginning to regret being quite so aggressive. His shocked, aggrieved look had been very out of character for a seasoned letch. If he was just being plain friendly he must now be thinking her a complete fool as well.

Life just didn't seem to be going at all well. Gone was the old Charlotte, bursting with confidence and self-esteem. She was becoming a silly woman who either jumped to the wrong conclusion altogether, or was blind to something that had been shoved right under her nose. Even the work wasn't going well. It wasn't that she was exactly short of commissions, it was just that it all seemed a little pedestrian to be sitting at home at the word processor all day, with only the occasional escape for an interview, or an odd bit of research, compared to the days when she had been responsible for the production of an entire magazine. Crisis management was what she thrived on, not laundry management or wifely politics. Every time she saw her colleagues from the old days, which she did as often as they could find time for her, she caught a glimpse of the old Charlotte. Here were people who actually talked to her as if she mattered, people who actually listened to what she had to say. They could make her laugh, make her feel funny and bright and witty, as when she had been a person in her own right, instead of William's doormat. Even he had found her attractive when she was a success. It was ironic that he'd forced her to give up work so that she could be a good wife to him, and now was so bored with her being a good wife that he obviously had to look for his excitement elsewhere.

The thought of phoning a friend, of sharing her misery with anyone else, she felt was too unkind, so she settled down for the evening in her dressing gown and woolly socks, with her hair tied up in a messy knot on her head, to a bottle of wine and a pile of unfinished articles.

When she heard the loud clatter of the door knocker she nearly leapt out of her skin. She looked at her watch. Who on earth would be dropping by at 9 o'clock? Unless Claudia had decided to come round for a natter. She hoped it was and hurried to open the door. She pulled it open the five or six inches the security chain allowed and peered through the crack, expecting to see Claudia's grin.

Instead, with a deep shock, she saw Daniel's tall figure outlined against the diffused amber streetlight. She closed the door in order to release the chain, half expecting the vision to have disappeared by the time she opened it again. But he was still there.

'What on earth are you doing here . . . ?'

'Charlotte, I have to talk to you . . . about this afternoon. Please, I must talk . . .'

She stepped aside to allow him in. She pulled the dressing gown tighter around her, conscious of looking a complete mess. He looked agitated and very wet, the water pouring off his raincoat, making puddles on the black-and-white hall tiles. He clutched a rather sodden bunch of pink roses which he held out to her.

'What's this?'

'A peace offering. I thought of bringing lilies, but they seemed a bit funereal.'

'That's very kind of you, Daniel.'

'It's the least I could do. I had to come, I do hope you don't mind . . . to explain.'

She led the way into the drawing room and poured a glass of wine. 'Here, you look as if you could do with this.'

He took the glass. 'I had no intention of compromising you, Charlotte. Whatever you may think, I'm really not that sort of man.'

'Oh, don't worry, Daniel, I've been thinking too, and I may have over-reacted. It's just been that sort of a day. Really bloody.' She stared down at her woolly socks. 'You must think I'm a complete neurotic, running out on you like that.'

'Not at all, Charlotte. If you really believed I was making a come-on, then you behaved very properly.'

She couldn't stop the small laugh that escaped her lips. It all sounded so dreadfully old-fashioned. Behaving properly. Again she giggled.

'What's so funny?'

'Oh nothing at all, really. Just the ironies of life.'

'Such as?'

'Sit down, Daniel.'

He did as he was told, and they sat facing each other on the two sofas on either side of the coffee table.

'Such as William being in Paris with his secretary.' Daniel raised his eyebrows, but he remained silent. 'After I left you today I called in at his office, to speak to Kate. Have you met Kate?'

He nodded.

'Well, they told me that she'd gone away with William.' She took a sip of wine and continued. 'So tell me, Daniel, what am I supposed to think? That he's taken her with him because he needs her? Why, I'm sure they've got secretaries at Reiser he could borrow. That all the rubbish he's spun me in the past about how valuable she is and how capable she is of running the office in his absence is true? Then how come she's not running his office for him now?'

Daniel knew exactly what Charlotte should think, but whether he should be the one to tell her what she should be thinking was a different problem altogether. He shrugged casually. 'He may have taken her because

93

he needs her help, I, er . . . often take my secretary with me.' In truth Daniel knew exactly the number of times he'd taken Sarah with him. Precisely none. 'There's no need to go jumping to the wrong conclusions, is there, Charlotte?'

She was looking at him with sorrow. 'Am I such a wimp that I have to be mollified like this, Daniel? Aren't I strong enough to take the truth?'

Again he shrugged. 'I don't know, Charlotte, I really don't know. Why don't you wait until you've got some proof, until you're really sure. That way you won't make a fool of yourself.'

'Something I seem to be getting rather good at,' she said drily. 'Do you remember what you said the other night – about how he probably wasn't easy to live with? Well, you were damn right.'

Daniel felt desperately sorry for Charlotte. She sat huddled up, defensively, in a corner of the sofa, like some hurt animal, and all because of that selfish bastard she was married to.

'He wants everything his way. Our relationship is a farce and I've just tried so hard . . .' Her voice broke into a kind of strangulated sob. Then she couldn't hold back any longer. Large tears welled up in her eyes and spilled down her pale cheeks. She sniffed loudly. 'He just seems to want to destroy me, Daniel.'

Daniel had been hovering on the edge of his seat and he couldn't stand it any longer. He crossed the short space between them and sat down next to her on the sofa. He pulled a large white handkerchief out of his pocket and handed it to her, whereupon she blew her nose loudly. 'That's it,' he said softly. 'You have a good cry, Charlotte, let it out.' Without thinking he reached out and placed his arm around her narrow, intensely vulnerable shoulders and pulled her close to him. For a second she resisted, and then relaxed towards him, seemingly bereft of any more fight. He continued to just hold her until she stopped shaking and her breathing became even again. Then, with the tip of his forefinger, he turned her chin towards him and studied her red, swollen features. Very deliberately, with a sense of wonder, he bent his head towards her face and placed his mouth firmly over hers.

At first she withdrew, and he saw a flicker of something like confusion in her eyes, then she too studied his face, as if it were the first time she had really seen him. Then she reached up and pulled his head down to meet hers again. Slowly, almost imperceptibly, their bodies slid together, so that they were lying across the sofa. She was breathing him, feeling him, tasting him. She felt a burning heat which started between her legs and slowly spread through her gut. She held her breath. She felt a wild mixture of fear and excitement. Her stomach turned long somersaults as she responded to his searching tongue.

Through a dim mist of ecstasy she felt him search inside her dressing gown for her breast. His hand rested tantalizingly lightly, making her want to squirm against him, and then it continued its delicious exploration down over her belly. His mouth followed the line of his hand and closed around her hard nipple. Then she cried out. She clawed at his shirt, lost completely, drowning with her own desire. And through the dim curtain, somewhere in her consciousness, came the realization that no man had had the key to unleash this wanton within her before. She reached down and her curious fingers tried to unzip him . . . and then the phone rang.

At first she didn't hear it, it was some kind of alien intrusion a million miles removed from where she was now. Then slowly, ring by ring, it dragged them both back to reality. Daniel pulled himself away from her. She watched him, not quite knowing what to do next. He started to shake his head, as if he were sorry. 'Don't you think you'd better answer it?'

His voice sounded hard. Suddenly she felt deeply afraid. Just what had happened between them? Was he now going to blame her? She pulled the robe back around her and struggled over to the telephone. Daniel picked up his jacket and looked over his shoulder. 'I'll let myself out, Charlotte.' And he was gone.

She lifted up the receiver and her hand trembled uncontrollably. She steadied it with her other hand. 'Hello,' she said, not quite trusting her voice. Then came the deliberate clicks of the long distance connection, and the slightly hollow sound of William's voice. 'Charlotte . . . Charlotte . . . are you there?'

She cleared her throat. 'Yes, William, I'm here.'

'Sorry to ring you so late, darling, but I've just got out of a meeting. Everything all right over there?'

'Er . . . yes . . . I think so.' In truth she could barely speak. She just had to concentrate on getting through this phone call.

'Are you sure? You sound a bit strained.'

'Yes, quite sure, William. How's Reiser?'

'Well, that's just it. I might have to stay longer than I thought. This thing seems to be blowing up right out of proportion. I'll have more idea after tomorrow, so I'll call you then, OK?'

'Night, William.' She put the phone down before he could talk any more. She stared at the empty space on the sofa, where only a few moments before she had very nearly made love to Daniel. They must have been quite mad. And now he had gone. Walked out. Just like that. No explanation, no understanding warmth. Just a great big painful vacuum. She pulled the robe around her shoulders and curled up, a small ball of confusion and frustration. She could still taste him on her lips. She lay unblinking as if in shock, in horror and disbelief.

Chapter Five

The constant drone of the traffic seeped irritatingly through the shutters, despite the double-glazing. A large cast iron radiator ticked intermittently, overheating the small but shabbily elegant room. William had vainly tried to get a room at the back and had been in a quandary as to whether to switch to a different hotel, but he was a creature of habit, and ever since his parents had brought him as a child, he had developed an especial fondness for the Louis Cinq.

He turned from his side on to his back and lay staring at the ceiling unable to sleep. His eyes followed the lines and contours of the mouldings. Plasterwork bunches of grapes and other fruits were entwined around lengths of rope and ivy leaves. Here and there small flecks of paint had fallen off, giving the impression in the dim light of myriad insects scattered unmoving across the ceiling. Car headlights threw strange patterns of light which travelled in window-shaped oblongs across the room.

Despite the sleeplessness it felt good to be away. He wondered vaguely what had been bothering Charlotte when he rang. She certainly sounded strange – no doubt she was in one of her moods again. Whatever it was he hoped she'd have got herself over it by the time he returned. She was just no fun to come home to these days, she seemed to have changed so much since he had first met her. Then she had been stimulating, interesting and irritatingly independent. She'd had much more exciting things on her mind than his working hours or his sperm count. But work had taken too much out of her, she'd been a tired wreck most of the time, and she'd felt guilty at not being able to devote enough time to their marriage. So it had been a good idea for her to stop. He just wished she could realize what her behaviour was doing to them. And stop this pestering about babies once and for all. Everything would happen in its own time without medical interference and there was absolutely no question about there being anything wrong with him. Oh no, he was certainly above average in that department.

His skin felt prickly dry, the starched linen scratchy to his sensitized skin. He threw back the sheet, sighing heavily. He swung his legs over the side of the bed, toes meeting the soft-piled red-and-gold carpet. He switched on the bathroom light, the cold glare of the chrome fitting hurting his eyes. He blinked. Trapped air inside the old water pipes knocked gently as he filled a glass with water. William smiled wryly to himself. The most exclusive hotels in Paris were the older and tattier ones. Newness was frowned upon as being gauche and tasteless. Modern plumbing, sophisticated air-conditioning, efficient double glazing – all were quite readily available. But still people flocked to the classy discomfort of the old.

He returned to the bedroom and slid back under the sheets as noiselessly as possible. The previously still form on the other side of the bed stirred, slowly surfacing from a very deep sleep.

'What is it, darling? Can't you sleep?' A slim hand reached across and stroked his bare chest. Long fingers curled through the short blond hairs across his breastbone. Gently they centred around his nipples, slow circles sending hot messages down through his lower belly to his groin. His cock started to stiffen. She rolled over and lowered her head over his chest. Giggling quietly she said: 'Don't worry . . . I know just what you need.' Her tongue took the place of her fingers, darting teasingly over the small pink bud of his nipple, its small

98

hard centre testimony to his response. Agonizingly slowly, her mouth travelled down. When she reached the soft warm inverse triangle of hair that rose up to his navel, she drew back, eyes already half-glazed with want. He gasped and stretched himself luxuriously, pushing his pelvis upwards; lifting his lower body. His arms stretched above his head, hands clasped around the bars of the gilt headboard.

Eyes closed, he waited, silently willing her to continue her delicious explorations, which set his balls on fire. Her mouth closed over his glans and then travelled expertly down to the base and back. His hips rose up once more and her mouth enveloped him in soft wetness, her tongue and lips squeezing around him, driving everything from his mind. He reached down, feeling for long silky hair. Twining a mass around his fist he firmly pulled her back up to him. Her lips were swollen and shiny wet. Quickly straddling him she guided herself on to him, moaning with pleasure. Her mouth lifted at the corners with her half-wicked smile as she carried her divine act of seduction to its conclusion, until finally, in sudden convulsive thrusts, they reached their climax, her moans mixing with his own grunts of gratification.

When he woke much later, she was gone. Had it not been for the sweet stickiness on his belly he could almost have dreamt it.

A sharp tap on the door heralded the arrival of breakfast. A silver tray bore a steaming jug of hot chocolate and warm fresh croissants. A small china bowl held carefully sculpted lumps of almost pure white butter. William frowned. The adrenalin was already beginning to pump through his body in preparation for the day ahead. He poured himself a cupful of the pale pinky-brown liquid and sipped slowly, thoughtfully. He had an outlined report of the proposal for handling the

Reiser crisis. This morning's meeting would be the first full one he had had with the directors and he strongly suspected they would be in a blind panic, aggressively resistant to any suggestions he might put forward. Public relations was one of the most vital ingredients in diluting a crisis. Handled carefully and subtly a vengeful public could slowly be brought around, even to find sympathy with a hapless company.

He glanced once at the croissants, deciding he needed no such heaviness in his gut this morning. A clear stomach and a clear mind.

Reiser's offices occupied an entire block on the Avenue Kléber, off the Arc de Triomphe. The redbrick building had a small and discreet brass plate announcing the identity of its occupants. William dodged past the two journalists already staking their position. He simply smiled at their questions. 'Later . . .' he promised. He took the elevator to the executive suite. The exterior office buzzed with fax machines and busy telephones. Two elegant young women, so alike they could almost have been sisters, were collating bits of paper and juggling with the telephone calls. He smiled at them appreciatively.

'Bonjour, monsieur,' one of them said smilingly. He nodded. 'Good morning.' The other woman broke into perfect English: 'Good morning, Mr de Sallis. How are you? I shall tell Monsieur le Directeur that you are here. One moment, please.'

She disappeared through a large mahogany panelled door. William waited patiently. Meanwhile the other girl was busy on the phone, obviously saying that she was not at liberty to make any comment and that a statement would be issued later. Despite being pressed for information, she maintained a calm, easy measure in her voice. Eventually she thanked the caller very much for their interest and suggested that they call later.

She replaced the receiver and looked up at William. He smiled back. 'Beautifully handled, mam'selle.' She raised her eyebrows questioningly. Then her colleague reappeared. 'You may go in now, Mr de Sallis.' William strode in past the heavy door. The large room housed an enormous board table around which was seated almost the entire executive committee of Reiser Holdings. He quickly scanned the twenty or so faces, searching for people he knew. Kate looked up at his entrance. He smiled. She winked at him and then returned to her notepad. He had briefed her to get there early so that she could make notes on any discussion prior to his arrival. Claude Bonnet gestured William to an empty seat, on the right of the Chairman, William noted. So he was an honoured committee member today.

Claude was speaking: 'Gentlemen . . . and Lady,' he added quickly, glancing at Kate, 'I would like to welcome and introduce to those of you who do not already recognize him, Mr William de Sallis. William handles our public relations affairs in London and is here to advise us, together with Paul Montigny, on how best to respond to the media questions we have flooding in.'

William glanced across at Paul Montigny, who was sitting on Claude's left, watching William levelly. William had met him on several occasions. Each time Paul visited London he would have a meeting with William to discuss joint strategies and programmes. On the surface they got on all right, but on a more personal level William sensed an air of suspicion, possibly fuelled by the ever-present edge of competition inherent in the business. Anyway, whatever the reason, William had not spent overmuch time worrying about his relationship with Paul. He knew that there was no way Paul could possibly handle the British PR campaign on behalf of Reiser. The only risk to William was if ever Paul developed his own relationship with Reiser to the extent that he 'had the ear' so to speak. Then he might decide to recommend a London agency which he had an interest in. Up to now, though, Reiser had seemingly enormous respect for William and his professional expertise.

Claude continued addressing the meeting. The only other sound in the room was the faint scratching of Kate's pencil flying over her notebook.

'Just to recap for everyone's benefit, the situation to date is this. Exactly one week ago today, last Thursday, routine checks showed contamination in one of the milk powder producing plants in Lyons. The next day reports started to filter back that some babies had been admitted to hospital with bacterial poisoning. Most fortunately all the children concerned have made a full recovery. However, naturally, as soon as the contamination was discovered we stopped production and closed down the plant until the source of infection could be located.' Claude paused and looked around at the intent faces.

'I am pleased to report that this has in fact finally been achieved. Every morning all the equipment is thoroughly cleansed and sterilized by a number of technicians, each one being responsible for his own particular area. It transpires that one of them was simply not doing his job properly. He had allowed one of the ducts to become blocked. The warm temperatures allowed the bacteria to flourish and multiply and, hey presto, the perfect recipe for infant gastro-enteritis. Unfortunately the secondary testing could only pick up the infection after it had developed.

'The situation now is that the entire plant has been closed down. All batches of milk processed prior to last week have been recalled from the retailers and wholesalers. As far as the consumer is concerned all new batches from today are absolutely safe. The plant has been stripped and rebuilt almost entirely. Production and testing have been running constantly over the past thirty-six hours and we are confident that everything is now safe.' Again he paused. His face looked pale and drawn under his neat dark hair. Blue circles of fatigue and strain appeared like bruises beneath his eyes.

'Financially the situation is devastating. Our share price has more than halved. We've lost production and we've had to reimburse customers for returned stocks. In all, taking into account the loss of investors and loss of confidence, it has probably cost us £5 million. It is most fortunate that Reiser Pharmaceuticals, our revered parent company,' he paused for the soft laughter to diminish, 'has had such a successful year and can, in effect, carry our losses.

'The reason I have called this crisis meeting today – and I know that we're all well used to them by now – is to discuss what our profile to the public will be. We have lost sales and faith. Our competitors are delighted. What do we do? William, I wonder if you would care to let us have your suggestions first?'

Claude sat down, watching William from underneath raised brows. William shifted the pile of notes around and quickly scanned the typescript for a few seconds. Slowly he stood, sliding back his chair. He stroked his chin thoughtfully, then looked around the table.

'Good morning, everyone, and thank you, Claude. Firstly, I would like to add my commiserations that this business has happened at all. It's all most unfortunate . . .' he paused, 'though *not*, I would like to stress, impossible to overcome.

'The plain fact at the moment is that sales have ceased completely and the public will need hard evidence to convince them that the situation has been rectified. The press have, in the absence of a full picture, taken it upon themselves to fabricate their stories which obviously

103

makes the situation seem much more dire than it actually is.

'We have in our favour a good historical relationship with the press and the overall image of the company is one of integrity and being worthy of great respect. On the one hand, of course, that makes it so utterly scandalous that such a thing should happen. But on the other, there is already an enormous amount of goodwill in existence that should help to carry us through. In view of that I believe it to be imperative that we tell the press the truth.' He stopped and glanced quickly round the intent faces. A few were frowning silently. Paul Montigny stared down at the table, slowly shaking his head. William's voice rose once more.

'That is the only way we can hope to retain any support at all. If we change the packaging slightly on the new batches of milk and schedule an advertising campaign around the packaging changes, the public will know that the milk is absolutely safe – in some ways safer than our competitors' because we've had to test *everything*. It follows the same principle as boosting confidence after an air disaster. You should be safer afterwards than you ever were before. *That* is the rationale I believe we should work to.'

He sat down and caught Kate's eye. 'Well done,' she mouthed silently. Claude remained seated.

'Thank you, William,' he said, and then turned to his left. 'Paul, now that you've heard our English colleague, do you agree with him, or do you have other ideas?'

Paul Montigny's face had reddened. His mouth had a firm, almost petulant, set to it. 'No, Claude. I'm afraid I don't agree at all. Why on earth should we give away that sort of ammunition?' He was speaking quickly, voice clipped and dismissive. 'I believe we should say that we have found no evidence to suggest any connection with the sick babies . . .' A murmur of agreement rose around the room. '. . . There have only

104

been . . . well, let me see . . .' he looked down at his notes '. . . six cases to date, and that is from a whole week. Is it not possible that these babies had a . . . a . . . what do you say . . . bug? We tell the press that everything was and is perfectly all right. If any independent investigators would wish to check it over why we'd be delighted to accommodate them, would we not?'

William looked at him in stunned silence. The man was out of his tiny mind. All the press had to do was sniff around a few technicians, take the odd clerical worker out to lunch and the story would be spilled like hot cocoa. And at that stage a denial would be out of the question. To be backed up by a newly created history of deceit. Now *that* really would wreck the company for a considerable time. He bit his tongue and waited with a burning curiosity to know how Claude would respond.

Claude scribbled down a few notes on his pad and then underlined them with a flourish of his pen. His expression remained inscrutable. Then he stood.

'We are most honoured to have with us today Monsieur Fleurac, the chief advisor to the minister for health . . .' Paul Montigny gasped. His face suddenly drained white, hearing his own death knell.

A very distinguished looking silver-haired man, handsome even in his advanced years, now stood to address the meeting. He was smiling benignly at Paul.

'No, no, monsieur, that will not do. Not do at all. Deceit will only serve to breed more deceit. If I have the facts clearly I have understood that the infection was confirmed by independent tests as certainly having caused these poor babies to become sick. A "cover up" as you suggest would be *immoral*. In fact I hardly think I need discuss the suggestion further. It is too . . . too . . .' he struggled to find the word, 'ridiculous!' His voice was level. 'I have to agree with our English friend,' he nodded towards William. 'He is of course, absolutely right in saying that Reiser's previous reputation is flawless. You are internationally respected and an often-consulted spokesperson for the industry as a whole. You have no choice but to issue a statement bearing all the facts.' He looked at his watch. 'Now I am afraid I am already late for my next engagement. I wish you luck with your statement.' He clicked his heels together and, nodding once at Claude, left the room.

Paul's face was now a picture of hate and revenge which he was fighting desperately to control.

'Shall we take a vote then, gentlemen,' said Claude. 'Firstly, all those in favour of Monsieur de Sallis's campaign please raise your hands.' All hands were raised. 'Then I think a further vote would be academic. Very well.' Claude turned to William. 'Would you like to advise us on the next steps to be taken?'

William had been busily scribbling down notes while Claude was talking. He twisted the pencil between his fingers, reading his hasty scrawl. 'Well, I think one of the first things to get underway would be the new can labels. Presumably you'll have to commission and approve the designs.' Claude was already reaching for the white telephone in front of him. He pushed a single button. Immediately one of the young women appeared, notebook in hand. 'Ah, Mireille, thank you. Could you please arrange for our designer to come up immediately. Then would you ask the advertising agency to come in.'

'Yes, monsieur.' She left the room.

'Claude, I'd like to draft a statement for your approval; then I suggest I return to London.' William paused, then added quickly, 'That is, of course, if you think that's a good idea. No doubt Paul will be handling things at this end.'

Paul had not spoken. His eyes had taken on a nasty, rat-like cast. He just watched William, waiting for Claude's reply.

'Yes, yes,' Claude said, too quickly. 'We'll sort that out after the meeting. You go ahead, William, Kate . . .' They both excused themselves and William held the heavy door open for his secretary. Upon request they were shown to an empty office.

Kate threw herself down on to the chair, stretching her legs in front of her. She let her glasses slip down her nose so that William was confronted with a stern schoolmarmish pose, contradicted by sparkling blue eyes, dancing mischievously. She pushed her glasses back on to the bridge of her nose.

'Phew, William. You do realize you're going to have a contract put out on you. I have never seen anyone so angry. He was so humiliated. Mind you, I can't believe how crassly stupid he was to suggest such a thing. Do you think Claude will fire him?'

'I don't see how he can *not* do so. The fact that Claude has a publicly quoted liar on his pay roll will not sit comfortably on his conscience. However, I don't know whether for convenience's sake he may decide to keep him on for now. *Someone* has to handle the press. Claude might find life a little tricky if he had to reappoint someone right now, unless . . . No, we couldn't . . .'

Kate interrupted him. 'What? William, what is it?'

'I had a thought. But it's impossible.'

'Well, go on. Spill the beans. Please don't keep me in suspense.'

'I was just thinking of how great the story could be. "Bent PR man fired in boardroom battle. Truth reigns supreme, etc., etc.," But of course Paul Montigny's career would be finished for ever.'

'He'd deserve it. Remember he would have denied Reiser's responsibility for those sick babies.' Her voice was full of contempt.

'I accept that, but I don't want to have his blood on my hands, thank you very much. He'd only be out for

107

revenge and I can do without that sort of hassle. No. Let Claude handle it.'

He began to dictate. Kate's head bent diligently over her work, her deep auburn hair falling across her face, one hand absently holding it back as her hand sped across the notepad. Her long slim legs stretched out, their fine black film of Lycra shimmering seductively. William noticed her delicate ankles as her feet described little arcs up and down, through the air as she concentrated on her work.

He was very relieved to have her with him. She was an excellent secretary, an easy companion and had a quick, lively mind. His only regret was that he couldn't have two of her – one permanently at his side and the other left to manage things in his absence.

William had started to dial the office in London when Claude came into the office and he replaced the receiver. 'It's not quite ready, Claude, Kate's typing it now.'

'That's OK, William. I wanted to talk to you about Paul. Naturally he's resigned. Bloody idiot. No doubt the whole story will somehow find its way into this evening's papers, but I just couldn't afford to take the risk of having him connected to us. You, William, are going to come out of this like a knight in shining armour, are you not?' William shrugged and permitted a half-smile to cross his lips.

'I want you to handle the entire European public relations for Reiser from now on. I need you here to handle the statement and all the interviews.'

William felt a heady sense of triumph. But there were problems. 'Claude, I can't possibly. What about the London end? I can't be in two places at once, and when the balloon goes up over there I won't be there to deal with it. It's impossible.'

'I will fly over *anyone*, from your office. I will send over our internal PR girl to London if it would help. All queries can come straight to us. I will fly over any journalists who wish a personal interview. I need you, William. And of course the fee will be commensurate with the amount of responsibility we are putting on you. Just think, William, I am giving you an annual contract worth £500,000. What do you say?'

'What can I say? Kate, have you finished that draft? Get me David on the phone. Book Anne-Marie on a flight. Claude, can you check this draft?' All three of them started to laugh.

'My God, William. If you keep up that kind of pressure I might even regret the decision,' said Claude.

'Just start reading, please.' William laughed back at him.

When Daniel first saw the headline he assumed that William had been compromising his integrity, but reading further it seemed that rather than being cast as villain, he was in fact the hero of the day. That was a turn-up for the books – William championing the cause of justice. It rather put Daniel in an invidious position considering all his brave thoughts about the injustice of William's behaviour. And now Daniel had very nearly seduced William's wife while the man was off in Paris making a brilliant job of being honest.

Daniel was livid with himself for what he had very nearly done the previous night. In fact, he was livid with himself for all the things he *had* done. His intentions had been quite proper, as he had told Charlotte. When he arrived there he had no thought of touching her or compromising her in any way. Just how the hell he had got to the point where he had damned nearly made love to her was simply inexplicable. If the phone hadn't rung when it did, he couldn't have said with any degree of certainty whether he would have returned to his senses.

It was several years since he had been as out of control as he had last night. Sex was great and very satisfying, but it wasn't like what had passed between him and Charlotte last night. That had been like there'd never been anyone else – almost like the first time, but without the hesitancy of inexperience. He had felt a passion stirring through him that he couldn't remember experiencing before. Was it because she was forbidden fruit? But, God help him, he wanted more of it. He mustn't have it. Daniel's principles were important to him. Without them he was unguided, directionless. He had to live his life by a certain code and having Charlotte was way outside of it. He knew he had the willpower to resist her. However hard it felt right now, it would get better.

A bit of distance between them was essential. He cursed himself for getting Charlotte to organize the party. It meant he would have to deal with her – or would he? Maybe Sarah could do all the liaising. And he could arrange to be conveniently out if Charlotte came into the office. Something would work out . . . His direct line buzzed. 'Hi. Cornwallis speaking.'

'Daniel.'

He recognized William's voice immediately. The sound of it made him feel guilty and underhand. To compensate, he started to gush, something completely out of character. 'Well done, William. Congratulations. I've read the paper. Sounds as if you did an absolutely brilliant job.'

'Wait till you hear the rest of it. We've been given the entire European PR contract. £500,000 worth of business, Daniel.'

Daniel whistled quietly, under his breath. 'Jeesus. How come?'

'Claude was so pissed off with Montigny and, I think, without sounding too immodest, he was impressed with our presentation.'

'Well done, William! When are you coming back?'

'Oh, not for another couple of days at least. We'll

have to stay through the weekend – there's a whole pile of shit to go through at this end. How's things over there?'

'Fine. Any leads on the advertising side perhaps?'

'I'm working on it. Though Claude seems pretty happy with the lot they've got. I must say they came up with the new label designs pretty quickly – just a couple of hours. Now they're dotting the "i"'s for the new campaign to let everyone know the milk's OK and the new packaging means a new batch.'

'Well, just keep plugging away.'

William put the phone down and turned to Kate.

'Hungry?'

'You bet,' she answered.

'Well, when we're finished here let's go and celebrate. Dinner and a night on the town.'

'Mmmm, sounds nice . . .' She smiled.

Then he picked up the phone again and dialled Charlotte's number. Her phone rang for quite a time before it was answered. He waited for her voice on the other end. There was silence.

'Charlotte,' he asked, 'are you there?'

'Oh, William. Yes . . .' her voice was barely audible. Just a faint whisper.

'Whatever's the matter with you? Are you all right?'

'What?'

'I said, are you all right?' He was almost shouting into the mouthpiece now.

'Fine. Just a headache. A migraine. When are you coming back?'

'I don't know. That's why I'm ringing. I've got to stay for a few more days. If you read the papers you'll understand. Reiser have fired their French PR company and appointed us in their place. I shall have to stay here for another couple of days at least.'

'Oh . . . that must be good news, I suppose.'

'Yes, it is. A coup and a half.'

'Congratulations,' she said weakly.

'Charlotte, whatever is the matter with you? You sound like death.'

'Nothing, William, really. Just this bloody awful headache. Look, if you're not coming back I may go home to Mum's. If I'm not here when you next call, try down there.'

'OK. Bye, darling.'

Charlotte sank on to the floor at the side of the desk, still nursing the receiver in her hand, her mind a million miles away. After a few moments the phone started to howl, the sudden noise bringing her back to life. She replaced the receiver on its cradle, her cold white hands slippery on the plastic, but it dropped out of her grasp and fell with a bang.

She had to squint to see clearly across the room. The shadows had deepened to blanket the room in a blue-slate light. Dusk. She clutched the side of her head as she raised herself back on to her feet. She bent and switched on the table lamp beside the telephone. The harsh circle of yellow which fell on to the polished mahogany exaggerated the micro-fine layer of dust. She blew at it absently. Then once more she sat on the floor, knees tucked up under her chin, and considered what do to next.

After Dan had left her she had had an overwhelming urge just to run away. The pit of her stomach had swollen in size and was now pressing urgently on her diaphragm so that she had no desire for food. She felt sick and unreal.

All his fine words about morality and high-minded intent were a load of unadulterated crap. He had obviously just turned up in the hope that he could get a quick screw. And the really dreadful thing was that she had very nearly let him. Had it not been for William's timely call, then she would have almost certainly begged him to continue. He was the strangest man she had ever met. He just seemed to have so many different sides to him. At first he had been arrogant and pushy, then he had been quietly dry and amusing. Over lunch he had been friendly rather than threatening and last night he seemed to be so caring. Before, that was . . . Which one was the real Daniel? Not that she ever wanted to find out. The last thing she ever wanted to do was clap eyes on him again. He was just the same as all the rest. An out-and-out bastard. William was at it in Paris. Daniel was at it over here. And what really hurt, deep, deep down inside her, was that both had now rejected her. What was left of Charlotte? Like the fairy in Peter Pan, nobody believed in her and she was now disappearing.

She felt engulfed by self-pity. She wanted to crawl into a large, dark hole and never come out again. How she could face William after what had happened last night she had no idea. How could she now accuse him of being unfaithful to her, when she had behaved like such a common harlot in her own home? And how would she ever face Daniel again? She wanted him to know how angry she was, somehow she wanted to get back at him. But how would she do that? In the meantime, she had to find the strength to go on.

She could do what she had told William she would do. That was to visit her parents. It would be good to see them and they would probably help her to feel better. But whether she would make *them* feel any better was something she should take into account. If she forewarned them her mother would go into a frenzy of preparation. Cakes would be baked, beds would be aired, the cat would be polished and her father would be dusted. She would just have to turn up. But if she turned up in this state they'd only end up being worried about her. And they'd had enough worries in the past couple of years without her adding to them. She was now their only child. All their hopes were channelled into her. She could not disappoint them. She could not give them a hint that her marriage was less than successful, or that she was unhappy with William. They would be devastated, just when they were beginning to sort out their lives again in their idyllic New Forest retirement.

No, it would not be fair. She would just have to pull herself together and behave like a grown-up twenty-nine-year-old woman should. She burst into tears.

Chapter Six

Daniel had been doing his sums. William's news had got him thinking. With the extra five hundred thousand that William had picked up from Reiser it might mean Daniel could bring his personal plans a good deal forward. He glanced at his watch. It was seven o'clock and that meant that in New York Bob could still be out at lunch. He'd leave it an hour and then put in a call to him. He refilled his glass with a large Scotch and sipped it slowly. All day he'd immersed himself in reports from his executives. Normally he would just give them a cursory glance, but today he'd read every colon and comma and had even brought more home with him in case he felt like dipping into them during the evening.

The sun was fast disappearing as he picked up the remote control device and pressed several buttons. Black halogen space age lights flickered into life one by one, and the curtains closed. Like his office, the basis of the room was monochromatic. Only here, large, vivid splashes of colour broke up the grey, black and white tones. Red and blue cushions on the white sofas complemented the vast canvas hung on the wall behind. A coal-black carpet spread across the floor to meet the ice-white walls. An almost pure white marble chimneypiece framed the flickering fire. Two black cylindrical vases stood on either side of the mantelpiece, each holding a casual arrangement of pure white tulips. His home was uncluttered, stylish, hi-tech and very much a bachelor flat. But Daniel was not in a mood to appreciate his surroundings tonight.

He had first met Bob Lester in London at an

international advertising conference, at which all the top agency guys had been present. Bob had invited him over to see his operation in New York. The snow in Vermont had been particularly good that year he remembered, with pleasure. Bob's majestic chalet had provided them with a base from which they skied their butts off every day. And after they returned exhilarated and exhausted in the late afternoon they were fed like kings. Daniel had skied before, but not with the likes of Bob. He had introduced Daniel to the thrill of off-piste territory, where your skis could sink a foot deep in powdery snow.

After that, Daniel decided he had to set a path for himself so that, like Bob, he could afford to indulge his expensive hobbies, and live in the style that he'd quickly grown used to. He told Bob just what his intentions were: 'I'll be back in two years and I'll have my own agency. Then, my friend, you and I are going to be transatlantic partners.' Six months after he'd started up Cornwallis Advertising he had returned, true to his word, and talked Bob into signing a split-share deal: twenty per cent of each other's companies, which at current value was no small fry.

Now Daniel had decided it was time to expand even further. Unlike many of their competitors, both Cornwallis's and Lester's companies were managing to weather the recession. Business was extremely tight, but they had always maintained the practice of keeping overheads low and working with a comparatively small, but highly effective number of staff. They had sufficient accounts and surplus profits from previous years to still justify the idea of buying up other, smaller agencies worldwide, who might not be surviving the storm quite so successfully. With the de Sallis merger imminent it had seemed prudent to wait and see how the new PR division would perform before skipping off on a grand tour and leaving London to fend for itself, but now, with this new account in William's pocket, Daniel could quite happily pursue his plan. All he had to do was sell the idea to Bob.

There was another advantage to being out of the country for a while, and that was the fact that he could avoid having to be around William and Charlotte de Sallis.

Just as his hand hovered over the telephone, about to call Lester's number, the doorbell buzzed insistently. It was the kind of buzz that usually meant Valentine. 'Fuck it,' he swore. 'Yes?'

'Darling . . . ' The voice confirmed his suspicions. 'Let me in. It's freezing out here.'

He was tempted just to say no. Instead he pressed the door release button and waited for the click of her heels on the landing outside. He slid the latch up and left the door ajar, returning once more to his position at his desk.

He looked up with lazy, disinterested eyes at the sound of the slamming door. As usual, visually, Valentine was stunning. A long full, black leather skirt circled her slender ankles. Her feet were encased in beautiful soft calf court shoes. A matching black leather jacket was slung casually over her shoulders, scorning the chill of the evening air. Bold slashes of red, black and white fell dramatically across her blouse. Valentine could have been made for the room. Her colours matched perfectly. And knowing her as he did, Daniel would not have been surprised to learn that that was exactly what she had planned. She knew how successful a chameleon could be. But unlike her lizard-sister, she couldn't keep still. She twirled around, as if posing for the cameras, to give him the full benefit of herself. He smiled, knowing that he would only have to wait a short while before she announced the purpose of her visit. She raised her eyebrows and pouted her crimson lips at him.

117

'Darling Daniel . . .' She moved closer so that he could smell her musky, heady scent. 'Aren't you going to ask me how Paris was?'

'How was Paris?' he asked drily.

'Oh Dan . . . you're impossible. You know, sometimes I wonder what I see in you. Anyway, seeing as how you've asked, it was great. I flew back this afternoon. Now the work's over . . .' she walked over to him and bent so that her lips were close to his ear, her voice low '. . . I thought we could perhaps play together.'

Unconsciously he drew away from her. He turned in time to catch a small flicker of hurt surprise cross her eyes.

'What is it?'

'Nothing. I was having a very quiet evening. No one to bother me, only myself for company. I was really enjoying it.'

Not to be deterred she rounded on him. 'Good, well you obviously need jollying up then. Dan, I haven't seen you for forty-eight hours at least. Aren't you a tiny bit pleased to see me?' Her voice wheedled childishly.

In truth it was so obvious that he wasn't in the least pleased to see her he wondered how she had the stupidity to ask the question. 'Valentine, you're here. Now if it doesn't seem too rude a question, what is your purpose behind the visit?'

'I'd like to take you to dinner.' She smiled sweetly.

He knew she was in one of her determined moods. She was going to be impossible to get rid of. He could either give in gracefully or spend the entire evening having to listen to her endless complaining. Of course the third alternative would be to throw her out, but he didn't feel strong enough in his present frame of mind to cope with the histrionics which would inevitably ensue. His stomach rumbled loudly.

'Ah ha,' she said, pointing her finger accusingly at his abdomen. 'There you are. The body's willing at

118

any rate. You should follow your baser instincts, darling.'

'Oh, all right, Valentine. If only to shut you up.'

She described another little twirl, victoriously. 'Oh goody, goody. Now as it's my treat you can choose where we go. Where shall we go?'

'Les Arcs?' he said, more than a small hint of malice in his thoughts. Her smile drooped for a moment and then she recovered manfully.

'Fine,' she almost squeaked. Les Arcs was one of London's most exclusive restaurants, and undoubtedly one of its most expensive.

'I haven't been there for months,' he yawned. 'Yes, I'm looking forward to it.'

'Do you think we should book – of course they may be full.' Her voice rose hopefully. Obviously the prospect of spending £250 on dinner was fairly disheartening. He shook his head. 'Do you seriously think they'd turn either of us away?' Under the circumstances the question was neither pompous nor arrogant. It was simply a statement of fact.

'No, no. I suppose not.' She squared her shoulders under the creaking leather. He had to admire her bottle. She was going to go through with it. He might just find out how much it took to break her cover. Suddenly he felt lighter than he had all day. The evening had possibilities.

They started well. They were shown straight to a table, though the restaurant appeared to be quite full. A waiter stood discreetly behind Dan's chair while he scanned the wine list, resting on the 'champagne' section. Valentine nonchalantly sucked on her cigarette and then rubbed off the lipstick smears transferred on to her fingers from the tip of the cigarette.

'The Dom Perignon please. But it must be extremely well chilled.'

'Of course, sir,' the waiter said, deferentially. Valentine's eyes narrowed, and her lips pursed, but she said nothing.

Next they were handed the menus. Dan looked at his quickly, then smiled. 'Right, lovely, what are you having?' His voice was guileless but he was clearly enjoying himself. A cold war had begun and neither side would admit there was a battle raging.

'Oh, I think just a steak and salad, maybe the ham and mango to start with,' she said, equally sweetly.

'Good. I'll have the oysters, then I'll have the lobster. I suddenly feel like seafood in a big way.'

Valentine choked. Her breath caught, her face reddened and she fought to clear her throat.

'Darling, are you all right? Here, let me help you . . .' *Thwack*. He hit her soundly on her back, her eyes now almost popping out of her head. She reached for the champagne and gulped it back.

Breathless she fought for words. 'Hmm. Thanks and no thanks,' she said. 'That really hurt, Daniel. I'm sure it wasn't absolutely necessary.'

'Valentine, you were choking. I thought you were going blue. My dear I was worried. I am sorry if it was too hard. Believe me, it was pure concern.'

She eyed him disbelievingly. The waiter took their order, his obsequiousness increasing in direct relation to the number of pound signs in his eyes. He was bowing so low that Dan could have sworn his nose nearly scraped the eau de nil tablecloth.

He flicked his napkin and grinned across the table. 'What a good idea this was, Valentine. Thanks for bringing me. I'm really enjoying myself . . . aren't you?'

'Yes,' she hissed. 'Of course I am.'

By the time the bill arrived Daniel was almost fit to burst. While Valentine studied the figures incredulously he silently gestured to the waiter and slipped him a small gold plastic card. Valentine was too busy reeling from shock to notice. Her hands trembled on her bag. He had managed to push their bill up to the splendid figure of £480.00. Valiantly she reached for her purse and credit cards.

Daniel could carry on no longer. He reached across the table and put his hand firmly on her purse. 'No, Valentine. You really must allow me . . .' She started to protest – a conditioned reaction. 'Yes, Valentine, I insist.'

Then she started to laugh. 'Daniel, you are an out-and-out bastard! You knew, didn't you, right from the start? How could you have let me go on? Why, I could even have enjoyed the meal, you shit!'

'Oh Valentine. I know. I'm sorry. But you have to admit it was funny. I just wish you could have seen your face.'

'Well, it would only have been funny to someone as warped as you. Honestly!'

The waiter returned Daniel's card. He was well pleased with his evening's work. His tip was more than double his day's earnings. He pulled the table clear to allow Valentine to stand unhindered.

Back in the cool night air Daniel's light mood seemed to evaporate. They drove home in relative silence. Dan drew into the underground garage below the block of flats near Tower Bridge and locked up the car. Valentine was already on her way to the door which marked the entry to the lift. Again his heart sank. She turned to him as they waited for the lift to come and nuzzled his neck. Her cold nose felt irritating against his warm skin. When the door slid open, she snuggled her hand into his.

'You know I'm not in the mood . . .'

She shrugged. 'We'll see,' she said lightly.

Daniel took a shower. When he came out of the bathroom she was already in his bed. The sight annoyed him.

'Look, Valentine, I'm really not in the mood. I meant

121

what I said. I really think it would be best if you went home.'

She climbed out of the bed and moved towards him, her tall, slim body wrapped in a very alluring lace and silk teddy. The thick lace rose at 45-degree angles from her crotch to her hips, framing a very beautiful curve. The two lines of lace met invitingly between her legs where tiny covered buttons waited to either be ripped off in a frenzy, or released tantalizingly slowly, one by one, to reveal their treasure trove.

The sight left Daniel cold. Valentine's arms went round his neck and she pushed her lower body forward, the silk sliding seductively against the towelling. He remained expressionless as she turned her face up to his, waiting for him to bend his head down to meet her mouth.

Then her eyes changed. Sultry seduction changed to anger, confusion. 'What's the matter with you? You've suddenly changed your tune. Why, only the other night you couldn't wait to rip off my knickers.' She studied him with furious eyes. Hands on her hips she faced him squarely. 'So, you don't want me any more. Well that's fine, Daniel. There's plenty more deserving than you. I shan't give you a second thought, don't you worry.'

She started to leave the room, then she stopped suddenly. Turning she said: 'I know what it is, or rather who! My God, how stupid of me. It's that little wimp William's married to, isn't it? What's her name?'

'Charlotte,' he said, his voice dangerously low.

'So that's it. My, my, that's living dangerously, isn't it? Though I can't for one moment imagine she'd be any good at it. Was she, Daniel dear? Is that what's biting your balls?'

He could contain himself no longer. He heard himself bellow, 'Valentine, that is a filthy accusation. Just get out of here, will you? Fast. Take your clothes, dress in the other room and leave quietly. I'm going to bed.' He pushed her through the door struggling, then picked up a stray shoe and threw it after her. A short time later he heard the slam of the door. He checked the sitting room. Everything seemed to be in place. But there was an atmosphere of high tension which hung like an invisible charge over the room.

'Phew,' he sighed, clutching his pounding temple.

When he finally slipped between the sheets he felt numb with exhaustion. But hard as he tried sleep did not come easily.

When she finally managed to throw herself into the back seat of a taxi, a good half hour or so later, Valentine was still shaking with rage. She seethed with a vicious anger. How dare he, the disgusting man, treat her this way when only a few days ago she had him wound right around her little finger? And why had he changed so abruptly? Because of that little cow Charlotte de Sallis, that's why. Valentine had more sex appeal in her big toe than Charlotte had in her entire being. Daniel had almost begged her for it a few days ago. And to turn her down for . . . Idiot . . . idiot . . . idiot . . . she chanted to herself as she turned the key in the lock of her flat, or rather the flat she shared with her absent brother. The flat that Daddy had so stupidly thought to leave in Mark's control until she reached the age of twenty-five. God, what a sense of humour that man had. He knew damn well how much rivalry there had always been between the two of them, and how they would fight over anything that was left in their joint control. But that was all part of Daddy's thing – his rather twisted way of seeing things.

Poor Daddy, Valentine mused. Mixed up and mis-understood. His huge building empire had netted him vast profits which he felt he must repent for in his weekly sermons to the people. He was a well-respected Methodist lay preacher, highly esteemed among the

Somerset community where he was the main employer as well as the spiritual leader. When Valentine and Mark returned from their long stints at boarding school he had felt duty-bound to instil his own tartarish sense of discipline into them. What he had failed to account for was the fact that both his children had inherited his rather keenly developed sexual appetite. As Valentine's breasts started to form, he started to come into her room late in the evening, on the pretext of checking that everything was all right with her. Valentine was a fast learner and it didn't take her too long to realize that her father was after more than a goodnight kiss and an assertion that she had washed all over. And she also learned the delicious sense of power she had over him if she lifted her nightie that little bit more, and spread her legs a tiny bit, until his tongue appeared at the corner of his mouth, and his eyes bulged.

She knew that if she brushed her hand over his thigh she could have anything she wanted from him. She read books and magazines. Sneaked into X-rated movies, and learned. Sex was something extremely powerful which she could use to great advantage. She loved him to look at her. She always knew that she looked better than most girls of her own age and she soon became addicted to the form of worship his letching took. After he died, followed by her mother only a year later, the only career she could ever conceive of was one where she could be admired and looked at.

Daniel was a bloody fool to turn her down. It was almost inconceivable that he should no longer admire or want to look at her. Her pride would not let either of them get away with it. She'd get back at them all right. Sooner or later both Daniel and Charlotte were in for a right old shock. Oh, he'd regret it all right, once her little secret was out. Both Charlotte and Daniel would realize that, of all the players, she was by far the most accomplished.

Chapter Seven

Now that Daniel was face to face with William he found himself, rather surprisingly, not half so guilt-ridden as he had expected. There was something about the smugness of the man sitting opposite that irritated him. William had filled him in on all the details of his coup with Reiser and Daniel had to admit he'd obviously done an excellent job. It wasn't his expertise that was annoying Daniel. After all, why else would he have agreed to join forces with him? His expertise was what Daniel had spotted and wanted.

William wasn't unpleasant or rude. On the contrary, he was charming and quintessentially English. Maybe that was it. The very Englishness of him – that sort of over-assurance he had, an over-large portion of self-confidence that could almost be seen as self-righteousness. Daniel wondered if he was the kind of man ever to question his actions or think that his behaviour might be less than acceptable.

During the last few days Daniel had done some quiet sleuthing in the office. What he had found out had confirmed his suspicions, but hadn't succeeded in making him feel any better about it. One of the account directors over at de Sallis Communications had amused William for a time, and still did, on and off as far as he could gather. As far as Kate was concerned, nothing concrete had come back on that. He felt bloody angry with William but in a funny kind of way it had probably helped Daniel's sense of guilt. What was so irritating was the fact that he could hardly think of himself as being above William in the morality stakes.

When William had finally finished talking Daniel just sat and looked at him for a few moments. 'You did a great job,' he said rather flatly. 'And I've been thinking that now the PR side's financially OK, for the next year at least, I might do what I've been thinking of doing for ages, but haven't felt confident enough about things at this end before now.'

'Oh?' William was obviously intrigued.

'If Bob Lester agrees, and I've already spoken to him about it and he's there in principle, I shall spend a bit of time going round some smaller agencies, see if I can do a bit of shopping.'

'Shopping?'

'Acquiring. Australia, Hong Kong, North America, maybe even China and Moscow.' He laughed. 'Whatever, I'm sure you'll all manage quite nicely while I'm gone. As I said, nothing's been agreed yet and obviously I want to get this merger settled before I go, so I'll certainly be around until after the announcement.'

'You're certainly full of surprises, Daniel.'

Daniel stood up, signifying the end of the meeting. 'So are you, William . . . so are you.'

Charlotte barely saw William these days. As always he left early and returned late. They were like the proverbial ships in the night. But she was glad. The more superficial their relationship, the easier it was to deal with her own feelings. Whatever he'd been up to in Paris hadn't left any noticeable mark on him, either physically or mentally. He was just the same coldly unemotional partner he had been prior to his trip. It was no good torturing herself with suspicions about his philandering. She was in no position to judge him. Anyway, the last thing she wanted was to encourage any kind of intimacy between them.

The only good thing about having agreed to organize the party was the fact that the days just seemed to fly by. The invitations were printed and sent out. The caterers were booked, musicians organized, florists, decorators and so on had all been briefed. All she had to get through was the visit to Daniel's office with Mr Hart, the caterer. He had taken her by surprise, insisting that she go with him to inspect the facilities. Sarah, Daniel's secretary, had guilelessly suggested that she let Daniel know Charlotte would be coming in, but Charlotte had listened to the days Daniel could not make, and quickly plumped for one of those, anticipating that he would be out of the office, and therefore she'd be unlikely to bump into him.

But when she did finally meet Mr Hart at the offices of Cornwallis Advertising she was dreadfully on edge, and found it hard to concentrate on Mr Hart's loving inspection of the state-of-the-art oven and the magnificent conference room with its sweeping views across London. She was almost hopping with impatience, trying to hurry him up, so that she could get out of the enemy camp.

Eventually he was satisfied and they headed back down the plush corridor and stood waiting, listening to the lift banging in the shaft, fast approaching. Charlotte was still busy thanking Daniel's secretary for her help when she saw Sarah smile over Charlotte's shoulder as the doors clanged open. She feared to look round. Every hair on her body rose. Her heart started to pound and the blood raced in her ears.

Sarah confirmed her worst fears. 'Hi, Daniel.'

Charlotte turned. Her mouth opened but no words came. She was dumbstruck. He looked devastatingly attractive though his face was paler and he looked a little leaner than before. She reached out to the wall, to steady herself. 'Daniel . . .' she heard a voice (surely not her own?) squeak.

His brows knitted. He clearly was not expecting to see her either. He stood in front of her. She waited. He held out his hand to shake hers and then quickly withdrew it – a ridiculously formal gesture. Sarah was watching first Charlotte and then Daniel, obviously aware of the tension between them.

'Charlotte,' Daniel said. Then, remembering they were indeed under direct scrutiny, he said, 'What a nice surprise. What are you doing here?' His voice sounded level, pleasantly interested; while his eyes, which only she could see, narrowed dangerously.

Sarah interrupted. 'Mrs de Sallis brought Mr Hart the caterer in to see the room for the party, Daniel.'

His false smile broadened. 'Can I offer you tea, my dear Charlotte?'

'No thank you, Daniel,' she answered politely, her green eyes blazing back at him. 'I had no intention of disturbing you, I know how busy you are. Thanks again, Sarah,' she said, turning away from him. Daniel stabbed the lift button. 'Mr Hart . . . ' she called, holding the door open for him. As it slid shut she caught a last glimpse of his angry eyes.

Charlotte picked up the phone to hear Claudia's enthusiastic babble on the other end: 'I've been trying to catch you for weeks – you're either engaged or out!'

'I'm sorry, life's been crazy. What's new?'

The truth was that Charlotte had been carefully avoiding Claudia because she knew damn well she'd only want to talk about Daniel. And she couldn't trust herself to listen to Claudia's crowing on about how much she fancied him. But it seemed she was to be spared once more.

'Listen, darling, I can't talk now, but any chance you can meet me for lunch – usual place at one?'

'Fine,' Charlotte sighed, relieved at being granted a reprieve for a couple of hours. 'I'll see you there.'

For once Claudia had actually beaten her. Charlotte's

Marguerita stood ready for her on the table.

'Lovely, thanks.' She took a sip of the icy, lemony cocktail. 'Mmmm, perfect.'

Claudia watched her, bursting to talk. 'Are you OK, Charlie? You look awfully thin and pale.'

'Thanks, it's nice to see you too.'

Claudia giggled. 'I'm only showing concern. OK, you look terrific. Will that do? I really was beginning to wonder if you were avoiding me. Ever since dinner with Daniel you've never called me back. I suppose you're angry with me, aren't you? But he is an awfully nice man . . .' She sighed. 'Needless to say I didn't get anywhere with him – more's the pity.' She frowned at Charlotte. 'I still can't understand why you don't like him. You know one of the girls in the office was telling me about a friend of hers who used to go out with him years ago. He sounded utterly delightful even then. Not at all like the playboy he's made out to be. He looked after her when she had terrible problems and . . .'

'Don't tell me,' Charlotte howled, 'and sent flowers to her sick mother and found her brother a job in advertising.'

Claudia shook her head in resignation. 'Well, honestly. There's no need to be like that. You're getting pretty spiky you know.'

'Look, let's not bicker about it. You're right. He's probably not half so bad as I think he is, it's just that we seem to have, well, a sort of personality clash, that's all. Let's drop him, shall we?'

'Oh, well. OK,' said Claudia, clearly disappointed. 'What about William? Is that a safe subject – or should I hide behind the napkin . . . ?' She laughed.

'He's all right – if you like that sort of thing. He took his secretary to Paris with him.'

Claudia's eyebrows shot up, but she said nothing.

'I really don't know if there's anything in it. He's certainly got every opportunity though. I hardly ever

129

see him. He works late every night, and sometimes over the weekends. But to be honest, Claudia, I don't know if it really bothers me.'

'And the baby?'

'On hold. I'm not even going to talk about it. There just doesn't seem any point really. I know what his answer will be and to tell you the truth I'm beginning to wonder if it really is what I want. We've hardly got the perfect marriage, have we?'

'No,' Claudia said, emphatically.

'I've been thinking quite a lot about what you said – about needing to get back into some real work, and I think you're right.'

Claudia rubbed her hands together, well pleased with herself. 'Oh good. Because that's exactly what I wanted to talk to you about. You know the night you left Daniel and I in the restaurant?' Charlotte nodded. She would hardly forget it. 'Well I spotted Giles Ferguson in the restaurant. Remember him?'

Charlotte frowned. 'No. Don't think so, who is he?'

'He's a publisher, he's just sold out in the States and he wants to set up over here. Come on, Charlie, you must remember him, he owned about five hundred titles and we used to syndicate a load of stuff between us.'

Charlotte shrugged. 'That may be, but I probably wouldn't have dealt with him, would I? How come you know him?'

'I met him in the States, when I was over there for that six-month trip, remember? He was after me for a bit, but he just wasn't my type. Anyway, I told him that you might want to get back to work. He certainly knows who you are, and he's very keen to meet you. I said I'd fix up lunch, if you agree.'

'Hang on a minute. Just what sort of magazine is he talking about?'

'A great big fat, glossy full-colour top of the market

130

women's magazine.' She paused for dramatic effect. 'Drooling yet?'

Charlotte shrugged, dead nonchalantly. 'Maybe. What's the plan then?'

'He's going to ring me when he's ready to talk to you. I expect it'll be in a week or so. I just wanted to sound you out first.'

'You're sure this isn't some harebrained scheme of yours, Claudia, that we're all going to go rushing about for, only to find it's a bag of wind!'

'Why don't you just wait and see. You've got nothing to lose, have you? I can't wait to move jobs. Ever since that Valentine rubber shoot things haven't been the same. They're so bloody small-minded.'

'Well, I've got enough to occupy me for the next few days. I've got this party tomorrow night . . .'

'Crikey, you must be going out of your mind, aren't you? I had no idea it was so soon. What are you going to wear?'

'Oh, some frightful creation. It's a sort of white jersey thing. Indian style trousers and a high-necked, long-sleeved blouse. I look a bit like an Indian houri.'

'Sounds interesting,' Claudia said, a little dubiously. 'Who's it by?'

Charlotte couldn't help laughing. 'We don't all spend our lives in designer creations, my dear. It's "by" someone I've never heard of and I picked it up in a backstreet boutique in downtown Richmond.'

Claudia sniffed. 'How quaint.'

'It'll be fine – certainly different. I'm going to put a silver sash around the waist and ask the hairdresser to put my hair up with silver braids.'

'Sounds stunning, I wish I could be a fly on the wall.'

'You could be. Why don't you come?'

'Sorry, darling. Prior commitment. But I can't wait to hear all about it.'

Chapter Eight

Charlotte drew back the kitchen curtains to reveal a ghostly grey, mist-shrouded morning. A thick veil hung over the trees and spilled down on to the shrubs. It concealed and muffled. Normally the sound of the rush hour would be drifting through the double glazing. Today there was nothing, it was deathly quiet. It was a fitting start to All Hallows Eve.

Charlotte's bare feet were icy against the chill ceramic floor. She stamped them to try to get the blood circulating. The kettle boiled and she quickly made the tea. William was showered and beginning to dress by the time she got back upstairs.

'Morning, darling. You're up bright and early.'

She set the tray down by her dressing table, answering his reflection in the mirror: 'There's quite a bit to do.'

He walked over to her and planted a kiss on top of her head. She smiled at him. 'You look very fresh, darling – just like when I married you.'

She raised her eyebrows at the compliment. 'Thank you,' she said, somewhat surprised. 'You're obviously in a good mood today.'

He pulled on his shirt and fiddled with his cuffs. 'Of course. I've got everything to celebrate. The move's gone well. The merger's a success. I'm looking forward to the party, and . . .' he placed his hands on her shoulders and stroked the bare skin between the thin straps of her nightdress with the tips of his fingers, '. . . I have a very beautiful wife.' He bent down once more and lifted her chin with the tip of his finger so that her mouth became level with his. He kissed her firmly, forcing her lips apart; his tongue invading the soft wetness of her mouth. He stroked her neck and then let his fingertip drop very lightly to her nipple which was outlined against the thin fabric of the gown. He slid the strap down and described small circles over her shoulders.

'Mmmmmm,' he sighed. 'Darling . . . I'll be late for work if I stay here doing this. You are so sexy . . .' He pushed himself away from her, leaving her to stare at her reflection: swollen, blood-gorged lips, and sprawling hair. Her nipples stood out proudly now, erect and aroused: teased by him.

She poured the tea without comment and then vigorously rubbed thick white cream into her skin tissuing it off quickly. The action brought healthy pink colour to her cheeks. William finished dressing and picked up his tea. He drank it in one gulp and then set it back on the tray noisily.

'What time are you coming into the office, darling?'

'Oh, about six. Everything was sorted out there yesterday. There's no point in my arriving too early, unless some emergency happens.'

'Well, if you need anything just ask Kate. I know she'll be delighted to help.'

'How very sweet of her,' Charlotte said, innocently. William finished tying his bow-tie and combed his hair. Charlotte had to admit that he was certainly attractive; his body still firm and athletic, his broad shoulders accentuated by the immaculate cut of the dark grey suit.

'I'll see you later, my love.' He bent to kiss her once more, this time a paternal peck planted firmly on her cheek, then he was gone.

Charlotte looked at her watch. Eight o'clock already. She'd better get moving if she was to be anywhere near organized. She dressed quickly and wolfed down her

133

breakfast. Then she set about making all the confirmatory telephone calls but the phone kept busy non-stop. Every time she finished a call someone would ring her. There seemed to be a hundred and one things to check and double check. Suddenly she realized she was due at the hairdressers in half an hour. The day had just disappeared. She tried to call Kate to check how things were going.

'I'm sorry, Mrs de Sallis, but I'm afraid she's still at lunch.'

'Oh.' Charlotte thought for a moment. William could pass on the message. 'In that case could you please put me through to my husband.'

'I'm sorry, Mrs de Sallis, but he's out too.' She hesitated. 'In fact they're out together.'

'I see,' Charlotte snapped a little abruptly. She quickly added 'Thank you,' before hanging up.

Well, she intended to give them a good looking-over tonight if she got half a chance. You'd have thought the pair of them would have had enough to do without buggering off to lunch, she thought, rather uncharitably.

The serene vision which emerged from the hairdressers some two hours later appeared somewhat removed from Charlotte's inner self, which was beginning to feel rather sick. A latticework of silver thread had been intricately woven through the blonde strands, and she looked like a mediaeval princess. She just hoped that she'd be able to bathe and change without the whole creation toppling into a sorry mess. By the time she returned to Richmond it was time to get ready. The cab was booked to take her to the office for six o'clock. That meant she had just over an hour to get herself tarted up.

She soaped herself slowly, enjoying the smell of the stephanotis-scented lather. She sat bolt upright so as not to let the steam damage her hair. Her toenails looked like disembodied red squares floating in the water – she'd painted them earlier, though why she'd bothered she didn't really know as her toes would be well hidden inside her shoes. It was all part of the ritual and it pleased her. She ran a matching fingernail around the edges of her toenails, easing away little flakes of lacquer which had hit skin instead of nail. Then she examined her fingers for any similar imperfections. Her nails were not long; just small neat crescents protruding above the ends of her fingertips. Finally satisfied, she hauled herself out of the bath and set about the business of getting ready.

Half an hour later she stood back to survey the effect. She was *fairly* satisfied. The soft white jersey pants fell loosely over her hips and tapered in to above her knees, where they were gathered into tight seams to her ankles. She'd managed to find some bautiful Indian slippers, emblazoned with mirrored sequins, ending in a point above her toes. The shirt top had loose box sleeves which fell to the elbows, and from there echoed the tight seams of the trousers to her wrists. A silver sash was tied in a bow at her navel. It was not a particularly elaborate outfit but it had style and, more importantly, it was very comfortable. Above all else, this was not the evening to be worried about escaping cleavages, drooping shoulder straps or wobbling heels.

She was just finishing applying her lipstick when the taxi arrived. She opened the window and shouted down to the driver: 'Give me two minutes and I'll be right with you.' She switched handbags, grabbed a jacket and raced down the stairs.

When she arrived at the office, just before six o'clock, the cloakroom attendant booked for the evening had already arrived. She was sorting out dress-rails and hangers in the room which ran off the reception area. Her make-up consisted basically of just three colours: black, white and green. Her skin tone had been

135

whitened out, and then 'shadows' painted on in green. Her lips were outlined in black. The white and green served only to exaggerate the redness of her eyes.

'You look wonderful,' Charlotte told her. 'I just hope you don't scare off too many of the guests . . . in the nicest possible way of course,' she added quickly.

The ceiling above the reception desk was hung with fine grey netting, like centuries-old spiders' webs. Charlotte raced on up to the fourth floor. Sarah's desk was now pushed to one side to make room for another one. Both desks were empty. She turned left down the corridor towards the conference room. The whole passageway had been transformed. Great swags of grey netting swept from the ceiling across the walls, to just above head height. Little black fur-like objects clung to the netting in places, small red beads glowing in bat-like heads. Charlotte walked through the pseudo gossamer into the conference room.

The windows had been blacked out – she'd supervised the blanket-pinning session the previous day. The lights had been covered with red, green and white tissue paper angled on to 'spray' webs which hung all over the ceiling. A fan blew tiny draughts up to the webs, wafting them gently, so that the light effect was even more surreal.

A vampire approached her. Two enormous white fangs protruded from either side of its mouth. A small dribble of black, or possibly red, though it was difficult to tell in the strange light, ran down its chin. It wore a black suit and an enormous black flowing cloak, which swirled about its body, showing flashes of red satin lining. 'Hello, Mrs de Sallis,' it said, holding out a hand. The hand squeezed hers so tightly she winced.

'Oh, Mr Hart,' she said. 'I didn't recognize you. You look absolutely terrifying.'

'Oh, thank you,' he said delightedly. 'Do you really think so? We had great fun, you know. It makes a nice change for us to do something a bit different, dress up, you know. Come on. I'll show you the others.'

He led her across the room. A huge black, steaming cauldron spewed green smoke over its sides. The awful, putrid-looking mist tumbled down on to the floor and then drifted upwards.

'Uggh. That looks really horrible,' Charlotte said, well pleased with the effect. It was a test run, supervised by Frankenstein's monster. Behind him stood a werewolf, a skeleton, sundry other vampires and the occasional ghoul. The girls were dressed as black cats. Fine Lycra stretched over skinny bodies; tails stretched skyward from their nether regions and long whiskers grew from their cheeks.

'Bravo, all of you!' Charlotte cried. 'You look absolutely wonderful.' They grinned. Not at all monsterlike. 'Don't smile too much,' she warned. 'You'll crack your make-up.'

'Hello, Charlotte,' said a voice behind her. She turned to see Kate's cheery smile. In the past she had always referred to her as 'Mrs de Sallis'. Now she bridled at the familiarity but let it pass. 'I didn't know you were here. When did you arrive?'

'Oh, not long ago,' Charlotte answered smoothly. 'I didn't want to disturb you, Kate. I thought you might be "tied up" with William.' She couldn't resist the barb in her voice.

'I was. But we're finished now. I've come to see if there's anything I can do to help before I change.'

God, she was cool, Charlotte thought. There was not one tiny hint of guile in her voice. 'No thanks, Kate. It all seems to be under control. I think I'll just pop along and see William.' She turned and left Kate to oversee the caterers.

William's name hung in bold, gold letters across his door: 'William de Sallis, JOINT MANAGING DIRECTOR', they announced proudly. She opened the door and walked in. He was not alone. Daniel was standing beside his desk.

'Oh, sorry . . .' she blurted. 'I didn't mean to interrupt. I just thought I'd say hello.'

Daniel turned to her, an unreadable expression on his face. 'It's all right Charlotte,' he said, his voice expressionless. 'I was just leaving. I'll see you both later.'

He walked past her, closing the door behind him. 'What's up with him I wonder?' William asked, puzzled. 'It's unlike him to be so abrupt. Why he hardly said hello to you, Charlotte. Can't think what's up with the man. He seems to have got that way lately. Moody and preoccupied. Strange, though. He's been fine all day. Kept on saying what a marvellous job you'd done with all the decorations. Let's hope he'll be all right for tonight.'

She shrugged noncommittally. 'Oh, he's probably just anxious that everything goes well,' she said in a much brighter way than she was feeling.

She couldn't help wondering if his mood had anything to do with her. Don't be ridiculous, she told herself. Why on earth should it? He's probably completely forgotten the whole thing happened. But she was unaccountably pleased that Daniel liked her efforts. She just hoped the rest of the evening lived up to expectations.

By the time the first guests arrived Charlotte had no time to think any further about Daniel or William or Kate. She was lost in a flurry of introductions, checking that all the food was being circulated and trying to control the volume of the string quartet who were providing the evening's music. Their gentle strains had a tendency to become louder during a particularly stirring phrase of music, and drown out conversation almost entirely. But at least they'd dressed suitably for the occasion. Two witches and two warlocks; clothed in black. She waved at the cellist once more and gestured slightly, patting the air with her hand. He nodded and waved to the others to damp it down a little.

There was a sudden kerfuffle over by the door. A buzz of interest seemed to be centred around a new arrival. There was a shriek of laughter and a blaze of bright, copper-red hair. Valentine's height alone made her conspicuous. As the bodies cleared Charlotte could see her more clearly. How apt, she thought. Valentine must feel very much at home.

She was dressed in the most extraordinarily dramatic witch's garb. An almost completely diaphanous drape of sheer grey tulle hung in uneven points down her legs. Her grey tights were shredded in places, and her upper arms blotched with grey charcoal. When she moved the light caught the shapes of her naked breasts below the tissue-thin fabric. The costume was almost obscene, but Valentine wore it as easily as she would an old sweater. She had achieved the effect she sought: she was noticed; she was admired; she was shocking and she would be talked about.

William was at her side, clearly appreciating the revealing garment. Valentine threw her arms around him, flirting with him outrageously. You needn't worry, thought Charlotte. You're not his type, dear – she glanced over at Kate who stood just behind William – he only likes mice. She narrowed her eyes and turned away, only to catch Dan's eye. He had been watching her. He turned back to Valentine and William, and Charlotte could have sworn she saw him mouth some expletive. Then he crossed the room to carry out his duty as joint host. William left Valentine's side when he saw Daniel approach. Valentine turned and scowled at Daniel, then she looked over in Charlotte's direction and spoke. Daniel too then looked at Charlotte before turning back to Valentine. She burst out laughing.

Bastard, Charlotte spat. They were clearly sharing a wonderful joke at her expense.

Valentine flounced over to her. 'Charlotte, my dear, what a sweet little outfit you're wearing.'

Charlotte smiled coolly. 'Valentine, I hope you don't get too cold. I can always go and find you a jacket if you like . . .'

'Don't worry a bit,' the younger woman retorted. 'I'm positively hot. William told me how much work you've put into the party. You've done awfully well!'

William bloody well would, wouldn't he? 'I hope you enjoy yourself, Valentine – mind you don't get bitten . . .'

Charlotte waved as a vampire appeared with a tray of glasses, and helped herself to yet another of the specially concocted cocktails. They were coloured green with chartreuse. She thought there was probably a vodka base but she wasn't really that fussy. Her job was just about over. She could relax and enjoy herself. She gulped back the drink.

A voice at her elbow said: 'Your glass is empty . . . here let me get you another one.' The man reached out and collected another glass from the tray and handed it to Charlotte.

'Thanks,' she said. 'I should be doing that for you.'

He looked at her questioningly.

'I'm supposed to be a sort of host, you see.'

'Well, you have my permission to take a break. Do you work here?'

Charlotte laughed at the suggestion. 'No, I'm just part-time really,' she answered. He must be one of Dan's clients. His voice had a slight transatlantic twang. He was handsome in a dark, foreign, sort of way. Brown-black eyes in a deep olive skin.

'Whoever did the organizing did a pretty good job, didn't they?' He looked around. Charlotte smiled. 'Have you met William and Daniel before?' he asked politely.

140

'Yes. I know William better though,' Charlotte said with a twinkle in her eye.

'I don't know him at all. It's Daniel I've had dealings with. I'm moving my business over here so I'm looking for an agency.'

'Oh.' Charlotte nodded. He was obviously expecting her to ask what he did. She was not going to be so predictable. 'Who else do you know here apart from Daniel?' she asked.

'No one really. Of course there are one or two I recognize. But no one I particularly want to get involved with.' He glanced at her hand. 'I see you're married. What a disappointment. I was hoping I might persuade you to have dinner with me. Wouldn't you like me to whisk you away from all this? I could give you a really very interesting evening.'

Charlotte laughed aloud. He seemed harmless enough. For all his clichés he was amusing. Dry.

Just then Daniel appeared at her elbow. 'Charlotte, there's somebody I'd like you to meet.' He led her away, almost pulling her.

'Daniel, what on earth are you doing? I was in mid-conversation, enjoying myself.'

'That was more than apparent. You seem to have forgotten that we're all working here tonight, and you're . . . you're . . . well, you're neglecting people.' Anger, if she wasn't mistaken, seemed to be blazing from his eyes. Why, she had absolutely no idea. His grip tightened on her arm as he brought her over to a silver-haired man standing on his own. 'Michael.' Daniel's voice flipped into velvet. 'This is Charlotte, William's wife. She was responsible for all the organization tonight.'

She politely acknowledged the introductions. Glancing behind her she saw her new friend seemed to have disappeared back into the sea of people. She concentrated on the conversation around her. The party was a success. The string quartet were still playing

141

valiantly. The buzz of conversation had grown to such a level that they were now really having to flog the cats to make themselves heard. The buzz drove into her ears and echoed in her temple, the beginnings of a throbbing head. She remembered that she'd left her pills in the handbag at home. She hadn't swapped them over. And she was feeling more than a little lightheaded.

Daniel disappeared off to make some more introductions, leaving her surrounded by a crowd of clients. She tried to listen attentively, but their voices were irritating, getting unbearably shrill. She had to get a glass of water, or a pill, or something. Then she remembered William always carried a pack of paracetamol in his briefcase. She knew she'd find it in his office.

Quite a few people were already beginning to drift off. She crossed the room amid a torrent of goodbyes and thank yous. Excusing herself, she made her way back down the corridor to William's room. She reached for the door handle, but was halted by a muffled noise, a sort of half shriek, cut off mid-way, and then a low laugh. It seemed to be coming from within. With her heart in her mouth and a thousand pictures passing through her imagination she clicked open the door. There was another laugh. This time a deeper, male chuckle.

Hands trembling, she slowly slid her fingers down the wall, trying to find the light switch. Once it was located, her hand hung suspended for a few seconds; she was terrified to reveal what she knew had to be faced. All her suspicions were about to be confirmed. By now she felt sick to her stomach. Already she thought her knees might buckle, and her head pounded interminably. Summoning up every ounce of courage in her body she flicked the switch. The light exploded into the darkness, her eyes blinking at the sudden glare.

The scene before her would have been almost comic

were it not so horrifyingly shocking. William was frozen to the spot, his trousers and pants in a messy heap around his ankles. His shirt-tails were half hitched up over his bare buttocks. He stood with his back to the door, half leaning over his desk. Kate's legs were straddled around his back, knees raised up under his armpits. Charlotte would never, as long as she lived, forget the expression on William's face as he turned his head. The mixture of shock and disbelief in that second engraved itself on her memory for ever more. His mouth hung open. A total time-suspension. He knew there was nothing he could say. Nothing to excuse or correct. If he moved he stepped back into time. The awful consequences of his action would follow with the speed and certainty of a high-speed train. She could not see Kate's face. She was raising up her head, awkwardly twisting to see who had come in.

But there was something not quite right. The pieces of the puzzle didn't fit properly. One of them was way off course. A slow suspicion was beginning to form into grave realization. Those legs? What had Kate been wearing? There were tears in those stockings. Those grey smudges . . . In the thousandths of a second it took for the legs to move Charlotte's mind raced. It couldn't be . . . How . . . And then she saw.

'Valentine!' she cried aloud. She put her hand over her mouth to stem the scream caught in her throat. Bitter bile rose. Her stomach churned dangerously. She felt dizzy. Dizzy, sick and disgusted. She stood, rooted to the spot for a few more seconds and then half stumbled back through the door. She fell straight into Daniel's arms in the doorway where he stood, open-mouthed at the scene. He caught hold of Charlotte as she fell against him. Using a superhuman effort and strength she would have denied she possessed, she threw herself away from him, and pushed him aside. Tears of humiliation now poured down her cheeks.

143

Dan chased after her, as she headed for the lift.

As Dan caught up with her she saw the man who had been so interested in her earlier. When he saw her, surprise and confusion were clear on his face.

'Take me out of here,' she demanded, dragging him into the open lift. The lift doors slid shut behind them. The eyes of Daniel Cornwallis, lit by a murderous glint, locked into her memory long after the lift had left them behind.

Chapter Nine

Giles helped Charlotte out to his car. Her teeth chattered uncontrollably and her body shook with huge tremors which Giles did his best to contain, cradling her gently, whispering 'Ssssh . . . it's OK . . . come on . . .' soothingly. Mindlessly and oblivious to the cold night she let herself be put into the car. Giles climbed into the driving seat. 'Where would you like me to take you?'

Charlotte stared out of the window not hearing, or seeing. He watched her briefly, and then started the engine, driving smoothly through the heart of London. Charlotte had no consciousness of where she was being taken or, even, barely who she was with. She just wanted to put as much distance as possible between herself and William . . . Valentine and her foul, mocking, triumphant grin . . . Daniel. The whole grim trio.

'Do you want to talk?' Charlotte jumped. The intrusion seemed to come from very far away. She looked in sudden shock at Giles, having momentarily forgotten about this stranger at her side.

'What?'

'I said do you want to talk about it? Whatever happened back there was obviously pretty upsetting for you.' She turned from him and shook her head silently.

She let him take her inside his flat, moving automatically, unaware of where she was. She heard from a distance a voice ask her if she would like a drink. She nodded, dumbly. A large glass with thick orange-brown liquid was handed to her – the colour of copper hair. She searched the depths of amber and then took a large gulp. The fiery liquid burned her throat. The pain was satisfying, reviving. She took another mouthful. 'Steady on . . . that's Armagnac, you know. You don't want to be ill on top of everything else, do you?' His hand rested gently on her shoulder.

A small bit of feeling began to creep back into her frozen limbs. She turned to her rescuer and studied him more closely. He was not overly tall but he had a powerful presence. She would not like to be on the wrong side of him. He was watching her, his almost black eyes unreadable. The reality of the situation started to dawn on her awareness. He was a complete stranger. Here she was, alone in his flat. What did it matter? She was completely drained of all emotion: including fear. The world could explode and what would it matter? She'd been duped, humiliated. The bitter irony of Valentine, the poisonous, conceited little brat. Anger and bitterness were drawn clearly across Charlotte's features.

'What is it?' Giles asked quietly.

Staring at the glass she said: 'I caught my husband fucking another woman!'

'Oh,' he said, quietly. 'I see.'

She laughed, a brittle high-pitched sound. 'It's really quite funny. You see I thought he was having an affair with his secretary. But it wasn't her at all.' She swirled the liquid around the bowl of the glass, biting her bottom lip, fighting for the painful words. 'I must have been blind,' she whispered. 'Valentine . . . How could he? Valentine . . .' She spat out the words, talking to herself. She stood and paced the room. Then she started to sway. Giles rose to steady her. He took the glass from her hand.

'Excuse me . . .' she said, 'but I think I'm going to be ill.' He pulled her towards the bathroom. Charlotte ran in, slamming the door behind her, lurching for the bowl. Her whole body was taken over by huge con-

146

vulsions as she retched. Finally she relaxed on to her
knees, pressing her hot brow on the cold porcelain,
composing herself. She filled a glass at the basin and
took a sip of cool water. She felt dreadful.

She curled up on the bathroom floor, letting un-
consciousness overtake her.

Daniel stormed back into the conference room. 'Where
the hell is Sarah?' he demanded, oblivious to the strange
looks the remaining guests were throwing in his
direction. 'Sarah!' he bellowed.

She scuttled across to his side as fast as her heels
would carry her. He grabbed her by the arm and pulled
her back along the corridor to her desk.

'Where is Giles Ferguson staying? God help you if you
don't know . . .'

Sarah winced. 'Ouch, Daniel. You're hurting my arm.
Let go.'

'Sorry, Sarah,' he said, genuinely. 'But it's really
important. Don't ask why, but please tell me fast.'

She pulled out a pile of cards from her personal index.
Turning to the 'F' divider she said: 'Here we are. We
sent him some credentials earlier.' She passed the card
to Dan.

'Thank you.' He touched her arm gently.

Turning to the lift he saw the two culprits coming out
of William's office. William saw Daniel and stopped,
mid-stride, registering the anger he saw on Daniel's
face, a cold dangerous rage.

'You bastard,' he spat at William. 'There's really
nothing like shitting on your own doorstep, is there?
Well done. That was a really inspired piece of behaviour.'
His lip curled in a disgusted sneer. 'Couldn't you have
been a little more discreet? I suppose you were just so
desperate to get your end away . . . ' His voice was
beginning to rise and he knew he was dangerously close
to reorganizing William's arrogant features.

William had paled somewhat. 'Listen, Daniel,' he began, rather weakly.

Valentine interrupted. She was sliding closer to him. 'Come on Dan,' she oiled, 'it was only a bit of fun. You of all people should understand that.' Daniel felt his hand twitch. He was using a superhuman effort to control it. 'After all, what's the difference? William and me . . . you and . . .' Daniel's hand cut her short with a resounding smack on the cheek. She reeled sideways, eyes registering shocked surprise. 'Why you . . .' she screeched, dangerous blood-red talons poised, ready to tear at his face. Her eyes blazed with the lust for revenge.

He caught at her hand and held it easily. 'Forget it, Valentine. You're just an evil-minded little slut.'

William just stood there, caught between a desire to help Valentine and the suspicion that he must not take his eyes off Daniel for one second.

Daniel straightened his tie. 'If you'll both excuse me I have some business to attend to.'

After he had gone, Valentine turned to William. 'Come on, darling,' she said, unabashed by Dan's outburst. 'The evening's still young. Let's go partying.' She started to pull him back towards the conference room.

'Don't you think we've caused enough damage between us for one night?' She shrugged. 'I'm going home to try and find my wife!'

She sidled up to him, pressing against him. 'But you'd have much more fun with me,' she simpered.

He looked at her coldly. 'Valentine, the games are over for tonight. Charlotte is my wife.'

'OK,' she said petulantly. 'But if I were you I certainly wouldn't bother.'

Daniel's foot hardly left the floor as he screeched along, racing to get to Chester Square. He slammed through the gears, punishing the car. Finally it screamed to a halt outside the tall regency terrace house that was number 18. There were three bells on the side of the door – he pressed all three simultaneously. The catch slipped and he leaped up the stairs three at a time and hammered on the door at the top. The door opened to reveal Giles, dressed only in a towelling robe. Daniel barged past him ignoring his look of outrage.

'Where is she . . .' he demanded.

'What the hell is all this about, Daniel?'

'Just tell me where she is?' he bellowed back. He started throwing open doors. Giles knew he was not going to be able to stop the assault of this madman. He watched silently. Daniel reached the bedroom door. A small lamp illuminated the room. He caught a glimpse of blonde hair strewn across the pillows, shoulders naked above the line of the covers. He turned, his face twisted with disgust.

'I can see I'm too late. Sorry to have bothered you, Giles. Do excuse me if I don't wish you goodnight.' He slammed the door shut behind him.

Giles went over to the bedside. He looked down and then, reaching over, picked up Charlotte's heavy arm. He quickly checked the pulse of the drugged woman. Satisfied, he went to the phone. He waited impatiently for the voice to answer.

'Get over here as fast as you can. Bring all the gear. We've got a busy night ahead of us.' Replacing the receiver he smiled grimly to himself. He was certainly looking forward to this one.

Daniel was disturbed to notice that his hand was shaking as he placed his key in the lock. Shaking with a cold, dangerous rage. Only sheer bloody instinct had made him chase after Charlotte tonight. He had known that he must find her and take care of her after witnessing that . . . that . . . well, that disgusting little scene between William and Valentine. Why the fuck she had chosen to run off with Giles Ferguson was something he couldn't fathom at all.

But what a stupid fool he'd been. She didn't need his help. She was already tucked up in Ferguson's bed, the little whore. They were all the bloody same. God, he'd had a skinful of women and screwing around. It made him nauseous. He'd be glad to get away from the whole bloody lot of them.

He kicked off his shoes and threw himself fully clothed on to the bed. Then he picked up the phone and punched out Bob Lester's number. 'So still working late are you?' he said when Bob answered.

'Yeah. It just wouldn't seem normal to get home on time. How'd the party go?'

'Fine,' Daniel said quickly. 'Listen, Bob, have you got time to see me tomorrow? If I can get a flight I'll be with you in the morning. Book me in for lunch, and can you get me in at the usual place tomorrow night?'

'Well, that's fine, Dan, but what's the big urgency?'

'Just business. Now that this jamboree's over I want to get started on our expansion plan. There's no time like the present.'

Bob laughed quietly. 'You don't change, Dan. I'll see you then.'

Daniel hung up and set the alarm for 6 a.m., knowing that his dreams would most likely be punctuated by both Charlotte and Giles Ferguson.

Charlotte slowly returned to consciousness. The pain in her head seared through her temple, causing her to wince when she moved. She clutched at the side of her head. Her eyes felt dry and prickly painful. Slowly she opened them. The curtains were drawn but she could just make out the shadowy contours of the room. It took her several seconds to realize she was in a strange bed, and then came the sickening jolt to her stomach as she remembered why she was there. She lay back, covering her face, wishing she hadn't woken up at all, not wanting to face up to what had happened. Her entire body felt stiff and bruised. Her legs and abdomen were sore. Her mouth was dry. She licked her lips to try and get some moisture back. There was a glass of water at the side of the bed. She took small sips then fell back on to the pillows and tried to remember what had happened. Where had Giles slept? The pillow next to her looked dented. The bed itself was in complete disarray, the covers half hanging off. Whatever had happened she certainly didn't remember it. And she'd never in her life been so drunk as to not remember. Hazy dreams drifted back to her and she gasped. Daniel making love to her. And William too. She'd given herself to them both. A complete wanton. She flushed.

The bedroom door opened and her rescuer appeared. 'Hello there,' he called cheerfully. He drew back the curtains slightly, sensitive to her need to adjust to the light. She shielded her eyes. Then he disappeared for a few seconds, returning with a full tray of breakfast. 'I hope you're hungry,' he said.

She didn't feel remotely hungry, but she smiled weakly. The tray bore scrambled eggs, buttered toast, fresh orange juice and a pot of tea. The smell convinced her that she was, after all, a little hungry. He sat at the foot of the bed, watching her. She wriggled uncomfortably, not knowing how to phrase the question that she knew she had to ask. 'I don't remember coming to bed. Did we . . . ummm . . . did we, you know . . . did we sleep together?' she blurted. He laughed. She was surprised at the hard edge to the sound. She certainly hadn't noticed that before.

He looked at her and spoke rather condescendingly. 'My dear girl,' he said. 'You were not in a fit state for anything last night. I'd have to be some kind of animal to have taken advantage of anyone in that state.'

151

Charlotte flushed. 'I'm sorry,' she said. 'It's just that I couldn't seem to remember and I felt . . . oh, never mind.' This was beginning to get very embarrassing. She reached over for the orange juice.

'That's it,' he said encouragingly. 'You'll feel much better after you've eaten. You look very pale, you know.'

'You've been very kind to me,' Charlotte said gratefully. 'I feel I owe you an enormous thank you.' She thought for a moment, and then laughed, the ridiculousness of the situation suddenly striking her. 'You know I don't even know your name. Here we are, sitting in a bedroom eating breakfast and we haven't even been introduced.'

He put out his hand. 'Giles Ferguson,' he announced.

'Charlotte de Sallis.' She put hers out too.

'How do you do,' they said in unison. She laughed once more and then thought better of it, the activity too much for her sore head.

'I'm glad to see you're a bit happier than you were last night,' he said.

'Your name seems familiar, but I can't think why.' She frowned. 'It's probably through the agency I should think.'

'If you'd like to take a shower I've put all your things in the bathroom. You'll find towels and soaps and hopefully everything you need. I took the liberty of putting your clothes in there.'

'Thank you,' she said, blushing once more, realizing she must have been 'put to bed'. And he'd obviously done a very thorough job of undressing her. He passed her a towelling robe.

'The bathroom's through there . . .' he gestured, 'in case you've forgotten.'

After her shower she began to feel a little more human. But still her body ached in the most extraordinary places. She dressed, glad that she hadn't been

152

wearing some awful flimsy creation. It was bad enough feeling she'd spent the night on the tiles without having to face south-west London in silk and taffeta mid-morning.

Giles had made a fresh pot of coffee by the time she reappeared. He smiled appreciatively. 'You look great, Charlotte. Now come and sit down, then I'll ring for a cab.' He passed her the coffee.

'You really have been so kind to me.'

'Don't mention it,' he said. 'I was just in the right place at the right time.'

'How long are you going to be staying over here?' she asked.

'Quite some time, I should think. It depends whether this idea of mine takes off or not.'

'Would it be presumptuous of me to ask what it was?'

'Well, no, not really. I'm a publisher. I'm going to launch a new magazine.'

'That's it,' she interrupted. 'Of course. Giles Ferguson. Oh my God, Giles. The world is full of coincidences.'

He watched her, not understanding.

'Charlotte Grange,' she said.

'Yes, I know of her. In fact I want to get hold of her.'

Charlotte stood up and did a little pirouette. Putting out her hand once more, she said: 'How do you do, I'm Charlotte Grange.'

'But I thought you said . . .'

'I did. But my pen name is Charlotte Grange. What a coincidence,' she repeated. 'Claudia told me you wanted to speak to me.' Charlotte was delighted. Giles's face, on the other hand, was showing a mixture of emotions. She could have sworn she saw a frown cross his features. He seemed to be fighting to control himself. But she must be mistaken. Now he was grinning broadly.

'Well, that makes life much easier, doesn't it?' he said.

153

'There I was chasing your contacts all over town. It's an interesting way of meeting people, isn't it?' He patted the cushion beside him. 'Come and sit down here and I'll tell you what it's all about.'

Charlotte was glad to have a distraction from her more pressing problem of what she was going to do about William. She listened attentively to Giles.

'I believe,' he was saying 'that there's a gap in the market for a really intelligent women's magazine. In fact I don't really like the phrase "women's magazine". I'm thinking of an articulate, intelligent publication that is slanted towards women. I see it carrying in-depth financial and current affairs stories instead of the normal what-to-wear for bed, or what to feed your lover rubbish, that I believe women are sick of. There's so much scope for a thinking woman's magazine. But it wouldn't seek to discriminate and segment a particular market. It will be aimed at career women and non-working mothers alike. There's to be no stereotyping . . .'

'Sounds amazing. Like complete editorial freedom.' Charlotte sighed. 'Do you think it might be a little too idealistic to work, Giles? After all, the advertisers like a bit of segmentation. They like to know which bit of the market they're buying into. But I suppose on the other hand we'd end up attracting everybody.'

'Exactly,' Giles agreed. 'And the budgets aren't a problem. We can make a loss for years if necessary. Now, Charlotte, this is where you come in. I'd like you to think about the editorship.'

She gasped. 'You can't be serious?'

'Never more so,' he nodded.

'But I haven't worked full-time for over a year.'

'That's all to the good. I want someone capable but fresh-eyed. I know your work, Charlotte. I know how respected your judgement is. I don't want to poach someone off one of the other glossies. They'd only bring

154

with them set ideas which have been drilled into them by their late masters, coloured by whatever office politics have caused them to decide to leave. No, I want someone who hasn't been tied in with a competitor. I want a woman, and I want someone good. Understand Charlotte, I'm not doing this blindly. I've talked to quite a few people in the business who have affirmed my regard for you. It's up to you whether you want to take the talks further or not.'

Charlotte was silent. The enormity of what he was saying had hardly sunk in. She was actually being offered an editorship on a plate. And what an opportunity. A completely new magazine formulated around the ideas that she had always worked towards. It didn't have to be stupid to attract women readers. A truly articulate publication. Unlimited budget . . . Her mind started to race ahead.

'What about staffing?' she said.

'Well, I have some ideas, but of course as far as the editorial staff is concerned you'd have final veto, unless there were extraordinary circumstances.'

'Premises?'

'Just about lined up. Near Waterloo. There's a magazine about to move out to Wapping. It's perfect and just about to be signed.'

'Timescale?'

'Realistically as soon as we could get it going. Naturally there'd have to be research, dummies and so on. Charlotte, if you take it on you'll get a large salary. Name what you want. You can have a flashy car. But what I must have from you is 100 per cent commitment, a minimum annual contract and a lot of hard work and long hours.'

'If you'd asked me yesterday I might have hesitated over that,' she said. 'Now what the hell do I have to lose? Going back to work full-time will probably seem like a holiday after catering to that bastard's needs. Look

Giles, I'm very interested. But I'd like to have a few days to sort myself out.'

'Of course, Charlotte. Under the circumstances I wouldn't dream of pushing you for an answer. And, of course, if there's anything I can do to help . . .'

'Thanks, Giles. But I think I'm going to have to handle it myself.'

He nodded. 'I'll call a cab for you.'

Giles retreated to the privacy of the bedroom. He opened his diary and looked up the number of the taxi company he always used, and booked Charlotte's car. Next he dialled another number. 'Come on, come on,' he said impatiently. Finally the voice he was waiting for came on the other end: 'Listen carefully. You're to hold the stuff. Process it, but don't send it on. I'll pick it up later. Got that?'

A grunt on the other end signified 'yes'.

He returned to Charlotte. 'They'll be here shortly.'

Charlotte was staring out of the window, lost in deep thought. 'I still find it hard to believe, you know, Giles. Valentine of all people. I can't understand it. I mean she's Dan's girlfriend, for heaven's sake.'

Giles's brows shot up. What an intricate little web he seemed to have uncovered. He'd drawn his own conclusions from Dan's visit the previous night. He had assumed that Charlotte was something to do with him. But if Daniel was screwing Valentine too . . . well, it was all getting a little confusing and he wasn't that interested in unravelling it. All he was interested in was catching Charlotte for his own little scheme.

The doorbell rang.

'That's it, Charlotte. Here's my card. Please call me as soon as you can.'

She stepped forward and gave him a small hug.

156

'Giles, how can I ever thank you, you really saved my life.'

'Not at all, not at all.' He waved her out of the door. 'And good luck.'

Chapter Ten

Charlotte half expected William to have left for the office. Instead he almost jumped on her when she opened the door.

'Charlotte, where the hell have you been? God, I've been so worried . . .'

His chin was blue-grey, unshaven. He'd clearly not slept well. His eyes were sunken. She looked at him: a pathetic creature waiting to make excuses, soft-soap her. She swept past him, not speaking. 'Charlotte, where are you going . . . ?' He started to follow her.

'I'm going to change, William. Please don't follow me. I'll be down in a minute. We'll talk then.' Her voice was ice cold.

'But where have you been?' he called after her.

'That's none of your business,' she retorted.

She threw off her clothes, noting that the bed had not been made. She swore at it. 'Why the bloody hell should I? You can damn well stay unmade.' There was a damp towel in the bathroom doorway. She stepped over it. She pulled out a black tracksuit, befitting her mood, and then scraped her hair back into a sombre black bow. Then steeling herself, she went back downstairs to face him. He was standing in the drawing room, leaning against the mantelpiece, eyes fixed on a small photograph. It was their wedding photograph. He turned when he heard her. 'Would you like a drink?' he asked.

'I think I would.' She nodded.

He handed her a large whisky. 'I really don't know what to say,' he began. 'Charlotte, I've been stupid, so stupid . . . How can you ever forgive me?'

'I don't know, William,' she said. She felt close to tears, but the humiliating image in her mind kept her anger foremost, refusing to let her give in to self-pity.

'Look, Charlotte, there really is nothing between us. It was just a stupid fling, for God's sake. Valentine means nothing to me.'

'Then why, William?'

'Well, that's what I'm saying, Charlotte. I can't excuse it. You know it happened. But it didn't mean anything.'

She snapped. 'But don't you see? That makes it worse. The whole thing is so horribly cheap. If you were in love with her, well, then maybe it could be justified. But if it was just for a thrill . . . God you make me sick.' She turned away from him, shaking her head bitterly.

'I swear it only happened two or three times, Charlotte.'

She whirled back at him. 'Two or three times – you mean it happened before last night? Jesus Christ, William, just how long has it been going on?' she demanded, her voice rising.

'But, but . . .' He felt cornered.

'Look, William, you might just as well tell me the truth now. I really don't want any stupid evasions. I don't intend to play games. Now just exactly how long has this been going on?' The strength of her own voice surprised her as much as it did William. The cold authority in it brooked no refusal.

'It started just before we signed the deal. I met her with Daniel a couple of times for drinks, then I bumped into her over lunch one day. We met for a drink and then ended up in bed.' The shame in his voice lowered it to a whisper. Charlotte fought to hide her emotions. Inside she felt as if a plough were going through her intestines. The whole thing was unreal. Could this conversation really be happening? She knew now what was meant by the expression 'being out of one's body'. That was just how she felt. She was an observer. Pulling strings. Watching these two people destroy each other. Her face remained impassive. Her limbs felt heavy. But her hands and feet were almost numb with cold. It was only when she sighed and moved slightly that she realized how very still she'd been holding herself. Her knees had been pressed tight together, her fists clenched, her shoulders hunched up. She made a conscious effort to relax her body, squeezing one hand tightly closed and then slowly unclenching it, releasing the tension with it.

'Go on,' she said quietly.

'It's not necessary, really, Charlotte.' He hung his head.

'Oh but it is, William. I'd really like to know.'

He searched her face but her expression didn't falter. He met clear green eyes, just waiting. 'I saw her in Paris.'

Charlotte bit her lip and nodded. 'I see,' she said. She twisted the glass in her hand. So this was how her marriage would end. It was a sort of quiet, unsatisfactory ending in a way. No great climax. No great explosion. Just an enormous helping of deceit unveiled. She'd been duped, lied to, played with. Suddenly all the anger evaporated. She felt drained, exhausted.

She let her mind drift back to the time he was in Paris. So he was with Valentine at the very time Daniel had turned up on her doorstep. She almost laughed. There was a certain neatness to it all. At least it had been kept in the family, so to speak. But was she any more 'right' than William? Hadn't she herself nearly screwed Daniel? He'd been the one to stop it. Therefore how could she accuse William of betraying her?

How her head swam. And what was the point of it all? She could berate him and make him crawl. But to what end? It wasn't as if she wanted to patch it up. No, it was certainly too late for that. She was sad, sad for the loss of her marriage. It was like a death. Something

160

familiar and at one time very dear could never be the same again. They were at a huge turning-point and neither of them could step back from it. Three years of marriage. Not a very long time. So, there had been a saving grace in her childlessness. For the first time in so many months she thanked God that she had not conceived.

What did they have to show for their marriage? A beautiful house? Joint names on the gas bill? Separate ends of a wardrobe? What else was there? She wasn't saying goodbye to a close friendship. In truth they hardly spoke at all, save to discuss practical arrangements. She didn't even think about their sex life. The money and security – well, she had the offer from Giles, didn't she? Poor William, she thought. Could he have foreseen the consequences? If he had, would he have done it? Or did his cock rule his head?

'Tell me, William,' she said. 'Did it occur to you that this could mess up the whole business deal? I mean she is Daniel's girlfriend, after all.'

'They haven't been together properly for months. That was plain to see. In fact I wouldn't be surprised if Daniel had known. I don't suppose he was that bothered really. He probably thought it wasn't any of his business. Valentine said they hadn't been lovers for a long time.'

Charlotte was surprised. 'Oh,' she said.

He sighed. 'But like you, Charlotte, Daniel wasn't too impressed by what he saw last night.'

'No, I suppose not,' she agreed. 'Right then,' she said, decisively. 'I think it would be a good idea if you moved out for a few days. Then I'll contact my solicitors and we'll take it from there. I suggest you do the same.'

'Oh Charlotte, come on. You can't be serious.'

Her mouth dropped open.

'Look, darling.' He came and squatted down in front

161

of her, resting his hands on her knees. They were a stranger's hands. She had to stop herself from screaming to him to take them off. 'I told you. She meant nothing to me. I don't want to lose you, Charlotte. I swear to you it'll never happen again, as long as I live. I can't tell you how sorry I am.'

She had an irresistible urge to kick him squarely on the breastbone. Suddenly she snapped. 'How dare you insult me by pretending it doesn't matter?' she cried. 'Whether you do it again or not is entirely your affair, William. I will not have you back.'

'But, Charlotte . . . that's just stupid.'

Her angry eyes blazed back at him. 'You fool, William. You've just no conception, have you, of what our marriage has been like for me. Your own selfishness has blinded you to every one of my needs. Your stupid pride that refused to do anything about me getting pregnant – refusing even to talk about it. You haven't bothered to talk to me properly for longer than I can remember. I'm just this sort of thing that you come home to – a vague blob of insignificance that you can step over and ignore.

'Well that's fine, William. That was your choice. Now it's time to make mine. One thing I won't be is a fool for you. Have you any idea how it felt to go into your office and be told that you'd taken Kate with you to Paris?' She saw his confusion. 'I suppose you're going to deny it, are you?'

He spluttered awkwardly. 'No, no . . . of course not. Kate did come with me to Paris. But I certainly didn't . . . do anything with her. I told you I was with Valentine.'

She could hardly believe how obtuse he was. 'I'm truly sick of you, William. I really loved you, you know, and I wanted to make you happy, do what you wanted me to, be who you wanted me to be. But you just couldn't play fair, could you? You wanted it all your own way. Now you've got it. I'm going out for a while and when I get back I'd be grateful if you could have left by then. I think it's best for both of us if we avoid any more painful scenes, don't you?'

He looked at her silently, as if he too had been kicked in the stomach. Hurt, confusion, anger and bitterness clouded his pale grey eyes. Charlotte turned away and left.

She drove out of the town and headed for Richmond Park. She pulled into the first car park on the way to Kingston. There she stopped the car. Her control finally broke and she howled.

Daniel leaned back in the large black swivel chair and grinned across at Bob Lester. The man facing him was greyer than when he'd last seen him some three or four months earlier, but he looked tanned and relaxed, super slim and fit for his forty odd years. Dan knew that Bob got up at 6 a.m. every morning and jogged around the park with the thousands of others who blocked the sidewalks, creating a joggers' jam, before New York was properly awake. He had poured Daniel a Perrier and as he sipped from his own glass Daniel saw a glint of light pass over the diamonds on his watch face.

Bob Lester had presided over Lester Advertising for some ten years during which time he had honed his reputation for avoiding the old school of brash sales-manship in favour of the more creatively inspired style of Britain's advertising. He had followed the lead of his transatlantic cousins and made a name producing the sort of mini-movies that drew industry awards like kindergarten stars. Unlike his uptown Madison Avenue competitors he shunned the sort of brash, 'repeat the product name sixty times in as many seconds' philosophy which epitomized America's highly paid persuaders. It was not surprising that the two men had found a common link. Dan had first visited Bob some four years previously, shortly after Bob had moved down to the trendy Fifth Avenue block which had fast become known as Madison Avenue South, where the truly creative hung out.

As Bob's good reputation spread, clients started to wear the agency name like a status symbol and, like Topsy, business just growed and growed. Advertising was becoming more and more global. With market saturation in home countries, advertisers looked more and more to international expansion and wanted their agencies to create desire for their products in those new markets. If an agency was slick and clever, instead of letting these enormous chunks of new business go to foreign agencies, they set up partnerships and take-overs, mergers and contra-deals so that they, in turn, could offer a truly international package to their clients. Bob and Dan had successfully tapped that market, but Daniel knew there was more to do.

'You look completely fucked, man,' Bob was saying. 'What's up? You been burning the candle again, haven't you? I keep telling you you've got to get healthy. Look at me . . . more than ten years older than you and a whole lot prettier. I s'pose you've been busy with that PR deal I'm not supposed to say anything about.'

'It's a good job you're not in PR – bloody rude bugger.' Dan laughed good-naturedly. 'Yes, I have had a fairly heavy few days and I didn't get that much sleep last night.'

'That's obvious. So, what's this all about? It's not often you jump on Concorde at an hour's notice, is it? Now either the Inland Revenue have caught up with you or it's this business deal you want to discuss. I wonder which?'

Daniel held his fingertips together and studied Bob Lester over the top of them. 'As I said on the phone last week, world expansion,' he said simply.

Bob nodded. 'Go on,' he said.

164

'Well you know we've been talking about it for some time.'

'Uh huh.'

'I've decided to take a sabbatical from London for the moment. It will do them good to manage without me. Maybe let them find their feet a little bit. I'll always only be a phone call away. And Tom Fraser's a bloody good MD. Let's face it, Bob, from our revered positions we're hardly necessary. How much good honest client handling do you actually do?'

'Not so much,' Bob laughed. 'You know, Dan, you're right. I mean we have high-flying lunches. I can put together a mega-deal over a cocktail at six. I can put together three production teams at three separate international locations just by doing a memo to my secretary. No, I don't do much "good honest client handling" as you call it. I suppose we're necessary . . .' he said, somewhat pensively.

'Oh, I'm necessary all right,' Daniel said firmly. 'But I'm going to leave the little babies to fend for themselves for a bit.'

'You still haven't told me what you intend to do and where I come into it.'

'I think it's time we started buying up agencies in other countries. I know we've got associates all over the place and contra-deals, but think of the amount of money we're losing. Instead of getting the odd ten or twenty per cent here and there we should be getting one hundred per cent on the deals. God knows our profits mean we can fund it at the moment.'

'And just how many agencies do you have on your shopping list?'

'Don't know.' Daniel grinned sheepishly. 'I thought you might like to help me work it out.'

'And how are you so sure that we should risk our capital on these acquisitions?'

'Come on, Bob, you know as well as I do the way

165

things are going. Look at cable and satellite TV. Millions of people from different countries all over the world can tune into the same channel. Now what ads are appearing on those channels? Global ones of course. An international message that can be recognized, understood and recalled by an immense audience. Tastes are becoming universal. Everyone drinks Coca-Cola. Everyone wants to wear Levi's. Smokers world-wide know Marlboro cigarettes. The bigger our clients get the more we need to offer them a global service. And that service has to have uniformity and accountability.'

'I see all that, Daniel, but I repeat, how do we fund it?'

'Simple. We offer agencies a downpayment at the beginning. Then we give them deferred payments over a period of years depending on their productivity and profitability. Obviously we immediately gain extra revenue through their existing clients. And they have the benefit of ours. Instant new markets. And the idea isn't a new one. It's well tried and tested by loads of other big agencies. I could do it on my own. I could do it from London. It would be better if you were behind me. Between us we carry a lot of clout and I think it's time to have a go.'

He sat back in his chair and waited for Bob's reaction. Bob was thoughtful for a few moments and then a slow smile started to spread across his tanned features.

'OK.'

'Knew you'd like it.'

'Tell you what. I'd like to have a talk with our vice-president in charge of overseas development, Sam Storey.'

'Fine.'

'Then maybe the three of us could meet up for dinner tonight?'

'Great. Oh, and Bob, there's just one other thing I wanted to mention.'

'Sure.'

'Giles Ferguson, what do you know about him?'

Bob's expression hardened immediately. The warmth in his eyes gave way to a steely hardness. His voice was cold. 'Stay clear. Well clear. That one is like a cobra. A moray eel. A tankful of piranhas – and that's on a good day. Smooth and deadly.'

Daniel's frown deepened. 'Doesn't sound too good.'

'I wouldn't go within fifty miles of him if I could help it. Nothing's ever been pinned on him. Not yet, anyway. He certainly covers himself well, and if you met him you'd be charmed.'

Daniel nodded. 'I have.'

'Then you know what I mean. He's big in publishing. He wanted us to work for him once. I did a bit of groundwork on him and came up with a whole can of snakes. He had some big titles over here, though he always keeps a low profile. He tended to push his editors as the figureheads rather than himself. Suddenly he sold up. Nobody really knows why. He keeps his nose too clean to be nailed as they say, but rumours fly about porn, drugs, protection. You name it, there's a sniff of it around that one.'

'Sounds more like mafia,' Dan said, his discomfort increasing by the minute.

'Well, he may not be of the family, but I'd say he's a pretty cute third cousin. I can't say it enough, Dan. If you're thinking of getting involved with him, take my advice, don't.'

'Well, thanks for that. It's er . . . someone I know was thinking about working with him.'

'Jesus Christ,' Bob growled. 'If you like them then tell them to stay away – and you too, Daniel. I can't say it enough, he's a bunch of trouble.'

'I know, Bob, I guessed there was something odd about him, though I'd no idea he was that bad. I get the picture.' Daniel wanted some space, some time to clear his head, decide what to do next.

'Now about dinner, what shall we say, the Plaza at eight?'

'OK Dan, we'll see you then.'

Daniel spent most of the afternoon just walking. His mind was too busy to settle to anything other than just the steady rhythm of placing one foot in front of the other. So he had been right to suspect Ferguson, but to have imagined any of the stuff that Bob had just filled him in on seemed inconceivable. He groaned inwardly at the thought that he had guilelessly thrown Charlotte's name at him. And what about Claudia, surely she must know something of the sort of man Giles was? Though judging from her reaction to him she maybe didn't. And now the pair of them were about to get involved with this dangerous criminal. He had to warn Charlotte, somehow he knew he could not rest easy until he had told her just what she was getting involved with.

The bloody woman. Indirectly she seemed to be running his mind these days. He'd tried to push her to the back of it, but there were too many times when, especially late at night, the memory of her stirred him to a kind of madness. The heat of her response had awakened in him a desire he had never felt before in his life. Even having seen her in Ferguson's bed hadn't put her out of his mind. Through his mentioning her name to Ferguson he now had a duty to warn her against him – but he had a feeling it would not be an easy task. All he wanted was to put thousands of miles between them. Now he had to go back and make Charlotte listen. Life could be a bitch at times . . .

Much later he made his way to the Plaza Bar. He was right on time. Bob was already sitting there, his head bent towards a gorgeous blonde seated alongside him on the tall bar stools. Daniel smiled to himself. Bob didn't change. He never wasted time when it came to the fast pick-up. The girl was laughing unaffectedly, revealing white even teeth between dimpled cheeks. Dan was a little regretful that he had to break up the happy duo, but it was a business dinner after all.

He strode up to the bar and patted Bob on the back. 'Hello, you old devil,' he said. 'Picking up poor innocents again, are you?'

The girl's eyes narrowed slightly and her smile drooped.

'Hi Dan,' Bob returned a little coolly. 'Sam, I'd like to introduce you to Daniel Cornwallis,' he said, addressing the girl. She turned towards Daniel and offered her hand, eyeing him levelly. Daniel felt as if his feet had grown by about ten sizes. You great ignorant buffoon, he told himself. Just why he had expected Sam Storey to be a man . . . Well, with a name like that you would, wouldn't you? But there was no earthly reason why the Senior V-P shouldn't be a gorgeous blonde bombshell.

'I'm sorry,' he said, clearly unable to hide his faux-pas. 'You must think me a dreadful chauvinist. I'm delighted to meet you, Sam, please forgive me.'

Sam smiled easily. 'Don't worry, Dan. You'd be surprised how often it happens. With a name like Sam I really only have my folks to blame.' She was charming, but Dan wasn't sure whether he was entirely forgiven.

During dinner she proved her worth as a business partner when Daniel quizzed her about the contacts she had already made with other agencies. She was obviously very clued up. Figures, budgets, turnovers, overheads, share prices, subsidiaries . . . she knew the lot.

Later, after she had excused herself to visit the Ladies Room, Bob leaned across the table conspiratorially. 'Brightest thing to come into the agency in years. She's destined for great things.'

'She can only be about twenty-three.'

169

'That's right, but since when has youth ever been an obstacle in advertising? Take my word, Daniel, she's one of our biggest assets. That's why I think you should take her with you on your trip.'

'What!' Daniel's roar made heads turn. He continued, more quietly. 'You can't be serious. I had no plans for making this some kind of firm's outing, Bob.'

'Be sensible. A team like the pair of you would be much better than just you on your own. You need back-up. When your arguments run out, you need reinforcement from someone refreshing like Sam. I want you to do it, Daniel.'

'I'll consider it.' Daniel watched the slim figure return to the table, long slender thighs showing through the slits in her tight business skirt. He sighed. Somehow he sensed even more complications but he knew that Bob was serious, and that this was his way of making it a joint venture, rather than just Dan's baby. To have Bob's full support, he'd have to agree to going with Sam. In that case he might just as well make friends.

By the end of dinner the seeds of an easy companionship had already been well sown. 'I'm going back to London tomorrow,' he explained. 'Sam, I'd like you to put together a suggested itinerary starting off with the biggest fish. If you agree,' he added quickly. 'Then if you can organize yourself at your end, I'll do the same at mine. I'll call you next week.'

Chapter Eleven

Claudia listened quietly. Here and there she nodded, or tutted, or simply said 'Go on,' letting her friend unburden all the dreadful trauma she'd bottled up.

Occasionally, while pausing for thought, Charlotte would gulp back some more wine. Claudia kept shifting across the floor, refilling the glass clutched absently between Charlotte's fingers. Charlotte was pale and drawn. Slight shadows were outlined faintly below her lower lashes. Her hair was untidy, and her nail varnish was chipped. She wore no make-up. Her lips were pinker than normal – from crying, Claudia guessed.

Claudia's face remained impassive. She showed no shock or judgement on the awful story Charlotte was relating, save for a small flicker of her eyebrows when she told of William and Valentine. Charlotte left nothing out. She told of her wrestle with Daniel. Of his coldness to her. Of her stupidity over Valentine and of her meeting with Giles. She talked and talked and talked until, finally exhausted, she lay back on the sofa, eyes closed, silent for several moments.

'Well, that's just about it, I suppose. The story so far.'

Claudia nodded once more. She spoke very gently. 'Well done, darling. You handled it marvellously,' she said soothingly. Then more fiercely: 'I'd love to get my hands round Valentine's bloody neck. What a she-devil that one is. She must have not one tiny essence of humanity in her entire body. I'll certainly not give her any more work. And as for William – fucking idiot. You'd think at his age he'd have more sense than to go sticking it in someone like Valentine.' She saw Charlotte flinch slightly. 'Oh sweetheart, I'm sorry. That wasn't very tactful of me, was it?'

Charlotte sighed a great long sigh. 'Oh come off it, Claudia.' Her voice was resigned. Unemotional. Flat. 'He's a bastard. They're all bastards. God if it wasn't Valentine it would probably be someone else. In fact it probably has been. Loads of them I shouldn't wonder. Why would Valentine be singled out particularly? Just because of the way she is it convinces me that he's probably always ripe for it. He told me himself he wasn't in love with her; that it meant nothing. So, if her, why not loads more as well – that "mean nothing"!

'I've been stupid. All this nonsense about babies. He's been so selfish. Claudia, I feel sick myself that even through all that I still looked after him, shared his bed, cooked his supper, ironed his shirts, washed his rotten underwear . . . uggh . . . ' She grimaced dramatically. 'Through all that shit I was still the little wife.

'Well, really. I feel I've only myself to blame. If I had that little respect for myself as to put up with it, then why on earth should I expect him to have any respect for me? I tell you, Claudia, that's it from now on. No man is going to take me for a ride like that again.'

'That's the kind of fighting talk I like to hear,' Claudia said.

'I intend to look after number one from now on. Stick my career back together. Get myself a house I want to live in. Liberate myself from the laundry.' She waved her arms to emphasize the point. 'Claudia, I shall be my own woman once more.'

'Bravo!' Claudia cried. 'I like it, Charlie.' She punched the air in front of her playfully. 'You show 'em. No-shit Charlie from now on.'

'Oh shut up and be serious, Claudia.'

'But I am, deadly. I mean it. And really, Charlotte, you have taken yourself terribly seriously while you've been with that prig of a husband you know.'

172

Charlotte rounded on her. 'What do you mean?'

'Exactly that. His awful Englishness, just sometimes, has reflected on you.'

Charlotte's eyes blazed. Claudia felt she had probably overstepped the mark. She backpedalled frantically. 'But I knew you'd shine through eventually. And here you are. A sane woman once more!'

Charlotte didn't know whether to laugh or shout at her. Then she burst out laughing. 'Bitch,' she cried between splutters. 'I don't know why you're even an acquaintance of mine, let alone a bosom friend.'

Claudia stuck out her tits and looked down at them, two chins resting on her chest. 'Well, I have to say they're pretty spectacular specimens.'

'Claudia, you're too much. You have to bring everything down to the basest level.'

'Well, at least I got you laughing.'

Charlotte poked her tongue out, feeling a lot better than she had all day.

'Remember how he wanted you in the early days . . . strange how things change, isn't it?' Claudia went on.

'He was desperate to have me. He was the one that pushed us into marriage, Claudia. My God. When I think about the times I hesitated. He pestered me to death with his phone calls and flowers. Mr Romantic personified. You know, I think he must have been in love with the image . . .'

'Of course. There's a pattern isn't there?' Claudia interrupted. 'While you were on the magazine he wanted you more than anything, and as soon as you became a "boring old housewife" – to coin the phrase – then he wasn't interested. You just weren't important enough to keep him interested. He's so into position and status that he couldn't see through the façade to the person underneath. That you are just the same woman he first fell in love with. If he's capable of love, that is.'

173

Charlotte stared into the depths of the carpet for several moments, deep in thought. 'He wanted me to live up to some glossy stereotype all the time. I suppose if I'd carried on working then he would have stayed interested. Been prouder of me.' Her voice got stronger. 'That's really disgusting, isn't it? Just to judge a person like that. It just goes to show how bloody shallow he is. And of course the irony is that as soon as I get back to work he'll come sniffing around again because I'll suddenly become very attractive. Whatever, it won't even be interesting to see. I frankly couldn't give a fuck what he does. I think my feelings for him probably died quite a long time ago – without me realizing it. And now it's time to move on. Maybe I've grown up a bit. I'll certainly be more careful with men and motives in future.'

Claudia suddenly felt brave. 'How do you feel about Daniel?'

Charlotte took a large slug of wine and then shrugged slowly. 'God knows. I can't explain it at all. I thought I couldn't stand him and then I couldn't help liking him. There's something very genuine about him, Claudia. I wonder about all those stories, whether there's any truth in them at all. He looks the playboy type, that's for sure. But he's a bit of an enigma. He was genuinely caring about me. He kind of sensed I was unhappy.'

Claudia filled her glass once more, willing her to go on.

Charlotte studied her hand absently. 'I suppose it was just one of those inexplicable things. You know, the defences are down. You each need something and you happen to be in the right, or wrong, place at the right time. Yes, I would have made love to him. God knows I wanted to. He was the one that stopped us. But Claudia, if you could have seen the expression on his face when he left. Sheer, bloody anger. He looked murderous.' She sighed loudly. 'So,' she went on, sounding a lot brighter than she felt, 'it's really not worth worrying about, is it? I'm going to forget all about it, as I'm sure he has. In the meantime I intend to see this divorce through as quickly as possible, so I can get on with my life – and my career. Where's Giles's number, Claudia? I'm going to ring him right now.'

'Are you really sure about it, Charlie? I mean, you're overwrought, and you don't want to make any rash decision while you're feeling so low.'

Charlotte looked at her in horror. 'Look, you old bag, I've never been more together. Here I am being offered the editorship of a new magazine and you think I'm being neurotic.' She punched out the digits purposefully. After a few seconds she said: 'Giles. Hi. It's Charlotte. Charlotte de . . . I mean Charlotte Grange.' They exchanged the formalities. 'Giles, I'll come straight to the point. I've been thinking about what you said – about the offer for the magazine, and I want to let you know I'm interested. Very interested indeed. In fact, how soon can we talk about it? . . . Well, how about lunch in a couple of days? . . . Fine. Thursday suits me fine. Whereabouts?'

After Charlotte had finished Claudia grabbed the phone from her. 'Giles. Hi, it's Claudia. I want to come too.' She laughed and then put the phone down. 'Phew! Looks like we might just have landed ourselves two pretty cool jobs!'

'I hope we've done the right thing,' Charlotte said uncertainly.

'Don't be so ridiculous, woman, of course we've done the right thing. Now let's have another drink and celebrate!'

The bathroom seemed different. The basin spare and uncluttered. All William's razors and shaving creams and shampoos were gone. No different really to when he went away on business. But this *was* different. She'd never really noticed the absence before. Overnight it had become a woman's bathroom. Only her own towelling robe hung on the back of the door. Her toothbrush looked pathetically solitary sitting in the double holder. His washbag no longer sat in its usual place, next to hers on the windowsill. It had moved, along with its owner, to a friend's flat in the Barbican, where he would be staying until he could find somewhere more permanent.

On impulse she searched the medicine cabinet. Two or three brown plastic bottles of sundry pills bore his name. She picked one of them up and read the pale typescript. His name and instructions. His indigestion pills from his ulcerated stomach two years previously. A large lump stuck in her throat and the tears welled up. She squeezed the bottle until her nails dug welts in the palm of her hand. She was not going to give in to self-pity that easily. She opened the bottles and tipped the contents into the lavatory, and then flung the bottles into the wastebin. She systematically sorted through the entire cupboard, removing anything connected with him. Then, still wrapped in a towel, she opened the wardrobe. Half his suits still hung there. Several pairs of shoes cluttered the floor.

She raced down the stairs and hunted for her address book. She called a removal firm and ordered some packing cases to be delivered. Then she returned to the bedroom and threw all William's things into a large pile in the centre of the room, emptying cupboards, drawers, shelves; anything which still held a trace of his presence.

A mountain of things finally settled. She rubbed her hands together, satisfied. Then she dressed, trying to ignore the mountain. She walked round it, half fell over it, caught sight of it from her mirror. In frustration she pulled a sheet out of the linen cupboard and threw it over the pile. It didn't make it any less conspicuous, but at least she didn't have to stare at William's shoes!

What was she supposed to do next? Edith Piaf shouted at her from the midi system '. . . Non, je ne regrette rien . . .' She sang along loudly, in firm agreement, convincing herself as she sang. Steeling herself to find the strength to face up to what had to be a traumatic time ahead. She knew a good firm of lawyers who specialized in divorce because she'd written an article on them about the way of the Eighties. The age of the quickie. Fast food and fast marriage. There could be no escaping it. She might as well dive in and see what she should be doing.

Rosalind Carter was delighted to hear from her. 'Charlotte, what a lovely surprise. How are you?'

'Oh, all right, Rosalind. This is a business call I'm afraid. I need your advice. William and I are going to get a divorce.'

'Oh Charlotte, I'm sorry to hear that.'

'Well, it's just one of those things. Look, Rosalind, I don't really want to talk over the phone. I'd like to come and see you.'

They fixed an appointment. Charlotte felt sick in her stomach. The cold reality of what was happening was reinforced. She'd actually spoken the words to an outsider. She'd arranged to talk about putting it into action. There was a mixture of sadness and fear. Fear of the unknown, of passing the point of no return. But there was no going back. It was right. However hard and unpleasant it was essential. She returned to the record player. She flicked over the Piaf and the strains of her inimitable warble again flooded the room. Charlotte curled up on the sofa, hugging a cushion to her breast, burrowing her chin into the soft feathers, feeling a little lost and very alone.

A few moments later she was jolted out of her misery by a sharp thud on the door. Her gut tipped over. It was

177

probably William. She stood up quickly, the sudden movement making her slightly dizzy. She unconsciously ran her fingers through her hair as she went to the door, her bare feet moving noiselessly over the carpet. She opened the door and then stood motionless, struck dumb with shock. For on the doorstep was Daniel. Her hand rose to her mouth to stem the gasp that escaped from her lips.

When she opened the door he was not only surprised to find himself there, but was shocked at her appearance. Her face was deathly pale and the skin around her eyes purple with fatigue and weeping. His heart went out to her, and he had to resist the almost overwhelming desire to gather her up in his arms. All through his long journey home Daniel had been planning just exactly what to say to Charlotte. He'd briefly even thought of letting her get on with it. But he could no more do that than drop a rabbit into a snakepit. He was honour bound to tell her. He did not know what sort of a reception he would get, but he sensed it would probably not be a warm one. And when she heard what he had to say, well, who could say what her reaction would be?

She looked smaller than he remembered, like some poor neglected waif, but even the strain could not hide the beauty of those green eyes, the defiant set of her mouth which drove him crazy and her long silky hair that made his fingers itch to stroke it.

Eventually he spoke. 'May I come in?'

She nodded, the stupefaction clear on her face. She was horribly conscious of her scruffy old jeans. The long sloppy sweater; her scrubbed face and her uncombed hair. She walked across and lowered the volume of the music. 'Please . . .' she said, gesturing to him to sit down. 'How are you?'

He smiled. 'OK, Charlotte. But how are you? You

look tired. I suppose you must be under quite a strain at the moment?'

She nodded. 'Things have been better. But I'm getting them sorted out slowly. Divorce is always a ghastly business, isn't it? You should be pleased you haven't married, Daniel. Probably best to keep it that way. Monogamy just doesn't seem to be the thing anymore.'

'I don't know about that. I suppose if I took the marital vows I'd try bloody hard to keep them. Anyway, it's academic.'

She sat on the very edge of the sofa, knees together, hands folded neatly in her lap. He could see the whiteness of her knuckles where she squeezed her fists together and her shoulders were hunched. She looked a bundle of stress. Once more he debated the wisdom of his decision to visit her. He was only going to add to her troubles.

'How's William?'

She shrugged. 'Don't know. In fact I thought it might have been him at the door. I really don't know where he's staying. I'm sure he'll be in touch soon. Daniel . . .' she went on falteringly. 'Did you know?'

He looked at her questioningly.

'About William and Valentine I mean?'

He shook his head. 'No, Charlotte, I didn't. For what it's worth I think he's a bloody fool. God knows Valentine and I haven't been getting on too well for some time. The relationship was dying a natural death. But as for playing around with William. I'm very sorry . . .' His voice tapered off awkwardly. 'I suppose if it wasn't for the merger this would never have happened.'

She laughed, but it was a mirthless sound. 'I'm sure it would have been someone else. Probably lots more in fact. Anyway, I'm sure you didn't come here to discuss William's adultery – or did you?'

'No. I didn't. And when you hear why I've come I don't suppose you'll thank me.'

Her mind was in turmoil. The distance between them felt like some vast, unbreachable chasm, more divisive than a forty-foot wall. She thought back to the previous time he had been there. When they had sat side by side on the very sofa she was now sitting on. How he had held her and kissed her. She searched his face. His mouth was as softly sensuous as before despite his worried frown. He looked tired though, and his thick dark hair was uncombed. She held herself very still, waiting for what he had to say.

'It's about Giles Ferguson,' he began.

Now she was confused. 'Giles? What about him?'

'He's a vice king, Charlotte. He's a pornographer. Probably involved in drugs too . . .' He looked at her, watching her incredulous expression.

'Giles?' she said again, disbelief clear in her voice.

'Yes. That's right, Giles. He's a crook. I can't tell you how I know, but believe me I have it on very good authority.'

'Don't be ridiculous, Daniel. Of course he isn't. He's a perfectly respectable publisher. In fact I'm probably going to work with him.'

'Look, Charlotte,' Daniel said slowly. 'I understand how difficult this must be for you. Especially after you . . . well . . . how shall I put it . . . have been so close to him.'

'What do you mean "close to him"?' she snapped.

'Oh come on. You know what I mean. There's no need to be obtuse, Charlotte.'

'No, really. I don't know what you mean. Really Daniel, I'm finding it very difficult to take in anything that you're saying. It all seems to be nonsense. Are you sure you're feeling all right? You haven't had a knock on the head, have you?'

'No. I have not. When I say "close to him" I mean you shared his bed.'

'What!' she exploded. 'Shared his bed? What the hell do you mean?'

'We do seem to be having a communications problem, don't we? The night of the party. After you left with him. Well, I followed you. I followed you to his apartment. I saw you in his bed. It was obvious what was going on.'

Charlotte's head was spinning. Daniel had followed her to Giles's apartment. Why on earth did he do that? She looked at him through a mist of confusion. Trying to piece together the strange things he was saying. 'I stayed the night there. That's right. But that's all. I certainly didn't screw him if that's what you mean, Daniel.'

He smiled at her. 'It's OK. You don't have to tell me. It's really none of my business.'

'But I am telling you. Nothing happened. What the hell do you think I am, Daniel, some kind of bed-hopping female who jumps into the arms of whoever happens to be available when she's just caught her husband fucking the arse off someone else!' Her voice was harsh and accusing. 'How dare you . . .'

'Well, let's face it, Charlotte . . .' He was on the attack now. All the resentment and bitterness of the scene he had witnessed tied in with her denial. Maybe he had been wrong. But he doubted it. His judgement never let him down. He felt the cold steel of cruelty pierce his chest. 'It wouldn't have been out of character, would it?'

She crossed the room like an uncoiling spring. This time Daniel found himself on the wrong end of a resounding slap on the face. He caught her hand before she could repeat the assault. She looked like a small, spitting she-cat, green eyes blazing with a hell-fire fury.

He forced her hand back to her side and pinned it there. 'Now, now, Charlotte, there's no need to be violent. I understand, really I do. It's understandable that you should be distressed about your lover . . .'

'But he's not my lover!' she screeched back at him. 'Giles Ferguson has never been anywhere near me, and even if he had, Daniel, it wouldn't be any of your damn business, would it?'

'No. You're right. It isn't any of my "damn business", as you say. I was worried about you, Charlotte. I felt I should warn you about the man.'

'Crap!' she hissed through barely parted lips. 'You're just jealous because you thought he was getting something you didn't dare take for yourself. Oh, don't forget that night, for I certainly haven't. You seduced me right here . . .' She stabbed the space in front of her with an accusing finger. 'Yet you sit there like some self-righteous, pompous guardian angel warning me about someone who's shown me nothing but absolute kindness and consideration at all times, unlike you . . . you . . .'

She pushed past him and paced across to the doorway. How could he possibly believe that there was anything between Giles and herself? The whole idea was just too ridiculous for words. She turned back and looked at Daniel once more; at the angry set of his mouth, the jagged line of his brow and his narrowed scowling eyes.

His voice was low, she had to strain to catch it. 'But I didn't seduce you, Charlotte, did I? You say you remember. You're right. I remember it too. I left, didn't I, before I let something happen I thought we each might regret. You misjudge me, Charlotte, for I came here to warn you, really . . .'

She shrugged disbelievingly.

'Why would I be interested in tormenting you over Giles? It's nothing to me what you do with your private life. I wanted you to know that you're playing with fire as far as Giles is concerned. He's a dangerous criminal and he's using you, Charlotte. Don't be a fool. Listen to me, for God's sake!'

A red mist of rage swam before Charlotte's eyes. Despite all his assumptions about Giles it was something else that had cut her deeper. For though she didn't want Daniel now, couldn't stand him in fact, the reminder of his cruel rejection laid open the wound again.

She squared her shoulders and spoke, her voice sounding oddly twisted, but carrying a cold authority and confidence. 'Get out of this house, Daniel. Just get out. Compared to you, Giles is the most compassionate man on this earth. I may well turn to him for . . . solace . . . maybe . . . but that's my business.' She paused and thought she caught a tiny flicker of something she couldn't quite define cross his eyes. 'And I don't have to remind you of the laws of slander, do I?'

'Oh, Charlotte . . .' He took a step towards her but stopped as she raised her hands.

'Don't come near me. We don't want a repeat performance of last time, when you half raped me.' As soon as the words were out she could have bitten her tongue.

'I didn't force you, Charlotte, and you know it. You were as eager as I was.' He quickly closed the gap between them and stood for a split second, towering over her. He leaned forward and covered her parted lips with his own. He kissed her angrily and thoroughly until he thought he sensed a slight softening in the fierce resistance of her body. Then as suddenly he released her.

'I hate you,' she spat at him. 'Get out of here and don't ever come back.'

'Don't worry, Charlotte. That would be the last thing I'd want to do. I'm going on a little trip. Good luck with your new job.' His voice was heavy with sarcasm. She turned her back on him and waited until the front door slammed behind him.

Chapter Twelve

By the time Charlotte was dipping her spoon into the *oeufs à la neige* she had decided that Daniel's warnings were a complete load of hogwash. The man sitting between herself and Claudia was no more a crook than she was. She was even tempted, through a bravado born of a rather good bottle of Pouilly Fuissé, to enlighten him with the facts of Daniel's accusation. The only reason she held back was that she didn't want to offend him when they were all getting on so well.

There were no two ways about it, Daniel was just plain jealous. She wouldn't let his twisted comments foul up her new career. The more she learned about Giles's ideas for the magazine, the more she knew it was a job tailor-made for her. She could visualize the cover already. Her mind swam with ideas for features, leading articles, layouts. Her fingers itched to get started.

It had been taken for granted that Claudia would take over the whole of the fashion and beauty side while Charlotte would take overall responsibility for the editorial content and commissioning.

'Tell me, Giles, why did you come to us?' Charlotte asked.

'I knew your work well. While I was in the States we used to buy and sell stuff through your syndication department. Your work is well known. And yours too, Claudia,' he added quickly. 'As you know, I approached Claudia first. I didn't know you were thinking of resuming your career. It was a great loss to *Today's Woman* when you retired.'

Charlotte blushed prettily, and murmured 'Thank you.'

'But why did you leave the States?' Claudia interrupted.

'The challenge of a fresh market. Besides, I was bought out over there. Someone made a very good offer for all the titles, one I simply couldn't turn down. For a while I twiddled my thumbs enjoying my own retirement, and then I thought why not set up here? I could see the gap in the market. I have the independent resources to finance the venture. All I need to do is find the right people to run the first title . . .'

'You mean you plan on more than one?'

'Why not? If *Amber* is successful then I shall increase the portfolio. Whether that means setting up from scratch, or buying out existing titles, well, we'll have to see. For the moment I just want to concentrate on this one. You see, I get very bored when I'm not making money. I need the stimulation of watching something grow and succeed. I suppose it's the challenge. There's always the risk it'll go wildly wrong.'

Charlotte shuddered. 'Let's hope not.'

Claudia looked at her watch. 'Giles, I'm sorry. I have a meeting this afternoon. I'm afraid I'll have to go . . . but thanks for the lunch. Let me know when you get the specimen contracts drawn up. Talk to you later, Charlie.' She was gone in a whiff of Calvin Klein.

Giles's voice dropped to a more intimate level. 'Did you manage to sort out your . . . er . . . problem?'

'William?' He nodded. 'Yes. Thanks. Giles, you were so kind to me. I really can't thank you enough.'

He raised his hands. 'Please, Charlotte . . . I did nothing.'

'But you did, Giles. You gave me somewhere to run to. You must have thought me a complete idiot really.'

'Considering what you had just witnessed I thought

186

you did remarkably well. A little too much brandy perhaps . . . ' He laughed.

'Well, at least I've got the house to myself for the time being. And I'm looking forward to getting my teeth back into work. So, Giles, what do we do next? I'm keen to get on with the next stage as soon as possible. As Claudia said, are you going to draw up contracts?'

'Just a formality, Charlotte. Name your figure. You'll get a car, expenses, and more or less complete editorial freedom. You'll have to do a bit of poaching, won't you?' Charlotte raised her eyebrows questioningly. 'For staff I mean. I thought you might be happier putting together your own team. After all, you're better placed to know who you can work with, and who's around, than I am.'

Charlotte's eyes had begun to take on a sort of glazed, trance-like quality. This man sitting across the table from her was handing her a title, loads of money, and the freedom to work with who she chose. A hand-picked team of journalists to mould *Amber* into the best magazine on the newsstands. She sighed happily. 'Pinch me!'

'What?' he laughed.

'I can hardly believe this is happening. I can't wait to start. I'll draw up a list of people straight away. What about dummies? And we need an advertising agency. Who's going to handle that side?'

'I'll leave it all to you. All I ask is that you finalize everything with me before you commit. Obviously we need to get a fair stock of articles ready before we launch. You might be wise to think of getting a few writers on retainers rather than on the staff. But you can work that out.' He handed her a card. 'Here. In case you haven't got the last one I gave you. It's got my home number and my office number in Mayfair. You can get hold of me on these numbers anytime you want.'

187

She glanced quickly at the card. 'What about the premises, Giles?'

'As I told you, we're taking over the place in Waterloo from the publishers who are moving to Wapping. You might like to come and look at them with me.'

She nodded enthusiastically. 'Of course.'

He signed the bill and stood up.

'Thanks for lunch, Giles,' she said. 'I'll come back to you when I've done some initial research.'

'Anytime. Ring me day or night if you need to.' He smiled. 'Good luck.'

She felt an odd mixture of excitement and apprehension. For the first time in years she had something to really get her teeth into. Instead of running around after William all the time she had a purpose. A dream of a job. Her own magazine. Yes, she had been an editor before. And she had had quite a lot of freedom to do more or less what she wanted with it. But to start something completely from scratch. Now that was a real challenge. Suddenly the divorce was little more than something to be got over with, an irritating thorn in the side.

Charlotte went into the first newsagents she passed on her way back to the house. She came out struggling under an enormous pile of glossy magazines, over £30-worth of light reading matter and heavy research material. She consoled herself with the fact that she could claim it back on expenses.

What with the formalities and hunting for elusive journalists without telling them why they were being hunted Charlotte had little time to think of anything but *Amber*, which was becoming a more tangible thing by the hour. But her visit to Rosalind Carter was a necessary evil. She had to get her house in order, so that she could move on.

The day after she'd met Giles she went up to town to

see Rosalind. The office was grey and uninspiring. The tall Georgian building had elegant windows defaced by the name of the company in huge brassy letters. Advertisements of the profession of the building's occupants which had appeared long before the advent of legal advertising.

Charlotte was reminded of her childhood visits to the dentist. She had the same nervous feeling of apprehension. Rosalind's door was painted a sort of dark, institutional red. There was a small glazed window at the top, with reinforced glass reminding Charlotte of a cell. She tapped on the door.

A reassuringly cheerful 'come in' echoed through the closed doorway.

Charlotte pushed open the door and smiled at Rosalind's cheery face.

'Hello Charlotte,' she said warmly. 'Come in, sit down.' She gestured to an easy chair which stood facing her desk, pale wood arms worn paler by nervous hands. 'Now, Charlotte. I'm sorry you seem to be having rather an unhappy time. Tell me about it.'

'I want a divorce.' She hated the cold finality of her words, her clipped, thin voice. All those years of marriage.

Rosalind looked at her steadily. No doubt Charlotte was the fourth person that day using exactly the same words. 'I see. On what grounds?'

'Adultery, I suppose.'

Rosalind was busy scribbling on a large pad in front of her. 'His adultery? Right. Do you know who with? Has he admitted it?' she asked quietly, professional sympathy in her voice.

'I caught him in the act. In flagrante delicto, as they say.'

'Oh dear. How unpleasant for you,' Rosalind said, the distaste clear in her disinterested eyes.

189

'Yes, it was rather. A short, sharp shock you might say.'

'Hmm.' Rosalind's pencil scribbled noisily across the sheet. 'And her name?'

'Good God, I'm not sure. I only know her as Valentine. She's a model, you see. She only uses that name. Like the Queen, there's only one . . .' Charlotte said, her words thick with sarcasm.

'We will have to cite her as co-respondent you see.'

'What does that involve?'

'She has to be served with a copy of the petition, admit that the adultery took place, that sort of thing . . . '

'Well, she could hardly deny it, under the circumstances, could she?'

'No. Not really. Were there any other witnesses?'

'Believe it or not, I should think there were probably at least two or three.'

'Where on earth were they doing it then, a goldfish bowl?'

'At an office party, would you believe?'

Rosalind raised her brows and pursed her lips. 'That wasn't very bright – or original, was it?'

Charlotte couldn't help laughing, in spite of the earnestness of the meeting. 'No. Rather pathetic actually. Still, it all helps with the anger. You know, the angrier you are, the easier it is to stifle the pain.'

'Oh I know. It does you good to hate them.'

Charlotte nodded dumbly, a cold claw of hurt clutching at her heartstrings. Suddenly the whole episode seemed such a travesty. She remembered all the planning for their wedding, all their hopes and expectations, all the things they had been building up together. For a moment she remembered just how she had felt when they had stood in the registry office. Her heart had been bursting with joy and love at the thought of becoming Mrs William de Sallis. She remembered how his parents had congratulated her happily, welcoming

190

her into the bosom of the family. Then hinting over the years about the joys of grandchildren. Once more she thought back to the way she and William had made love. She bit her lip and swallowed hard, almost choked by the lump in her throat.

After the wedding William had whisked her off to Cannes. He had booked the honeymoon suite at the Carlton, and they had spent two weeks of conjugal bliss – between the marital bed and the beach mats. Devouring the French delicacies as hungrily as they devoured each other.

That was the beginning. Now this was the end. A tawdry request for the marriage certificate so that it could be obliterated. A note of the place of solemnization so that it could be wiped from the records. They were another failure to add to the ridiculous divorce statistics.

She caught herself suddenly. 'I'm sorry,' she apologized. 'I was just . . . er . . . thinking.'

'Don't worry. It's always very hard.' Rosalind gestured to the large box of tissues on her desk. 'These aren't here for my use, you know. Will you be asking William for any maintenance? Though I doubt whether you'd get anything substantial. It depends on what you are doing regarding work.'

'I couldn't bear the thought of his maintaining me, Rosalind. Obviously I would like my share of the house. After all, I need to buy something else. But as far as asking him for any money after that. No way,' Charlotte said vehemently.

'In such cases,' Rosalind said slowly, 'what we generally advise is for a nominal amount of maintenance to be agreed, be it only fifty pence a year. That way the door is always open for you to claim against him should your circumstances change. And of course, conversely, should his circumstances become dire, and you find yourself in a more secure position than him, he can claim off you.'

'I do understand, Rosalind. But I want nothing. Not even a penny a year. I want no lingering ties with that man. He can sue me in the future if he wants. I won't worry about it. But as for me asking him for anything, forget it.'

'Think it over, Charlotte. There's lots of time. It takes a good few months to get everything sorted out.'

'OK. But I am already resolved, Rosalind.'

By the time they had finished a few minutes later Charlotte was completely exhausted. Her limbs felt heavy and her head ached. All the emotional turmoil of the past few days seemed to be welling up, knocking her sideways. She huddled into the corner of the taxi on the way back, the cold November day making her pull her coat closely round her. She crossed her legs tightly and wrapped her arms about herself, shivering. As they sped through the Piccadilly underpass she caught sight of her reflection in the cab window. She looked white as a sheet.

She was surprised that she had not heard from William. She supposed it was probably because he was too ashamed. The alternative was that he was too busy rogering Valentine. In some strange way, Charlotte was missing him. She did not want him back, but after always having him around her, whether physically or on the other end of the phone, she felt disordered now that she had no contact with him. It was as if she couldn't start really to sort her life out until he resurfaced. She had to unlearn the habit of constant referral to another person. Not only had she lost her lover, albeit a pretty unsatisfactory one of late, she had lost the other person she could tell about her day. Whether he listened or not, William had been a sounding board for her spoken thoughts. That realization made her feel very isolated.

Yes, she had her career. She also had financial security. But the one thing she never realized William had given her until it was gone was company of sorts. He was not the kind of soul-mate she had always desired but he had been another body in the house. Somebody to tell when you were going to be home late. Somebody else to listen out for – the key in the door. As she stared out at the shop windows, being gaudily prepared for the Christmas rush, she guessed she was suffering a kind of withdrawal, something the books didn't warn you about. She knew about feelings of dissatisfaction. She knew about the sharp blade of jealousy, the poison effect of betrayal. But she had not been prepared for the simple fact that no matter how bad the relationship was, the severance carried its own, masochistic, sense of loneliness and failure.

In fact her ego had taken a severe knocking in the past few days. Since Daniel's visit she had gone over what he said, trying to make sense of it. Why had he followed her to Giles's house? It couldn't have been because he was worried about her. He seemed to hate her too much for that. She just couldn't work him out at all. He could swing from being a softly caring Sir Galahad to a fire-blazing demon. He had come to warn her about Giles, he said. But Daniel himself could be labelled more of a crook than Giles. After all, Giles had not jumped on her the minute he had the opportunity. Daniel must be jealous. For him to be jealous meant he must care for her. But if he cared he couldn't be so foul to her . . . She clutched her temple and screwed her eyes up tightly. It was all too much.

Fortunately one of the best antidotes to morbidity is activity, and Charlotte found that getting a national magazine off the ground, even in embryonic form, was a gargantuan task. First of all she drew up a list of the many journalists whose work she admired. Some she had worked with in the past, and some she knew by reputation only. She tried to draw up a list balanced between the literary giants and the new 'cult' figures of almost underground fame. Weighty in-depth features and snappy diary-type pieces needed to be blended together to produce the new, 'intelligent' kind of magazine profile she was after.

Next she had to decide who she would invite to join her on the staff. To begin with she did not want a large number. They could 'buy in' talent on a freelance basis. Once the magazine was announced she knew she would be flooded with such writers suggesting pieces either already written, or attempting to find a 'commission'.

She needed to surround herself with extremely capable and committed people who could bring a fresh eye to a jaundiced profession. Firstly she needed a features editor, someone who could deal with the day-to-day commissioning and editing of pieces. Then she would need a picture editor to supervise all photography and illustration. Claudia could take care of the fashion side of things. And Charlotte knew from experience that she worked best by being given a free rein to run her own department.

A managing editor was essential to chase up outstanding pieces from writers, make sure the layouts were finished to printing deadlines and generally handle the day-to-day administration of the magazine so that Charlotte could be left free to get on with the more journalistically productive side. Then she would need sub-editors who would carefully check all copy, then subsequent proofs for literals and grammatical errors. They were also vital in the fine tapering of pieces to fit certain layouts. A good sub-editor could make a magazine, a bad one ruin it. She had her own ideas already about whom she would ask in that regard.

Over the next few days she dug out her old address books and methodically went through lists of her old associates. Whether they were wise to her motives or not, nearly all were keen to meet her for lunch, a quick evening drink or even, in a couple of cases, an early breakfast. In between catching up on what they were up to, she slipped in casual questions as to who was doing what with whom, who was disenchanted with their job, who was worth watching out for in the new generation, who had moved on to new pastures. Slowly she began to gather a broad picture of just who might be ready to think about her proposals. The one thing she could not do at this stage was let on to anyone just what she really had in mind. She had to maintain a complete mantle of secrecy, or once the word was out it would spread like wildfire. There were times when judicious leaks were beneficial, but that time wasn't yet.

After several undercover meetings Charlotte had more or less decided on exactly whom she wanted to approach. They were nearly all under thirty years old. Most were at the stage where they had taken a first job on one of the national magazines and were now ready to move on and upwards to head their own department. In other words they had learned their lessons in Fleet Street's manners and were now ready to step up from the shadowy world of deputies and put more of their own characters into print.

When Charlotte's shortlist was prepared she called up Giles.

'OK. This is it. Tell me what you think.'

He listened carefully. 'Sounds great. All new talent, just about. That's exactly the way I would have played it, Charlotte.'

'Well, I'm glad you agree, Giles. The point is I think it's getting to the stage where I'll have to start approaching them and telling them why. That means I'll have to start offering them money.'

She heard him laugh quietly. 'Yes . . .' he said.

'So, Giles. How much of a free rein do I have on the

salary levels? Do you want to give me some limits or what?'

'Charlotte, I'm more than happy to leave that entirely up to your judgement. I know you will only pay what you have to. You go ahead. I'll just write the cheques. All right?'

Charlotte shook her head slowly, smiling into the mouthpiece. 'Well, yes . . . fine. Of course. And thanks – I'll let you know how I get on.'

He was a strange one indeed. Not to be given a limit on what amounted to six or seven major salaries was some responsibility. She was beginning to wonder if he intended to have any input into the magazine at all other than signing cheques. There weren't many publishers who, to her knowledge, were prepared to throw a limitless budget into an untried book. Still, who was she to worry about it? She had asked and she had her answer. Total responsibility.

Now her real campaign began. First she fixed up more quiet, seemingly innocent, lunch dates with her targets. Over these interludes she probed to see just how satisfied they were with their jobs, and what their attitudes would be if they were to be approached by, say, someone who was making them a very good offer to start on something completely new. By definition a journalist's make-up is ninety per cent natural curiosity and ten per cent avarice, therefore without exception they all said that if such an opportunity was presented they would think seriously about it.

Charlotte always came away from these meetings laughing inwardly. There were the two of them talking about something that was clearly not a hypothesis, but a very real proposition that she would undoubtedly make given the right response from the relevant quarter. It was almost as if they were rigorously adhering to the movements of some primeval mating dance.

By the time she had spoken to the five major editors

she required, discounting Claudia, she was ready to put together the presentation where she would bring them all together and pull the inaugural ribbon. She was taking a calculated risk; there was the possibility one or more would not be interested in pursuing things once they knew what was actually in the offing. She had her own contingency list of people should the first choice decide to renege in the final counting. But the secrecy of the scheme would be undermined.

She decided to make her presentation an informal one and to this end she booked a table at Julie's Wine Bar in Holland Park, where they could all sit round a large table in a secluded alcove, without too much risk of being overheard. Naturally Claudia would be involved in this preliminary meeting of *Amber*'s creators.

Getting everyone together on the same night had not been an easy task, but eventually at 6.30 p.m. on the duly appointed day Charlotte found herself in an extreme state of nervous excitement, counting out glasses around the reserved table in the trendy wine bar. She glanced through her notes for the last time and tucked them away into her briefcase, which she then slid under the chair, between her feet. She pulled up the sleeves of her sweater and carelessly tossed her hair back, ready to get down to business. A few minutes later, Claudia arrived and with a sweep of her expensive riding mac slid into the seat opposite.

Charlotte splashed white wine into Claudia's glass and she drank thirstily. 'Mmm,' she said appreciatively. 'I needed that. What a bloody awful day I've had. Funny isn't it, once you've made the decision to leave a place, no matter how tolerable it was before, you immediately become bored and impatient. Frankly I can't wait to get on with this magazine. Trouble is, it takes such a long time to pull everything together.' She paused for another sip. 'Seen Giles lately?'

Charlotte shook her head. 'I thought I'd get in touch with him after tonight. If all goes according to plan I can then introduce him to all the staff at once. It's about time he had some input. After all it is his title.' She broke off, recognizing the tall, slim shape of Colin Gray. His pale, rather long face was overshadowed by a dramatic black trilby hat. When he saw Charlotte he doffed his hat and, clutching it to his middle, leant over the table and took her hand.

'Charlotte,' he said in beautifully modulated Oxford tones. 'How wonderful to see you.'

She grinned back at him. 'Colin, I think you know Claudia.'

'Very well,' he purred.

'Hi lovey,' Claudia beamed back. 'How's life at *Titbits*?'

He burst out laughing. 'God, you're such a bitch, Claudia. Since when has *Tatler* ever resembled *Titbits*?'

'Well, the tits are smaller, I grant you that. But the gossip's pretty much the same. It all comes down to nobs and knockers at the end of the day, doesn't it?'

'Claudia, you're the end,' Colin said, guffawing loudly. He was only twenty-five years old but he had the sophistication of a forty year old. He was an ex-*Isis* editor who had been snapped up by *Tatler* where he had graduated from writing inane but snappy photocaptions for the nouveau-aristos to producing sharply witty features. He wrote with a natural perception and had the unnerving aptitude for extracting just what you didn't want him to know. He had earned as many enemies as he had admirers, but successful journalists were made of stronger stuff than most. Truth, however banal, must out.

He was the man who had discovered the truth about Lady Ruth Tremayne's penchant for wearing thermal long johns under her silk taffeta. Who found out that Richard, Earl of Brighton, took his afternoon nap curled up in a battered dog basket in the corner of a draughty kitchen, snuggled up next to his favourite cocker spaniel. Such snippets as these had matured into more in-depth revelatory articles, only fifty per cent of which ever saw the light of a printing plant.

He was more than ready to move on to something a little harder. Charlotte liked him enormously and was looking forward to working with him. He was the kind of character every staff needed, who could ease the pressure on deadline day with his light wit.

He sat down next to Claudia and helped himself to a glass of wine, glancing at the remaining glasses. 'So, you're expecting quite a few more, Charlotte.'

'Yes,' she nodded.

'You know rumours have started already.'

'I'm not surprised,' she said. 'There's bound to be a lot of speculation as to what I'm up to.'

He looked at her questioningly, a small smile on his lips. 'Well . . . ?'

She smiled at him enigmatically. 'Wait and see.'

Within a few minutes John Gillespie, Frances May and Edwina Robinson arrived. They all looked faintly surprised to see each other. Not one of them was a stranger. Now the only person missing was Bob Steele, whom Charlotte had earmarked as managing editor.

Edwina grinned at Charlotte. 'You seem to have started some sort of club, Charlotte. And none of us yet knows what the membership entails.'

'You will soon.'

Edwina Robinson was the deputy art editor on *Architectural Digest*. It was not a particularly high profile magazine, but the quality of the layout was excellent. Charlotte knew she was going to have a bit of difficulty coaxing Edwina away from such a beautiful tome.

The oldest member of the party was John Gillespie. In contrast to the others he seemed shy and rather quiet. He had a pipe-and-slippers kind of face which crinkled into a lovely, cheeky grin when amused, and he had a habit of running his hands through his thick salt-and-pepper hair. Both Charlotte and Claudia had worked with him before on *Today's Woman*. But he had left after their first six months to join the *Telegraph* magazine as their picture editor. A lot of his colleagues had recently been prematurely retired by the new editor and Charlotte had learned of his awkwardness with the new leader.

At last Bob Steele appeared, slightly breathless, rushing across the bar towards them. 'Sorry . . .' he said between gasps. 'The one night I decide to commit my destiny to London Transport I wait forty-five minutes for a bloody number 73 bus. When it finally came it was full. I tell you I could have smashed the conductor's face in. Then I decided to get a taxi. Everyone's going to the frigging theatre – so could I get a bloody taxi?' He snarled and threw off his coat. 'Ah good,' he said, reaching across the table for the bottle. 'Evening, everyone.'

While the others had shown their surprise at all being thrown together, Bob Steele took it to be the most natural thing in the world. It was almost as if he knew already whom he would be meeting, and what it was about. Charlotte studied him wryly. It was precisely his dryness that made him just right for the job of managing editor.

'Don't worry, Bob,' she began. 'You haven't missed anything. Everyone was just wondering why I had brought you all here together. Though I should think by now some of you have a pretty shrewd idea of what it's all about.'

Colin raised his hand. 'Miss . . . Miss . . .' he mocked. 'Yes, Colin.'

'You're going to start a new magazine and you want us to staff it . . . oof!' he exclaimed as he felt Claudia elbow him in the ribs. 'What was that for?'

'Subtlety,' she said.

'Now, now, children,' Charlotte said. 'Absolutely right, Colin. How did you guess?'

'It wasn't easy,' he laughed. Suddenly everyone seemed to relax, to visibly lean back in their chairs. Colin had managed to take the tension out of the situation by making a joke out of it. They felt part of a team already. That was a good start.

'I've been approached by a publisher who's previously had titles in the States and wants to launch a magazine over here. He has asked me to formulate a team to run it and that's why you're all here.' So far so good. At least they looked interested. No one interrupted her.

'It's going to be a high profile, AB1 magazine, mainly targeted at the thinking woman's market, with a strong emphasis on business. We feel that there is a gap in the market between titles such as *Options* and *New Woman* across to *Business Magazine*, *The Economist*, *Newsweek*, etc. What we want to produce is a monthly, topical, glossy publication which will appeal not only to the highly segmented top-end women's market, but also to the business executive. I want high-calibre features from classy writers. I want topicality coupled with wit and style. I believe that all of you could fulfil a very exciting role within such a magazine.

'Obviously we have all had preliminary meetings during which I think it is fair to say you expressed interest, in principle, so I thought it a good idea for us to meet up informally so you can get a feel for the sort of team I want to put together. Above all, I want this magazine to be based on very close working relationships. I want absolute commitment and dedication and a forum for some great creative production. I want a young team . . .'

'How flattering,' John laughed.

'You're not over the hill yet.' She continued: 'So here

201

we are. At the moment there are no firm ideas as to launch dates. No dummies have been designed. We're still very much at the embryonic stage. But if you are all interested I'd like you to have an input from the beginning. All of you have your own distinctive styles. There's little point in me doing all the groundwork and ending up with a product which has only my stamp on it. To make it really excellent, I want us to work together from the outset. So far as remuneration is concerned I feel we won't have too much of a problem. The budgets are more than generous. Your present salaries can and will be bettered. So . . .' She paused to look around the table. 'The next stage is for you to ask me any questions and let me know whether you intend to join me or not.'

'You can count me in.' Claudia was the first to speak. 'Frankly I can't wait. It's one of the best opportunities to come along for years. Obviously it's a risk. If it falls flat on its face we're all out of a job. Somehow,' she grinned across at Charlotte, 'I have a feeling it won't.'

Bob Steele was next. 'We know what you can do, Charlotte. God knows there isn't a journalist in town who doesn't know about your success with *Today's Woman*. There's no question of your ability as an editor. It's no secret that I'm ready to move from the *Radio Times*. I'm well and truly game.' He raised his glass in salutation. 'Here's to you, Charlotte Grange.'

'Thanks, Bob.' She smiled gratefully.

There was a lot of shuffling in seats and crossing and uncrossing of legs. Edwina cleared her throat loudly. 'The trouble with something completely new is the risk. I mean you could fold in a month. We might all give up our nice little earners and then find ourselves with a large amount of egg on our faces. There's quite a few who'd like to jump into my chair on the *Digest*.' She paused and looked around the table. 'I mean I really do enjoy what I'm doing at the moment . . . although to get on I can't stay there forever. What about this publisher, Charlotte. Who is he?'

'His name is Giles Ferguson. He was involved with a load of titles in the States. Sold out, retired, and now wants a new hobby to get his teeth into. Financially I'm told we're safe as houses. We can afford to run at a loss if necessary. I do see your point, Edwina. Obviously it's a risk. I can't give you any guarantees about the future. But we can all help to bloody well make it work. For myself I'm completely confident. But I can't and won't talk you into it. That's a decision you must make for yourself.

'If you want the job of art editor it's yours. If you don't the magazine will be worse off for it and I shall be very disappointed. But if I have to persuade you to join then the job's not right for you. I need total commitment and involvement. The only way this team can work together and make the magazine a success is if we all truly believe in it. You don't need me to tell you what the career rewards will be if this magazine is a success. We'll all be classed as innovators. Leaders in design. Your style will be the magazine's hallmark. You won't just be taking over someone else's job, someone else's way of running a magazine, with the same layout, for the last five million years. Maybe once every six months you can alter a column width. Maybe you can juggle the ads a bit to give you more space – but maybe not. And as for that new typeface you've been dying to have a go with . . . well . . . change the house style – you must be out of your tiny! As I said, Edwina, I don't have to talk you into it. The advantages are obvious.'

She looked around the table, her eyes carrying the earnestness of her message. 'And that goes for all of you. If you need me to "sell" the magazine to you well I'm not interested. You must decide for yourselves.'

She took a silent but very deep breath and exhaled slowly. She was taking one hell of a risk. Of course she wanted to sell the magazine to them. She needed them all, desperately. But as well as their acceptance she wanted their inspiration and dedication. If she could convince them that they would be gaining a real forum for their talent then she felt the battle was won. Security was one thing, but real job satisfaction was something rarer.

Edwina nodded slowly. 'You're right, Charlotte. I have a great job. There was a lot of competition for it. But I'd like to put my own mark on something.' She started to laugh wryly. 'You're a clever woman. You said you wouldn't talk me into it. But you certainly have.' She raised her glass in Charlotte's direction and Charlotte grinned back. 'Here's to us!'

So two down, three to go. Frances, John and Colin seemed all to be waiting for the others to speak first.

'Of course if you'd like more time . . . ' Charlotte offered.

'As soon as I get the contract I'll hand in my notice.' Frances was the first to speak. 'As Edwina says, I really enjoy my job, but I work with this man who's been in the department since about the year dot. He rather treats me like an indulgent grandfather would. He thinks he's doing me a kindness by checking everything I do, and I haven't got the heart to hurt his feelings by explaining that I have the ability to do the job. Really he's a dear old stick but he drives me round the twist. I feel I've well and truly served my apprenticeship. A challenge is just what I need. How soon can we start?'

Charlotte's grin grew broader. 'Terrific!'

So, just John and Colin left now. Still they said nothing. Charlotte looked at the bottles on the table which were now just about empty. 'So, gentlemen,' she said. 'Do I make the next order one for champagne or not?'

'I have a reputation to think about you know,' Colin stated grandly.

'I know.'

'And connections.'

'Yes.'

'I have a certain style and flamboyancy which requires careful nurturing, understanding and a certain amount of . . . er . . . shall we say, artistic licence.'

'Of course, Colin.' Charlotte's voice was level and her face was set. Only her eyes glittered with amusement at Colin's monologue. 'I quite understand your idiosyncrasies. I want you as features editor.'

'How can I resist?' he shrugged.

'John?' Charlotte said finally. 'Looks like you're in a bit of a minority now. Are you going to be our picture editor or not?'

'There's one proviso.'

'What's that?'

'I want to bring my researcher with me. I can't survive without her. Really she's so brilliant. I couldn't possibly leave her behind after all the training I've given her.'

'OK. That's fine. I'll take your word for it. God knows decent researchers are hard to find. I'll leave it up to you whether you mention it to her as yet. I have no need to tell you all about the importance of extreme discretion at the moment.'

'Well, seeing as none of us has given in our notice it would hardly be in our interests to start yacking about it, would it? And we don't have any contracts as yet, do we?'

'Absolutely right. Well, now how about we have that champagne and get down to the serious business of celebrating the beginning of the most successful magazine this century?'

Chapter Thirteen

'So tell me about this new house of yours, Charlotte,'
William asked politely. The business of the evening was
nearly over. It was a semi-labelling session, deciding
which spoils each would get. Charlotte's head was
throbbing but she tried not to let it show. As usual
William seemed to be coming out of it extraordinarily
well.

He clearly felt obliged to ask her – it must seem only
polite after she'd given him such an easy ride, she
thought more than a little bitterly.

'I think "house" is a bit of an exaggeration to tell you
the truth – spacious wardrobe would do.'

He looked at her oddly and then smiled. 'Ha ha, oh
really darling. I'm sure it can't be that small.'

Claudia was right, he never had had much sense of
humour.

'No, William. It's not that small. Just small. Big
enough for me. I like it. It's cosy and homely.' She
sniffed and looked around the vast high-ceilinged room.
No, this could never be called 'homely'.

William too was following her gaze, but his expression was somewhat different. It was covetous. Smug.
No, she thought. You haven't done so badly, have you,
darling William?

'I must say, my dear, it's a great relief to me to be able
to keep the old place on.'

God. He made it sound like an ancestral home. Why
was it that within the space of a few weeks his
mannerisms, which before had been mildly irritating,
had suddenly become maddening to the point of

206

distraction? She squeezed the chair arms and smiled through gritted teeth. 'I knew how much it meant to you.'

He missed the note of sarcasm in her voice. He nodded. 'Yes, yes. It certainly does. And I'm grateful, Charlotte. You've been an absolute brick. I know that I haven't always been the best husband . . .'

'William, stop,' she said. 'I don't want to hear it. No, you haven't been the best husband, that's why I'm divorcing you. Yes, you've got the house. It always meant much more to you than to me. I'm pleased you're pleased. But I really don't want your gratitude.'

He jumped as if bitten, his eyes taking on a hurt, hang-dog expression.

'I was only trying to be nice, Charlotte. Sorry I spoke. Anyway how's the rag?'

She bridled at his expression. The man had about as much depth and sensitivity as a disused puddle.

'The magazine is fine, thank you. We're all set to launch in a month.'

'You must be thrilled,' he said in a manner similar to that of her father when she had come home with a highly commended rosette for coming last in the tack-cleaning class.

'Yes, I am rather excited,' she answered tonelessly. 'And how's your work?'

'Oh, going great guns. Reiser settled down and we all came out smelling of roses. It was a major crisis for them, but the agency did pretty well out of it. Shame about poor Paul Montigny though. He's going to be tried for fraud. It seems he was charging all his clients huge expenses for non-existent expenditure. One of his clients – Reiser in fact - decided to investigate his invoices and uncovered a whole history of deception and swindling. He's out on bail at the moment but it seems likely he'll eventually go to prison. Silly man.

'But business is pretty good. Despite old Daniel's absence. Strange about him going off like that . . .'

Suddenly all Charlotte's nerves jangled. 'What do you mean?' She tried to keep her voice even.

'Didn't you hear the story?'

'No, William.' She was trying very hard to keep the impatience out of her voice.

'Well, he's been gone for quite some time now. Must be a couple of months I s'pose.'

'Where?' Her curiosity was threatening to swallow her up whole.

'Round the world on an overseas development trip with some flashy bird from the American agency. I speak to him on the phone once a week. He seems to be taking some sort of extended sabbatical but I wonder if it is really a euphemism for some romantic liaison he's stumbled into. I keep asking him when he's coming back but he just says "not yet".'

Charlotte's green eyes narrowed.

'Still, can't complain. Everything is ticking over very well without him. If he doesn't come back soon he may well find we've staged a coup in his absence.'

'Hmmm,' she said noncommittally.

He looked at his watch. 'Oops. Sorry Charlotte, I'm afraid I have to go.' She stood, relieved, offering her cheek as he bent to kiss her. 'I'll be in touch.'

She nodded. 'Give my fondest regards to Valentine,' she couldn't resist saying.

Christmas came and went with Charlotte barely noticing. She was too deeply into preparing dummies of *Amber*'s format. The new team had had weeks of secret meetings often held after eight o'clock at night and through to the small hours, working on the layouts and features for the first issues. Charlotte's hunches about the candidates were proving to be well founded. All of them, without exception, were as enthused as she herself. Sometimes she was the one who had to tell them to go home to bed before it was time to go to their other jobs. They were quite literally moonlighting.

Giles had kept his word and more than matched their salaries. The contracts had been signed and sealed and the new offices were just about ready to move into. Charlotte's advertisement manager, Brian Cox, was already selling space in the first couple of issues.

Giles had given an official presentation, a sort of 'meet your maker' affair, when all the staff had gathered together in a private room at the Intercontinental and the complete profile of the magazine had been unveiled. Everyone had been delighted with the presentation. The dummy of the magazine looked fantastic: attractive, readable, but above all, intelligent. Giles's talk about his background in publishing and loose financial details seemed to inspire confidence in everyone. Charlotte felt proud of him. When he invited her to outline her editorial plans she had taken the floor and listed the writers they hoped to approach and the special issues that were already planned. She answered any questions easily. This was her baby. She knew it intimately, and had very definite ideas as to its future development. Like any proud parent she defended its weaknesses, of which she knew there were none, passionately. At the end of the meeting the magazine had become even more of a reality and she begged the designers for her own personal copy of the dummy.

Amber was going to be printed in Holland. At first Charlotte had been surprised at Giles's choice of location, but he assured her that the benefits far outweighed the inconvenience of constant flights to Amsterdam – which at the end of the day could be faster than travelling to Watford, he argued. The quality of the presses was far superior, the technology more up-to-date, and there were no union problems to worry about. This also meant that the lead-time (the pre-publication run-up from closing the copy to publication) would only be three weeks, a vast improvement on the eight to ten weeks usually required to set up, proof and run.

After the official presentation and announcement it was impossible and impractical to keep *Amber*'s development secret any longer. All the staff must tender their resignations on their various publications. Although most were bound by three months' notice not one was expected to work it through. In the competitive world of journalism you became an enemy in the camp immediately your resignation hit the editor's desk. Ideas could be pinched, writers cajoled and exclusives no longer be exclusive.

So it was fortunate that the offices were just about ready to accommodate all of them. Over the past few weeks Charlotte had been spending more and more time at her desk in the office off Waterloo Road. The decorators hadn't quite finished their task but the inner sanctum, which she had quickly named her office, was just about ready. Huge windows let in floods of daylight and views of the north bank of the River Thames. She had a large table around which most of the editorial conferences would take place, a light box on which to view transparencies, and a computer. This was part of the system networked throughout the entire magazine, allowing all the journalists to put their work directly through to her and the typesetters.

The outer offices were mostly open-plan. Half-installed telephones and paging systems ran like thick spaghetti over desks which were still covered with polythene. Bright red swivel chairs had been delivered and stood awkwardly between the rows of desks like novice tarts. Everything was deliciously shiny and new, the ultimate in hi-tech publishing. Charlotte's layette was prepared. All she needed now was the baby.

Chapter Fourteen

Daniel leaned over and brushed the fly from the rim of his fruit punch. He took a sip of the icy cocktail: the lemon and lime juice was tartly refreshing, complementing the sweetness of the passion fruit and orange. He shielded his eyes against the glaring sunlight and lowered his knees, so that he could see the pool. At first he couldn't see her, then a shadowy form surfaced from the depths, hair plastered flatly to her head, the tip of her nose pinker than the rest of her healthy deep bronzed face. Her mouth opened in a smile of recognition, revealing those perfect white teeth. He raised his arm and waved.

'Come on in, you sloth,' Sam called in her smooth Californian drawl. He screwed up his nose and raised his glass. 'Aw, come on, Dan, finish it later. You're an old chicken.'

He stood up and stretched. The sun had warmed him to the core. He felt good. Very good. Deeply sensuous, like a satiated cat. His body had turned from London white to deep sienna. His limbs shone with the coconut oil mixture Sam had insisted he cover himself with, its exotic smell heightening his sense of erotic awareness.

He walked to the edge of the pool and stood for a few moments, watching Sam's easy fluid strokes through the water. She was a natural athlete. Hardly a splash disturbed the azure liquid as she practised her lazy crawl. The thousands of miniature waves caught the sunlight, holding it in blinding points of pure diamond light.

She was level with him. He waited until she passed

and then plunged in. The contrast of the cold water against his sun-warmed body was shocking. He surfaced, gasping and then sped across the pool, letting his body cool.

Sam was resting at the other end, her head in the crook of her arm, the skin covered with droplets of crystalline water. She laughed at him. 'Wonderful, isn't it.'

'Cold you mean.'

'Come on, Dan, I'll race you. Last one out buys dinner.'

She had a head start. He waited for a few seconds and then propelled himself away from the edge. When he felt himself level with her he eased off and kept apace so that they finished in a dead heat.

'You dirty cheat, Dan!' she spluttered. 'You did that on purpose, didn't you? Now we'll have to go Dutch.'

He ducked under and picked her up, lifting her over his shoulders and up above his head.

'Now I have you in my power are you going to retract that slanderous accusation?'

'Put me down!' she shrieked. 'Daniel, I'm warning you . . .'

'Retract it,' he laughed.

'Shan't,' she said.

'OK. Have it your way.' He threw her as high as he could and deposited her unceremoniously head first back into the water. She came up kicking and screaming, but he was already out of the pool.

'I'll get you back, just you wait,' she threatened, laughingly. She sank down on to the bed at the side of him and towelled her face and hair. She dabbed at the rest of her body, so as not to rub off the remains of the water-resistant sun cream. After much wriggling and squirming she eventually settled back on to the sunbed, letting out a sigh of contentment, stretching out long graceful legs. After a while she raised her arms above

213

her head and crossed her hands, seemingly unconscious of the highly seductive attitude she'd assumed.

Dan's cock stiffened involuntarily, the sudden rush of blood through his groin taking him by surprise. Suddenly his balls started to ache. Jesus, he felt horny. He found himself following the golden line of down which glistened on her belly down to the point where it disappeared into her bikini pants. It was an almost invisible path beckoning the finger down, enticing it to trace where it led.

He picked up the towel from the ground and surreptitiously draped it across his trunks, in an effort to hide his erection. Luckily Sam kept her eyes closed. He tore his gaze away from the admiration of her silky-smooth skin and picked up his copy of the *Financial Times*, already two days old, trying to lose himself and his lust in the pages of doom, gloom and despondency over interest rates, share prices and inflation. Sam breathed softly and evenly beside him, apparently asleep. Her lips were slightly parted and again he found his imagination drifting back to wonder what it would be like to hold her. To have her sleep nestled up to him. To touch that soft skin . . .

'Damn it!' he swore and threw the *FT* back on to the ground. He adjusted the parasol over Sam's body so that she was shaded from the fierce, burning rays, then he left her. Picking up his keys from the reception desk he took the lift up to the plush suite he and Sam were sharing at the Hong Kong Mandarin. A central sitting room divided their own bedrooms and bathrooms. The sitting room was half living area, half portable office. A fax machine occupied one of the coffee tables and piles of notes and figures sprawled across another. He glanced at the papers, took a step towards them and then changed his mind, heading instead for a cooling shower.

He and Sam had been sharing this nomadic lifestyle for several months. They had covered twenty cities

214

in half as many countries. Between them they had managed to sell their strategy of income-related purchase to twenty new agencies. A one hundred per cent success rate, which increased their client portfolio by 180. Lester Advertising now had an annual fee income of $250 million dollars – a sudden increase of $50 million. Although seventy-five per cent of that $50 million had to be repaid to the new agencies annually for the next three years, it meant that all fee income after that would then be owned by Lester Advertising.

Both he and Sam would never have believed their success rate. It seemed that everyone had the scent of fear in their nostrils about high interest rates and the falling dollar. Anyone wanting to buy must be out of their minds. These small, independent agencies did not have the resources, or the balls, to ride out the recession in the same way that Lester's did. And with the deal based on actual fee income over three years, Daniel knew if they lost profitability then their purchase price would drop too. Both he and Bob knew that they couldn't lose.

The hardest man to convince had been a tough Australian called Dick O'Halahan in Sydney. Two days ago they had both arrived in his office ready with their presentation which was becoming like a long-running show. But after Dan had followed Sam into Dick's office Dick had turned to Sam and suggested she might have some shopping to do. While Daniel had been almost as appalled as Sam at the man's disgusting chauvinism, he had had to control an irresistible impulse to giggle. Her face was a picture of shock, disbelief and dislike.

Then Daniel thought he had better step in before she scratched his eyes out. 'Dick, I would like to introduce you to Sam Storey. Sam is Vice-President of Lester Advertising in New York.'

Dick had given Sam a complete appraisal from head to toe while she had stood, cheeks burning and eyes blazing, but too uncomfortably aware of the reason she was at this meeting. The agency billed a cool $14 million and she wanted it under Lester's umbrella.

'Sam,' Daniel said, 'why don't you start the meeting off. Tell Dick what we're up to.'

'Sure, Dan.' She grinned. 'I'd be delighted. If that's OK with you of course, Mr O'Halahan.' She had switched over to his formal mode of address, Dan noted with amusement.

'This should be interesting. Go on . . .' Dick said.

Daniel felt himself shudder. What a country this must be, that still allowed men like this to breathe. He'd be lynched in London or the States. He was the kind of narrow-minded bigot that hindered development of any kind and Daniel had the feeling that if they did acquire the agency the sooner this one was off the board the better the profits would be.

'I think you've already had a chance to look over the corporate accounts of Lester's, haven't you, Mr O'Halahan?'

'I did see something of them, yeah.'

'We're expanding. Over the past few weeks Daniel and I have visited nineteen agencies and you're the twentieth. Of all those we visited, every one of them has seen the advantages of being bought out by Lester's.' She paused for the words to sink in.

'Go on,' he said, giving no sign of interest.

'We want to set up a deal with you over the next three years. You keep seventy-five per cent of all fee income, we take on the interest payments on the property mortgage, you get twenty per cent of the shares with an option to keep them or sell out at market rate in three years' time. I don't need to tell you that those shares will be worth a heck of a lot more when the sale is announced. Your client list will double because we shall open up markets through you for other clients over here. Look, see this list . . . ' She handed him the prepared list of clients who would immediately want representation in Sydney.

Dick O'Halahan whistled softly. 'And if I wanted to retire after three years?'

'As we said, you'd be able to sell your shares at market rate. That should give you a nice little nest egg to retire with. Certainly a hell of a lot more than you're likely to get at the moment.'

'And if I retired now?'

'Well as major shareholder we'd give you three years' salary but retain all your shares. Obviously you'd do better if you hung out for the period. You see, the more profitable you become, the better we all do out of it. And the deal is what's going to make you more profitable. If you want to get out before that – well, it's up to you, isn't it?'

Dan knew that Sam was just dying for him to get out. If she had her way she'd have kicked him down the stairs fifteen minutes ago. Instead she just smiled disarmingly at him.

'I don't know. We've been independent for quite a long time.'

'Eight years to be exact. You have a fee income of $14 million. You have outgoings of $5 million. That leaves you with $9 million. You borrowed $2.5 million to buy this building, didn't you?'

His mouth had dropped open. He was clearly dumb-struck at this Sheila's audacity.

'Well, you did. The interest rates are about to go up. So if you borrowed at eighteen per cent . . .' She looked up at him. Still he said nothing. 'Which you did, and you go up by another per cent, well let's say twenty per cent for the sake of argument, that's another $500,000 per annum, which leaves you with $8,500,000. Sounds like a lot, doesn't it, but you have to remember that nice little chocolate bar account, you know, the one with six different brands totalling a spend of $3 million – well, they're on the move.'

Dick gasped. 'No. How the hell did you know about that?'

She ignored his question. 'And Proctor and Gamble – that's another $5 million. Seems like the wilderness years are upon you, Dick. And that we're your guardian angels . . .'

'Fucking hell,' he exclaimed in his inimitably genteel style. 'How did you know all this?'

'It's my business to know. When I'm not shopping that is . . .' she couldn't resist.

'Draw up the papers. Let me see them, then I'll get a lawyer to look them over and put them to the rest of the board. Though their shareholdings are so small they won't be a problem. But what about this business? You know for a fact we're about to lose it?'

She nodded.

'And Lester's will put the business back on?'

'Well, we wouldn't take you on if we didn't think you could be profitable. You've got a great creative team here who have won world acclaim for some of their campaigns. We'd like to channel them into some other stuff. There's a lot of satellite space waiting to be filled. But you need us, Dick.'

He had his back turned to them. He was staring out of his window, clearly deep in thought.

Dan didn't feel too sorry for him. It was true Dick was being rescued from a very slippery slope but he just didn't have the grace to accept it for what it was. Dan caught Sam's eye. She winked at him and put her thumb skywards. Then she poked her tongue out at O'Halahan's back.

'Now, Dick, can we take you out to lunch?'

'No no. I've got things to do. Call me this afternoon, would you? After four. I'll have had time to think by then.'

Daniel stood and shook his hand. Sam followed. 'Great doing business with you,' she said.

'G'day,' he said.

Yes, Sam was certainly a great kid.

Dan pulled himself up short. For one thing Sam would never have called herself was a kid. She was young, but not that young. Twenty-three was pretty mature in business these days, particularly in the media business. When you got to thirty you were almost ready to be put out to grass. She was sexy as hell and had a brain in her head most men could do with.

Why had he not pulled her into bed before now? She had all the right ingredients. He liked her. In fact he liked her a hell of a lot. Maybe that was it. They had too good a relationship to mess up with the business of sex. Women friends, true women friends, had been very sparse in his life. And it wasn't that he treated women as sex objects, it was just that he had perfectly normal, physical needs which invariably led to the inevitable. Friends became lovers and then everything soured.

He hadn't thought about it before, but he seemed to have put himself into a kind of celibacy. There was a part of his mind he had blocked off. Locked away was a woman who had caused him to wake, soaked with sweat, in the middle of the night. Haunting green eyes had watched him through the darkness, eyes which would suddenly blaze with hatred. He would get up and pace whatever hotel room he happened to be in, as if the pacing in itself would wipe the memory away. Then he would fall back into bed, exhausted, wiping her name from his mind and denying her very existence.

As the weeks went by the dreams stopped tormenting him. Ferguson was welcome to her, and she to him. To whatever perverse relationship they must share. Daniel was all right. A continent lay between them and that was the way he liked it right now. Soon he would go back, but he was not quite ready. Not yet. There was Sam to think about now. And the lovely Sam could finally lay that particular ghost to rest for good.

The needle jets poured over him and he started to soak himself. His skin was still ultra-sensitive – sexually charged. He soaped his groin, his hand slipped easily over his genitals. The warm slippery wetness regenerated his erection. He needed a release. All those weeks of physical denial and today he was like a cat on a hot tin roof. He held his cock in his fist and slid it up and down the length, letting his mind wander where it willed. He closed his eyes and groaned loud. Sam's legs were sliding invitingly over each other, the soft brush of skin, her mouth opened, she was arching while he drove himself into her. He felt his cock go hot. Burning with intense heat. The ache in his balls was unbearable but exquisite. He came and came, in spasms of release, his seed pumping out, to be washed away. He leaned back against the cold tiles, his breath and his heartrate slowing. After a time he picked up the soap and continued, feeling relaxed, unwound. When he had finished he towelled himself dry and then lay down on the bed.

When he woke, much later, he could hear Sam's low voice on the telephone. She was fixing up their next list of meetings, no doubt, getting the rundown on the company histories, doing her homework. She never let up. Today was one of the first days when they had actually taken time out for themselves. After her confrontation with the Australian he felt she deserved a break.

She called to him, tapping softly on his door. 'You OK, Dan?'

'I'll be out in a minute,' he called back. He dressed in jeans and a black polo shirt, with black moccasin shoes.

He whistled when he saw Sam. She looked good enough to eat. 'You look gorgeous.'

'Why, thank you.' She blushed, and unconsciously pushed a hand through her hair. She was wearing a softly quilted cream silk kimono, her long brown legs accentuated by the light, short dress. The large square sleeves hung softly to the elbow, where the fabric had been rolled up to show quilted cuffs. A single gold chain at her neck was her only jewellery.

He looked down at his jeans. 'I feel under-dressed,' he confessed. 'Would you like me to change?'

'No, no,' she laughed. 'It's a relief to see you out of a suit. So terribly English.' She imitated his clipped London accent.

'I could put a tie on.'

'Oh, old school, I suppose?'

'My parents were too poor to buy me a tie,' he grinned.

'Come on then, Oliver Twist, let's go play hookey.'

They walked through the buzzing network of streets lit with neon, restaurant upon restaurant vied with tourist shops, tailors, china dealers, a real shopper's paradise. It was noisy and exciting. Chinese hieroglyphics mixed with Americanese. They eventually picked up a rickshaw which took them to the restaurant Sam had booked earlier.

Delicate glass wind-chimes tinkled gently in the evening breeze – generated more from the air-conditioning than the city night. They sat on opposite sides of the low table, their legs crossed beneath them. Dan couldn't help his eyes straying to the opening of Sam's dress, the slit where her legs crossed.

She reeled off a list of suggestions to eat. Daniel was happy to let her take charge. After they had ordered Sam looked around the restaurant. Most of the other tables were occupied by businessmen – half oriental, half occidental. Dan caught her eye.

'Stop ogling, Sam.'

'I was just thinking what an appalling selection of malehood,' she whispered. 'Daniel, sometimes I wonder how they can let themselves go to pieces so completely. I mean, look at them . . . Jesus they're gross. Just take the one over there for instance. Look at the size of his stomach . . . uggh. He probably hasn't caught sight of his penis in years!'

'Sam, really,' Daniel exclaimed in mock horror.

'It's true. My pregnant girlfriends have told me that it must be like that – not being able to bend down to pull your socks on and things . . . '

Daniel found his own lip curling in sympathetic distaste.

'And the one next to him . . . look at his hair, Daniel . . .'

Daniel looked. Then wished he hadn't, for it was not a pretty sight. The grey-black mass was plastered down with grease and the parting showed large white flakes of dandruff which had spilled over on to his shoulders.

'You can get shampoos to treat things like that these days. There's just no excuse.'

'I wonder what their wives are like,' Daniel mused.

'Oh, definitely very unhappy.'

'Yes?'

'Certainly. Well I know I would be if I had that to sleep with.'

'But they might be just as bad themselves.'

'Aw come on, Dan. If women were the same the fashion industry would die off and every suburban hairdresser would go out of business. Don't you have a blue-rinse brigade? Women take a pride in themselves. They wear make-up to look more attractive. For men at first. But when the men stop taking an interest, which I bet neither of these do, well, they do it for themselves – or for their lovers more like.'

'Women like that don't have lovers.'

'You'd be surprised, Daniel. Bored women all over the world have lovers. It's just that the men are too dumb to realize it. They're complacent. They think they

222

earn the money, that they're the big providers. They shake their willies in the general direction – rarely the right one – once a month and think they're pretty hot shots.'

'Sam, if you'll excuse me for saying so, that does sound to be a rather jaundiced view of the male species. Are you a secret man hater by any chance?'

'Me? Man hater?' she said incredulously. 'God, no. I love them. I'm just aware, Daniel. I have my eyes open. It's called realism. Sure I want to meet the right man and settle down and live happily ever after. But I won't settle for second best and I won't ever accept complacency. I want a soul-mate. Someone who'll put as much emotional energy into the relationship as me, and if they can't – well, I won't wait around getting my hair dyed blue to make up for it.'

Their food arrived. The delicate porcelain dishes were placed on a tray over burning candles, keeping the food sizzling hot so that they could savour and experiment with the different piquancies. Sam wielded her chopsticks expertly.

'You've obviously done this before.'

'Don't forget I grew up in LA. The original Chinatown. Mom and Dad had a passion for Chinese food. That's why I know my way round a menu blindfold.'

'These are delicious, Sam. What are they?' He pointed to the small balls which were coated in a spicy orange sauce.

'Don't ask. I'll tell you later.'

He wasn't sure if she was joking or not, but he decided to take her at her word.

'Sam,' he began slowly, 'if you think I'm prying, tell me to shut up, but you sound as if you've been through it. As if you've been badly hurt sometime. What happened? We're not all that bad you know . . . If you want to talk about it . . . If not I'll understand.'

223

She stopped mid-mouthful, the humour and the colour drained from her face. 'How did you know.'

He laughed quietly. 'Oh, just something you said.'

'Oh. Right. Hmm,' she grinned sheepishly. 'That obvious, huh?'

'Fairly,' he said.

'I met someone. I fell in love with him. Deeply. Work was more important. That's it, in a nutshell.'

'I take it you mean his work?'

'Yes. His work. Oh, not that it shouldn't have been important. It was just that I never got a look in. The hardest part was coming to terms with having given so much of myself, body and soul, as it were, to someone who basically threw it all back. It wasn't wanted. Sometimes he'd just forget to come home. He'd never ring to tell me. He told me I was a nag. I felt like one until I could see clearly enough that I wasn't nagging – I was loving. Falling in love again comes hard after that. It took me a long time to get out of it, to break the cycle of destruction. Next time I will be treated with love, respect and dignity. I have a basic human right to that.'

Dan reached across the table and squeezed her hand. 'He was a very silly man.'

'I know,' she laughed.

He was almost asleep. Slats of light fell through the Venetian blinds across the room so that he was lying in a striped box. He was naked, the quilt lay in a rolled heap at the end of the bed. It was hot, but not humid: his skin was dry. He closed his eyes which then flew open at the sound which rose across the traffic noises coming from the window. It was the click of the door opening.

His first thought was one of defence. He lay hardly breathing, fists clenched, ready to spring into action against whatever onslaught might come. A shadowy figure stepped through the doorway. He could see the contours of a woman's body beneath a gossamer-fine gown. She smiled knowingly as she crossed the room to stand in front of him. Very slowly she lifted the gown up over her body, so that the neat triangle of down was revealed first, almost level with his head. Teasingly slowly she lifted it to reveal her firm proud breasts, nipples erect. Then she was naked. Arms at her side she watched him watching her. His eyes travelled over her. They returned to her face and then back to her sex.

'Beautiful,' he whispered. He took her hand and gently pulled her down next to him. She lay down beside him and he kissed her. She tasted of honey. Sweet and pure. She pushed her body against his. Then she guided his hand down over her belly to the soft mound of curls. She rested for a moment, her breath quickening. She shifted slightly then opened her legs and placed his hand there. She moaned and arched against him. She was very ready for him. Her soft pink flesh was ripe and wet. Yielding. Inviting.

She was running her hands down his back, sending small shocks, messages to his stiff cock. He wanted her. He pushed himself over her, so that she lay below him. He parted her legs and slipped between them, sliding easily inside her. Her hands tightened on his shoulders and she threw her head back with the ecstasy of the moment of penetration. Then she started to move with him, in unison with him, the most basic and instinctive rhythm known to humanity. He slipped in and out again while she arched up, pushing her pelvis hard against him, rubbing herself on his pubic bone, opening her legs wider to feel him deeper. He started to kiss her frantically. He pushed his hand through her hair and kissed her eyes, her face, her lips, her neck . . . He could feel she was near so he gave in to the rapturous waves coursing through him, feeling the life within him driving uncontrollably up through his manhood.

'Oh my God,' he cried out. 'Oh Charlotte . . .' He felt

225

the body below him stiffen. Then go limp. He looked down and saw two bright tears on her cheek. For a moment he didn't understand, then the full shock of what he had said hit him. He shook his head.

'No, no,' he cried. 'Oh Sam. I'm sorry. So sorry.' He hugged her to him but she curled away. 'Come on,' he said. 'Forgive me.'

She pulled free of his grasp and picked up her robe from the end of the bed. She huddled herself into it and bent to pick up her nightgown from the floor. She gave him one last look. 'Seems I'm not the only one with a past,' she said weakly. Then without another word she left the room.

Daniel was confused, mortified, hating himself. Charlotte was past, forgotten, denied. So what the hell was he doing calling for her?

Chapter Fifteen

The KLM early morning flight circled once over the landing strip and then broke the low cloud cover, its belly almost scraping the passenger terminals below. The noise of the reverse thrust roared in his ears and the wheels bumped down on to the tarmac as Giles snapped shut his briefcase and checked his watch. It was 10 a.m. With any luck he should be through the terminal in fifteen minutes and be well in time to meet Kurt as arranged. They taxied slowly to one of the satellites and the concertina seal snapped on to the plane's doorway like a giant, rubbery leech, great jaws agape.

Giles pushed through the crowd of trippers, through the immigration desks and past the customs hall to search the waiting faces. Kurt had already spotted him. 'It's good to see you, Giles.' He patted his old friend on the back.

'You too, Kurt. I know I haven't been able to get over for a while but I expect you've held everything together pretty well.'

'Wait and see. I think you will be more than a little pleased.'

Knowing the Dutch art of understatement Giles knew he must indeed be in for something pleasurable. 'Good.' He smiled.

They collected the car and drove the few miles into the heart of the city, drawing into the vast works of Van der Heim. Their heels rang out crisply on the tarmac surface. The earlier frost was almost gone, but the air retained its chill and their breath hung in white clouds around their heads. Giles flexed his fingers in an effort to stave off the biting cold.

Kurt led the way into the building. Vast glazed doors almost ten feet in height opened onto a marble hallway flanked by mahogany-panelled walls. Two serious-looking security guards, with pistol-clad hips, looked up at their entrance. They nodded to the two men.

Kurt pushed open a pair of wooden doors at the side of the hallway and Giles followed him through a kind of ante-room, and then on through another door. The roar in his ears got louder and louder and a strange kind of whipping sound echoed through. Giles knew it was the sound of the paper web speeding over the rollers of the printing presses. They skirted the edge of the printing room and went up a small, narrow staircase, then along the corridor until they came to Kurt's office. The noise could now barely be heard and the sudden peace reminded Giles once more of the purpose of his visit.

A fresh pot of coffee stood ready on Kurt's desk. He poured them each a cup. Kurt then quietly re-opened his office door, looked out into the corridor and then closed it once more. He turned the key in the lock and returned to his desk.

Giles was sipping his coffee. Grateful for the heat of the cup on his cold hands.

'It seems we are alone,' said Kurt. 'We can talk. Tell me about London.'

'Perfect. Just perfect. I think I might even make some legitimate money for once in my life. They're all buzzing around like little worker bees putting the whole thing together. Of course that damn silly woman I put in charge of it is taking it all terribly seriously. Really the whole thing is very amusing.' He yawned conspicuously. 'I suppose I really should take a proof back with me . . .'

'It's here, ready, if you want to see it.'

'Good God, no. Can't think of anything worse. Just

don't let me forget to take it back, or I'll never hear the last of it.'

'So she suspects nothing – what's her name – Charlotte something, isn't it?'

'Yes, Grange. No. Nothing. They're settling into offices in Waterloo – where, incidentally, I shall be moving too. There's a whole team of quite respectable journalists – most of whom would commit professional suicide if they knew what they were connected with. But all they seem to be worried about is their blessed budgets.'

'Well, they won't have any worries on that front, will they!' Kurt laughed.

'I keep telling them that. I think that's why they're so eager. Greed touches everyone a little you know. Not just you and me, old man.'

'I'd noticed.'

'We should be able to start shipping soon. When the first issue of the magazine is ready, that is.'

'Well, if all goes to plan the official launch date is next month. *Amber* should be on the news-stands by 1st April. That means we can ship, say, mid to late March. Included in the first shipment of 200,000 copies of *Amber* will be twenty kilos of heroin valued at . . .'

Giles was ahead of him already, '. . . one million. With a street value of double that. Correct?'

'Spot on. As the circulation increases we'll ship more, of course. But that's quite a healthy quantity for the first month, is it not?'

'Certainly. Once it arrives in Felixstowe the shippers will deliver it to a warehouse near the docks. From there it will be collected by a different haulage company and taken up to London's Docklands where our distributors are based. I have someone there who will remove the "interesting" cases and deal with the merchandise. He can be trusted. From there it will be delivered to various wholesalers around the country. And of course they have no idea where the stuff is coming from. They're only interested in keeping their supplies going. All we have to do is publish a magazine . . . Talking of which, don't you have something else for me, Kurt?'

Kurt leaned over and opened a cupboard to reveal a heavy lead safe. He quickly went through the combinations and then twisted the lever to release the door. It swung open slowly. He pulled out a copy of a magazine which he handed to Giles. Wordlessly Giles flicked through it. Kurt watched his expression which, as always, was unreadable. Now and then his mouth would twitch slightly and he would rotate the pages, all the better to see the position. He opened up the centre spread and laid it on the desk before him, clearly satisfied at the vision before him.

A naked woman was spreadeagled across the pages. One cock filled her mouth, and another her cunt. Every detail of every crack was more than clear. This was no cosmetic set up. This was the real thing. Pure, hard pornography. Pimples and all. Page after page revealed deviation upon deviation. Animals – even children – a paradise for perverts.

Kurt viewed it only with a business eye, but Giles devoured it hungrily. It was his own personal hobby – a rather unpleasant diversion but lucrative enough. And harmless in its way, Kurt thought as he saw Giles swallow hard and loosen his tie. His breathing was a little harsher than before. Kurt continued to watch him patiently and indulgently.

Finally Giles came up for air. 'Excellent, Kurt. Excellent,' he breathed. 'You have done a great job. Tell me about the video listings.'

Kurt handed him a single sheet of paper. Seemingly innocent titles were listed down one side of the paper, with boxes on the opposite side for orders to be placed: 'The Nun's Story; Hang 'em High; Three into One.' He laughed at the innuendo. 'Not very original, are they?

But I suppose they'll serve their purpose.' At the end of the day the content of the films didn't really matter. Just the degree of degradation and debasement.

The magazines and videos were a sort of side-line for them. They were easy enough to produce and almost came within the boundaries of the law. Almost. Of course some of the steamier stuff could send them to prison for several years under UK law, but a sophisticated system of clearing houses prevented the films and movies ever being traced back to Van der Heim, or to Giles himself.

Kurt threw another magazine across the desk. It landed under Giles's nose which he screwed up in distaste. 'Oh. That.'

'For your lady friend.'

Giles glanced at the cover and then put it straight into his briefcase. 'Let's go,' he said.

They drove silently across the city until they reached the outskirts. After about fifteen minutes' drive they turned down a long track which eventually led to a derelict windmill. A low barn was tucked away behind the ruin. Theirs was not the only vehicle at the lonely spot. Several other cars were already there. A large generator was humming noisily and several bits of lighting and wiring equipment ran from it towards the buildings.

As they walked across the courtyard a heavy door swung open in front of them and a huge monster of a man stood aside to let them in. He had no hair at all. His eyes were a very bright, almost manic, blue. He smiled at the two men, but it was a humourless twist of the mouth.

'I hope we're in time for the entertainment, Manfred.'

Manfred threw back his head and laughed out loud, spittle bouncing off his lower lip: it was a thin, almost cruel, sound. Their heels clipped loudly over the concrete floor as they walked to where the arc lights spilled stark yellow glare. They picked their way carefully through the mess of black leads and metal stands until they stood bordering the edge of the makeshift proscenium.

Kurt noticed that two chairs had been discreetly positioned just beyond the ring of light and gestured for Giles to join him. Wordlessly they sat, wondering what particular show they would have the privilege of witnessing today.

Several yards away, towards the centre, was a large tank, with transparent sides, three feet high. The bottom of the tank was filled with a thick, brown sludge, shining like melted chocolate under the illumination. Lighting and sound checks were underway. Giles and his partner settled back into the shadows, invisible except for the small red glow of Kurt's reefer.

After much to-ing and fro-ing and arguing with the bald man, a naked girl was led out. Her body certainly could never have been called perfect, voluptuous might have been more apt, and she unconsciously scratched her arms where bruises and scabs were testament to her addiction. Her long hair looked clean – no doubt specially washed for the occasion, ironic under the circumstances. Leather bracelets were clipped to her wrists and ankles. A second girl followed, a blonde. She was thinner and taller than the first, her breasts scrawnier. She too had tell-tale blemishes across her arms.

The two women climbed into the mud and the cameras started to roll. The dark-haired girl lunged for the taller but weaker-looking blonde, who staggered backwards but kept her balance, clutching great fistfuls of the dark girl's hair and pulling mercilessly. The other kicked out as hard as she could, winding the blonde, who released her grip and fell to the ground, her pale skin streaked with the thick brown sludge. She pulled the other down and they started to writhe over each

232

other. Soon it was almost impossible to tell them apart, but the skinnier of the two seemed to be weakening, her struggles becoming less and less vigorous. Each time she fell into the mud she took longer to stand again, until she eventually flopped, resigned and defeated.

The victor stood and raised her fist at the cameras triumphantly. She looked like a melting sculpture, mud oozing down over her breasts and belly, her flesh streaked pink and brown. Her hair was wetly plastered round her head and fell in filthy ringlets to her shoulders. She spat a jet of mud and spittle and stood brazenly, hands on hips, before the cameras – fiercely defiant. Then her prize appeared.

Giles shifted in his seat. He took a long greedy draw on the joint Kurt passed him, holding the smoke deep in his lungs until he almost gagged, coughing silently with the exhalation. This was the part he had been waiting for. This was where it would get really interesting.

The 'stud' had arrived. The girl turned. Her mouth dropped open with amazement, her face now split by three bright patches of white. He almost glided across to her, his powerful body oiled, muscles rippling under deep ebony skin. His penis was enormous. The woman slowly ran her tongue over her top lip and smiled appreciatively as he towered over her, twisting the strips of leather he carried. He stood in front of the girl for a moment, frowning angrily. Then, with a sudden movement, his hands shot forward and grabbed her arms, squeezing them tightly, making her wince in alarm. He took one of the leather thongs and threaded it through the bracelet on one of her arms. Then with another thong he did the same on the other wrist. Soon both ankles and wrists had leather leads attached to them. The girl seemed almost mesmerized by the man's genitals. Her eyes had never left the spot at the top of his legs where arousal had begun to take over from the previous relaxed state.

A hard wooden frame stood nearby – like a bed with none of the comforts such as bedding or even a mattress. Its only distinguishing feature was the four posts, or stakes, at each corner. A small iron ring was attached to each stake. He took hold of her arm leads and pulled her to the bed. Then he pushed her down on to it. First he tied her ankles, splaying her legs and revealing her vulval area to the cameras. Satisfied that the bindings were secure he tied her arms to the other two posts. She lay spreadeagled like a sludgy starfish with a deep pink centre.

Giles could see her bosom heaving, her breath accelerating. The man walked around the bed, appraising his prey. The girl twisted her head, following him as he moved, lips parted, eyes glazed. He stood at one side down by her feet and looked at her sex. Slowly, agonizingly, he slid his hand up the entire length of her legs, stopping short of the visible pink slit. The girl moaned slightly. Then he bent over her and flicked his tongue across a pale brown nipple. She tried to arch her body but the belts restrained her. His hand cupped her pubic bone and then a long black finger parted the soft wet folds and thrust upwards inside her. She screamed out in climactic ecstasy. Whether real or simulated it was impossible to say but its eroticism was undeniable.

Giles's own trousers were bulging. His blood pulsed red heat. He cursed the disease which had made raw fucking so difficult. He'd wait and relieve himself in his own inimitable way. In the meantime he just sat and watched the show.

Charlotte studied the cover with extremely mixed emotions. She was as anxious to tear the magazine open and look at the contents as she was to leave it shut. Fear gripped her intestines. Fear that all the design, creativity and innovative risk would not have worked.

Giles watched her benevolently. 'Aren't you going to look at it?'

She sighed. 'Yes.' She swallowed hard as she began to turn the pages uncertainly. The clarity of the colour was exceptional, a real triumph of modern technology. And the typeface – crisp, clear characters on the glossy pages. Gaining confidence she began to flick through it more quickly.

All the past weeks of worry, labour and commitment rested between her hands. She went through it once more, this time more slowly, studying the look of the pages; the style of the typeface; Edwina's clever layouts; the quality of the photographic reproduction. It looked nice, very nice. Her tentative smile was breaking into a broad grin. 'Wait till the others see it. Is this the only proof, Giles?'

'More coming over by courier tomorrow. I think another two or three.'

'Fantastic. Well, what do you think?'

'I think it's wonderful, Charlotte. You've done a marvellous job. I can't tell you how pleased I am with *Amber*. I knew when I first approached you you'd come up with something pretty special.'

'Just look at this,' she squeaked. She thrust a double-page spread of a female seemingly suspended from some sort of hang-glider. He had to admit the colours were pretty magnificent. She was wearing some kind of fluorescent swimsuit – the horizon of the photograph dividing it from azure blue into brilliant white – a backdrop for a deep orange and blue para-glider.

'Claudia's first feature. Isn't it brilliant? I thought she was taking a bit of a risk. And she had a hell of a job finding models who were qualified to do it. But look at it, Giles. What a fantastic piece of photography . . .'

'Yes, yes . . .' he agreed, trying to sound enthusiastic.

'And this . . . look.' She thrust another page under his nose. This time it had a space-eye view of the earth, with cloud patterns clearly marked like smoke-wisps. An artist's impression of a cross-section of the earth's atmosphere showed the growing threat of the greenhouse effect with a piece entitled 'Enemies of the Earth'.

He glanced over it and said, 'Yes, yes . . . It looks very nice, Charlotte. So can I take it that you are satisfied?'

She nodded happily. 'Oh yes. More than that.' She threw the magazine on to her desk and jumped out of her chair. 'Thank goodness. And thank you,' she said. She gave him a great big hug. 'Oh Giles, I'm so excited.' She kissed him on both cheeks. Had she had the strength she would have picked him up and spun him around.

'Steady on, Charlotte,' he laughed. 'I'm glad to see you're so excited. Come on, I think I'd better buy you a celebration drink.'

Charlotte sipped her champagne contentedly. She felt as if she'd reached the end of a very long, hard road. But the journey had been more than worth it. She had a magazine to be proud of. All the planning had paid off. Between them they had achieved what she considered to be an exceptional quality publication.

Although Giles was ultimately responsible for the whole magazine ever taking off, she couldn't help wishing that the others had been here to share it with them. It was just sod's law that they had all decided to leave at a reasonable time tonight and had missed Giles's surprise visit at seven o'clock. The good news would have to wait until tomorrow. She consoled herself with the fact that she had had an opportunity to study it privately, and get used to it, before sharing her baby.

'I should think you're going to find yourself rather busy over the next four weeks, Charlotte.'

'You're not kidding. I've got interviews coming out of my ears. It's hard to get used to it being this way round.

236

Usually it's me doing the interviewing. But once that promotion machine gets going it's like being on a non-stop express train. It seems every other magazine in town wants to know what I'm up to. I'm booked for *What the Papers Say*, and *The Media Show*. It wouldn't surprise me if it was *Wogan* next. Still, any hype is good hype. There won't be many people left who haven't heard of *Amber* by 1st April. Frankly I shall be glad when I can get on with the job of editing the magazine, rather than flogging it. It won't be long. Once we get the first issue out it'll be self-perpetuating. The product will almost sell itself. If we've pitched everything correctly the magazine will be such a status symbol – sort of magazine chic. If you want to be cool you've got to have a copy of *Amber* under your arm, or poking out of your bag, or whatever.'

'You'll have plenty of time to get back to your desk I should guess.'

'Oh, I know. I suppose the last thing I should be doing is complaining really. I should just be happy people are interested. And talking of interest, Giles, you seem to be creating an enormous amount of speculation, you know.'

He raised his eyebrows questioningly. 'Really?'

'Well, yes. I think mainly because you've chosen to take such a back-seat role.'

'But I'm the publisher, for God's sake, not the editor. I'm just the one that provides the money and the end product.'

'Yes, yes, I know. I s'pose it's because you seem to shun the publicity side of it. I mean the staff have hardly seen you. You do all your liaising through me.'

'Well, that's only because I have the utmost confidence in you, my dear.'

'Thank you,' she said. 'Would you like to do an interview with me, maybe – I mean with all your titles behind you in the States – coming out of your retirement

237

– you know, the angle of the venture and what you hope to do? London's publishing world is buzzing with curiosity, wondering what you're going to do next.'

'I'm sure they are. Well, they'll just have to wait and see, won't they? I'm afraid I prefer to take a back seat. A bit of speculation never did anyone any harm.'

Charlotte laughed. 'I see. The enigmatic Mr Giles Ferguson.'

'If you like. Anyway, I'll be seeing more of the staff when I move into the office.'

'I didn't know you were.'

'I've decided to take over the top floor. I shall be putting a secretary in there in a couple of weeks. I have a few other . . . er . . . business interests, and I might as well take advantage of the space.'

'Why not? It seems only sensible.'

'We shall be mostly self-contained. You know, separate phone lines and so on. So I won't be bothering you too much.'

Charlotte greeted this news with rather mixed feelings. She had been rather enjoying her autonomy. But if Giles continued in the style of his past behaviour she would have nothing to worry about. Through all her decision-making and magazine-building, she had always been aware of her status as Giles's employee. But it had been nice to feel completely in control for a change. She hoped she wouldn't now have to adjust to Giles running *Amber*.

'What are your other business interests, Giles?'

For a moment Daniel's words sprang unbidden to her mind. 'He's a pornographer . . . a criminal . . . mafia connections . . .' Somehow she just couldn't see it. Even so, she was curious to know just what else he was up to.

'Oh, you know the sort of thing. Wheeling and dealing. A bit of property here and there, import/export,' he said blandly. 'Quite separate to the magazine – another world completely.'

238

His manner was dismissive. Whatever it was, he clearly was not interested in sharing it. Naturally she let the subject drop.

Giles looked at his watch, rather obviously, she thought. 'Charlotte, my dear. I'd love to buy you supper, but . . .' He sounded regretful. 'I'm afraid I have another meeting. You understand . . .'

'Yes. Of course. I have to be getting back anyway. Don't worry about supper. I had a huge lunch and couldn't eat another thing.'

He smiled at her benevolently. 'I'm glad you're happy with *Amber*. I think you've done a wonderful job. Thank you.'

He ushered her out of the wine bar and hailed a cab. Foolishly she imagined it was for her. She was opening the door to get in when he stepped lightly in front of her. He grinned at her from the open door. 'Good night, Charlotte.'

She hid her surprise and smiled and waved, then squared her shoulders and walked briskly up the dark, deserted street, heels ringing loudly across the stone flags, in the vain hope that another taxi would appear.

Chapter Sixteen

'We did it, we did it,' Charlotte cried. She kicked off her shoes, did a twirl across the office and then sank down into her plush swivel chair, swigging from the champagne bottle. She grinned at Claudia smugly, then passed her the bottle.

'Did you see all the competition came? *Harpers*, *Vogue*, *Tatler*, *Cosmo* – not to mention the weeklies. They must be on their toes,' Claudia giggled.

'Of course they're on their toes. Within four hours we were sold out on the newsstand downstairs. I kept going down to check. The man said he was sick of people asking if he'd got any bleeding *Amber* left. More like bleeding gold, he said.'

'The advertisers are queuing up to buy space in the next issues and my pockets are bulging with suggestions for articles from God knows who tonight.'

'Are the others all right?'

'Seem to be. There's just a few hardened hangers-on left out there. And Colin's as pissed as anything. Maybe we should suggest going out to eat. That way at least we'd get everyone out of the office. Hungry?'

Charlotte scowled. 'Hardly. I stuffed myself silly with those canapé jobs. Frankly I feel a bit sick.'

'Then a meal would probably do you good. I'll round everyone up and we'll go to the Italian across the road. Put your shoes on.'

By the time they reached the restaurant there were just eleven of them left. The fresh, chill air seemed to have done wonders for Colin's sensibilities; outwardly at least. All the editorial staff were there: Claudia, John,

Frances, Edwina and Bob, and the three secretaries who had been recruited – Suzy, Philippa and Laura – together with Fiona Brevington, John's indispensable researcher. It had taken Charlotte all of two days to realize that Fiona's research skills were not the only thing indispensable to John. Charlotte had been on her way to the loo late one evening when she had interrupted their clinch as they stood waiting for the lift. They hadn't noticed her come out of the swing doors on to the landing. "Night you two,' she had called pleasantly. They had broken apart and both grinned sheepishly, caught like two mischievous kids. Charlotte said nothing – after all, their personal lives were none of her business. She had only met John's wife once and could not have said what she looked like if her life depended on it. She did know that they had two young children for they had smiled up at her from the twin picture-frame that stood on a corner of John's desk. To Charlotte it was yet one more nail in matrimony's coffin. Her own marriage had foundered partly because there were no children. And here was marriage blessed by two lovely kids, but they had proved incapable of holding their parents together.

John's face was relaxed, happy, his arm nestled protectively around Fiona's shoulders. She was young, probably no more than nineteen, Charlotte guessed, and protected by her own naivety. Not for her the experience of broken marriages or the searing pain of childlessness. Watching the two lovers, Charlotte decided she had no wish to know more of whatever burdens John bore in the battle with his conscience, whatever agonies of decision or indecision he felt about his wife and his girlfriend. Or equally of the disdain of the single girl sophisticate for the brood back home and their undoubtedly dowdy dragon of a mother.

Claudia interrupted her thoughts. 'You look as

though someone's just died, Charlie. We're supposed to be celebrating, for God's sake. What's up?'

'Just dreary thoughts, that's all. I guess I'm just a bit tired. You know what I'd like to do most in the world, Claudia?'

'What's that?'

'Go home and sleep. It's been a long day and I'll be bloody glad when it's over. You know, for the last five months I've done nothing but eat, sleep, breathe *Amber*. Now we've done it I'd like some peace. Just time to myself. Can you understand that?'

'You know I can. But for everyone else you've got to be on form tonight. They've all worked their butts off too. And you're the one that pulled them together. You owe it to them, Charlie, to look grateful. Just a couple more hours, that's all. Then you can go home to sleep. And tomorrow you can lock yourself away in your office all day or treat yourself to the hairdressers . . . Now come on. Snap out of it!'

Charlotte leaned forward and gave her old friend a peck on the cheek. 'You're so right. And what would I do without you?'

Claudia shook her head in despair. 'Fuck knows, Charlie!' she said, and then she burst out laughing.

The restaurant staff managed to find them a very large table at the far end of the room for, they had a shrewd suspicion, this crowd of latecomers might prove a little too noisy for comfort. They shuffled into their seats: Fiona and John superglued together, Claudia and Edwina either side of Colin, Bob next to Claudia, then Charlotte, Frances, Suzy, Philippa and Laura.

Bob leaned across to Charlotte. 'I noticed our Mr Ferguson was too busy to come to his own launch. Unless I missed him . . .'

'No, Bob. You didn't miss him. Suzy took a phone

message from him this afternoon. What was it he said, Suzy?'

'He was out of the country and wouldn't be able to get back. He did say he was extremely sorry and wished us all a great party – and he passed his "warmest congratulations" to all of us!'

'How terribly thoughtful of him,' Bob said with thick sarcasm. 'He's a cool bugger that one. I've never heard of a publisher keeping such a low profile before. You'd think he'd want to share in a bit of the glory wouldn't you?'

'Well, yes, I would. But he just seems to want us to have autonomy. He's a businessman, not a journalist. I don't even think he's particularly sociable. Probably a bit shy I'd guess. You know the type – a real genius at making money and doing business mega-deals, but hopeless at people generally. I must say I don't find him particularly easy to get on with, but then as he's around so little it doesn't really matter, does it?'

'Charlotte, did I tell you about when I met his secretary the other day?' Suzy chipped in.

'God no. I didn't know she'd been in. What secretary anyway?'

'I was putting some packing cases away on the sixth floor – you know in that space behind the dark room. There's a sort of huge storage cupboard . . .' Charlotte nodded. 'Well, when I came out I came face to face with this blonde bombshell.'

Bob's attention perked up immediately. 'Really?'

'Yes. Looked as though she'd just stepped off the set of *Dynasty*. All lip gloss and shoulder pads and cascading blonde hair. She gave me a fright, I can tell you.'

'That bad huh?' Bob asked.

'No. Her looks didn't frighten me. It was her appearance.'

243

Bob was beginning to look confused. 'I see,' he said. Not seeing at all.

'She made me jump.' Suzy was giggling now. 'Bob, you know what I mean. Don't be so daft. When I came out of the cupboard she was just standing there. I hadn't heard anyone come upstairs. And to be honest it's a bit scary up there anyway.' She looked across the table. 'Next time you're coming up with me, Laura.'

'Did she say what she was doing?' Charlotte asked. 'I mean, we didn't see her downstairs. You'd think she might have popped her head round the corner, just to say hello.'

'Well, obviously I introduced myself when she explained who she was. At first I thought she might be a model – something to do with Claudia.'

'Excuse me, but since when have I used plastic tarts in my features, Suzy!'

'I know, I know. But then she just said she was employed by Mr Ferguson and that they would be moving into the office shortly and she wanted to acquaint herself with the equipment.'

'Your words or hers?'

'And just how often have you heard me use words like that, Bob?'

'Oh, bloody hell. Not only is she plastic, she's po-faced as well. What were her legs like?'

'Bob Steele, that's a wholly chauvinistic remark and I'm truly surprised at you,' Charlotte exclaimed. 'I can't imagine that Suzy would have taken any notice of the poor girl's legs . . .'

'Well, of course I did. I couldn't help but notice. She was wearing a miniskirt and heels at least four inches high.'

'Sounds better and better.' Bob sighed happily.

'I'm sure she's a very nice person and we should all do our best to make her feel at home. She might feel very isolated up there, with just Giles to work with. And the amount he's out of the country she'll probably be spending a lot of time on her own. We'll try and make her feel part of the magazine . . . one of us.'

'Delighted. I'll make sure she's given a warm welcome.' Bob laughed.

'Just make sure you don't frighten her off, you dirty old bugger,' John shouted up from the other end of the table.

'Just what business is Giles going to be running from his eyrie on the top floor, Charlie?' Now it was Claudia's turn to voice her curiosity.

'He hasn't told me. But then why should he? We run the magazine, he finances it. How he does it is no business of ours. I really don't feel I should go prying into his other business life. Whatever it is I'm sure he must be damned good at it.'

Charlotte was surprised to hear a note of defensiveness creeping into her own voice. It was as though through his absence she was turning into a sort of front line, protecting him from the insatiable nosiness of her colleagues. She equally would dearly love to know what it was that Giles was doing, and what he spent all his time on, and where. But she felt she had some sort of professional duty to maintain his reputation, to remain above the tap-room gossip of her workmates. Giles had placed her in a position of responsibility and she had a duty to respond accordingly, even if that meant defending him despite her own suspicions.

'Tell you what. When and if he ever decides to tell me, I might let you know. Is that fair?'

'Oh, I'll do better than that,' Bob said bravely. 'Just you wait till I've smooth-talked Bo Derek upstairs. I'll find out just what makes Mr Ferguson tick.'

Charlotte shook her head slowly at him. 'And I always thought you were the shy, retiring one, Bob. The type we women can trust. Those gentle eyes of yours and cheery smile. All pipe-and-slippers homeliness. When in actual fact you're a raving gigolo.'

'Think yourself lucky you don't have to sit with him all day,' Philippa said. 'I've started wearing trousers to work because he liked watching me make the coffee too much. At least now he gets it himself. I'm training him slowly.'

Charlotte raised her eyebrows at Bob. 'Well, you'd better behave properly or Philippa will be in purdah soon.'

By the time the cappuccinos arrived Charlotte had developed quite a good idea of just how her staff were getting on with each other – the 'inter-relationships' as some transatlantic tome would no doubt put it.

A newspaper or magazine staff is one of the tightest, most claustrophobic groups of employees generally found. Once knitted together it becomes all for one and one for all, even down to the lowliest typists. And Charlotte had decreed from the very beginning there was to be as little hierarchy as possible. Many long hours spent toiling over achieving as near perfection as any of them dared go; an enormous respect for each other's abilities; and the unavoidable proximity of their working environment, all created a large, but incredibly close, family of sorts.

As Charlotte had found from her days of working during the marriage, you were in danger of being swallowed up whole by it. You became intimates. You told each other all your hopes, aspirations and, indeed, problems. You all rooted for each other, protected each other, lied and covered for each other if necessary. When you were depressed the whole staff knew it and acted on it. When you celebrated they celebrated too. With all this emotional support, coupled with the sense of pride and achievement at producing a brilliant piece of publishing, relationships outside the workplace were almost superfluous. Apart from sex, of course. That was

246

when the natural step seemed even to seek that from within the office environment.

For now it was good. She wanted to see her team this happy. It meant they all had a common purpose to make it succeed because it made them happy. But eventually, as in all close-knit families, there would come a time when tensions would surface with the power of nuclear fusion. When they did, they took on all the importance of World War III. They were life-threatening, lifted out of all proportion by the intimacy shared. That was when a shrewd editor became a hard editor and a sense of discipline must be instilled into the family. There might be a department change to settle things, or in extreme cases a summons of the culprit to Charlotte's office with a suggestion they might be better off moving on. She just hoped she was a long way away from that day. This was day one. The magazine was a success, and her staff were justly proud of themselves. She pushed her chair back and stood up. 'I'm not going to make a speech. But I want to say thank you to every one of you. It's a great privilege for me to be working with you all and I hope you all feel as proud and happy as I do tonight. Here's to you and to *Amber*.'

She raised her glass and took a large gulp, feeling the strange prick of tears behind her eyelids.

Charlotte had her keys ready in her hand as the cab dropped her outside the neat little terrace off Battersea Rise. She threaded her way between the two skips which blocked the pavement to the right of her front door. The original red-brick façades had long since been abandoned in favour of a tasteful co-ordination of soft pink, dusky blue and pale peach. Neat little window-boxes contained the remnants of narcissi and tulips, outside windows where nets had been replaced by festoons of Designers Guild and Laura Ashley. Intricate nylon lace had been swapped for ruched interlinings and plaited tiebacks, brass poles for swagged valances or tailored pinch pleats.

The old Cortinas and ageing Audis had long gone and a mixture of Porsches, BMWs and Golf GTis now lined the street where the occupants' occupations could be listed on the fingers of one hand. It was the kind of street to which the city newly-weds migrated after the obligatory flat in Clapham. After two or three years Jeremy would get a promotion in the bank, or the firm, or the agency and Louise would get broody. The house would make way for family extension and the previous incumbents would move on to three-beds in Fulham or points further west while Louise took extended maternity leave to scour the pages of the *Lady* for the ideal nanny.

Charlotte had not taken much notice of her neighbours, though she felt sure that in among the newly-weds would be a liberal smattering of newly-divs. Well-heeled, middle-class exes ready to return to cast-off careers from a no-man's island in a sea of idealistic couples.

She unlocked the door and switched on the lights. The house still carried the smell of new carpets, an unmistakable blend of wool and rubber. She heard the warning bleep of the burglar alarm and hurried to the tiny understairs cupboard to switch it off.

Her legs and feet felt like lead weights and she could already sense her body's outrage at the rubbish she had poured into it during the last twelve hours. The champagne had made her head ache and the mixture of canapés and spaghetti carbonara had given her indigestion. Her eyes, though heavy, were prickly red and sore. She looked in the hall mirror and saw a strained face stare back at her. The past few weeks had taken their toll. The tiny crow's feet under her eyes had deepened. She looked sallow and drawn. But she had come a long way. She had launched a magazine, was in the middle of divorce proceedings, and had just moved house. The woman looking back at her was far removed from her corporate wife days. That time seemed like a thousand years ago.

How easy it had been almost to sink without trace into the role of second-class mate, criticized, patronized, or merely dismissed. She had a wonderful antidote now. Something which truly stimulated her. Her old confidence had returned, and with it a measure of self-esteem. She no longer needed to reflect off anyone else and it was a heady thrill. Her life lacked nothing. She was at last fulfilled. Even her exhaustion seemed worthwhile.

The one small crevice that threatened her happiness would eventually heal, especially if she continued to deny its existence. But what Charlotte refused to admit was that sometimes small crevices have a tendency to develop into consuming ravines.

Chapter Seventeen

The plane juddered. The wheels clicked down into place, ready for landing. Sam's nose was pressed hard against the window, watching the incredible New York nightscape roll out below them. Millions of pinprick lights winked like yellow eyes watching from tall dark buildings. She'd seen it a hundred times before, but still found it a breathtaking approach. Even Daniel found himself craning over her, so that he could get a better view of it. In the distance they could see the Hudson River winding its shiny black path. He still got that same thrill; a sort of heady anticipation, that he'd felt on his maiden trip, some thirteen years before. Still wet behind the ears, but fired with a steely ambition to conquer New York's advertising world in the same way he had London's.

He squeezed Sam's arm. 'Glad to be back?'

She shrugged. 'Huh?' She considered for a moment, still frowning at the growing buildings beneath them. 'I guess . . . It's been an exciting few months though, hasn't it? All that dealing. All those cities . . . Yep, I guess I'll be glad just to sink down into my own bathtub, and not have to remove the courtesy cover from the pan; or look at another room service menu for a while. New York'll never be "home", you know. And the office might seem real draggy for a while. But it's nice to be back.

'How about you, Dan? What will you do now? Heading back to London? I'll come and visit you if you ask me. It's funny, isn't it? We've spent such a long time together and I feel I know you pretty well, yet there's a whole slice of your life I don't know anything about. I just can't picture your office, your apartment, your car, your Mom . . . Why, I don't even know if you've got one of those?'

'What?'

'A mother, for God's sakes.' She shook her head slowly. 'Just what did we talk about all those weeks?'

'Business. And more business. And when we weren't talking about business we were asleep.'

'Yeah. You're right there. Hardly a holiday, huh!'

'They won't believe us. Just look at the colour of you! You look as though you've lain on a beach for a month.'

'So do you. We must have caught the sun through the taxi windows rushing between meetings – and of course the odd afternoon we've managed to steal by the pool. What the hell. The results speak for themselves, don't they? We couldn't have done what we did lying by the pool all the time!'

Thirty minutes later they found a cab. Sam settled back in the seat, eyes invisible behind black shades, despite the hour. Neither had voiced it, but each was feeling pretty low.

That night, the night Sam had paid her visit to his room, still hung between them. Like a silent denial, neither had mentioned it since. The following day's breakfast had brought a cheery Sam who was as far removed from the midnight siren as ice from a flame. He had taken her lead and kept his mouth shut. But her eyes gave her away. He would turn and catch her looking after him, and then she would look away. Underneath her smiles lay disappointment which her pride would not let her admit. So he played along with her.

He liked her. She was funny and clever, young and beautiful, and Daniel had never before turned down such an attraction. He handled women as smoothly as he did an advertising brief. There was just something perverse that had suddenly, after thirty-six years, decided to enter his nature. Daniel was used to getting his own way. Not through devious means, or by bullyish aggression; it was just the way things had happened for him. Things just fell in his path. Work, money, and women. Now he wanted the one he couldn't have, and no matter how hard he tried to convince himself of the contrary, his heart wouldn't listen. Even Sam, who at any other time in his life would have been heaven-sent, had not weaved a stronger spell.

His heart was heavy at the prospect of returning to London. The distance he had so desperately sought to put between them had not eased Charlotte from his mind. Every mile he had travelled only served as a reminder of the futility of his attempt. The distance tore at the hurt and the aching hole he had felt after he had seen her with Ferguson. The stupidity of his desperate visit to her home, to warn her. He had succeeded in making her hate him and mistrust him, and there was fuck all he could do about it.

He studied Sam silently from his corner of the cab, locked in her own private misery. If only he could let go then maybe he could make this wonderful girl happy. Until then he had no intention of adding to her history of betrayal. A half-hearted affair was not what she needed to reinstate her faith in male nature.

As they pulled up outside the canopied entrance of the Plaza, Daniel leaned over and kissed her. 'I'll see you in the office tomorrow morning, love. Get a good night's sleep 'cos I think Bob's got a heavy schedule planned for us. De-briefing time and all that.'

'You too, Daniel.' Her voice was almost a whisper, and she didn't look at him.

'Sam . . .' he called to her through the open door. 'Look . . . I'm sorry. It's just . . .'

She lifted her glasses off and looked at him levelly. 'There's nothing to be sorry for, Dan.' She replaced her glasses and tapped the cab driver's shoulder. 'Let's go,' she said. He watched the cab turn down the street and then let the porter take his bags. He suddenly felt on the verge of collapse. His legs wobbled and his head felt light. What he needed was a damned good sleep.

Daniel was only ten minutes behind Sam when he arrived at Lester's next morning. He went straight up to the main man's office and, finding no one at home, settled back on the futon-style sofa with a pile of trade magazines from the past few weeks to see who had been doing what with whom and how much it had cost them. He was pleased to see that there was a fair smattering of London mags which Bob obviously felt he should keep up with. After all, as Dan kept telling him, New York may be the biggest, but London was the best.

After a good half hour's read he flicked through a copy of *Campaign*, the bible of London agencies, an informative gossip rag that no ad-man could afford to be without. In amongst the scandal pages of who had left which agency and which client was dissatisfied with their lot, there were profiles of agency, media people or clients. Daniel nearly fell off his futon when who should he see but Charlotte gazing back at him from the centre spread.

The photographer had caught her in typical *Campaign* style, leaning against a doorway in what was no doubt her workplace. She looked stiff and businesslike – an attitude no doubt enhanced by the harsh monochrome blow-up. It was a serious pose and the familiar lift to her mouth was not evident. Her eyes gazed levelly into the lens. Her hair was piled up neatly behind her. She looked a woman to be reckoned with. He realized he must have been staring at the photograph for several moments, studying every detail of that face he had first seen what seemed like a century ago. This was an altogether different woman. The girl in the silver dress had been built for love. She exuded an animal attraction that night in Langan's, though little did she realize it. This woman, looking coolly back at him now, brooked no such intimacy. She meant business. And he found himself liking this new image of her and wondering just how clever an editor she was. In truth, although he had listened to Valentine's catty comments, and Charlotte's own descriptions, he had never thought about her career. Hadn't he been the one who forced her, unwillingly, into organizing a party, because he had heard she was bored?

He dragged his eyes away from her image and back to the headline: 'Grange to head up new magazine'. There were a couple of quotes in bold type: '. . . thinking women's literature', 'emphasis on current, rather than affairs . . .'

He started to read the interview, suddenly hoping that Bob didn't materialize before he had had a chance to get through it. But he had just got to the third line when he heard a gasp and an 'I don't believe it,' behind him. Reluctantly he closed the paper and slipped it into his open briefcase.

'I didn't think you were due back till next week.'

'We weren't. Bracy cancelled and we decided to come back. We can always fix that up again. So here we are.'

'So I see. And where is my infant prodigy? I hope you've brought her back safe and untainted.'

'Sam's fine. She's probably in her office.'

Bob nodded. 'Well, I'll give her a chance to sort herself out, but first you can come in and tell me all about it, Dan. We've got a shareholders' meeting at 2 p.m. I think I might even get you to give them a little presentation, seeing as how you're the main reason for the meeting.'

'Shit!' Dan swore. 'You obviously had it all prepared

yourself, you bugger. Why don't you just go ahead with it?'

'Come on, Dan. We'll talk about it. Straight from the horse's mouth and all that.'

'But they won't like my accent. I'm foreign and threatening.'

'Daniel, since when have you ever backed down from a presentation?' Bob was leading the way into his office. He gestured to Dan to sit down.

'Never. And I'm not now. I'm just knackered, old pal, that's all. Too many hotels, too many flights and too much booze I should think.'

'Funny thing is you look so damned healthy. Are you sure you haven't been holidaying it somewhere?'

'No, I haven't. But I intend to quite soon.' The two men laughed and Bob started to sort through a file of papers he took out of his attaché case.

He handed a bound report to Daniel. 'Here. Have a look at that. It makes pretty impressive reading.'

Daniel leafed through the pages and smiled wryly. 'Seems Sam did a thorough job keeping you informed. Twenty new agencies to go under the Lester's umbrella – it's a good job we had such high profits last year. $40 million is quite a downpayment in one hit.'

'Well, next time you call me in the middle of the night try and make it a little less expensive can you, Dan. I don't think even Lester's can run to that kind of investment on a regular basis.'

'Don't worry. I've had my fill of shopping for a while. But once we start to cream off some of the income from those little agencies, the deferred payments are going to seem like nothing. You know damn well now that they've got Lester's name to tag on their letterheading they'll have clients kicking down their doors for the privilege of some decent advertising.'

'I know, I know,' Bob laughed. 'You two have become a bit of a legend. All these acquisitions have doubled our share price. The financial press have been going crazy trying to keep up with you. The Board quite rightly have asked to be informed of what's going on. They want some reassurances that this isn't just hype which will cost us in the long run. That's why you're coming with me to the Park Lane at two o'clock. I'm sure you'll find 150 shareholders a piece of cake after what you've just done.

'I'll introduce you, and explain what you've been up to. Not that they don't know, for God's sake. Then you can give them details of share deals, percentage splits, new client opportunities . . . You know the sort of bullshit they like to hear. After that I'm going to take you and Sam to dinner. This time it's on me.'

They sailed through the meeting. At the end of it, Bob insisted that Daniel and Sam stand up and take a vote of thanks. The audience stood and applauded them, much to their mutual embarrassment. Daniel had gone through the report and Sam had fielded the questions. As usual she was a deft communicator, even through the tiredness.

Afterwards Bob stood between them, an arm round each. 'Well done. We seem to have wooed them successfully. Could you see how happy they looked? Grinning all over their faces. Smiles of greed, weren't they? I could just see them with their pocket calculators, totting up their share values. Not that I wasn't doing exactly the same thing . . . I'll see you later at Harry's Bar. There's a client I want to talk to you about, Sam, and I think I might have a nice surprise for you too, Dan. Might fit in very well with what you were saying earlier about taking a break. See you at eight.'

Chapter Eighteen

'That's it. I can't stand it any longer. I swear I'm going to punch her on the nose.'

'Who, for God's sake?'

'That . . . that . . . blown up excuse for a bird upstairs, that's who.'

Charlotte lifted her nose from the third revise of the property scandal exposé she had commissioned from Alistair Smith. He had come to her with the story of how a major land deal had been financed with drug money. It made fascinating reading, but needed a lot of tightening up – and a lot of fact-checking. She was almost beginning to despair of it. Her last resort would be to pay him for the work he had already finished, and either write the piece herself, or pass it to Colin to do.

'What's she done now, Laura?' She looked at the girl in despair. Giles's secretary had been in situ precisely three weeks. Already Charlotte had had to mediate twice and it was beginning to get on her wick. She was an editor not a personnel officer.

'I have just received another memo.'

'Oh.' This was about the sixth memo and Charlotte had to admit, the girl upstairs did have an unfortunate turn of phrase. 'And?'

'Would we please ensure that any mail for either herself or Giles is taken up to the sixth floor immediately upon its arrival and is not left, as happened this morning, for half an hour on the fifth. Now, Charlotte. Correct me if I am wrong, but as Suzy so rightly pointed out when she first met her, the girl does have a good pair of legs, does she not?'

Charlotte nodded.

'Then why the bloody hell can't she get off her skinny little bottom and come down and get it herself? We're busy down here. She may well be working for the publisher, but I do not intend to jump about being her mailboy – and neither do the others. It wouldn't be half so bad if she was a tiny bit friendly. We've tried asking her out to lunch but she declined. I've tried chatting to her in the loo. Why, on her first week I even took her a cup of coffee up a couple of times. And you know what happened then . . .'

'She rang and asked what had happened to her coffee on the third day, right?'

'Right. And then there was the telephone. Could we not answer her telephone line under any circumstances, or engage any of Mr Ferguson's guests in conversation if they came into the office, and we happened to meet them on the stairs, as they were far too important to engage in "banal chitchat". I know you're busy, Charlotte, but I think you're going to have a riot on your hands soon. Either that or murder . . . and as for calling her Miss Pointer . . . aaaaagh!'

'Look, Laura, I will see what I can do, but I can't promise. Really the girl is nothing to do with us. She's working for Giles – as are we all. If he's happy with her there's not much I can do, except for having a few subtle words. I should think the best thing is to leave her alone as much as possible. Freeze her out if she's doing the same thing to you. I know it's a shame, especially when we've got such a friendly staff down here, but she obviously doesn't want to seem part of us. And frankly, that's no loss, is it? But I will have a quiet word with her, especially about things like the post. I certainly don't want you going up and down stairs all day running errands for her.'

Laura sniffed. 'Thanks, Charlotte.'

Then Charlotte's internal phone buzzed. 'Yes,' she

answered. Her voice had a tightness about it, resulting from a wish not to be interrupted.

'It's John.'

'Hi,' she said, sounding short.

'Those trannies of David Bloomstein, the New York property tycoon, have just come back. They're dreadful. There's a thin line running through so it looks as if the emulsion on the film could be damaged. Shall I go to the picture library and see if they can come up with anything?'

'Oh shit. The whole reason we wanted those was because his ex-wife was poking her tongue out at him. Have you spoken to Colin about it?'

'Yes. "Fucking amateurs" to quote his exact words.'

Soon she was lost once more in the depths of bribery and corruption. She put her pencil through long paragraphs, and scribbled down amendments of her own. When finally she looked up from her work, she realized two hours had passed. The phone had not rung, no one had been in to see her – not even Laura with her always-welcome cup of tea. Her angle-poise lamp flooded the desk with light, but the rest of the office was gloomy and dark. She got up, turned on the main light, and ventured out of her office wondering whether there was anyone else left in the building.

Laura's desk was deserted, but her jacket hung over her chair.

'Laura . . .' she called softly.

'Here . . .' She heard the voice, muffled, coming from somewhere underneath the large desk.

'What on earth are you doing?'

'Filing.'

'On the floor?'

'Well, sorting actually. It's just that the desk isn't really big enough to stack all the papers on.'

Charlotte looked down to see Laura stranded in a sea of paper, dealing out sheets like playing cards.

'Are we the only ones left?'

'Just about. Giles is in upstairs. He poked his nose round the door at about five to say he was here, but he hasn't been down since. And Claudia rang in to say she'd be in the wine bar at eight o'clock if you wanted to meet her for a drink. Oh, and this arrived by hand this afternoon.'

She handed Charlotte an envelope marked for 'The Personal Attention of Ms Charlotte Grange' in beautifully scripted italics. The paper was high quality – not the usual scrappy business stuff. Charlotte looked at it curiously. 'Wonder what's in here,' she said, almost to herself.

'Open it.'

'Thanks. I will.'

It was an invitation. At first she just glanced at it, expecting it to be some boring press do for a car launch or similar public relations extravaganza but then the word Caribbean caught her eye. This time she read it more slowly.

'What's this? The grand opening of Lux Hotels' flagship the Royal Anguilla, on Anguilla . . . Where's that, Laura? I've never heard of it. It says it's in the Caribbean.'

'Oh yes. I think it's actually British. Wasn't there some story about British Bobbies going out there to sort out some kind of trouble a few years back? Though I can't say I know anything about it. Go on, what else does it say.'

'It says I'm invited on an all expenses paid trip to the opening of a new hotel out there. Four days in the Caribbean . . . God, wouldn't that be wonderful?'

'Then why don't you go?'

'Me? Go out there? Don't be daft, Laura. I've got a magazine to run. I'd love a holiday some time, but I couldn't go just yet.'

'But it's not a holiday. It's work.'

'Well, whatever. There's no way I could go. Maybe we could send someone else.'

'I'm sure I could find my passport in time . . .'

'I'll remember that, Laura. Now, if Giles is upstairs, maybe this is a good time to have a little chat with him about Linda.'

'Well, if he's there, she probably is too. You usually find her guarding his door like a desk-trained rottweiler.'

'Thanks for the warning.'

Charlotte took the stairs two at a time, and as she went through the swing doors at the top she was assaulted by the smell of Rive Gauche. Linda was sitting at her desk, immaculately groomed and glossed, but she was not alone. Seated on the edge of her desk, head bent towards her intimately, was a stranger. Both of them looked up, startled by the slam of the doors.

Charlotte immediately felt intrusive. 'I'm sorry . . .' she blurted. 'I just wanted to have a quick word with Giles. Is he . . . ?' She gestured towards the office.

'He's busy,' Linda snapped. 'You can't see him. He won't be free tonight.'

'Oh, I see. Well, in that case I'll catch him tomorrow.'

'He's not here tomorrow.'

'I'll see him next time he's in then. When might that be, Linda?'

Charlotte's tone was beginning to be less than apologetic. This jumped-up tart really did have a most unfortunate manner. She was almost glowering at Charlotte.

'I really can't say. You'll just have to wait and see.' She turned back to her companion. 'She's the editor.'

He turned to Charlotte. 'Ah yes.' An American drawl. He nodded in her direction but was obviously not interested in a formal introduction. He eyed her impudently and Charlotte felt her cheeks grow red with anger. She squared her shoulders and summoned all her dignity. 'Then perhaps you would be kind enough to tell Giles that when he has a moment I'd like to see him?'

'All right,' Linda said with complete lack of interest. Charlotte fully understood Laura's urge to lay one on her.

'Thanks.' Charlotte turned to go.

'Hey!' She turned. The American had called her.

'Yes?'

'Don't slam the door, OK!'

Charlotte could not believe her ears. She swept through the doors and ran down the stairs, hearing with satisfaction the enormous crash as the two doors met behind her. How ever could Giles accommodate such pigs in the same building? Next time she saw him she'd have a few words to say about the company he kept, her business or not.

Laura had left and Charlotte picked up her bags, shut off all the lights and turned off the machines. The cleaners would be in later to lock up. She ran down the four flights of stairs and crossed the road to the cellar wine bar. Several of the tables were positioned underneath the structural arches of the old cellars and so it was difficult to see who was sitting where. Charlotte walked up the line of brick crescents and eventually found Claudia and Colin wrapping themselves round a bottle of Bordeaux.

'Boy, am I glad to see you two.' She squeezed into the alcove and sat down heavily, reaching for an empty glass.

Colin filled it for her. 'Bad day huh?'

'Not exactly. The day was all right. The usual crises.'

They both waited. It was obvious she couldn't wait to spit out whatever was bothering her. When she had finished relating her trip up the stairs, Claudia shrieked. 'Bloody hell. What a pig. I think I would have hit him.

262

And as for that little madam. I really do think you should have a word with Giles about it. That's too much, really it is . . .'

'Funny, isn't it? You'd think Giles would have drummed a bit of respect into his secretary. The magazine's doing very well. We're a pretty hot team, and we're probably making quite a bit of money for him. A modicum of reverence should be shown to all of us. It's almost as if Giles doesn't really take *Amber* terribly seriously.'

'I'm afraid you might be right, Colin. Things like not showing up for the launch and not having any interest in what's going on. I thought it was because he just trusted us to get on with it. Now I think it may be because he really couldn't give a damn. Whoever that man upstairs with Linda was – he was just awful!'

'I think we should stage a cold war. Let's freeze her out as you said to Laura. If she wants her post she'll soon learn to come and get it. Let's speak if spoken to and nothing else. What do you think?'

'I agree. It will be an interesting exercise if nothing else. We'll tell the others. There's no point beating around the bush and trying to be diplomatic about it. It's not as though nobody's noticed what's going on. Everyone's sick of Linda. And we've got a magazine to run. The last thing we want is a pain in the arse trollop upsetting everybody. If Giles notices – well, it's one good way of drawing him out, isn't it? Might make him realize there are certain things which even hardened journalists find unacceptable.'

'Right, now that's settled will you tell her or shall I, Colin?'

'Tell me what?'

'We've got some good news for you.'

'Well that makes a change. What is it?'

Claudia was digging into her handbag, which was more shopping- than hand-sized. 'Now let me see . . . I had it here not long ago.' Her voice was muffled as it disappeared into the depths of the tardis-like accessory. Finally she pulled out a small white envelope, which she then waved under Charlotte's nose. 'This is the good news.'

'It looks like an invitation . . . I got one this afternoon.'

'Not an ordinary invitation. A freebie in the Caribbean invitation.'

'That's the one. Some hotel chain, isn't it?'

'Yep.' Claudia read out the invitation with relish. 'And guess who's going?'

'You are. I thought you'd be sick of exotic locations by now. You've only just come back from Klosters.'

'That was eight weeks ago. And I'd hardly compare Klosters with the Caribbean. Besides, I'm not the one who's going.'

'Colin!' Charlotte shrieked. 'I somehow can't imagine you beefing it around a swimming pool. You don't look like a hothouse flower at all.'

'Can't stand the sun. It makes my skin come out in ghastly red bumps. Then I start to itch. I get third-degree sunburn and I hate swimming – you get chapped in the most intimate places.'

'Then who?'

'You!'

'Me!' she screeched. 'How the hell can I go? I've got a magazine to run, a mortgage to meet, a divorce to finalize, a publisher to sort out. It's completely out of the question, and . . . and . . .'

'Yes? Go on.'

'Well, Claudia, isn't that enough to start with?'

'No.'

'Look, you two. It's not that I don't want to go. Who wouldn't? I've never been to the West Indies and God knows I could do with a break, but there's just no way. The magazine is barely two months old. We've got our

264

next issue coming out in three weeks. I'm surprised you mentioned it.'

Now it was Colin's turn to chip in. 'Tell me about the schedules.'

'What do you mean?'

'How much have you got to do for issue number four?'

'Well, not much. But that's not the point . . .'

'Look, Charlotte, I know you and what a workaholic you are. You know damn well you've got every article planned until September at least. Don't you think we could manage for a week without you? We could reach you on the telephone and there's such a thing as a fax these days you know. You could edit from the hotel if you really wanted to. Though you'd be crazy if you did. Why don't you find yourself a nice young photographer to take with you, and take a break. You can ease your conscience by writing a wonderful travel piece about the place. Anyway, the point is that Claudia and I have made up our minds. You're going and that's all there is to it.'

'Well, that's awfully kind of you two mother hens, but you might at least give me the privilege of having a say in my own destiny, don't you think?'

'Not in this instance. You don't know what's good for you. You've worked yourself to the bone these last few weeks. And it's none of my business what's going on in your private life, but I do know that you had a shit of a husband that you're now getting rid of. In my estimation that's enough reason to take a break.'

'Charlotte knows she needs a break, don't you, darling? Please don't think we're trying to run your life. We just think it's the only way we can persuade you into it. Why don't you sleep on it? We'll talk about it again tomorrow morning.'

'I'll agree to think about it, that's all. No promises. No pressure. OK?'

'Agreed. It's a deal,' Claudia said.

Giles handed Frost the whisky bottle. 'So what is it you want me to do exactly with this Mark . . . what's his name . . .'

'Foster.'

'Yes. Mark Foster.'

'Well, we figured that after we gave you such an easy time when you decided to clear out from the States you might feel you owed us a small favour.'

Giles raised his glass. 'Of course. That is fair. But whether that runs to taking on what amounts to your unfinished business – well, I'm not sure. My operation's running really nicely here. Sounds like a whole load of hassle, Michael. Just because some stupid arsehole has got in too deep with his money handling. Go back and tell Eddy I'm not interested. The guy's too much of a liability. I don't want to take it on. I'll help you in other ways. How about a few little master tapes, huh?' Giles unlocked his desk drawer and pulled out a film canister. He held it up for Frost.

'I can guarantee you wouldn't be disappointed with these. There's twenty movies on this master. You can take them back. Tell you what, just for Eddy I won't even charge you. Now there's a gift horse for you. If you distribute these in the right way you should be able to stretch to half a million dollars.'

'Forget it, Ferguson. Unless there's any snuff . . . ?'

'No. Too select a market. I don't think Europe's quite ready for it yet. We'll see in a while.'

'In that case Eddy won't be interested. The other rubbish is two a penny. Good snuff is hard to come by. It's difficult getting the models to come back, see . . .' He laughed loudly at his own joke. The models didn't come back because they were murdered on screen.

'Eddy told me not to go back until I had it agreed. And you know what that means. I have to do what the man says.' He shrugged and knocked back his whisky. 'So you could save both our time by agreeing to it.'

Giles sighed deeply. The last thing he wanted was to take on Eddy d'Angelo's problems. Up until now he had got along with him pretty well. Eddy just about had the monopoly on all smack shipments through New York, along with a few other 'business interests'. He owned a good slice of real estate on the East Side of Manhattan; and, in one of his more respectable guises, sat on the board of Simmonds and Stein financiers. Giles's drug running had been almost a side-line. Secondary to his publishing venture. Up until now that was. He did not intend to sour their relationship. He knew that Eddy had a long reach and could indeed stretch as far as the refiners in Pakistan and Afghanistan. He was a big customer over there, and Giles did not want a word from Eddy to dry up his own supply.

'So, just what is it you want me to do?' There was no point in drawing it out any longer. He knew what both of them had known from the beginning of the meeting. There was no way Giles would turn down Eddy's request.

'I knew you'd agree, somehow.'

'Yes, I'm sure. So you'd better tell me.'

'We'll send him to you. Don't worry about that side of things. Set him up. Get rid of him. We can't have that kind of failure passing off without us doing anything about it.'

'Just what kind of failure was it?'

'He paid three million dollars towards half a shipment coming in from Pakistan. They tried the old suitcase trick – you know, one suitcase comes all the way from Pakistan full of drugs, someone else joins the flight at the stopover, carrying an identical suitcase . . . only full of clothes. The second courier goes through first with a ticket saying he's come from a country that's not on the drugs circuit, except he's got a case full of drugs. Well, he fucked it. That shipment is still in the hands of the Federal Drugs Bureau and Foster hasn't got the money to pay us back. Silly boy didn't think about his insurance policies when he started to live the high life. Now he can't meet his debts. And as you know, Ferguson, Eddy can't stand a bad debt. Have I made myself clear?'

'Oh, I think so. From what you're saying, Eddy isn't interested in the money any more.'

'Right.'

'What about the Drugs Bureau? They must be keen to know just who is behind their little hoard?'

'Right again, Ferguson. That's why Eddy's staying low at the moment. He thought it might be better if his business was taken care of over here.'

'I see.' Giles didn't like it one bit. He had to involve himself with a hot property. For all he knew this guy Mark Foster might be under surveillance himself. He was taking a big risk by agreeing to Eddy's request. But somehow he had to do it.

'Well, if there's nothing else I can do for you, Michael . . .'

'Oh, but there is.'

Giles was beginning to feel mildly impatient. This particular henchman of d'Angelo was a slimy bastard and the sooner he was out of his office the better. He wanted to open the windows, to get rid of the sickening smell of cheap aftershave. But his slickly charming smile carried no trace of the rising resentment he felt inside. 'Really. And what might that be?'

'The er, little lady, the one outside . . . ?'

'Linda?'

'Yeah, that's right, Linda. Cute little arse, she's got.'

Giles raised his brows and smiled indulgently at the stinking little turd. 'Oh, indeed she has.'

'I'd like some entertainment tonight. Know what I mean? To see the sights, keep me company, look after me. D'you think she'd be free?'

'Oh, I think she'd be very free.' He leaned across his desk and pushed a red button on his telephone. Immediately Linda appeared through the doorway. 'You wanted me, sir?' Her quiet, deferential tone was such that if any of the staff of *Amber* had heard, they would not have believed it.

'Mr Frost would like you to look after him tonight, Linda. Would that be all right?'

Her voice dropped to a smooth purr, almost a whisper. 'Oh, I'd be delighted.' She walked over to where Frost sat and leaned over him so that he could get a fuller view of her cleavage. Then she reached out and stroked his cheek. 'Anything you want,' she simpered, suggestively.

'OK, you two. Have a great evening,' Giles said conclusively. 'Oh, and Linda . . . don't rush in tomorrow. Take it easy, huh?'

'Yes, sir. Thank you, sir.'

The minute they left Giles threw open all the windows and then dropped the empty whisky bottle into the wastebin. He locked himself into the office and pulled a small, slim wallet out of his inside breast pocket. Next he unlocked the safe hidden behind the Matisse on the large wall in front of his desk, and pulled out a small bag of what looked like flour. He scooped up about an eighth of a teaspoonful of the white powder and dropped it carefully on to a hand-sized mirror he pulled from his wallet.

With minute care he took a silvered razor blade and deftly arranged the powder into two thin lines, like furrows, along the mirror. This done to his satisfaction he pulled out a short golden straw. One end of the straw he poked carefully up his left nostril and, bending over the cut lines of cocaine, he snorted up one line of white powder. He sniffed hard, and then bent forward and repeated the operation with his right nostril. Then he leaned back into his chair, savouring the hit of the drug.

Before he put the mirror away he scraped his forefinger over the surface to scoop up any remnants of coke. He rubbed the traces on to his top gum, feeling the familiar tingling sensation that signalled the onset of a pleasant time to come.

Chapter Nineteen

'Well?' Claudia poked her head round her door.

'You haven't wasted much time, have you? I've only been here five minutes.'

'I know. I was looking out for you. I had to make sure . . .'

'That I'd say yes I s'pose?'

'Uh huh. And you will, won't you?'

Charlotte looked at her earnestly. 'Well, I've thought long and hard about it, Claudia.' Her voice was deadly serious. 'And really it's just . . .' she could see Claudia frowning, knowing she was going to say no, '. . . too good an opportunity to miss!'

'Wow! That's great! Brill. Now ring them up. Come on, call them now to let them know you're going. And you want to take a photographer.'

Charlotte put her hands up in protest. 'For God's sake, woman, slow down, don't be so hysterical!'

'Hysterical? Huh! We've got work to do. Come here, where's the phone, what's the number . . . ?'

The next four weeks flew by in a flurry of schedules, visas and wardrobes. Claudia had revelled in her role as chief 'dresser' and grand organizer, haranguing and cajoling every fashion house in London for their summer collections so that Charlotte could have her pick of the next season's offerings.

The photographer they managed to line up was a mammoth figure of a man called George Berry. It had been a toss-up between him and James Harris. Charlotte had lunched with them both but on reflection had decided that as her own interest in dinghy sailing didn't anywhere near match James's, she'd be hard pushed to converse with him for four days, it being his sole topic of conversation. Conversely, George was a hilarious companion. The only problem with him was that she had to prise him away from his new baby daughter, born to him and his ex-model wife some three weeks before. But even he eventually had to give in to the attractions of four days' break in a Caribbean paradise.

It had been some two weeks before she had the chance to let Giles know of her intended trip. His lack of reaction to her news would have been astonishing were it not for his earlier uninterested behaviour. The staff had all stuck to their cold war strategy of freezing out Miss Pointer and ignoring Giles's rare visitations but neither seemed to have particularly noticed.

'Jolly good for you,' he had said when she told him she would be away for four or five days in May. 'Have a good break. Why don't you stay longer?'

'I might be tempted. But don't worry about the magazine,' she had added, the note of sarcasm in her voice only thinly veiled.

'Oh I won't,' he said, grinning. 'I know you'll have everything under control.'

And now here she was, four weeks and three suitcases later, in need of a sherpa's services, vainly trying to find a luggage trolley in the bowels of Heathrow Airport. Why she had three suitcases for what amounted to only four nights away she couldn't imagine. She had swimsuits coming out of her ears; shorts, T-shirts, a couple of evening dresses, at least four sexy cocktail dresses; even a couple of Janet Reger nightgowns which Claudia had surreptitiously slipped into the packing pile.

'What on earth are you putting those in for?'

'You never know when you might get lucky – talking of which you'd better take these too . . . '

272

'Claudia Williams,' Charlotte screeched, 'get those things out of here this minute. What happens if customs go through my suitcase and the first thing they see is a packet of Mates? Go on, get them out!'

'I'm sure they'd think you were a smart, sophisticated lady who was capable of taking care of herself in a hard world.'

'And you'd know about that, wouldn't you? I suppose you always take a crate of them when you go away?'

'I certainly take a couple of packets. Can't be too careful, and you never know when you might need them. I was a Girl Guide once – weren't you? – "Be Prepared" and all that . . . '

Charlotte giggled. She picked up the offending packet of condoms and threw them back at Claudia. 'Here, have one on me!'

By the time she had squeezed the enormous pile of clothes into the three suitcases and packed up a large handbag which had her tickets, passport, money and other vital bits and pieces, she could barely move. She found a trolley in the bus queue, loaded it up and wheeled it up the zigzag walkway to the international departures hall.

Searching through the crowds she saw the huge bulk of George Berry ahead of her in the check-in queue. He was quite unmissable, flamboyant both in his looks and his dress. His blond hair fell in long curls, almost like ringlets, to his shoulders and his chin was buried beneath a vast bushy beard with blond and ginger lights. He wore a thin cotton jacket over a stark black T-shirt and trousers, the other unusual feature being the fact that the jacket fell almost to his ankles. He was in heavy discussion with the girl at the desk over his cameras, gesturing to three large metal suitcases. 'I'm afraid that I will not put them in the hold. They are extremely valuable pieces of equipment and should not be entrusted to clumsy baggage handlers. Yes . . . yes . . .' he was saying, desperately trying to control his temper and maintain his patience '. . . of course I understand the security risk . . .' By this time Charlotte was at his side '. . . you can examine the whole lot in minute bloody detail. Show me a professional photographer anywhere in the world who would put his cameras through.'

A smooth voice came from behind them:

'What seems to be the problem? I wonder if I might help, I'm . . .'

He broke off as Charlotte gasped: 'William!'

'Charlotte!' he said simultaneously.

George, for all his argument, couldn't resist saying, 'Do you two know each other?'

They ignored him, shock obvious on both faces.

'What the hell are you doing here?'

'I might say the same to you!'

'Oh my God.' Realization suddenly registered on William's face. 'I should have thought. *Amber*, of course.'

'Of course what?' The issue of the camera cases was temporarily forgotten.

'Lux Hotels. They're my client. Who do you think is organizing this trip?'

'Oh no. Oh, I don't believe it.' Charlotte's heart sank somewhere below the level of the ankle straps on her white trainers. 'Oh William. Tell me this is a bad dream.' All hopes of the holiday seemed to be shattering slowly, bit by irreparable bit. She felt cold, bitter disappointment. How could she possibly hope to enjoy the holiday with him along?

'Listen Charlotte.' William took hold of her elbow and gently guided her away from the queue of now curious onlookers. 'I'm sure we can be sensible about this,' he was saying.

'Oh, how?' Her voice was razor-edged.

'Well, I assume you're not going to turn tail and run?'

'The thought doesn't seem that unattractive a prospect.'

'Well, if you'll forgive me for saying so, and at the risk of sounding pompous, I think that would be a little silly.'

'Hmph!' she said.

'Why can't we be grown up about this? We're going to have the Decree Absolute in a couple of days. That's rather ironic, isn't it? It's usually honeymoons that are celebrated in the Caribbean, not divorces. And we could stay a long way from each other – there's load of others going, some from America too.'

She had to admit that the prospect of unpacking her suitcases was probably a worse alternative than braving her way through the trip. 'Well, I suppose. But William, you must promise that you'll do as little as possible to upset me. We can keep our distance and not interfere in each other's affairs.'

'Of course. I'll promise, Charlotte – if you'll promise too.'

'OK. Agreed.'

'Great,' he said.

'William,' a voice drawled behind them. 'Darling. How are you?'

Charlotte turned. This time she really did feel sick. 'Fucking hell!' she mouthed silently and took an unconscious step backwards. 'This I really don't believe.'

Six foot of foul-mouthed, red-headed witchery was throwing its arms around her soon to be ex-husband.

'Valentine,' she breathed. 'William,' she hissed, 'I'd like a word with you . . .'

Once more they retreated to a quiet spot at a vacant check-in desk. It was becoming farcical. Now almost the entire queue had cottoned on to the comedy show.

'What the hell is she doing here? Come on, William. How do you expect me . . . ?'

'Charlotte, I didn't know.'

'Rubbish!'

'I swear. I didn't know. Ask her. I haven't seen her for weeks. She's probably somebody's model. I didn't check the passenger lists as you well know. Otherwise I'd have known you were going to be on the plane, wouldn't I? And I'd have thought you'd see my surprise was as genuine as your own. Charlotte. Look, does it really matter? Didn't we just promise each other that we'd leave well alone? Come on. We've caused enough of a spectacle already.'

Charlotte cursed herself for the hasty promise. 'Snake,' she hissed at him. 'Just get George's cameras on the plane would you,' she snapped.

She ignored Valentine's 'hello', whacked her cases through after George's and raced through the Passport Control area with George in hot pursuit. The only person missing now was Daniel. That really would complete the happy quartet.

After a long, tedious flight the plane finally made its descent to the island of St Martin. St Maarten, if you happened to hail from the Dutch side of the island. Two separate French and Dutch cultures had vied with each other for sovereignty, with neither becoming victorious. Instead a kind of status quo had been achieved by dividing the diminutive island in two. Half spoke Dutch and half spoke a kind of patois known as Papiamento.

As they shuffled through the corrugated steel barn grandly entitled the Arrivals Hall Charlotte studied the posters. Dutch and French hospitality competed for the tourist money gushing on to the island. To make matters worse, the centre of the island was flooded by a huge lake, depleting the pocket-sized land mass even more.

They were directed through the airport to another departure lounge. Charlotte could see, through the dusty, sun-blistered windows, a very small plane waiting by the runway. The hostess was counting heads and explaining as best she could that unfortunately two trips would have to be made as the plane could only seat twelve people. If the first twelve would volunteer they could start and minimize the delays for everyone. In typical British fashion everyone hung back, desperately afraid of appearing pushy. George, she noticed with satisfaction, was not having any of it and was already at the door. 'Come on, Charlotte,' he called.

A quarter of an hour later the small Islander aircraft took off, its wings shaking unsteadily. Charlotte watched the island grow smaller below. The perfect pale aquamarine sea and the stretches of white deserted sands were breathtaking. All thoughts of William and Valentine were pushed to the back of her mind and she surrendered to a delicious, let out of school feeling as the plane began its quick descent to the tiny, eel-shaped island of Anguilla.

They walked across the scanty tarmac to a tin hut, grandly entitled Wallblake Airport, a very temporary looking erection with flaps of corrugated panels falling off its roof. Two West Indian officials smiled at them from underneath incongruous peaked caps.

The first real heat was beginning to touch Charlotte. The wind blew hot as a winter fan. A haze bathed the countryside. Everything was still, seemingly held in suspension, a coach waited on the other side of the rickety airport hut. It looked almost surreal against the backdrop of corn-yellow dryness with its sleek chrome lines and the proud exclamation 'Lux Hotels – No Better in the World.' Charlotte and George made their way towards the rear, ducking down into their seats. Charlotte was next to the window but George craned over her to get a view himself. Just coming along the track to the side of them was a small boy with a stick, at least twenty goats trotting and cantering before him. Their colours, all varying shades of beige, forced George back out of the coach, camera poised, soon clicking away madly as their little heels kicked up clouds of dust. Beyond them was an enormous bougainvillaea, its lushly purple flowers splashing colour into the picture.

George returned, blowing the dust from his camera. His shoes, too, were covered with fine sand. 'Looks like water's a bit of a problem,' he remarked. 'I'd better stick to the whisky.'

Charlotte was grateful when the coach started to move. The air-conditioning felt blissful and she settled back to watch the countryside. There didn't appear to be any road signs as such, what would be the point if everyone knew precisely where they were? Soon, though, she noticed the hotel had seen fit to broadcast its whereabouts on an enormous hoarding, completely out of touch with its surroundings. She made a mental note for future copy.

They passed no towns or anywhere which could even be classed as a 'village', just solitary bungalows, set back from the road, red-tiled roofs over yellow or pink-washed render. Small children waved to the coach. The impression was one of extraordinary welcome and friendliness, indicative of the fact that the natives were fairly new to tourism and hadn't yet suffered the bitter experiences of some of their neighbouring islands.

A few minutes later the coach pulled into the hotel drive. Charlotte was immediately reminded of a part of the Algarve. Amid all the parched landscape there were perfectly manicured English-style lawns, lush from the water sprinklers running throughout the day. The flower-beds were crammed full of splendid colour. It all looked beautiful, but as George had suggested earlier, it somehow just didn't seem quite right in a country where water was almost certainly at a premium. She had no doubt that the hotel would pay dearly for the privilege, but even so . . .

Turning a dog-leg bend in the drive she caught her first glimpse of the hotel: modelled on an eighteenth-century colonial mansion with white steps sweeping up to the magnificent portico flanked by two enormous pillars. The entire building reflected the sun off its brilliant white walls. Many windows showed black in contrast. To the side of the drive she could see at least four tennis courts already in use. Hot work in this heat, she thought admiringly.

'Must be bloody mad . . .' George had followed her gaze and grunted, unimpressed.

'Come on, George. I thought you could give me a game later.'

'I haven't played since I was at school, but I'll have a go.'

Charlotte cringed. The thought of big George lumbering around the tennis court filled her with little enthusiasm to follow through her invitation. 'We'll see,' she said.

While they drank refreshing fruit punch in the cool marble foyer, William dealt with the formalities of signing in and assigning rooms. Charlotte wondered just how many floors he could manage to put between them. It was with much delight that she discovered the extent of her ex-husband's guilt. He had seen fit to put her in one of the luxurious suites. She had her own sitting room, fully air-conditioned, and a balcony with sweeping views across the hotel's rolling lawns and beyond to the sea. There were several hours before seven thirty, when they were due to meet downstairs. She had a quick shower and fell into bed, where she lay listening to the ceaseless buzz of the crickets and the soothing drone of the outboard engines drifting across the bay. And soon she slept.

*

Daniel wiped the drips from his forehead with his Lacoste sweatband. He positioned himself ready, then he tossed the ball high. His serve sent it whistling straight down the line and veering slightly to the left, leaving Sam helpless at the far side of the net.

'Cool ace, Daniel! But that still makes it three-five, second set.'

They both walked towards the net, ready to change ends.

'God knows how you can play in this heat.' He took a slug of cool mineral water from the bottle on the bench. 'Phew. I must have sweated off a stone in the last hour, and you look so bloody fresh.'

'I'm used to it. We get sun in LA. All you get is rain, isn't it? Come on, this should be the last game. Brace yourself, Daniel.'

She sent over a beautifully sliced serve and it spun out sideways, away from him. He didn't have the energy to run after it. He walked slowly back to the baseline. The next serve came over and he sent it flying back, low over the net, but she returned it equally hard. She was at the net waiting for his return and he ran towards it, but it bounced high and caught him on the arm.

She laughed over at him: 'Thirty-love.'

'Just giving you a chance to warm up.'

Then she served a double fault. 'Thirty-fifteen, love,' he said, with relish.

'Just wait.' The ball whistled over the net, and his racquet made contact, but the ball died on it, causing him to wince as his arm absorbed the shock. 'Have you been taking some of those drugs?'

'No. Just coaching. Forty-fifteen.'

He ran in to meet the ball which she had sent deceptively short of the service line, but slipped ungracefully and landed flat on his backside. 'Oh dear, Daniel. Looks like that's game, set and match.'

He shook his head in disgust. 'Bloody inferior courts. That wasn't fair, Sam.'

'Oh yes it was, and you know it.'

She picked up the towel hanging over the end of the net and rubbed her face dry. Daniel's cotton shirt was sticking to his body as if someone had thrown a bucket of water over him, but Sam showed no effects from the heat other than a slight pinkish tinge to her cheeks. She put out her hand and shook his. 'I really enjoyed that, Dan, thanks. Let's play again tomorrow.'

'I may not make tomorrow. You forget I'm quite a bit older than you.' He looked at his watch. 'Listen, I've got to go and change now. I'm meeting William in the bar at six. You can join us if you like.'

'No way. You two guys haven't seen each other for what, three months now?'

'Five actually.'

'He's your partner in London and you haven't seen him for five months, and you ask me to join you for a drink. No thanks, Dan. I think you two must have quite a bit to talk about. I'll have a shower and a rest and see you at dinner.' She slapped him manfully on the back. 'Hope it goes well. Remember there's always an office for you Stateside.'

'Thanks.'

He watched her tall, slim figure skip off the tennis court, admiring her grace. Fate really did seem to be throwing them together. Bob had offered them this little jaunt partly as a 'thank you' for what they had achieved for Lester's during the trip; and partly because Lux Hotels would be impressed to see that the agency had fielded its celebrities for their launch. Lester's had just started a campaign for the chain of fifty hotels, and the Royal Anguilla was the newest, and the best, of the lot. They were really going to town. A total of five hundred guests had been flown in from the States and Europe – journalists, corporation executives, travel agents – to sample the delights of this five-star palace of a hotel for four days, in a programme crammed with briefings and festivities.

It had been Sam who had talked Daniel into coming. At first he'd been reluctant – he knew he was putting off too long returning to London – but in the end he had decided to come mainly as a sort of farewell to Sam. And, he couldn't help but think, he might even fall in love with her after all.

He watched her disappear across the terrace and then collected his racquet and balls. Could he justify taking her to bed one more time? He knew that was what she wanted, but he certainly didn't want to repeat his previous performance. It must be the ultimate insult to be called by another woman's name when you've just made love. It still made his stomach turn to think about it. In the time since they'd been back he had tried once more to push Charlotte to the back of his mind. But seeing the article in *Campaign* hadn't helped. Sooner or later she'd have to be exorcised for good, but he didn't know whether his conscience could stretch to trying Sam out again.

By the time he'd showered and changed it was 5.45 p.m. He walked down the stairs to the bar and ordered a well-spiked Bloody Mary. He was just getting used to the agonizingly hot liquor when he heard his name. 'Daniel. Hello!'

He turned and was somehow surprised to notice how pale William seemed. Maybe it was because he was so used to seeing bronzed faces around him these days, but still, he looked anaemic and sickly. His short blond hair was, as usual, styled in a no-nonsense schoolboy cut, and even in the heat of the Caribbean he wore a suit – not a dark pin-stripe of course, but a cream linen outfit, with a pastel blue shirt and beige tie. Daniel had donned a pair of white jeans and a navy polo shirt but even in that he was feeling the heat badly.

'What will you have, William?'

'Gin and tonic please, Daniel, if I may.'

Daniel ordered the drink, wishing he did not still feel that same degree of dislike for William. William's conduct at the Cornwallis de Sallis party was a matter that had not been resolved between them. Daniel had fled the country before they had had time to discuss it. He very rarely found himself at a loss for words, but now small talk evaded him.

William was the first to break the silence. 'So . . . Daniel . . .' He paused. 'You look really well. Must have been a damn good trip. I read all about it in the papers of course, and Sarah kept me up to date on your phone calls.' He tailed off and took another sip of his gin.

'Yes. It was. And how's London? I shall be glad to get back to my desk – if I still have a desk that is,' he laughed.

'Oh yes. No need to worry about that.' There was another awkward silence.

'So, you'd better tell me what's been going on.'

'Nothing major really. We've put on three accounts on the PR side. I think the advertising side has been static since you left. You've been kept informed of all developments I think.'

'Yes, yes. I always knew if I was really needed I would have been called back. Luckily I wasn't. I'd have been hard pushed to fit in a trip to London with our hectic schedule. Tom did OK, didn't he?'

'I don't suppose you'd have left him in control if you weren't confident in him.'

Daniel shook his head. 'That's why I made him MD.' Then he laughed wryly. 'Still, I don't expect he was aware he'd be dumped in the deep end quite so quickly. I'm glad he's had a chance to prove himself. And as for me, well, I like my role as chairman. It was high time for me to step backwards a bit. I've spent too long wiping clients' noses for them. But how's the PR side coming along?'

'It's very profitable – at the moment. We've put on another £250,000 worth of business since the merger, and I've hired some more staff.'

The bar was beginning to fill up around them, the atmosphere rowdy and happy. William drained his glass. 'So when are you coming back, Daniel?'

'Two weeks. Unless anything unforeseen comes up. I'm going to fly straight back as soon as this thing here folds up. Not that I'm exactly looking forward to my return,' he added quietly.

'No?'

'It's been a real pleasure to be away from that shithole of a city and all the crap around it.' Finally he couldn't stand the farce any longer. 'How's Valentine, William?'

William flinched slightly as if stung. His chin pushed forward and he touched his tie awkwardly. 'I think she's OK. Not that I've seen much of her. I'll probably see more of her here than I have since you left.'

'What?'

'Didn't you know? Some magazine's brought her along as a model.'

'Oh Jesus Christ!' Dan exclaimed. 'That's all I bloody need. Four days of Valentine. So, do I take it that your little affair is now off – not that it's any of my business of course.'

'It was off from the time we were . . . how shall I put it . . . er . . . discovered.'

'Hmph.' Daniel shrugged. 'You were a fool, William.'

'Yes, I know. Anyway, I'm having to live with the consequences now. Charlotte's gone and I miss her. It was really quite a shock finding she was coming on the trip . . .'

Daniel choked on the last dregs of his Bloody Mary. 'What did you just say?'

'I said it was a shock finding out that Charlotte was coming on this trip.'

It was lucky for Daniel that his tanned face hid the fact

284

that he blanched. His grip tightened on his glass, but his face remained impassive. His mind raced back. Back to the last time he had seen her. Their row over Ferguson. He wondered if she were still carrying on with him. Well, good luck to her if she was. Fortunately it was none of his business.

William was still talking. '. . . strange that we'll be getting the Absolute through while we're actually away together, isn't it?'

Daniel dragged himself back to the present. 'What?'

'Our Decree Absolute comes through in a couple of days. While we're here. It's normally honeymoons that are celebrated in the Caribbean, not divorces.' He laughed weakly.

Daniel did not respond. He looked through William as if he no longer existed. All that was now on his mind was how the hell he could stay out of William's ex-wife's way for the next seventy-two hours.

Chapter Twenty

Charlotte woke to darkness. She stretched and slowly let consciousness seep over her. Then, fully awake, she opened her eyes and wondered about Claudia's wardrobe. She was beginning to wish that she hadn't allowed Claudia to take over the decisions. Charlotte's idea of a sexy dress was one which concealed and hinted subtly at the delights under it. Claudia, on the other hand, just let it 'all hang out'.

It wasn't as though she was particularly looking forward to the evening ahead. It was a sort of obligatory introduction from their hosts. All the guests had been summoned to attend a drinks reception and dinner at which they would be given information about the hotel, and the facilities in the surrounding areas. Charlotte could predict the format of the evening. Half an hour to get lubricated and generous of feeling, followed by a lecture on the wonderfulness of Lux Hotels, the beauty of the island . . . yawn . . . and then a dinner of local specialities to get to know one's fellow freeloaders. Just so long as they weren't expected to wear name badges, something Charlotte considered the ultimate indignity.

Getting up from her bed, she opened the door of the floor-to-ceiling wardrobe and riffled through the clothes she had hung up earlier. Her fingers fell upon a beautifully beaded and sequinned sheath of a gown, the weight of which had surely given the baggage handlers a hell of a time. Behind that was a black jersey mini dress, ruched down one side so that the fabric would stretch into soft pleats horizontally across her body, hugging the contours of her breasts and thighs. It had a high polo neck and arm holes which were scooped out so severely they almost met the rise of the neck roll.

Then she found a beautiful wisp of a skirt, in a creamy material like muslin. She pulled it off its hanger and held it in front of her. It almost reached her ankles. Beautifully soft and feminine, it reminded her of a ballerina's petticoat. The fabric was so fine and transparent that it was in fact in two layers, but the hems were of staggered lengths. It would do. She reached further into the wardrobe and found a biscuit-coloured tailored linen jacket which was long enough to wear over the skirt and conceal her knickerline.

By the time she was ready it was 7.30. She heard a knock at the door and opened it to find George standing there looking magnificent, having swapped his funereal black for tropical cream. She took a step back and laughed delightedly. 'My God, George. What will they think? Look at the pair of us – Fred Astaire and Ginger Rogers. Cool in cream, eh?'

'You look great!'

'Why thank you,' she grinned happily. 'You don't think it's a little risqué?' She bent forward and looked down at her legs. They were clearly visible through the diaphanous skirt. The single-breasted jacket was held in place by two buttons and just managed to hide the top of her bra. Round her neck hung a large coral and mother of pearl necklace which flattered her skin tones and picked up the soft rust of her suede slippers.

'Certainly not. Unless you decide to take your jacket off.'

'Well, the minute I do, just remind me not to, would you?'

'I'll try. Come on, otherwise we'll miss all the fun.'

Charlotte trotted along behind George whose mammoth strides made it difficult for her to keep up. Whenever she looked at him she was reminded of a Hollywood Moses. His piercing honest blue eyes and flowing blond curls could have come straight out of Cecil B. de Mille.

When they stepped out of the lift on the lower ground terrace they saw hundreds of people already standing around the swimming pool, perching at the little tables, or strolling through the floodlit gardens. Charlotte inhaled deeply on the deliciously scented, heady evening air. Magically, a waiter appeared at her elbow and offered what seemed like fruit cocktail. She looked at it suspiciously. 'What's in it, please?'

The waiter grinned. 'It's very good for you. Lots of fruit juices – mango, passion fruit, orange, pineapple . . . crushed ice.'

'Is that all? Just a fruit punch?'

'And the rum of course!'

'Ah . . . a rum punch. Silly me.' She giggled happily and took one of the large, sugar-frosted glasses and then raised it in George's direction.

'Here's to us having a good time,' said George, raising his glass too.

'Mmmm. That's really something.' Charlotte took another large gulp of the deceptively harmless-tasting drink.

'Go easy on these.' George's eyes twinkled. 'They've caught me out before. You drink them down like orange squash and then wonder where your legs have gone. And as for the hangover . . . Uggh!'

She followed him over to the poolside, her arm companionably through his. The smooth water glowed an incandescent aquamarine, generated by the underwater floodlights. It looked wonderfully inviting.

The sky had changed from a perfect sapphire blue to a deep shade of violet. Barbecue flares complemented the spotlights secreted around the flower beds, and the floodlights on the terrace above. If one listened carefully, above the hum of conversation, the buzz of the crickets could be heard, the lapping of the waves and

288

the far-away calling of the sea herons on their evening patrol.

Charlotte sighed. 'Oh George, can you imagine just what it would be like without all these people around. Wouldn't it just be heavenly. You know, if I ever had to go through it all again, marriage that is, I'd make damn sure I found somewhere like this to spend my honeymoon.'

'Yes. Would be nice, wouldn't it. Lesley and me went to some unpronounceable Polynesian island.'

'Well, that must have been fairly romantic. Even more so than here I bet.'

'Don't you believe it. If you think two weeks in a mud hut with no water or electricity is romantic you need your head testing. And Lesley with morning sickness into the bargain.'

'Oh dear. I suppose it must have been a bit wearing then.'

'You can say that again. I got the squits and she got prickly heat and dehydration. We spent more time at the local clinic than on the beach. Mind you, I lost a lot of weight which I needed to do. Of course Les went from eight and a half stone to seven and three quarters so she looked like an advert for Bonio. But we got a tan. You've got to look on the bright side, haven't you?'

Charlotte was laughing in spite of the horrific tale. 'Sounds like a complete nightmare.'

'It was. And the ironic thing was that when I came back I sold some shots to a picture library and they were used for a promotion on how marvellous the place was. I expect we were just unlucky. Always seems to happen whenever we go away together. Separately we've had some great times. You know, all these exotic locations we get sent to. She's been all round the world modelling, and I've been all round snapping pictures. But the minute we get on a plane together some disaster happens. Remember that heatwave in Greece when temperatures reached 130? Well, we were there. Christmas before last we thought we'd go skiing. There was no bloody snow that year. Once we decided to spend a long weekend on the Isle of Wight. Even then they stopped the ferries because of gales.

'It's not funny, Charlotte,' he said, unsuccessfully trying to stop Charlotte's helpless laughter. 'I tell you, together we're jinxed. That's partly why Les let me come on this trip without too much fuss. She knows we'd never survive it together. They'd have a hurricane or tidal wave or something.'

'Just so long as it's not you personally. God knows what might happen here otherwise.'

George took another slug of his rum punch. 'No sweat. I tell you, solo we're OK.'

Charlotte looked around the enormous crowd now spilling off the terrace on to the surrounding lawns. Then something caught her eye. There was something remarkably familiar about that back. Something about the dark curls and wide shoulders that inexplicably caught at her throat and started her pulse racing. Suddenly every nerve in her body was held taut. She stood transfixed, willing him to move, so that she could confirm her fears. It couldn't be. He turned so she got his face in full profile. She felt her heart stop. There was no mistake. Not more than fifteen yards from her was Daniel Cornwallis.

Her thoughts spun back to the last time she had seen him. The angry scene in Richmond, when he had come to warn her about Giles. It was as if all the months in between had passed as nothing. She remembered the feelings of hurt and disappointment as clearly as if it had been this very day. He had come to her house and accused her of being a cheap whore.

Almost six months had passed since that day. Six months during which time she had founded a magazine. She had not allowed herself to think about him

290

during that time, and it had been a hard task. He had a habit of creeping into her consciousness when she least wanted him to. Those times when she lay in bed, late at night, exhausted from her labours at *Amber*, when she realized that even the magazine could not fulfil all her needs. When she curled up in bed and reached out to an empty pillow, her body crying out for him.

In the few seconds she watched him she saw now how good he looked. He was deeply bronzed, and appeared smooth and relaxed. She saw he had company, and felt an almost irrational envy. He was deep in conversation with a gorgeous blonde. She was laughing unselfconsciously, then, in a movement suggestive of great intimacy, she reached up and brushed a fleck from his shoulder.

As if from a great distance Charlotte heard George's voice. She dragged her attention back to him. 'Sorry . . .' she said vaguely.

'I said, are you all right? You've gone as white as a sheet. Have you seen a ghost?'

'I suppose in a way I have.'

He looked at her strangely; questioningly.

'I've just seen someone I didn't expect . . . someone I'd rather wasn't here . . .'

'Oh dear,' George said. 'Who?'

In spite of her shock, Charlotte found herself laughing at him. Most people would have retreated into an embarrassed silence at her obviously private turmoil. George was refreshing in his almost childlike lack of sophistication.

She stared at her glass for a moment, deciding whether to burden him with her secret. 'Just an old flame.'

'Oh go on. Tell me.'

'No, George, I won't. It's best not to know. There was never anything in it. And I'd feel embarrassed all the time we're here. Please . . .' she pleaded.

George shrugged good-naturedly. 'I'll find out anyway. Odds on bet by the end of dinner I'll tell you which one it is.'

Charlotte raised her brows and pouted at him, but she did not answer. Inside she was trying to work out just why Daniel was out here in the Caribbean when she had believed he was gadding round the world on some mega-business deal. And just what was his reaction going to be when he saw her, as he surely would given that they presumably had to spend the next three days in each other's company. Along with five hundred or so others, of course. But even in that throng she'd find it difficult to avoid him all the time.

Up until now she had not allowed herself to wonder just what his feelings had been, or were now, towards her. She had not dared to nurse even a faint hope that he might sometimes think of her. And now, as she gazed across the short space between them, and watched him laugh and talk with the leggy blonde girl, she could see why she had not asked herself. The reason screamed back at her as clearly as if he himself was shouting the words. He had a new lover. Charlotte had been a small misalliance on a rainy night. He had forgotten her as easily as if she were an umbrella on a crowded train. True to his reputation he was a woman-eater. 'Love 'em and leave 'em.' Except in her case whatever small vestige of conscience lay buried in the man had surfaced in time to stop their adultery. Her cheeks coloured at the unbidden thought: she wished with all her heart that he had not held back.

Just then his companion raised her head and looked over in Charlotte's direction. For a split second, their eyes met. Then she turned and spoke to Daniel. Daniel immediately turned and looked over in Charlotte's direction.

Very slowly, he smiled that same lazy, half-mocking grin and waved in recognition. She could read no other message other than acknowledgement of a casual acquaintance.

'I take it back,' George whispered to her. 'I don't have to wait until after dinner. Charlotte, if you're going to survive this you'll have to do better than that. You've got Daniel Cornwallis plastered all over your lovely little face.'

'Shit!' she snapped, the tension broken. 'What the hell am I going to do, George?'

'A lot better than that. I don't know what passed between the two of you but you'll have to hide your heart or he'll just laugh at you. I didn't know tough editors could ever look that vulnerable.' His voice had softened and his expression oozed sympathy.

'Well, now you know. Don't worry. It's just the shock of seeing him. I can't understand what he's doing here.'

'Come on, Charlotte. The rum must have addled your brain. Isn't he in partnership with William?'

She nodded, but not understanding his drift.

'And Lux Hotels is William's client?'

'Jesus you're right. I suppose I just thought of it as being a London connection, not thinking it's probably part of the States' set-up as well. But I wonder who she is?'

'Charlotte, for someone who's supposed to be a shit-hot hack you're not doing very well. Too long in retirement I guess.'

'What the hell does that mean?'

'That is Sam Storey. Vice-President of Lester's in the States. You don't get to be an international fashion and advertising photographer without knowing which side of your bread is buttered. And that lady pays for quite a lot of my butter when I venture Stateside. Nice-looking and very clever. No wonder Cornwallis is sniffing around . . . Oops, sorry, Charlie. That wasn't very tactful.'

'Huh,' she said bravely. 'It doesn't matter to me a bit

what he's up to. I'm certainly not jealous if that's what you think . . .'

'Right,' George said, obviously unconvinced. 'Thing is, Charlotte . . . Looks like we're being called in to dinner.' All the guests were beginning to shuffle through the vast French windows.

'Umm, let's just wait a while, shall we, till the general rush has died down.'

'Until Daniel Cornwallis and friend have gone in you mean?'

'Subtle aren't you, George? I mean you let a person off lightly, don't you?'

'Never!' he grinned.

'Remind me never to bring you away on location again, OK?'

'Do you want to go into dinner on your own?'

'No, I do not. This is my hour of need.'

'Then you'd better be nice to me.'

They waited for a few moments, Charlotte in tense silence, and George in gentle amusement, while the main body of people surged into the hotel building. Finally, when they were almost the last left they stood up and slowly followed everyone into the elegantly mirrored and gilded dining room. Charlotte saw with relief that there wasn't a seating plan. One of the things which had most worried her in the garden was that, knowing her luck, she would end up at the same table as Daniel. She followed George through the sea of tables until they found some empty seats. Charlotte's appetite, not surprisingly, seemed to have been left somewhere between the swimming pool and the rum punch, and she concentrated on making inane small talk about consumer competitions with a couple of American travel journalists, and trying to force down the slightly warm melon, tastefully cut and fanned on the plate before her.

She had made an iron resolve not to look around the dining room for Daniel. She did not intend to give herself away so easily a second time, and would assume the same nonchalance he had. The task would have been easier if the conversation had been a little more involved than the prices of air fares.

Charlotte could tell that George was trying just as hard as she was to stifle yawns, but when coffee finally came, and she was locked in deep conversation about the latest in-flight movie headphones, she was horrified to notice George's head nodding forward at a dangerous angle, his long hair about to fall into the coffee. She was caught between rudely interrupting her American friend or letting George suffer a graceless accident.

She could bear it no longer and reached across the table, sending the wine bottle flying over, tipping the red liquid across the white tablecloth and into the chequered lap of the American 'callmeBob'. George woke with a start at Bob's exclamation.

Charlotte said, 'Oh no . . .' pure mortification in her voice.

Then George, unbelievably, started to laugh. 'I say, Charlotte, excellent targeting I call that. That means you probably won't be able to wear that suit again, doesn't it, Bob?' he said cheerfully.

Charlotte glowered at him, fighting the laughter lurking under her abject apologies. 'You must let me pay for the cleaning,' she said.

'Too damn right I will,' he said, coldly.

'I'm so sorry,' she kept saying. She gave the man her suite number. 'Here, charge it to this,' she said.

George stood up. 'I think it's time to retire, Charlotte, don't you?' he said pointedly.

'Yes, yes. Well, sorry again,' she said, 'and goodbye.' They almost sprinted from the room. 'You do realize we're going to miss all the speakers, and the talks about the place. George, how could you, that was horribly rude.'

'Oh come on, Charlotte, they were so bloody boring . . .'

295

'I know, you fell asleep. I was actually trying to rescue you from a coffee shampoo – that's when I spilt the wine.'

'Thanks,' he grinned. 'Anyway, it livened things up a bit, didn't it? And I meant what I said about the suit – God, it was awful!'

'Wasn't it?' she agreed. Then she started to laugh. They both laughed. And they laughed until the tears streamed down their cheeks. 'You're wicked,' she said, through strangled sobs.

'I know. Let's have a brandy to celebrate, shall we?'

They were well into their second brandy in the bar with no sign of the other guests being released from their lectures when Charlotte leaned forward conspiratorially in her seat. 'Come on then, George. What am I to do?'

'Well that mostly depends on what you want, doesn't it? I mean if you hate the guy then just forget he's here. Have a good time. I'll take some great pictures and you can think about some great copy. Lie in the sun, get a good tan, eat a lot, drink even more and go home brown and fat.'

'Well, I suppose that's what I should do, isn't it? Just ignore him. Forget he's here altogether.'

'Uh huh. That's right. He's only some tin-pot advertising tycoon who happens to earn hundreds of thousands of pounds a year, has one of the best reputations for smooth operating in town, is devastatingly handsome, kind to old ladies, etcetera etcetera . . . Who needs him?'

'Ha ha, very funny.' Charlotte chewed on her fingernail, frowning thoughtfully.

'Don't bite your nails, Charlie,' he warned. 'Of course the other alternative is that you find out exactly what his relationship is with Miss Storey and, depending on what the answer is, let him know you're still interested and available.'

'You must be off your head. I most certainly will not go chasing after him, George. After all, I do have some pride.'

'OK, OK. Sounds like option three then.'

'And what might that be?'

'Easy. Make him jealous. If he wants you he'll come and get you. Why don't you let him think we're together.'

'What do you mean?'

'You know, together. Not that we will of course. Les would castrate me if she ever thought I'd done anything naughty like that. And I'm not the type. Much too lazy. I always preferred home cooking.'

'So, what is it you're suggesting exactly?'

'Well, there's no harm in us pretending a bit, is there? We just seem a little close. Draw him out, eh? What do you think?'

'Dunno,' she said, dejectedly. 'I'll sleep on it. I'll let you know tomorrow. I think I'll go to bed before they all come back.'

'Running away, huh?'

'Yes, if you like. That's exactly what I'm doing. Running away. 'Night, St George.'

Charlotte spent a fitful night, tossing and turning, George's suggestion spinning round her head. By six o'clock she felt as though she had barely slept at all, mulling over how she felt, how he felt, what she should do, what he would do. She thought she would go mad if she stayed in bed any longer.

She got up and hunted through the drawers for a swimsuit. She quickly slipped into it, and then pulled out a rather creased matching sarong. She opened the shutters and breathed in the perfumed air. Even at this hour of the morning the balcony was warm to her bare toes. She could see the pool from her balcony, as still as a millpond, irresistible virgin water. She wanted to be the first to break it.

297

Barefoot, she ran silently down the stairs which opened on to the impressive, grey marble foyer. Her feet skidded over the smooth surface, icy to her soles, then out on to the terrace. It was still deserted but she could not believe what she saw. Nearly all of the wheelbarrow-style sun loungers had towels draped over them, as if their owners had gone for a quick dip before returning to reclaim the bed. But there was no one around at all. And as far as her eye could see the beach was deserted.

She shook her head and laughed to herself, wondering whether Lux Hotels had shipped over guests from Germany, and if these same guests had either snuck out at 5 a.m. to claim the beds or, even worse, draped their towel-stakes before retiring to bed the previous night. Feeling angry at their childish possessiveness, and a little mischievous, she collected up all the towels and rearranged every one of them on a different bed, wondering what angry scenes might ensue later in the morning over who had bagged which one. She did not realize she was being watched from above.

Finally satisfied that she would cause just the right degree of chaos she dived into the pool, and then shivered to the surface, shocked by the freezing water. She swam three quick lengths, then rested for a moment, enjoying the feel of the water lapping around her shoulders. Then she did a duck dive down and swam as far as she could below the surface until she felt her lungs were about to burst. She came up, gulping down air, panting loudly. She focused her eyes and was pleased to note she was only two or three yards from the end. Then she noticed a pair of strong masculine legs walking towards the pool. She rubbed her eyes.

Damn. Just as she was really enjoying her solitude. She turned and swam towards the opposite end of the pool away from the intruder. Then she turned and swam back, just as he dived in. He came up level with her about mid-centre. Charlotte choked on a great wash of pool water, fighting for breath. Dan got hold of her and helped her to the poolside where she clung, slowly regaining her breath. He watched her, his amusement clear on his features.

'It would be you! Just what the hell are you doing here, Daniel?' she said, between spluttered gasps.

'Same as you, Charlotte, only more successfully, by the look of it.'

She looked at him, not understanding.

'Swimming, aren't we?' he said, innocently.

'You know damn well that's not what I meant,' she hissed, her eyes blazing. 'What are you doing here with your, your . . . floozie?'

He looked at her in surprise then a look of dismay crossed his brow. Charlotte could have bitten off her tongue. All her resolve of the previous night to play it cool had just gone out of the window. She was behaving like a jealous fishwife. How was it she just couldn't seem to talk to this man without it becoming a slanging match between them?

'Anyway, it seems you're not exactly idle as far as the opposite sex is concerned are you, my dear Charlotte? First Giles, and now this blond Adonis. You're certainly getting a reputation as a fast worker. And all before your divorce is final.'

God, she wanted to hit him. The teasing, sardonic, insinuating bastard. 'I shall treat that remark with the contempt it deserves. George is my photographer.'

'That's novel,' he said.

'Oh shut up.'

His sarcastic grin widened. 'You know, for someone who's editor of one of Britain's leading new magazines I'd have thought your vocabulary might stretch a bit further than "shut up".'

Charlotte's mouth dropped open. Why, the self-righteous, slanderous little creep . . . and she had had

299

the foolishness to remember him even the remotest bit fondly. How she could ever have fooled herself that this . . . this . . . completely arrogant excuse for a man could have been in the least bit attractive?

She strode to the edge of the pool and looked down on him. Summoning all the haughtiness she possessed, she stood, hands on hips. Her eyes blazed at him like a furious she-cat's. 'Just for the record I did not sleep with Giles Ferguson.' She spat out the words through tight-lipped anger. 'And even if I had it's none of your God-damned business. Neither am I having an affair with my photographer. Unlike you, Mr Cornwallis, I am not in the habit of sleeping with any bit of flesh that happens to come my way. My reputation' – she stressed the words heavily – 'is still intact. But as for yours . . . Well, it never did amount to much, now did it? After all, your morals were so low that you would have taken advantage of your own partner's wife.'

He shrugged. 'I seem to remember you were quite willing . . .'

'Vulnerable! You took advantage of me when I was extremely vulnerable. There's just one thing I'd like you to do for me now.'

'Really? And what might that be?'

'Stay away from me!'

She spun on her heel and almost ran back into the hotel, her throat choking with sobs.

Daniel lifted himself out of the pool. Slowly he shook his head. Him and his big mouth. In the deep, dark silence of the night he'd lain awake thinking about her, trying to extinguish the searing pain he'd felt seeing her with that gangly blond hippy. All through dinner he'd surreptitiously watched them. And he'd seen them leave before the others, giggling to themselves as they disappeared. Of course he knew what they were up to. It was written all over them.

300

Just what he had been trying to achieve this morning, when he had watched her head for the pool, he did not quite know. But he knew he had to try and talk to her. Alone. It just didn't make sense but he wanted her more than anything he had ever wanted in his entire life, and somehow he had to make her realize.

Yet, once again, everything had gone wrong. As soon as he opened his mouth the words that came tumbling out were the very opposite of how he felt. Just why he couldn't grab her in his arms and show her. Instead he had seemingly jumped to the wrong conclusion again. First with Giles, and now with this . . . this photographer person. But hadn't she done just the same thing? Sam – his floozie? It was utter nonsense. To Charlotte though it must look like that.

They were behaving like a couple of idiot teenagers, fraught by wrong assumptions and misunderstandings. The closer he tried to get to her the further apart they became. He sighed heavily and wrapped his towelling robe around him. So she wanted him to stay away from her. Trouble was, all his life he had never been able to resist a challenge, and this was proving to be one of the hardest. He also had the rather sick feeling that he was beginning to lose. And losing was something he never had time for. He allowed himself a small smile. She was certainly giving him a good run for his money.

Chapter Twenty-one

Some two hours later, after a delicious al fresco breakfast, George and Charlotte went out to the small mini moke they had commandeered for their planned private excursion around the island. It was with some satisfaction that they watched the hordes climb aboard the hotel coach, laden down with cameras and location equipment. Charlotte caught a flash of brilliant red hair. 'There goes Valentine, on the charabanc, George. Wish you were there?'

'Not on your life. You can imagine what she'll be like after an hour working in this heat. She's professional . . . but she likes to be comfortable. You can bet your life she won't like sweating! It was an inspired idea of yours, Charlie, to hire this thing. Now, who's going to drive?'

'I will,' she said decisively. 'Then you can take pictures and look at the scenery.' They climbed into the tiny vehicle. George's knees ended up somewhere beneath his chin, and his head scraped the canvas roof. 'You look really uncomfortable. Why don't you take the roof off?'

George looked at her and frowned thoughtfully. Then he carefully clambered out of the car and began unpopping the weathered piece of fabric.

It took Charlotte about two or three miles to master the idiosyncrasies of the clutch, but George didn't seem to mind too much. They were just relieved to be away from the mass of people and the over-zealous hospitality girls who thought their guests could only have a good time if every minute was orchestrated by Lux Hotels.

George unfolded the map and studied it. 'Seems there's only one road that goes right the way around the island, with a few lanes off it.'

'In that case I'll just keep in a straight line until you tell me to stop.'

Already the heat of the sun felt fierce against their chalk-coloured skin. At least it was cool driving – the warm, scented breeze caressed their hair and softly ruffled their loose T-shirts, leaving them pleasantly refreshed.

Charlotte squinted against the glare of the mid-morning haze. As she became more confident at the wheel, she started to take in the surrounding country-side. Every several hundred yards or so, set back from the road amid an arid landscape of thirsty palms, stood a house. Walls of dried clay were washed in soft pastel colours of dusky pinks, pale mint greens and faded mustard yellow. Sometimes there were slatted shutters of bright green, or purple or red, adding contrasts of vivid colour to the sienna countryside.

Sometimes George would nudge her and she would stop the car while he took shots of the cheerful, welcoming little houses whose crumbling verandahs echoed the timbered masterpieces of their grand colonial cousins. With childlike curiosity their inhabitants would pause for a few moments from their washing or conversation, grinning amiably in saluta-tion. Long-limbed children would race towards the newcomers, waving frantically, shouting, 'Hello . . . hello!', climbing on to the moke and riding for a few yards down the road when the car moved off again.

Charlotte and George found themselves under a barrage of questions. Where did they come from? Did they live in London? Had they met the Queen? Had they had tea with her? When Charlotte explained that no, they had not, confusion and disappointment spread over their wide-eyed expressions. For this small island of only some 7,000 inhabitants nurtured more patriotism for the motherland than did Britain herself. When neighbouring St Kitts and Nevis had declared their independence from the Crown in 1967, Anguilla had politely declined the opportunity to join them and seceded itself, avowing gently that they could never love St Kitts as much as they did Britain. The parents of these children would still remember the help that the Crown had given them upon the foundation of their constitution. The British had supported the Anguillans by sending a couple of frigates, a contingent of para-troopers and several London policemen in a show of solidarity: something the island would be slow to forget, the reminders of their sovereignty now relegated to a postage stamp and a day's holiday in recognition of the monarch's birthday.

But gratitude for this support made British visitors feel they had been personally responsible for providing it. The Anguillans seemed to want more than anything in the world to demonstrate their warmth of feeling towards anything British. Their brief experience of the influx of tourism had not yet hardened them. Crime was non-existent, save when an excess of rum and emotion drove someone to slaughter a relative, or inflamed a feud over the ownership of a stray goat. Petty pilfering was beyond their comprehension. But for how long, Charlotte thought cynically.

She was still torn between her desire to promote this small unspoilt island paradise and her wish to protect its quaint naivety from the poisoning onslaught of mass tourism. People would not be satisfied with merely a hotel stop. They would be clamouring to buy up building plots for their own holiday homes or time-share condos, while the initially grateful Anguillans would sweep up their new-found riches and head for Ruislip and their distant relatives, and the lure of afternoon tea at Buckingham Palace.

304

Within a few years the face of this charming enclave would change beyond all recognition. The population would diminish as the young would, for the first time in hundreds of years, have the means to travel, and the old industries of fishing and farming would disappear to make way for the more lucrative burden of tourism. It was a sad slippery slope; and one which Charlotte knew she herself could easily perpetuate. This was brought home to her when they turned down a lane with a home-made 'fish restaurant' sign planted into the bank, to find it opened out on to what must be one of the most beautiful beaches in the world.

The road petered out into a dusty clearing with a tumbledown hut. A pile of empty crates seemed to give the only clue that this indeed could be the restaurant. They looked at each other uncertainly and climbed out of the moke. A small gap in the slatted palm walls was the only thing akin to a doorway and Charlotte followed George's huge bulk inside.

It took their eyes a few seconds to adjust to the gloom, but then they could see that there were about fifteen tables, only one of which was occupied, and a bar. The room formed a rectangle, and two sides of the walls were open to the beach. The whole erection looked as if a strong wind could uproot it and deposit it unceremoniously in the sea beyond. Charlotte immediately chose one of the tables where they could see straight out on to the pink-white coral sand and watch the pale turquoise water chase foam over the washed-up conch shells.

The unassuming little restaurant did nothing to advertise the adeptness of its Parisian chef-owner. As they dipped into a delicious fish soup he told them he had emigrated to St Martin some few years previously and had eventually decided to settle on the virgin Anguilla. Now he was looking forward to the influx of tourists and had already allotted half of his beachside land for a coastal marine park.

Charlotte wondered if the four local fishermen feasting at the other table would give him their patronage when the menu included such things as burgers and chips. Yes, she supposed. They'd probably welcome it. It was a battle already won. The course was pre-ordained. And the arrival of Lux Hotels sent it forward at a galloping rate. All she could do now was enjoy lunch and savour this last outpost of Caribbean quaintness before it became a memory.

They drank a lot of wine. Charlotte gazed out across the waves towards a US warship anchored menacingly on the horizon; no doubt on 'training manoeuvres' in the peaceful waters well north of South America. An occasional pelican would hover for a few moments before swooping down into the water, to reappear a few seconds later, its sack of a beak drooping like a giant chin – a parody of Alice's Duchess – bobbing on the surface, before taking flight once more.

George was debating whether to take more pictures or to return to the hotel for a post-prandial nap. The soporific effect of the wine and the delicious food and the lulling of the waves decided them, and they headed back the way they had come to prepare for the suspicious-sounding 'Caribbean style' evening ahead of them.

Charlotte went to bed, but, instead of sleeping, which her body told her she could easily do any second, her mind insisted on going over and over her meeting with Daniel. All day long she had managed to throw thoughts of him aside and concentrate on the magnificent simplicity of their surroundings, yet now, in the peace and quiet of her own suite, she found she could no longer evade her emotions.

She was twenty-nine years old. She was a successful

editor, almost single again, and she could not stop herself from lusting after this dark-eyed man who only communicated with her through a series of well-spaced slanging matches. She must need her head examining. Hassle was one thing she did not want in her ordered life. She had had the courage to turn away from an unsatisfactory marriage and the lessons from that were clear enough. She was an independent, free spirit in control of her own destiny once more. Yet she only had to look at him and her guts felt like they had turned into warm, slippery oil. The memory of his body, glistening from his morning swim, made her senses cry out. She ached for him. But she could never let him know how she felt. She could just imagine him gloating with self-satisfied amusement at yet another conquest to chalk up. The only way she could possibly get through the next couple of days was to avoid any contact with him, and failing that, if she did happen to run into him, she would let him see that he mattered not at all to her.

Her thoughts turned to William and Valentine. Every time she saw the viperous Valentine she was reminded of that ghastly night. Valentine did not need to say anything, her triumph was there in her eyes. It said: 'I laid your husband!' Not that Charlotte cared any more what she had done. It was just Valentine's particular brand of smugness which rankled, yet another pain in her life that she wanted to put behind her. Like William . . . He who vacillated between sickening remorse and a kind of arrogant detachment, depending on what he was after at the time. At least Charlotte's anger towards him was beginning to subside a little. He was just a victim, as they all were, in their different ways, of a career philosophy that glamourized executive stress and glossy affairs. William had been sucked into the black hole of the media world and seduced into believing the long hours he worked and the recreation he sought spelled success. If he stopped and looked at himself he would realize that he was just a puppet in a self-serving industry; but to admit that would be for him to deny his whole *raison d'être*. He just didn't have the depth to do that. At least Daniel had the honesty to admit he liked enjoying himself.

William would continue to burn himself out and then, belatedly, at the age of fifty, wonder just what the hell he had done with his life. Charlotte guessed there would be plenty of other Valentines for William. At least now he could enjoy them without the complication of a demanding wife to satisfy as well.

She must have drifted off to sleep, for when she opened her eyes, it was to the sound of a steel band warming up. She slipped out of bed and went out on to the balcony. She smiled to herself. She could see the band were doing the native music justice. A lithe body was limboing down to a thin pole stretched between two jump-like posts with height-adjustable pegs. It was certainly going to be a traditional evening.

She pulled out a bandeau bra garment and a matching skirt with a pannier-like top that split in two arcs at the front, like an inverse tulip. She was pleased to note that her legs had lost some of their glaring whiteness, but all the same she rubbed on some tanning make-up. Then to finish off the outfit she pulled out a matching sash which she flicked under her hair and pulled into a large bow on top of her head. Yes, she decided, studying herself in the mirror, it was highly suitable for the evening's character.

As before, George knocked on the door to see if she was ready. She was just putting in her ears the large gold hoops which Claudia had told her were absolutely essential to the overall effect. George raised his eyebrows.

'Very nice, Charlotte. Does this mean you might be trying out some limbo later?'

308

'No. But thank you,' she said. 'I feel in the party mood.'

After a mouthwatering supper of melons and mangos, kiwis and passion fruit, ham and fresh pineapple, curries and salad, chocolate mousse and cheese, the entertainment commenced. A heavy drumbeat accompanied the entrance of the limbo dancer. He had oiled his beautiful, deep brown body and his muscles caught the light like a fine wood carving. The pole started off at an easy height. After each successful attempt the pole was ceremoniously lowered, until it lay approximately nine inches from the ground. Even the most inveterate talkers had now been silenced and were intently watching the artiste. The drum had slowed to a louder, more insistent thump, a single rhythm. The dancer moved with each beat, his legs splayed out sideways, his knees bending. He was rocking all the time, each movement compressing his body a little more. Eventually his knees were level with the bar, the sides of his ankles just about flat on the floor. He drew every ounce of drama by touching the bar very slightly, most probably purposefully. Then very, very slowly he eased himself under. Once through, he turned and kicked up the pole, catching it in his left hand, and the drums sped into their previous sophisticated voodoo rhythm. He gestured to his audience, inviting them to try their skill.

Charlotte turned back to George, not in the slightest bit interested in anyone making a complete fool of themselves, and she finished her cheese and coffee. Eventually the steel band started to play and the dancing commenced.

'Come on, George,' Charlotte said after a while. 'Wouldn't you like to dance?'

'Love to, darling heart,' he said, mock camp.

He turned out to be a brilliant dancer. Between the two of them they just about stole the floor. Charlotte

309

kicked off her shoes and was completely immersed in the heavy reggae music, twisting and swaying to the hypnotic sound. All eyes fixed on the sway of Charlotte's slender figure. The bandeau top, soon soaked with perspiration, moulded itself to her breasts so the outline of her nipples was clear to see. Daniel, from his seat near the bar, could hardly take his eyes off her. He felt eaten up with desire and jealousy.

They danced for a long time, until George's thin white voile shirt clung to him in dark wet patches and his hair stuck to his shoulders. 'Charlotte, I need a drink.'

She waited at the table and then looked over to the bar. George seemed deep in conversation with someone she didn't recognize. On sudden impulse she decided she wanted to feel the sand between her toes. She got up and followed the little path down through the lit shrubs to the sea shore. The sand felt cold and soft under her bare feet and she wiggled her toes around, feeling a more intense coldness in the damp substrata. The moonlight shone on the pale sand, and sent silver shimmers across the waves. The music drifted lightly across, dulled by the breaking water and the slight breeze. Charlotte sighed in contentment, drinking in the atmosphere of this paradise through all her senses. How precious it was to be given the experience of this beauty. She started to move to the distant music, rocking her hips backwards and forwards, sliding her toes through the sand. She closed her eyes and hummed the familiar melody.

'Charlotte! What the hell are you doing?'

Her eyes snapped open. For a moment she was speechless, disorientated, as if woken from sleep.

'You could be raped or something. What are you doing down here all by yourself, you foolish girl?' His voice was cold and accusing.

'Daniel. How dare you. What business is it of yours where I am? What danger am I possibly in?'

'Danger? Did you not see those men watching you dance? Don't tell me you weren't aware of their eyes, ready to eat you up just about. Why, any one of them could have followed you down here . . . and God knows what would have happened.'

She looked at him incredulously. 'You're not serious, Daniel. Oh I don't believe it.' She started to laugh. 'So I suppose I'm now safe, am I? Lucky that Daniel Cornwallis was the one to follow me to the beach. That's pretty rich, isn't it? When the closest I've ever been to rape in my life has been at your hands. The only man I've ever needed protection from was you . . . You're the most dangerous, arrogant, pigheaded excuse for a man I've ever had the misfortune to come across. Now if you'll excuse me I was actually enjoying my solitude.'

She turned and walked away. Eyes blazing with anger he looked after her. Perhaps on thinking about it he had overreacted, responding to the deep emotions within him. Damn the woman. Why could she affect him in this way? He kicked up the sand, turned on his heel, swore under his breath and marched straight back to the hotel.

The following day passed relatively quietly. They were free to amuse themselves. Charlotte and George continued their exploration of the island during the morning, then returned to the hotel for a buffet lunch beside the pool, shielded from the burning midday sun by huge yellow and white striped parasols. They lazed quietly and peacefully by the pool during the afternoon, hardly talking, just basking in the glorious warmth and occasionally slipping into the lukewarm pool for a semi-refreshing dip.

It was almost three days since Charlotte had spoken to the office. She reluctantly realized that she would have to contact them. She booked the call before her evening shower, and was already dressing when the

311

phone rang and Claudia's cheery voice came through.

'Hi. I told Laura to let me know as soon as you called. Hope you don't mind.' The line crackled, but Charlotte could hear her very clearly. 'I couldn't wait to know how you're getting on. How are you?'

Charlotte laughed at her friend's familiar warmth. 'The place is just beautiful . . . a real island paradise. And George is great company. I think he's probably got some terrific photographs. The hotel is a pretty standard luxury hotel, the sort you'd find anywhere in the world – you know the sort of thing. But wait till you hear this.'

She paused for dramatic effect. Even through the thousands of miles that lay between them, Charlotte was aware Claudia was holding her breath. 'Go on then,' she finally said, impatiently. 'Don't tell me you've met a man.'

'Not exactly.' In spite of the situation, Charlotte couldn't resist a quiet giggle. 'William's here.'

'Oh no!' Claudia shrieked. 'How dreadful for you . . .'

'And Valentine!'

'Jeesus . . . Oh, Charlotte. What a terrible thing to happen. The rat – taking her out there on some freebie. Just shows what a bloody cheapskate worm he is.'

'But they're not together.'

'Well then, what are they doing?' Claudia sounded most confused.

'And Daniel's here too.'

'You're joking. Oh now I know you're having me on. You can't be serious.'

'Never more so, Claudia. And I seem to remember it was all your idea that I came on this little excursion. As a sort of break, wasn't it? To get away from it all. Well frankly, Claudia Williams, you've landed me right in it. If I ever speak to you again when I get back it will be a miracle of forgiveness and high-mindedness.'

'Shit, Charlotte. Sorry. But there was no way I could have known. God. I'd give anything to be there. I mean

. . . in a funny kind of way, it is rather ironic, isn't it? The four of you there. Do you think someone's trying to tell you all something?'

'Yes. That we're all a bunch of imbeciles.'

'Well, how is it?'

'Well, William's organized the trip from London, as he does the PR for Lux Hotels. So we should have guessed. But he's seen fit to put me in one of the best suites. Obviously 'cause he still feels so guilty. As for Valentine – I've hardly seen her. George and I have managed to keep ourselves pretty much to ourselves, and as for Daniel . . .'

'Yes. What about Daniel?' Claudia was hanging on Charlotte's every word.

'I've only come face to face with him twice, and we had a bit of a slanging match each time. He thought I was here with George in a more intimate way. And I thought he was with this rather glamorous blonde bit in a very intimate way. So we had a good go at each other about it. Then he almost accused me of enticing a rape attempt when I went for a stroll on the beach last night. Hardly a harmonious series of meetings, would you say?'

'And how do you feel about him? After all this time?'

'Passionate, if you really want to know. I fancy him something rotten. I'm jealous as hell and I want him. Satisfied?'

Claudia was silent for a moment. She knew that Charlotte's flippancy was a cover-up for something that went much deeper. Daniel had obviously got to her. And to be in such a volatile set of circumstances must be a considerable strain. Suddenly she had an idea. 'Why don't you stay on for a few days? When does the official visit finish?'

'Tomorrow.'

'Right. Stay for another few days. As long as you like. I'll make sure everything's OK at this end. So far absolutely nothing has happened. No dramas. No artistic tantrums. Haven't seen Giles at all.'

Charlotte was protesting. 'I couldn't . . . don't be daft. I've got to come back with the others.'

'Why?'

'Because it's all arranged.'

'Well, I'll just unarrange it. We can get you booked on another plane. Just charge it to your Am-Ex and then put it on expenses when you get back. You could even try some writing while you're out there. I mean it hardly sounds as if you had a proper rest with that lot there. Are you mad or something, woman? Take it while it's offered. It's dreary here. And as soon as you get back you'll wish you'd stayed on, and wonder why the hell you didn't!'

Finally Charlotte sighed in resignation. 'OK, OK, I will. But this is going to have to stop soon you know, Claude. I can't have you bossing me and running my life for much longer. This is the last time I let you nanny me . . .'

'Yes, yes . . . 'course it is.'

'And thanks, you old bat.' Charlotte laughed gratefully. 'Ring me if anything happens.'

Claudia screeched in exasperation. 'I've got the number. I know where you are. But I won't bother you unless it's an absolute emergency. This is your holiday, OK?'

'Agreed!'

Claudia replaced the receiver and returned to her pile of transparencies, thinking over Charlotte's conversation. Then she smiled to herself. A small glint of mischief flickered in her eyes. She picked up the telephone and looked over at the notice board for the number Laura had pinned there, in large figures.

After what seemed like an age her call was answered. 'Daniel Cornwallis, please.'

Her pulse raced. She would either be damned to kingdom-come, or made a saint. But whatever, she wasn't about to go back. After a very short time she recognized his smooth, sexy voice. 'Daniel Cornwallis.'

'Daniel, you may not remember me, but my name's Claudia, Claudia Williams. I'm a friend of Charlotte's . . . '

'Really,' he said, his curiosity stirred.

Charlotte said goodbye to George in the foyer. William was close behind. He waved a fax in her direction. 'Look, Charlotte. See what it is.'

She read the faint, waxy paper. 'Oh, I see. Do we celebrate or what?' she said somewhat gloomily.

'No. Probably not, I suppose. But that's it, isn't it? All neatly packaged up now. Where's your suitcase?'

'I'm staying on for a few days.'

'What about the magazine?'

'It's at their insistence actually.' She suddenly felt awkward. She wanted to be alone. She'd had three days of just about solid company. And now William was irritating her with his stupid Decree Absolute. 'I think I'll go and lie down . . .' she said vaguely. 'Oh, thanks for everything, William.' He looked a little surprised. 'I meant the trip . . . not the marriage.'

Then he laughed. 'Of course. Ha ha. Take care then.' His arms hung awkwardly at his sides. She sensed he was wondering whether to hug her or not. She put him out of his misery by stepping towards him and giving him a peck on the cheek.

'Bye,' she said.

She collected her beach things, her book and a towel and made her way down to the sheltered bay owned by the hotel. It was completely deserted. She made her way to the middle of the crescent and then settled herself down to an afternoon's serious sunning. She lay on her stomach, her head on her crooked arms, supporting a book against her beach bag. As her body warmed, she stretched luxuriously and closed her eyes, thinking over the events of the past few days, and what she was going to do with her time over the next few. She dozed off.

When she woke it was with a start. She looked at her watch. Almost an hour had passed. She rolled on to her side.

'You could get sunstroke if you fall asleep in the sun, Charlotte.'

She twisted round quickly. He was sitting a little way from her by a large beach parasol planted securely in the sand. He was lying on an adjustable couch complete with mattress, and was putting his iced drink back on to the table at his side. She just looked, pure astonishment written all over her features.

Not so much as an hour ago the beach had been deserted. Not one parasol, or bed, or body had cluttered the sands. Yet here, not more than five yards away, was a kind of mobile cocktail bar. He picked up an empty glass and filled it from the jug on the table. He gestured to Charlotte to join him.

She remained motionless, still taking in the situation. 'How on earth did you get there?'

'I walked.'

'I mean, the parasol, the bed, the drinks . . .'

'The hotel.'

'When?'

'About half an hour ago, I suppose. They freshened the jug about ten minutes ago. I was going to wake you up soon, but you looked so peaceful lying here, with your mouth open, snoring . . .'

'Oh, Daniel . . . I wasn't.'

'No, of course you weren't.'

'But you mean I had a whole procession of waiters just about stepping over me with all this nonsense, and I had no idea?'

'That's right. Pretty sound sleeper, eh Charlotte?'

'Hmm,' she said, still confused.

'Why didn't you leave with the others?'

'Now that is the question I've been pondering while you were sleeping. Dan, I said to myself. Why on earth are you here? What is it about this woman who irritates you beyond belief? Why would you want to risk her razor-sharp tongue again? Are you some kind of masochist or what? That, my dear Charlotte, is exactly what I've been asking myself.'

'Oh really?' she snapped. She got up and raced into the water, scattering shoals of tiny black fish. She swam out, away from the shore.

He was close behind her. She stopped swimming, her limbs tiring, and trod water, looking at him. He closed on her, both of them breathing harshly. He looked into her eyes and then dropped his gaze to her mouth. Then she twisted away from him and swam back towards the shore. Again he followed her. Eventually she was waist deep. He grabbed her hand and pulled her towards him. He swept her into his powerful clasp, hands closing like steel behind her back. Then he kissed her. He kissed her on and on until her world started to spin and her head felt disembodied. Her knees started to buckle under her and her limbs trembled. His body felt hot against her. The waves broke around their thighs but she was oblivious. Unwittingly she raised her arms and twisted them round his neck, holding him tight against her, and moaned with pleasure at the feel of his hard chest pressed to her breasts. She was tired of fighting. All she knew was that she wanted him, and that she wanted him urgently.

He pulled away from her, reading the answer in her eyes, which were hooded with passion and want. He nodded slowly, then picked her up and carried her gently out of the water and back up the beach. He put her down on the mattress and then, in front of her curious eyes, took off his swimming trunks and lay down on top of her, covering her body with his own.

317

She pushed him a little away from her and looked down at her bikini pants. He grinned and hooked his finger into the side, as she helped him pull them down, off her legs. Then he unhooked her top. She arched against him, feeling the most wonderful, warm, almost wanton need for this man.

There were no preliminaries. Too much time had already been wasted. Now all that was left was a surge of desire that had to be satisfied. She slid her legs up and he thrust into her. She cried out at the exquisite sensation and then tensed her pelvic muscles as he pumped into her. Ripples of pure ecstasy ran over her. She was lost. Abandoned. Aware only of the feel of him. Suddenly, she felt herself coming. She arched up and moaned again, her mouth open in an expression which could almost have been pain. Dan sensed her climax and quickened his thrusts, until they cried out together, their bodies convulsing. He held her tight and whispered her name over and over. 'Charlotte. Oh my love, Charlotte . . . at last. Oh my darling.'

She too held him tightly, brushing his face with light kisses, smiling in utter contentment. She never wanted him to let go. She didn't want to speak in case they ended up fighting once more. She sighed happily, relaxed for the first time in many months, truly content, fulfilled. Eventually he rolled to one side and propped himself on his elbow, his eyes half closed. She studied him. His thick black lashes, his black curls much tighter now, thanks to the recent dip. He was deeply bronzed. She couldn't resist tracing a line from his forehead down to the end of his nose. Suddenly he opened his mouth, as if to snare her finger. She moved it quickly away, and giggled.

'I'm glad you stayed, Daniel.'

He opened one eye and then the other. Pretending shock and disbelief. 'Charlotte, that's the nicest thing you've ever said to me. Aren't you going to call me something terrible? I think you'd better. Otherwise it just won't feel right, you know.'

She placed a finger over his lips. 'Sssh,' she whispered. 'I meant it. I don't want to fight you any more. Well . . . not today anyway.'

She turned over and looked back towards the path which led to the hotel. 'Daniel, do you suppose anyone can actually see us from up there?'

He placed a hand on her naked buttock and squeezed it lightly. 'Well, if they can they're having a very scenic afternoon, aren't they? Do you think we should give them another show?'

'Mmmmm,' she sighed.

He looked at his watch. 'There are things we've got to do . . . before dark.'

'What things?'

'Surprise things.'

'Oh?'

'Do you want to play or not?'

She grinned. 'Oh yes. I want to play all right.'

He held her bikini out for her. 'Seems a shame to cover you, Charlotte, but I don't want to share you either.'

They collected their things together and followed the path back to the hotel. Charlotte automatically turned towards the side entrance which led up to the lift.

'Where are you going?' he asked. 'A surprise, remember. You just have to follow me, and say nothing!'

She again looked at him, puzzled, but said nothing. He took her hand and pulled her towards the front of the hotel. A white jeep stood in splendid isolation to one side of the car park. A huge white ribbon was draped in a bow, tied over the radiator grille. Dan led her towards it. A single white rose lay on the passenger seat.

He answered her questioning look. 'For peace,' he said simply. He gestured to her to get in.

He seemed to know exactly where he was going. They took the main road for a short distance, and then headed off up an unmade track, bouncing over many a bump. The afternoon sun was cooling, the daylight softening. Pink clouds were taking shape above the distant horizons. There was no breeze at all, only the draught caused by the jeep, blowing Charlotte's hair back and cooling her newly-tanned skin.

She couldn't help looking at him. She kept stealing quick glances, meeting his wry smile, then almost blushingly turning away. He seemed to have the peculiar ability of making her stomach turn triple somersaults when he grinned like that. Or maybe it was the recent feel of him hard inside her that did it. Whatever the reason, she was happy to be where she was.

They passed a couple more houses and then turned off to the left, following an even rougher track. She bit her tongue to stop herself from questioning him. Then suddenly a beautiful house appeared as if from nowhere. Dan slowed to a halt in the middle of the drive. Slowly Charlotte climbed out of the car, drinking in her surroundings. The house was a delightful bungalow-style villa, with balconies of wrought iron and creeping climbers nestled between a wall of trees on either side. Its pink-washed walls echoed the changing tints of the early vening sky.

'Whose is it, Daniel? It's lovely.'

'Come and see.'

A white-jacketed houseboy stood to one side, welcoming them. 'Good evening, Mr Cornwallis,' he said. 'And Mrs Cornwallis.'

Charlotte raised her eyebrows, but said nothing.

Daniel held her hand and led the way through the house. She caught a glimpse of a sitting room, with an enormous inglenook fireplace, a pile of logs ready at the side, more for show than for use. On the other side of the hall she could see two candlesticks on a dining table: a sea of flowers tumbling around them. But Daniel was pulling her up the stairs. She almost fell up after him, her bare feet slipping over the pale terracotta tiles, as he led her into a light airy room.

'Daniel, who lives here? Whose is it?'

'Ours.'

'What do you mean "ours"?'

'Exactly that.'

Then she saw her robe hanging on the back of the door. 'How on earth . . . ?'

She opened the wardrobe door and found all her clothes inside. 'Daniel, what are you, some kind of magician? How did my clothes get here? What are we doing here? – I just don't understand.'

'I've rented it. For us, my love. I took the liberty of having your things sent over earlier.'

'You must have been very sure of yourself,' she interrupted. 'How did you know I'd be willing to come with you?'

'Well, I wasn't sure, of course. The way you've behaved to me in the past pointed towards you certainly not agreeing to it. I just had a hunch. A gut feeling. Intuition. Whatever. Charlotte, I knew the time had to be right for us. For so long now we've done nothing but fight. I think about you nearly all the time. God knows I've tried to get you out of my head – you've certainly made me angry enough on occasion – but I just don't seem to be able to. You've woven some kind of spell over me. I need you.'

'Oh Dan.' She turned and threw her arms around his neck. Her eyes were bright with tears. Tears of happiness. 'I know. It's been the same with me. Whatever has happened, however busy and preoccupied I've been, there has always been a kind of emptiness. I wouldn't let myself even think about you. I guessed that you were involved with that pretty blonde . . .'

'Sam? No. We work together. That's all. But what about you and Ferguson?'

She sighed. 'Daniel, I told you. I've never lied about him. Nothing ever happened between us. He was just very kind to me. And as for the pornography . . .'

He put his fingers to her lips. 'Sssh. Come on. Let's not talk about it. We've got better things to think about and the important thing is that we're here. Together. Nothing is going to come between us now, Charlotte. We are going to have some peace and a lot of loving.'

With that he picked her up and carried her over to the doorway, kicking it shut. Then he returned to the bed and gently lowered her on to the covers.

'Now I seem to remember we were sort of in the middle of something.'

He cut off her giggle with his kiss.

They were like a pair of kids. Suddenly everything became wildly funny. The world was full of private jokes and hidden meanings. They were inseparable. They ate the marvellous food provided by the resident chef; they sailed on the twenty-seven-foot yacht at their disposal; they lazed on the beach; they fished in the sea from a glass-bottomed boat; and they made the most wonderful, slow, exquisite love that either of them had ever experienced. Charlotte had never been happier. She glowed inside and out. She never wanted to be separate from him. He was everything she'd dreamed of and he loved her as much as she did him.

On the second night they ate supper on the terrace. James the houseboy served them unobtrusively. They feasted on oysters and lobster, exotic fruits, salads and pavlova. Dan kept filling her glass and gazing at her across the table. They didn't talk much. And Charlotte found her appetite sparse. She was too full of him. Afterwards they went inside and fell into the feather cushions of the enormous cream sofa, the only light in the room being the pale moonlight filtering in through the windows and the soft yellow light from the flickering candles on the mantelpiece. Dan held her close. She felt safe, protected, completely at home in that heavenly circle of his grip. He breathed softly into her neck, the little draughts of air sending delicious tremors down her spine.

'I love you, witch woman,' he murmured against her ear, nibbling the lobe lightly.

She snuggled harder against him, and sighed happily. 'Mmmm,' she said.

'But I know nothing about you. All I know about is that joke of a husband of yours and your frightfully successful career. I know you're strong, capable, intelligent, sensitive, and pig-headed and daft at times – but I want to know all about you. Darling, tell me the story of your life.'

'Don't be so daft,' she laughed. 'You sound like something out of a corny Sunday afternoon movie, Dan,' she mocked him. Then she stopped, seeing the fleeting look of something akin to hurt pass his features.

'Oh, I'm sorry, my love.' She kissed him quickly and ran her fingers lightly through his curls. 'You do want to know, don't you? You'll have to forgive me. You see I'm not used to having all this intense interest lavished in my direction. Yes . . . I suppose I feel the same way. I want to know everything about you. I'd like to crawl inside you if I could.'

'And I'd like to crawl inside you . . . mm.'

'Oh Daniel, really. You're insatiable.'

She squeaked as his hand closed on her breast. She lifted it playfully and moved slightly away from him, so that she could see him properly. 'Where shall I start?'

'Tell me about your family.'

He drew her back into his arms so that she was cradled by him once more, but her back nestled against his chest, so that she had to turn her head round to see him.

She told him briefly about her parents and how they lived a very quiet but well-organized lifestyle in Hampshire, and how she was really quite close to them.

'They must regret seeing you so rarely then, Charlotte.'

She thought for a moment. 'Yes, I suppose they do in a way. But they were never really dependent parents you know. It's sad, isn't it, how some poor people dedicate their whole lives to their children to the exclusion of all else. One day they wake up and their children are grown. Ready to fly – quite rightly. So what happens to those poor people? Their lives leave with them. Their whole *raison d'être* for eighteen years suddenly walks out with a suitcase and a bank account and a promise to ring. What do they do then? Ring their children nightly? Pine for their lost progeny? Pester and smother them and inevitably push them further away?

'Oh Dan, if I have children I shall never fall into that trap. They'll be more important than anything else, of course, but I won't lose myself in them. Not on your life.'

Daniel was silent for a while. 'Was your mother like that with you, being an only child? I suppose that must make things worse?'

'Oh God no. No, she wasn't. Not at all. Quite the reverse in fact. And I wasn't an only child. I had a brother . . .' She felt his fingers tighten against her back. 'James was killed seven years ago in a car crash.'

'I'm sorry,' Daniel said weakly. 'That must have been dreadful.'

'Yes, it was. I was with him. He was driving. Some idiot overtook on a blind bend and went into us head on. All I know is that I woke up with a headache and this,' she touched the thin white line across her temple.

'My poor love.' Daniel pulled her tightly to him and kissed the top of her head.

Charlotte continued. 'So it wasn't his fault. The other

driver was killed too. I was the lucky one. Though at the time it was so ghastly that I sometimes wished I had been killed too. Seeing my parents' agony. Daniel, they were destroyed. My mother didn't speak. Dad and I cracked. We cracked a lot. We cried. We talked about James. We did our textbook mourning. Mum seemed to have been turned to ice. She just didn't seem to react. Even at the funeral she never shed a tear. It was almost like she had turned to stone.

'Dad and I didn't know what to do. We thought about speaking to a psychiatrist. It was so unnatural. And then her mare foaled. And the foal was stillborn. We heard this kind of wailing. God it was eerie. It was late, we'd gone to bed. Neither Dad nor I had realized what had happened. Of course Mum was always hyper-sensitive to the animals. She must have known this mare's time had come. But the first we knew about it was this frightful noise. A sort of keening. Naturally we went to her. At first we were petrified, thinking she must have flipped. And then we realized that at last, almost six weeks afterwards, the dam had finally burst. The blessed release had come. We just let her wail and cry and let it all out. Released thanks to that unfortunate little foal with the cord around its neck.'

For a long time Charlotte stared into the fire, remembering that time. Thinking about her brother. How vital James had been. A bright young barrister. Handsome and successful. And so full of life. She still missed him dreadfully.

When Dan stirred next to her she was so lost in thought she had almost forgotten where she was. His face was a picture of love and sympathy.

'Poor, poor Charlotte,' he murmured. Then he started to kiss her. He kissed her until her blood started to race and the spark of passion flared into life. He kissed her until her own kisses were as demanding as his. Fiercely demanding. They almost tore off each other's clothes.

Charlotte sank down from the sofa on to the rug in front of the fireplace. She pulled him down on to her, becoming desperate. Panting for him. Opening up to him. She gasped with the feel of him and held him so close to her. His body weight was almost crushing her. But she wanted to feel him. Wanted to be crushed. She needed this man so badly it was like a searing pain deep within her. When finally they reached their shattering climax, she felt tears burn her cheeks. A great sob escaped her lungs. He quickly pulled himself up so that he could see her, worry and concern and confusion on his face.

The tears flowed down her cheeks. 'Don't worry,' she said, between sobs. 'It's just that I love you, Daniel. I love you so much.'

'Oh my darling,' he cried and held her as tightly as he could without snapping her in two.

Chapter Twenty-two

Valentine replaced the phone. Damn him. Damn her darling brother. Why did he always pick the worst possible times for his surprise visits? She just wished he'd stay in bloody New York and leave her in peace.

For the ninety millionth time she cursed the stupidity and lack of foresight on her parents' part of leaving the trust in her brother's hands. He'd probably spent all the cash. Of course if he had she'd slit his throat, but for the moment she had to be content with the fact that she had got the family home until she came of age – hah! That was a joke, 'came of age' at the grand old age of twenty-five. Her father certainly had a wild sense of humour.

And now her evening had been ruined. All her plans kiboshed by bloody Mark. She had her nails to paint, her hair to wash, maybe a face pack . . . the odd eyebrow to weed out. God. Things she really needed to do. And now her idiot brother wanted to use the flat. Could she possibly be a dear little sister and vacate the place . . . ? She went over the words in her mind, mocking his 'frightfully' English upper-class accent, . . . as he had a frightfully important meeting. 'Absolutely private, old gel, know what I mean?' She blew a raspberry. Bloody private. How dare he. Snotty-nosed little tick.

She rang a friend, and booked herself in for a couple of hours of bitching and Perrier. Then she set about collecting up all the sundry bits of clothing that littered the flat. She pushed the whole lot under the duvet. Then she shoved all the grubby plates into the dishwasher, out of sight. Not that she gave a toss really. It was just that she would hate whoever was meeting Mark at the flat to get the wrong idea.

But when she opened the door to him she was shocked. Her handsome brother had aged. His deep auburn hair was streaked with grey, and his face looked gaunt. He must have read her expression.

'What's up, sis, aren't you thrilled to see me?'

She frowned. 'No. Of course I'm not thrilled to see you. Nought minutes' notice and I'm told to get out of my own flat . . .'

'Our flat,' he corrected.

'Huh. Well, even so. What exactly are you doing here, Mark? I assume this isn't a social visit. You rarely venture back across the Atlantic without a particularly good reason. Is this a flying visit, or what?'

'Valentine,' he drawled. She found herself looking into a mirror of her own orange eyes. He could almost have been her twin. 'I'm negotiating a very important deal. In fact I would say it's rather in your interests, my darling little sibling.' His thin lips curled into a smile of haughty condescension. He turned to the drinks tray and poured himself a large vodka, then sneered at the empty ice bucket.

'I can't imagine anything you do could possibly be in my interests. Tell me how long you're going to be here.' Her temper was rising. 'You can't just walk in and take over my life like this, Mark. Really it's too much.'

That taunting, slightly effeminate smile of his always made her furious. She wanted to pinch him as hard as she could, to wipe it off.

'And just who are you meeting? Another one of your little bumboys I suppose?'

She saw him wince. He recovered quickly. He was used to her taunts. He couldn't care less what she thought of his proclivities, knowing they were just a threat to her need for constant adoration. And the fact that the men he brought home were heedless of her

328

charms nearly killed her. Yes, he took a vaguely sadistic pleasure in winding up poor little Valentine. But he had other things to do. This was not the time to play cat and mouse with his sister. He was growing impatient.

'I know you understand really, dear girl. Now just run along and do whatever it is you young girls do, and don't come back before, say, ten o'clock!'

She picked up her coat, swore loudly and slammed the door behind her.

Mark refilled his glass, wondering for the fiftieth time just what it was that Eddy d'Angelo wanted him to get from this man Ferguson. He was sick to the back teeth of being d'Angelo's puppet, but there was fuck all he could do about it. Ever since the Federal Drugs Bureau had got wind of the shipment from Pakistan and opened up the suitcase he'd been trying to pay back the debt. Three million dollars didn't seem like such a great deal of money when you had it in front of you on a gaming table. But when you owed it to the Cosa Nostra and you didn't have it in readies, then suddenly it seemed like one hell of a lot of money.

Still things could have been worse. They could have been in jail. At least the suitcase trick had worked for them. His partner had been able to deny that it was his suitcase, and prove it by returning to pick up the decoy case. That meant so far as the authorities were concerned they were fairly clean. Though sometimes Mark couldn't help wondering whether the Drugs Bureau might have been the lesser of two evils, now that he ran the risk of getting on Eddy's wrong side.

Until he could pay him back he had to do what Eddy told him. His hand shook nervously and he could feel the cold sweat already prick across his brow. He wiped at it in irritation, and looked at his watch once more. Fatalistically, he knew whatever he was asked to do, he had no choice but to agree. Whatever it was, he was about to find out. His guest had arrived.

Almost as soon as he opened the door, Mark questioned his decision to invite Giles to see him at the flat. Even as Giles squeezed his hand in greeting, he felt a cold grip on his bowel, wrenching his gut. The man had a vulture's beak of a nose. His eyes were cold and deadly as a cobra's, black and inscrutable, while his skin had a kind of deathly pallor about it. Yes. That was it. This man had an air of the angel of death, the grim reaper. As Giles grinned at him, Mark had the terrifying feeling he was looking at his own hangman. He tried desperately to compose himself. To shake off these completely ridiculous, irrational thoughts. He hadn't even spoken to the man and already he felt like a piece of chicken-shit.

'Hi Giles,' he said, his voice sounding calm and friendly. 'I'm glad you found me.'

'Hello. Yes, I found you with no trouble at all.' He smiled back, but the cold hard lift to his mouth did not reach his eyes. Giles continued to stare at him.

Mark offered him a drink. Giles refused. Mark gulped down the remains of his own vodka and then gestured to Giles to sit. He waited for him to speak. There seemed little point in making small talk.

'Eddy told me you'd be getting in touch with me. Did he say why?'

Mark shook his head. 'No. I guessed you'd tell me that.'

Giles nodded. 'I see. Well, that's what we're here for, isn't it?'

Mark looked at him steadily. Waiting.

Giles looked around the flat. 'Nice place you've got here. Do you have a lady?'

He had noticed the many pictures of Valentine spread over the walls, and the little feminine touches like flowers on the table and an odd stocking peeping out

330

from under one of the chair cushions. He thought he knew her face.

'My sister. She lives here. In fact I only use it when I'm in town. Most of the time she has it to herself.'

'And where is she tonight?'

'Out. Conveniently. I explained I had a private engagement.'

'Good. Well, it seems that there's some very good smack coming in from Afghanistan. Very pure. Almost a hundred per cent in fact.'

'Whew,' Mark whistled under his breath.

'It's coming in from Spain to the west of Ireland. And what Eddy wants is someone to pick it up from Cork and courier it back to me so that I can sample the goods.'

'But that's one of the worst runs in the world.'

Giles looked at him levelly. 'That's precisely why Eddy thought you should handle it. He wanted someone capable.'

'I see,' he said slowly. Eddy was certainly going to make him pay in more ways than one for his bad luck. Security was always extremely tight on any runs from the Republic. It would be like playing Russian roulette. All these thoughts buzzed angrily round his head, while all the time he tried to maintain an outward appearance of coolness. 'So, when's it to be?' he said decisively.

'Soon. In the meantime why don't you book yourself a little trip to Ireland. That way you'll be well placed to do the pick-up when it's ready.'

'When's that likely to be?'

'Hmmm? Oh, in two or three days,' Giles said casually.

This time Mark could not contain himself. 'Two or three days? That's impossible. I can't possibly organize myself in three days!'

Giles shrugged. 'In that case I'll tell Eddy you said no . . .'

'No! No . . . don't do that! I'll see what I can do. On second thoughts I've been meaning to visit Ireland for ages.'

Giles grinned back at him. 'Funny, isn't it? I had a feeling you might.'

At that moment they both looked up at the sound of the front door opening and closing. Giles looked at Mark in alarmed surprise.

Valentine swept majestically into the room. 'Mark!' she boomed. 'I flatly refuse to walk the streets of London all night just so that you . . . oh.' She saw Giles looking at her with cool interest. Her jaw hung open. 'Oh, sorry,' she said insincerely. There was something terribly familiar about Giles. She studied him openly. Finally she said: 'Have we met?'

His voice was slippery smooth. 'Well, if we haven't, we certainly should have.' He stood up and graciously kissed Valentine's hand. His manner was charming and effusive. 'Mark, your sister is very beautiful.' His eyes didn't leave Valentine's.

So, Valentine thought to herself, this wasn't one of the usual fags Mark surrounded himself with. This one was obviously one hundred per cent hetero.

'Aren't you going to introduce us, brother dear?' Her bad temper, which had flown into the room along with her, seemed to have miraculously blown away.

Mark, on the other hand, was having a very hard time keeping his feelings under control. His mind whirled. He was cornered and desperate. He could hear his own death knell, but he had no choice other than to accept Giles's offer. Eddy was after him and he would just have to play along. If he didn't he would end up somewhere set in concrete boots. He struggled to keep his voice even. 'Of course, Valentine, this is Giles Ferguson.'

'Hello . . .' she drawled back at him. 'And how do

you know my dearest big brother?' Her cat-like eyes slanted curiously at him.

'Giles is in publishing,' Mark jumped in quickly, and then looked to Giles for affirmation.

Giles smiled as easily, as if he and Mark had been discussing the weather prior to her entrance. 'That's right.'

'And what do you publish?' she said, her lack of interest clear in her voice.

'*Amber*.'

'Not Charlotte Grange's *Amber*?'

'You know her then?'

'Oh, I know Charlotte all right.' Valentine's interest had suddenly magnified tenfold. 'Through my modelling.'

'I thought I recognized you. Maybe you should do some work for us, Valentine. A cover or a centre-spread perhaps.'

Valentine shrugged. 'Maybe. Call me.'

'I'll have a word with my fashion editor.'

Valentine was smiling at him as seductively as she could manage. So . . . Charlotte's boss. What a coup. She intended to have him eating from the palm of her hand before tomorrow's breakfast.

'I'm hungry,' she said. 'I've hardly touched a thing all day.'

Giles rose to the bait. 'Then why don't I buy you dinner? Mark, how about you? Will you join us?'

'What? Oh no, no thanks. You two go ahead.'

'I expect you've got a few things to think about, haven't you?' Giles said pointedly. 'Come on then, Valentine. I'll ring you on the same number tomorrow, Mark, same time.'

Valentine found him wildly attractive. His very aloofness was a turn on. In truth she found it impossible to tell whether his charm was a come on or just his

333

natural manner. But there was a mystery. Something underneath she couldn't quite put her finger on, but she knew she wanted him. He was powerful, that was for sure. She wouldn't like to get on the wrong side of him. But there was no fear of that. She giggled at him over the dinner table. Turning on her best smiles. Dazzling him with her best wit and beauty. Towards the end of the meal she surreptitiously slipped off her shoe and let her stockinged toe creep up his trousered leg, and gently tickle his thigh. His action hidden by the white damask cloth, he reached down and grabbed her foot. He pulled it up and rested it on his lap, so that she could feel the bulge beneath his fly. As she wriggled her foot, ever so slightly, she felt him stiffen. His eyes flickered and he wet his lips. 'I think it's time to get the bill.'

Valentine could hardly speak. Her voice was lost in her passion-constricted throat. Her crotch was wet. She had to have him soon. She nodded dumbly, sliding her foot across the soft wool of his trousers, feeling the hardness of his cock, and the softness of his balls. In return, he stroked her toes, grabbing her foot firmly so that she couldn't escape his teasing tickles.

'Come on, Giles,' she said. 'I want you. Let's go.'

'My my. An impatient lady. An impatient hot, horny, lady. I like that, Valentine. It's nice to meet a woman who knows what she wants. But be patient, little hot pussy. It'll be worth waiting for, I promise you that.'

Valentine retrieved her shoe and held on to his arm as they left, pressing it tightly against her breast. She was like a bitch on heat.

As soon as he closed the flat door she turned on him. Her long arms twined around his neck, she craned for his mouth, moaning with lust. He pushed her back gently. 'Come on, Valentine. There's no hurry. I'm going to slip into something a little more comfortable, as they say. Would you like some grass?'

She nodded. He handed her a little wooden box

containing the marijuana and cigarette papers and left the room.

Valentine undressed down to her silk camisole and then prepared a joint. She lit it and was exhaling the aromatic smoke when Giles returned. He was wearing a short, silky-black dressing gown that failed to hide the thick dark hairs covering his legs and chest. She passed him the reefer and stretched out on the sofa, unselfconsciously splaying her legs. Giles handed her the reefer once more and then opened a cupboard in a corner of the room, revealing a stack of video-tapes. 'How about a little entertainment, sweetie?' he asked.

Valentine squinted at him curiously. But he was already pushing a video into the machine, pressing buttons. She waited for the fuzzy lines to subside.

It was a very slickly produced movie. Valentine wasn't exactly sure of the plot, but she understood the movements pretty well. The dialogue was stilted because the woman had a penis in her mouth. The man didn't say much because he was too busy moaning. They looked like a pretty straight couple, apart from the fact that he was wearing stockings and suspenders. It looked surprisingly erotic, Valentine decided through the haze of the narcotic. She turned back to Giles, wild for him now, and started to perform the same service for him. Giles continued to watch the action, his eyes bulging with lust. Valentine knelt on the floor stroking herself as her head bobbed up and down, until she felt Giles about to come. She slipped him out of her mouth and into the hot wet folds of velvet between her legs. Giles, she noticed dimly, had a strange air of detachment throughout. It was as if he was still a voyeur. He wasn't really participating in the action. He was set back, outside of it. Valentine was driven to an almost greater frenzy in her desire to crack his aloofness. She had never come across such steely control. He could almost have been bored. Yet she knew better than that.

No man could ever be bored making love to her. But when she felt herself coming, she knew he stiffened. He teased and held himself still, eyes closed, mouth open. But she still could not be sure, not entirely, if he had been fulfilled or not. A strange fish – but very exciting.

She woke much later. Giles was breathing deeply and evenly at her side. She looked at her watch: 3.30 a.m. She lay and thought about what would happen if she spent the entire night in his bed. It was certainly easy to turn over and go back to sleep. On the other hand she hated not having a change of clothes. And she wanted to make sure that Mark wasn't planning on making himself too much at home. She sighed and silently slipped out of the bed, tiptoeing across the dark room. She gently clicked the door shut behind her, desperate not to wake him. She grinned to herself, imagining his surprise at finding her gone in the morning. If anything, that should make him even hotter to see her again. She found her clothes which hung off the side of the sofa. She sat on the chair opposite the television screen and put on her shoes. She looked up and saw the half-open cupboard which housed a stack of video tapes. It looked as though Giles had got himself quite a library together. She wondered if they all had a similar content to the one she'd seen. She glanced through the titles. They sounded fairly innocuous. She pulled one out. Unlike the others there was no title on its spine. Valentine was curious. She slipped it into her bag and then quietly left.

Chapter Twenty-three

Claudia's head was almost buried in a large trunk. She was busily riffling through a mass of tights, belts, handbags and make-up kits – you name it, most of it was chucked into the loot box, as she had nicknamed it –' in order to find the tights of a particular shade she remembered seeing in there a week before. Suddenly she had the strangest sensation. The tiny hairs on the back of her neck prickled, and she shivered. 'Someone's just walked over my grave,' she muttered out loud.

'I hope not, Claudia. Be a little premature, wouldn't it?'

She nearly jumped out of her skin. 'Giles! What the hell are you doing?' she exclaimed loudly.

'Well, that's a nice greeting I must say.'

'You gave me one hell of a fright sneaking up on me like that.'

'I don't sneak up on anyone, Claudia. I just walked into your office. You were obviously too buried in your work . . .'

Claudia looked at him and frowned slowly. He bloody well had sneaked up on her. He always did. He didn't walk around the place, he crept. All of them had noticed the rather disconcerting habit he had of suddenly appearing at their shoulder, making them jump in alarm. Claudia, with her penchant for plain speaking, did not intend to let him get away with it either. 'Do me a favour in future, Giles, would you, and cough loudly or something. Really you could give us heart failure, you know.'

Reluctantly she turned from her rummaging and

stood up, so she was level with him. As far as she knew, he had not been near the office for days, if not weeks. She was tempted to ask just how long he intended to stay around this time, but thought better of it. She didn't want him to think she was encouraging him.

She returned his look. A smile played around his mouth, but as usual it did not touch his lifeless black eyes that reminded her so strongly of a killer shark.

'I'm collecting everything together for a shoot to-morrow . . .' She gestured towards the box.

'Yes, well, I wouldn't know about that. I wanted to talk to you about a rather nice model I've come across. I don't think you've used her before, Claudia. I said we'd get in touch with her. She looks great. In fact you'll probably have heard of her.'

'Oh? What's her name then?'

'Valentine.'

'Valentine!' Claudia's voice was a high-pitched whisper. She sank back to the floor. 'You can't be serious, Giles.'

'Why not?'

'Well, for one, she's one of the most over-exposed faces in the business, and for two I think you'd probably lose your editor if I so much as suggested using her to Charlotte.'

'What on earth do you mean by that?'

'I mean, Giles, that if Valentine were put in *Amber*'s pages, Charlotte would leave. So the answer is "no". I will not use Valentine.' She raised her hands as Giles started to protest. She could see he was furious. 'Do you remember the night Charlotte went home with you? The night of the agency party? When William . . . ? When he . . . you know . . . When Charlotte caught him with another woman?'

'Yes, I remember it. But what's that got to do with it?'

'The other woman was Valentine. Charlotte caught William having it off with Valentine. That is why she

338

would not wish to edit a magazine that featured the harlot. And quite frankly neither would I. I'm sorry, Giles, if that puts you in an awkward position so far as she's concerned . . . if she's a, well, a friend of yours. But as long as the decision is still mine – or Charlotte's – the answer is no.'

Giles looked thoughtful for a few moments. Claudia guessed he was probably wondering how he was going to tell Valentine.

'I see. Come to think of it I do remember her mentioning something about Valentine. Well, that does make things a little sensitive I suppose. And I'm sure I don't have to tell you that I don't intend to lose my editor over something so trivial. And . . . er . . . under the circumstances it's probably best if we don't mention it to Charlotte, eh Claudia? No point in upsetting her over the thing.'

'Fine. Sorry I couldn't be more helpful, Giles. I hope Valentine's not too disappointed.'

She thought she detected a hint of a scowl as he turned on his heel. Then she had the almost irresistible urge to laugh. Poor pathetic Giles, caught up with Venomous Val. Well, they were two of a kind all right. She waited a few moments and then headed off through the open-plan offices to the end room where the illustrious editor had once more taken up residence.

Charlotte was leaning over her lightbox for about the fiftieth time that morning, drinking in the beauty of George's transparencies. He had taken some absolutely magnificent shots and Charlotte glanced over them all, once more remembering the delicious days she had spent. There was the hotel, in all its splendour, white façade reflecting the sun's pale gold. The beach where she and Dan had made exquisite love. She closed her eyes to savour the feeling once again. How she missed him! But only two more days, just a few bits of unfinished business he had to attend to in New York, and then he would be back with her and they could start to build a real relationship, based on love and understanding, all their previous battles forgotten.

Charlotte knew she was behaving like a lovesick teenager. In the two weeks since she had been back she had lost weight. Her appetite was almost non-existent. Most meal times were spent chasing food around the plate, in the vain hope that it might disappear if she chased it for long enough. Instead she usually ended up tipping it into the bin and nearly half a stone had disappeared off the scales.

She looked up from her reverie when Claudia came in.

'Drop everything. I need a drink. We're going to lunch. Come on.'

'What do you mean "drop everything"? Can't you see I'm busy? I've got some serious reminiscing going on here.'

'Yes, yes, leave all that. I need you. And I've got some gossip for you. Get your handbag. Put your lipstick on. Come on . . . please.'

Charlotte laughed. 'All right, all right, but it had better be good gossip.'

After they had collected their salads from the counter they jostled their way to a table. Claudia's plate was piled high with quiche, cheese, coleslaw, green salad, rice salad, tomato salad and loads of dressings, while Charlotte's plate boasted only a small spoonful of lettuce and tomato. Claudia looked at the amount disbelievingly. 'That wouldn't keep a self-respecting rabbit going. Why aren't you eating?'

'Don't know. I'm just not really hungry.'

'You've lost weight, haven't you? I thought you were looking skinny.'

'Not much, just a bit.'

'Are you feeling all right? You look terribly pale, underneath your tan, that is.'

Charlotte laughed. 'If it's underneath my tan how on earth can you say that I look pale?'

Claudia shrugged sheepishly. 'Well, you do. I just know you do.'

Suddenly Charlotte felt defensive. 'I'm just not that hungry, OK? Anyway, you're the one that dragged me out to lunch. Just what is it that you're so keen to tell me?'

Claudia took a huge mouthful of her salad as she started to talk, bits of coleslaw appearing at the corners of her mouth. 'I had a visit from Giles this morning.'

'Oh?'

'He asked me to use Valentine in a fashion feature.'

'You're joking.'

Claudia shook her head. ''Fraid not.'

'What did you say?'

'No, of course. What do you think I said? "Giles, I'd be delighted – and so would Charlotte!" No, I told him that if Valentine appeared in *Amber* then we probably wouldn't have an editor left.'

'Too bloody right you wouldn't. She'd just love that, wouldn't she? My husband and my magazine. Huh!' She almost spat. 'But just what the hell is Giles doing pimping for Valentine?'

'That's just what I'm dying to know. Do you suppose they're having an affair or something?'

'If they are, they certainly deserve each other, that's all I can say.'

'But can you imagine how upset Valentine will be when she knows that we won't use her? Revenge is sweet, they say, and I'm sure she'll get up to something.'

Charlotte looked thoughtful. 'Yes, she probably will. But I won't let that bother me. She's got the looks, but she certainly hasn't the intellect.'

341

Claudia frowned. 'I hope you're right. The last thing we need right now is some kind of vendetta from a bitter model. I wanted to tell you . . . just in case. Giles decided he wouldn't mention it to you himself.'

'Very wise. I'd probably have bitten his balls off.'

'Oh God,' Claudia screwed up her face. 'What an unsavoury thought. So – I'm glad I did the right thing. Now, when's Dan coming back to London?'

Charlotte beamed back at her as if someone had switched on the light behind her eyes. 'The day after tomorrow. And I can't wait. It seems like ages since I saw him and it's only been a couple of weeks. It's strange, isn't it? In one way I'm excited and in another I'm apprehensive. I keep thinking things like, will we still want each other as much? You know . . . Will we still find things to talk about? Will he have gone off me? Stuff like that. Trouble is when you nurture a fantasy for so many months, which is what both of us did in a way, well, the fantasy builds up to a desperation level. I just hope that the reality lives up to it.'

Claudia looked at her thoughtfully, realizing the truth in what her friend was saying.

'The other really strange thing is,' Charlotte said, pensively, 'that it's only two weeks since I saw him, but I can't for the life of me remember what he looks like. I can remember his voice. I can remember the smell of him, but I just can't picture him. My God – if this goes on, I wonder if I'll even recognize him.'

'Of course you will. Don't be so daft. Everyone goes through that. It happens with those closest to you, don't ask me why. I suppose that's why people carry pictures of their families with them. To remind themselves.'

Charlotte stared into the middle distance, dewy-eyed and far away. Claudia looked at her despairingly. 'Do you know, sometimes I think I preferred you bitter. At least you had some spunk then. Now you're like a lovesick cow.'

'Thanks. You're only jealous.'

'Yep. I'm jealous all right. And it's all thanks to me that you met up with him at all. I mean, if I hadn't insisted that you go on that little jaunt you might never have got it together at all. And,' she went on somewhat smugly, 'if I hadn't persuaded you to stay on for a few days . . .' (and spoken to Daniel, she thought privately).

'Yes, yes, I know. You did it, Claudia. You played Cupid. If I ever get married again you can be chief bridesmaid, how's that!'

'Good. That's just what I wanted.'

Charlotte yawned loudly. She took a sip of the cool white wine and winced. It tasted terribly acid. Then once more she yawned. 'Oh Claudia. Excuse me. God, I'm sorry. It's just that I feel really tired suddenly.'

After a few more minutes and several more yawns Claudia could stand it no longer. 'Come on, Charlie, we're going back to the office. You're exhausted, aren't you? Whatever's the matter? Didn't you get any sleep last night?'

'Oh, for God's sake stop nagging me,' Charlotte snapped as they walked out. 'You know sometimes, Claudia, you're like a mother hen. Yes, I did get some sleep last night if you really want to know. I'm just tired now. I don't know why.'

'I was only showing concern about you. There's no need to snap my head off.'

'I wasn't, I was trying to get you to stop fussing. And I'm all right. Really. It was just the atmosphere in the wine bar. It was so hot and smoky in there it's enough to make anybody feel ill.'

'Funnily enough it made me feel rather at home,' Claudia said quietly.

'Huh! It would, with your forty fags and two bottles of wine a day. You're pretty unhealthy Claudia – and you could do with losing some weight.'

Had she been looking, Charlotte would have seen a

343

flicker of hurt appear in her friend's eyes. 'Charlotte, are you premenstrual or something? You seem remarkably short-tempered a lot of the time!'

Charlotte looked at her. 'Am I? What? Just because I give you a few home truths. God, you sound just like a man, Claudia.'

They were back at the office by then. 'Oh forget it, Charlie. I'll see you later – and thanks for coming.'

Charlotte didn't answer but strode off purposefully in the direction of her office.

Laura looked up from her desk. 'Charlotte, you had some calls while you were out . . .'

'I don't want to know. Save them, OK!'

'But . . .'

'No buts, Laura!' she snapped. 'I said save them.'

Laura sank down into her chair and glowered at Charlotte's back. A few seconds later the intercom buzzed angrily. 'No calls, please, and don't let anyone in my office until I tell you otherwise.'

'Certainly.'

Charlotte kicked off her shoes, lay down on the floor behind her desk and closed her eyes wearily. Within a few minutes she was sound asleep.

When she woke, she looked at her watch. It was four o'clock. She had crashed out for two hours. She was beginning to wonder just what was the matter with her.

After she had had a good stretch and a walk around the office to ease her stiffened joints, she went out to see Laura. Her mood had lifted completely. She smiled cheerily at her secretary. 'Right. Now, Laura. You said there were some messages.'

Laura regarded her slightly sullenly, still smarting. 'Daniel phoned while you were at lunch.'

'What?' Charlotte screeched. 'Why the hell didn't you tell me?' Her mood did an abrupt about-turn once more. 'Laura, what time, and what did he say?'

344

'He rang at about one o'clock and he said he wanted you to call him back before three as he was going into a meeting for the day.'

'Why didn't you tell me?'

'I tried, but you snapped my head off. You said you didn't want to know.'

'Oh fucking hell!' she cursed and disappeared back into her office, leaving Laura on the verge of crying. She slammed the door behind her and strode angrily over to her chair. Then she burst into tears.

It was much later, on the train home, that she finally pondered Claudia's words. The train was particularly crowded and she'd had to stand for the last three stations. She felt unbearably hot and was swaying with more than the judderings of the unsteady commuter train. She was beginning to feel sick and sensed the colour drain from her face. She knew if she didn't sit down soon she would faint. She gritted her teeth and took some deep breaths as the world started to go black. Her knees seemed to be crumbling beneath her. Then they arrived at Battersea and she almost staggered off the train. She sank gratefully down on to a bench, placing her head between her knees in best first-aid fashion, oblivious to the curious glances. Once outside the station she hailed a taxi to take her the couple of blocks to her home.

As soon as she was inside she took herself upstairs and lay down on the bed, giving in to the onset of an almighty headache. What a bloody awful day it had been. She knew without a doubt that she had been a real bitch to Claudia. And she knew that she had treated Laura abysmally. Her behaviour had been worse than appalling. Maybe she was premenstrual . . .

Then a thought hit her with the force of a nuclear

345

missile. She started to count off the days since her last period. It had been well before her trip to the Caribbean . . . at least five weeks ago in fact. And she was never late!

She started to piece together her symptoms. She was extremely tired. She was ratty. She had nearly fainted. She felt nauseous. How could she have been so dumb? She was pregnant. She knew it beyond any doubt. She'd done enough research into the subject to write a book on it.

She stared up at the ceiling, wide-eyed, and sighed. After all those barren years with William. All that time of trying to conceive a child. All the unhappiness and dissatisfaction, the self-destruction of obsession. Now after just one week with Daniel she was pregnant. And what the hell was he going to say? They'd spent an idyllic week together, and he had told her he loved her desperately, but would he be quite so enamoured at the prospect of a third party joining them? She didn't even know if he liked children. He might well be turned off at the prospect of a swelling belly and nappies and real commitment. She just had no way of judging how he might react.

But one thing was sure, she was going to have this baby no matter what. There would be no talk of abortions. She had craved a child so desperately that she would not tempt providence by letting this one go. Whether Daniel wanted her to or not, she would have his baby.

She clutched her belly in a gesture of protection and defiance. This was her child. She stroked the surface of her stomach tenderly and thought of the minute life growing there. Well, she didn't have long to wait to find out what Daniel thought. He was back the day after tomorrow. And then she would break it to him gently. But just in case . . . she'd better get used to the idea of being on her own once more.

Except that somewhere very deep within her she had the feeling that Daniel might be rather pleased too . . .

Chapter Twenty-four

'I don't believe this, Giles,' Valentine almost spat down the phone. 'This has never happened to me before. What do you mean, they wouldn't use me? I thought you owned the magazine. Do your staff tell you what to do?'

'Really, Valentine. This is most unfortunate. I did my best for you, my dear.' Giles's voice was smooth as ever. 'You really mustn't react like this. It's quite unbecoming you know. Sometimes I do have to listen to them. Under the circumstances you can hardly blame Charlotte for feeling things are a little delicate, now can you? You were messing around with her husband, were you not?'

'Giles, this sounds as though you're defending her.'

'Well, in a way I suppose I am. She's an excellent editor.'

'Rubbish!' Valentine snapped. 'The only thing she's excellent at is looking pathetic. She's a complete wimp, Giles.'

'She's a well-respected journalist Valentine.' Giles was beginning to lose his patience. 'I'm afraid I have to go now. I'm sorry, Valentine, but I think we'll give everything a rest, shall we?'

'Oh!'

'Goodbye.'

The phone clicked down.

'Damn and shit!' she said aloud. How dare Charlotte treat her like that? Boring little cow. She had never been able to see what Daniel found so attractive about her. Huh! And what a shame that her relationship with Giles had blown apart. She couldn't remember when she'd had such an exciting evening.

She wrapped herself around a very large vodka and tonic, kicked off her shoes and curled up in a corner of the sofa, remembering the previous night and their passionate coupling. Her eyes drifted around the room. Then she saw the small black video-tape sitting on the mantelpiece. The one she had 'borrowed' from Giles. Maybe whatever it contained would help her unwind after her particularly trying day chasing her brother around town. He had gone almost as suddenly as he had arrived, explaining he was to be staying with 'friends' for a few days. Probably gone off on some unpleasant binge, she suspected. He had rather a penchant for S & M since their dear departed father had excited him with regular beatings as a child.

Her lips curled up in a sly smile as she put the video into the slim black machine. She could easily have become one of these porn stars. Except for the fact that she liked to be in control of who touched her. Most of the fun was watching their faces, just wanting her. She wouldn't like the competition of some sweating stud stealing the show. And she certainly didn't need the money.

The screen crackled and hissed until finally a dimly lit room could be seen. Valentine curled up on the sofa with a fresh drink, eagerly anticipating the erotica to come.

A shadowy form was asleep on the bed. It looked very small, a girl's body. A male hand came into camera and slowly peeled back the cover to reveal long naked legs. The man stepped in front of the camera, revealing that he too was naked. He turned slightly so that his profile was visible. She recognized him immediately. It was Giles! My oh my. She rubbed her hands together gleefully. This certainly promised to be interesting. He parted the girl's legs. Then the camera moved in for a close-up shot. Giles smiled a leering, suggestive, almost sadistic kind of smile and started to probe the tender flesh with his fingers, while at the same time masturbating his stiff cock.

Then, for the first time, the legs moved. She heard the girl moan slightly. Valentine felt her breath quicken as she watched, tense, on the edge of her seat. Giles raised his body over the girl, his penis huge and erect. The camera caught the penetration in full glorious detail. He was swift and aggressive. The camera moved upwards to her breasts and lingered there for a moment, and then moved on up to the twisted face. The girl's head tossing and turning.

Valentine's mouth dropped open. She could hardly believe her eyes. This could not be real. Every muscle in her entire body tensed, forcing her concentration. It was. She knew it was. Nobody else could look so like her.

'Charlotte!' she said aloud. 'Fucking hell!' What the hell was she doing in a pornographic video? It was impossible to tell whether her moans were of pleasure or pain. Valentine strongly suspected the former. Why the little whore!

A ghastly smile lit Valentine's face. She felt as though she were on the brink of one of man's major discoveries. The sort that made poor men wealthy and rich men kings, that had the power to change the world.

Giles had withdrawn in order to finish his business: the obligatory 'cum shot' as his seed spilled out over Charlotte's thigh. Then he smacked Charlotte firmly on the rump and pulled the covers back over her unceremoniously.

So, the cunning little hausfrau. All the time she'd been so holier than thou when really she was just a whore. Valentine had to admire her. She had some spunk after all. She grinned to herself. And no wonder

Giles was so protective about her. So the two of them seemed to be sharing all their men at the moment. First William, then Daniel, and now Giles. Maybe they had more in common than Valentine had first thought.

But she didn't suppose for one minute that Daniel would know about Charlotte's 'hobby'.

Valentine had work to do.

Charlotte was too excited to get much done in the way of work. She had had quite a busy morning so far. The first stop had been at the chemist's to pick up a pregnancy test, and then the florist for flowers to make her peace with Claudia and Laura. As soon as she had reached the office, handed them out and made her apologies, she rang her hairdresser and booked an appointment for later in the afternoon. She intended to look her best if nothing else when Daniel returned the next day.

Then she followed the instructions on the 'easy to use', 'instant' pregnancy test, which involved sticking a piece of paper into her pee to see if it changed colour. It was as she thought. She was, indeed, pregnant.

To the rest of the staff she was a woman transformed. The miserable, snapping tyrant of the previous day had been changed into a sweet and gentle angel. She smiled bounteously and laughed with them all day long. And when the anonymous package arrived for her, parcelled up in a rose-coloured paper and bound in a white satin ribbon, she popped it in her bag as a treat for herself that evening.

She sailed through her visit to the hairdresser's as if walking on air. As Trevor snipped away, her reflection beamed back at her. Even her nausea didn't seem quite so bad now that she knew there was a good reason for it. She was a woman with a secret, and a knowing smile.

Instead of her customary evening glass of wine, she poured herself some mineral water, with a dash of ice and a sliver of lemon. She was feeling extremely light-hearted, fulfilled and important. She refused even to consider that Daniel would be less than pleased.

She pulled out the little package with the neat white ribbon, and carefully untied the fastidious bow. Inside was a small black video with a black-edged card resting against it.
It read:

> Dear Charlotte,
> When you have read this note, please watch the enclosed video. I think you will agree that it is probably in your best interests that certain people do not get hold of it, or witness its contents. I will endeavour to keep my own copy of it away from Daniel if you would like to use me as a cover girl for *Amber*.
> My fee is £10,000, by the way.
>
> Love,
> Valentine.
>
> PS I never knew you had it in you!

Charlotte turned the video over in her hand as if expecting to find the answer. What on earth was she talking about, 'cover girl and fees' and Daniel getting hold of it? What was that to do with her? Oh well, she'd better have a look at it and see what it was all about.

She settled back on the sofa and waited for the fuzzy lines to subside. As soon as she saw the opening shot she guessed what kind of film it was. She had only ever seen one 'blue' movie in her life before. That had been at a party in college days. She hadn't stayed to watch it all. She'd found it gross and, above all, boring. There was no titillation for her in any sense. Just a sadness that certain people could derive a perverse pleasure from it.

She saw an anonymous naked back. Then he turned

to face the camera and her heart jumped. In that split second she remembered Daniel's warning words about Giles. He was a pornographer. He was a crook. He was probably into drugs too. He used people to front his vice empires. Giles. He was unmistakable. Daniel had been right. And she worked for him. She gripped the edge of the sofa, unable to tear her eyes away from what happened next. She recognized the room as being the very same one she had spent the night in. Then she saw the girl in the bed and a seed of terror took root. She held her breath. She watched the legs as if in slow motion. Small red dashes of colour marked the pale toes. Her head started to shake from side to side in a silent denial.

She willed the camera to reveal the face, so that she could be released from her fear. That it wouldn't be true. At the same time she already knew it was. She felt she was going to throw up. She had double booked someone else's nightmare. For she knew she was watching her own body, that Giles was mauling and assaulting *her*. She fought the bitter bile, the temptation to throw something at the screen. Incredulity and rage clouded her mind. How? How could it have happened? How could she have been so unaware?

She knew damn well when it had happened. There had been only one opportunity for this . . . this . . . disgusting vileness. And she remembered her feelings the next morning. Her body had certainly felt as though something had gone on during the night. She had even tried to ask Giles the next morning, but had felt ashamed of doing so, for fear of affronting him. Hah! That was a joke! And now she worked for the bastard. He must have drugged her. She knew herself well enough to know that even when drunk she would never have submitted to such treatment. She had certainly been upset. And vulnerable. But not that upset.

She stood up, pressed the off button and pulled the video out of the machine, her resolve already made. As for Valentine and how it had got into her hands, well, she'd deal with her later. Right now she had some urgent business to attend to that meant sorting out Giles Ferguson for good. She wanted to tear him limb from limb. Slit his throat. He'd pay for this, the bastard. She picked up her car keys and ran out, slamming the door shut behind her.

Chapter Twenty-five

❦❧❦

In the dimly lit shadows of Chester Square an old Volkswagen van was parked incongruously among the Mercedes and BMWs. Its parking permit was up to date, and a passerby would assume that it belonged to an occupant of one of the flats just around the corner from the luxury properties of the square. It was dusty and grimy and the chrome was dulled by marching rust. Its interior was hidden by small curtains drawn across the windows. For some weeks it, and several others like it, had parked at various points around the square. In what was typical of any London neighbourhood, nobody paid it any attention and, indeed, several residents would have been hard pushed to recall it was ever there at all. Which was fortunate.

Detective Inspector Murray Preece and Detective Constable Tim Davis were settling down for a night in the uncomfortable vehicle, the next in a long series of nights and days, depending on their shifts. A mattress lay unrolled on the floor in the back so that they could take it in turns to doze in the small hours. It was pushed up to the side of the van, to escape the fumes of the small camping lavatory half-heartedly curtained off in the opposite corner.

Murray spotted her first. 'Look! There's a blonde bird at the door. Haven't seen that one before, have we?'

Tim squinted through the windows, being careful not to move the tiny curtains, or jolt the van.

'Bit classy too. Wonder what she's up to. Maybe he's got a new girlfriend. Anyway, we'll soon find out.'

The two policemen watched the woman press the

doorbell. The special video camera, equipped with its low-light lens, whirred quietly, the small red light easily visible in the gloom. At one frame a second, the three-hour tape would last about three days and record all the toings and froings in Chester Square.

But 'Sedge' Davis wanted to make extra sure. 'Better take a couple of stills . . . just in case.'

His colleague clicked down the shutter on the camera, which was already trained on the house.

'I wish we'd managed to get that bloody mike into his place. Make life a damn sight easier. What's she doing there?'

Murray picked his nose thoughtfully as he watched. Sedge curled his lip. Several months on the plot had made each other's habits irritatingly familiar. Some nights it took a supreme effort of will to swallow a biting remark when your colleague farted in a confined space such as this. Murray was the older of the two. At twenty-four his gut was spreading a little more than he would have liked, and since they had been dispatched to Operation Amber his twice-weekly game of squash had been abandoned. His large frame made it almost impossible for him to stretch out in the small van. But, like most officers assigned to this kind of work, the occasional rewards made it more than worth it. Hundreds of hours of painstaking work could suddenly culminate in the 'busting' of major drugs rings. All their meticulous reports of suspects' activities during the preceding months would then be assimilated as evidence to charge some of this new generation of master criminals, who were often owners of vast business empires and whose sophisticated trinkets included private jets and million-pound yachts.

The success of each such undercover operation hung on absolute secrecy. Discovery could result in an entire network of criminals disbanding themselves overnight and huge drugs runs being abandoned as the scent of detection caught their noses. The surveillance operation stretched far across Europe via Customs and Interpol through the ports of entry to the network of importers, distributors and dealers. Many more of Murray and Sedge's team were employed in situations such as their own. Many were even worse off. Some had gone further underground, mingling with the dealers and posing as dealers themselves, involved in complicated systems of drug swapping and large sums of money changing hands. Both Murray and Sedge had been at the front line in past operations. They knew the drugs scene inside out and could as easily set up a bona fide exchange as stand besuited in a court witness box. But they were happiest out of uniform. Murray's quick wits had kept him out of trouble for his seven years with the Met. His companion would probably get his promotion to inspector as soon as this operation was complete. In looks, both men would have passed for students. Murray's black hair was swept back into a thick pony tail. He wore a singlet-style vest and grubby jeans. Sedge Davis had a lion's mane of long curls and intense blue eyes which he could turn into a 'spaced out' stare at a second's notice. Both knew what it meant to be 'spaced out'. When you have to mingle with junkies as part of your job; and when those junkies have ultra-sensitive antennae which can smell a pig ten miles off, you've got to be a pretty convincing operator. Part of that conviction involves doing drugs too. Hard stuff was out, but neither man had bothered to count the number of times they'd had to smoke dope.

Sedge was a good worker and had an eye for detail which Murray counted on and would emphasize in his final report, when the time came. This was the first time they had worked on a stake-out together and although things got a little touchy at times, on the whole they made a pretty good team.

'Can you see what's going on?' Murray asked. Sedge

was now craning into the viewfinder of a large telescope trained somewhere around the third floor of the Chester Square house.

'He's closed the frigging curtains,' Sedge said in disgust. 'We'll just have to wait and see when she comes out again.'

'Charlotte,' Giles said, his voice as slickly charming as ever. 'What a lovely surprise. How nice to see you, my dear . . .' But she pushed past him and waved the video under his nose.

'Your time's up, Giles, you've been caught.' She faced him then gave him a sharp thwack across the face.

He caught her wrist in a grip of steel. 'What on earth . . . ?'

'You bastard! You absolute bloody bastard!' She fought to escape his grasp, but his hand just tightened in a seemingly effortless squeeze.

'Now, young lady, just what is this all about?'

'This!' she spat, hurling the video down at him. 'That night I stayed here,' she hissed. 'Tell me about it, Giles. Tell me about the night you "rescued" me from the party. My gallant hero. Providing a safe haven. A den of vipers would have been preferable.' Her voice was rising. 'How could you, Giles? You raped me!' Her voice dropped to a whisper. Shame and humiliation flooded through her at the thought of his violation. All the time she had worked for him. Made his magazine a success. She was nothing more than his paid prostitute.

'You can thank Valentine for drawing my attention to this . . . this . . . piece of filth. Oh I'm sure you must have both had a great laugh at it. What a coup for you. I'm surprised you didn't try to blackmail me before. Except you wouldn't dare. Well, your time is up now, Giles.'

'How so?' Still his voice was even, unruffled. He seemed in some extraordinary way almost amused. Like

358

a cat toying with a defenceless mouse. Defenceless. The thought struck her like a return slap in the face. She was indeed defenceless. In Giles's flat. He was a criminal. He was unscrupulous. And probably extremely dangerous. He let go of her wrist. She rubbed the red welt his fingers had left on her skin.

'Now, Charlotte, what's all this "time's up" nonsense?'

'I intend to expose you, Giles,' she said firmly. As she spoke she took a backwards step towards the door. His face changed and she realized her foolishness. She had to get out fast.

His eyes became menacing. He barked: 'Who knows you're here?'

'The police. I told the police, Giles.' Her voice faltered. She was sure he could see through the fabrication. 'They'll be here any second . . .' Her hand was on the door handle. She pulled it open and almost fell in her panic. He moved like lightning, crossing the space between them in a fraction of a second.

'You're not going anywhere, Charlotte.' He grabbed hold of her arm. She winced in pain. 'Come on, come back.' He squeezed her arm tighter still so that the pain made her dizzy. He pulled her after him, through the door into the bedroom which had become the seat of her nightmare. He snatched his dressing-gown cord off the back of the door and, with a deft slip of his hands, pulled both her arms behind her. He twisted the cord around her wrists and then pulled it tight, pinioning them together.

His voice, when he spoke, sounded calm; almost conversational. 'This really is a pain, you know. And after we were doing so well with the magazine. It's a shame that Valentine had to go meddling in my affairs. Most unfortunate . . . And you're such a good editor. Seems such a waste . . .'

'What do you mean "a waste"?' Charlotte asked, trying to keep the fear from her voice.

'I'm going to find it very hard to put you back to work, aren't I? I mean you have threatened me, dear girl, and that's something I really can't afford. Still I'm sure there are others who would be willing to step into your shoes at the magazine. Now, the question is, what am I going to do with you now? I can't have you skipping off to the police in the middle of the night, full of your little tales, now can I?'

He crossed the room and peeled back the curtains slightly. 'If you *had* informed them already, they'd be swarming outside by now, would they not, so I think I can safely assume you did no such thing.'

Charlotte bit her lip so that it almost bled, but did not answer. She followed him with her eyes, watching his every move. He studied her for a few moments, frowning deeply. Finally he said: 'Maybe we should take that trip you've been going on about eh? Go and see Holland.'

He picked up her handbag and then riffled through it. 'As I thought,' he said triumphantly. 'No self-respecting journalist would ever leave this behind. A good habit to get into . . .' He held her passport under her nose. 'You'll need this where we're going.'

'You'll never get away with . . . with . . . kidnapping me, Giles. People will miss me . . . they'll come looking for me. They'll know I'm with you.'

Giles smiled at her, undeterred. 'Charlotte, Charlotte,' he said quietly. 'Don't you worry about details like that. You must let me deal with things. I think you'll learn that's best. Now if you'll excuse me for a few moments . . .'

He flipped her over on to her stomach and then drew her ankles up behind her, so that they were level with her wrists. Her neck and shoulders felt as if they would crack but Giles paid no attention to her protesting screams.

'I'll be back in a moment.'

He left her alone for what seemed like an eternity. Over and over again she cursed herself for being so stupid. How could she not have realized what he would do? She had let her rage blind her completely to the dangers. Giles would no more let her go than surrender himself. She choked back a sob. He would probably murder her. She didn't know the extent of his activities, but if he were ruthless enough to drug and abuse her in the way he had already, then a few murders were probably just a necessary part of life to him. She shivered and tried to concentrate on relaxing her limbs, the ache across her upper arms and shoulders becoming more and more painful.

Giles was busy. First of all he went to the phone and quickly dialled Linda Pointer's number. He was clipped and to the point. 'I shall be out of the country for a couple of days. I need you to do something very important while I'm gone. You'd better get over here quickly.'

Murray and Sedge's radio leaped into life. 'Wakey wakey, you two . . .' the crackly voice alerted them, and while Sedge continued his watchful vigil, Murray answered the voice of his colleague.

'The phone's been used. Someone's coming to see him. A bird. Keep a look out for who it is.'

'He's got one with him already. Sure it's not the same one?'

'How long has she been there?'

'About fifteen minutes.'

'Well, number two only rang a minute ago. Maybe they're having a party. If you could get your box brownie into action.'

'Thanks for the tip . . .'

Murray grunted and snapped the ringpull off his low alcohol lager. He took a large gulp and then belched loudly. 'Seems we might have something to watch tonight.'

Giles opened a cupboard in the bathroom and pulled out a bottle containing small yellow pills. He crushed three on to the sheet of glass which formed a shelf below the mirror. Then very carefully he swept up the powder into a small china eggcup and added a few drops of water from an Evian bottle. He slowly shook the eggcup, watching the small grains dissolve. Next he took a syringe from the cupboard and stripped it of its sterile seal. With the utmost care he sucked the contents of the eggcup into the syringe and then carried the equipment through to where Charlotte lay, scared and unblinking.

Holding his hands behind his back he sat down on the bed next to her then put the syringe down carefully behind him so that she couldn't see it. He was on top of her almost before she saw him move, sitting astride her while her face was almost buried in the pillow. His weight pressed down agonizingly on her already over-stretched limbs, immobilizing her. He picked up the syringe and then quickly stabbed it into her upper arm. She shrieked at the sudden searing pain of the needle and tried to struggle, but she was powerless. 'No . . . no . . . please . . .' she screamed. But he just laughed quietly and then slowly, almost leisurely withdrew the offending article.

'What have you done to me?' she sobbed.

'Just something to quieten you down a bit,' he said. 'Don't worry, I haven't put you on the hard stuff. Yet . . .'

Almost immediately she could feel her head start to spin. She felt horribly sick and then cold and shivery. Her body started to shake. She closed her eyes and concentrated on trying to keep her breathing even. Maybe that way she might fight the drug. She must keep a hold on herself . . .

*

362

Ten minutes later Linda Pointer stood in Giles's flat.

'That was quick,' he said appreciatively.

'I know. I got a cab straight away. You said you needed to speak to me quickly.'

'I'm going away. Something very important needs attending to.'

She nodded. 'OK.'

'The safe. You know the combination, don't you?'

'Yes.'

'Take a couple of ounces of snow. Take a straw with it – you know what to do – and put it in Charlotte's desk. In her drawer or somewhere where it will be easily found by anyone who's snooping.'

Linda looked at him unquestioningly. 'OK. Anything else?'

'Do it before tomorrow morning. And I want this card put by her telephone at her house. I'll give you her keys now.' He walked to where Charlotte's handbag had been abandoned and pulled out a set of keys. 'You'll have to work out which one is hers. Oh, and take her car back for me, would you? So that it's parked outside her house. You'd better make sure no one sees you.'

'Right. You want me to put coke in her drawer; return her car to her house and leave that card by her telephone.'

'Well done, Linda. And don't fuck it up! Leave her house tidy. Make it look as though she's gone off on a trip. You know, draw the curtains back, cancel the milk, turn the lights out. Empty the fridge. You know what to do.'

'Terrific!' Linda said sarcastically.

'As I said, Linda, don't screw it up. You wouldn't like to be in her shoes would you?' He gestured to the small crack in the door behind which Charlotte's bent-up form could just be seen.

'You know me better than that. And it will be a pleasure.'

'Goodnight, Linda,' he said in a cool dismissal.

After she had gone he looked at his watch. It was 9.30 p.m. If he got a move on he might be able to get on to the one o'clock sailing. He looked at Charlotte's sleeping form. He'd have to wake her up to get her down to the car.

He picked up a few things and put them into an overnight bag. Then he picked up Charlotte's coat and bag. He fetched a large jug of cold water and started to tip it over her head. Then he stopped for a moment and slid her body off the bed on to the floor. He didn't particularly want his bed flooded out. He tipped the whole jug of freezing water over her. She moaned and opened her eyes slowly. Giles was untying the cord and she started to squirm with pain as the circulation began to return to her numb limbs. Giles tried to make her stand up, but the pins and needles made it impossible. Impatiently he stood and waited while she attempted to stand herself.

He gave her his arm for support, and then draped her coat around her shoulders. With the amount of barbiturate he'd just pumped inside her, she was not about to put up much of a fight. He half pushed her out of the flat door, down the stairs and then out on to the street. His black Mercedes was parked immediately by the front door and he quickly bustled Charlotte into the back, tripping the safety catches into place so that she would not be able to escape.

Murray and Sedge radioed their team-mate. 'Freddie's flying. Get ready to move. He's pulling out of the square going east. He's got a woman with him, unidentified as yet. Get on it.'

'Roger,' came the reply. As Giles drove out of the square a small brown Vauxhall Cavalier pulled out from the shadows. In it sat a young man and woman who a moment ago had been apparently canoodling

364

quietly in a shady spot. They picked up the black Mercedes and sat as close on its tail as they could without being spotted.

Murray got back on the radio. 'Bird number two came out and went off in a red Peugeot 205 registration G231 YVN. Identified as suspect's secretary, Linda Pointer. Check car registration details please, as she arrived in a cab, and by the way, chief,' Murray said hopefully, 'do you want to call us in now he's gone off swanning, or move locations, or what?'

'Stay put for a bit lads,' came the weary reply.

Claudia breezed into the main office. 'Is Charlotte here yet, Laura?'

'No, not yet. She'll be here any minute though. Anything exciting happening in the fashion department today?'

'Nothing. God, what I wouldn't give to be in Charlotte's shoes right now, eh? Just back from an exotic trip. A gorgeous hunk of a man potty about her. That's what I need, Laura. Someone to sweep me off my feet. Instead, all I get are petulant models and gay photographers.'

'I've told you I'm always available,' Bob interjected from his corner. 'It's just that you won't give me a try . . .'

'Really, Bob, you don't give up, do you?' Claudia said exasperatedly. 'When I'm really desperate I'll let you know, OK?'

He sighed and continued to flick through the morning's post. He collected together a whole pile of correspondence and chucked it in the bin.

'How can you be so sure that there's nothing you should read in there?' Laura asked.

'Because they're press releases. And by definition, if they send the same information out to all the magazines and newspapers, it's not of interest. If they want to

365

contact us direct and give us exclusives then I'll be more than happy. This lot' – he gestured to the pile of letters in the bin – 'is just crap.'

'So now you know, Laura,' Claudia added. 'Luckily my junk mail consists of free samples. Tights mostly. Hundreds and hundreds of pairs of tights. Trouble is I've got the most bloody awful legs. So whenever you want a pair of tights come and see me, OK?'

'Thanks.'

'Yeah, me too,' Bob added. Claudia looked at him sideways.

'Isn't it today that Daniel comes back, Laura?'

'Uh huh. Why do you think Charlotte was in such a good mood yesterday?'

'Funny she's not in yet. Maybe she's catching up on her beauty sleep. Do us a favour and give me a buzz when she comes in, will you, love?'

'OK,' Laura smiled.

It was midday by the time Claudia came back into the office.

'Still no sign, Laura?' Her voice showed clear concern.

The secretary shook her head. 'No, nothing. No calls, no messages. Strange, isn't it?'

Claudia picked up one of the outside extensions and quickly dialled Charlotte's home number. She let it ring for a while and finally replaced the receiver. 'No, she's not there either. Laura, she hasn't done this before, has she? Just not come in without letting anyone know?'

Laura shook her head. 'Never.'

'Well, she has been acting a little strange lately, but it's not like her to just go off somewhere without saying anything about it. I wonder if Daniel arrived early or something. Laura, do we have his office number?'

Laura riffled through the office Filofax and read out the number of Cornwallis de Sallis while Claudia punched out the digits. Eventually she got through to

366

Daniel's secretary. She spoke quickly to Sarah, and then thanked her.

'He's not arriving until late afternoon. Apparently he was meeting Charlotte at her home this evening. Ah well, let me know if you hear anything, OK?'

They had travelled through the night on the vast car ferry that took them into Calais.

'Remember the syringe, Charlotte. It will be next to you all the time. I warn you. If you try anything you get the full dose, whatever that is!'

They had filed up the stairs, right to the top lounge, where they were alone save for a few travelling lorry drivers who had their own private club and were not interested in anyone else around them. Charlotte was sandwiched firmly between Giles and the wall.

'Now tell me,' Giles began softly. 'Just what do you mean about the video, Charlotte?'

'That night,' she said sullenly, 'you must have made it that night. After the party.'

'Ah yes,' he said. 'I remember. That was when you and I . . .' He felt Charlotte's body tense. 'But then of course you wouldn't remember, would you? You were drugged. You're going to have to be careful, Charlotte. All this drug abuse could turn into a habit. Question is, how did you know about it? Through Valentine, you say . . . ?'

'She sent it to me. She was trying to blackmail me into using her in *Amber*.'

'Was she now?' he said thoughtfully. 'How on earth did she get it?' He was almost talking to himself. Where had he left it? He remembered giving strict instructions not to have anything done with it. Either the processors had acted wildly out of order, which was unlikely, or something else. Suddenly he remembered. That was it, it had been at the flat. Valentine had obviously lifted the tape when she had been round the other night. God, the little bitch. She'd have to be taught a lesson, he thought grimly.

They raced through the motorways of Belgium, on into Holland, and eventually the suburbs of Rotterdam, the dawn splitting the night sky, outlining the tower blocks along the city ring road. The traffic was light. Charlotte's wrists had been retied. Her arms ached unbearably. She just couldn't get comfortable. But her eyelids were heavy. The drug had almost worn through her system, but she still felt tired and eventually she fell into the sleep of the exhausted.

She was being shaken. A hard voice was calling her name. Someone was slapping her. She tried to raise her hands to stop the onslaught but they were caught. She opened her eyes, the effort painful, and a bright light hit her full force. She realized with a shock it was the sun. It seemed incongruous. She was pulled out of the car, stumbling and falling. Giles grabbed her arm and dragged her across a sort of courtyard. She could see a windmill and a building like a warehouse or barn behind it. Her heels slid over the old stone slabs. Two enormous wooden doors creaked open. Again she had to let her eyes adjust, this time to the dimness. She was in a sort of studio. Arc lights and cabling littered the area. There were no windows. It was a huge dark bunker-like place and she felt as if she had stepped into hell.

An immense bull of a man appeared from nowhere. He grunted at Giles. Then he looked at Charlotte appreciatively, poking at her as if she was a ripe pig in a marketplace. Giles spoke: 'We need to find this lady some accommodation.' The bull man's cruel face split into a hideous grin. It was almost devoid of teeth, other than a couple of black stumps. His breath was fetid.

'Charlotte, this is Manfred. He's going to be looking after you. You'll find him a wonderful host. You see he's particularly fond of blondes, aren't you, Manfred? But he won't say much. He's a mute.'

Charlotte's flesh crawled. The great monster was pushing her down some stairs, through an open door. She turned. 'You'll never get away with this, Giles. Someone will come looking for me.'

'But my dear, they won't have any idea where to look, will they?'

'They'll know. Everyone knows you're a crook, Giles. It won't take them long to work it out.'

'Let's hope not, because you don't have that long, Charlotte.'

With that they were gone, slamming the huge door shut behind her, leaving her alone in the total darkness. Not one tiny chink of light split the black. She closed her eyes and tried to stop her imagination from conjuring up the hundred red eyes she knew must surely be sitting waiting for her, small furry bodies that could so easily rip her to shreds. She tried to stop her ears from hearing the dreamlike squeaks from between sharp yellow teeth. She hugged her knees up under her chin like a small child, and wept.

Chapter Twenty-six

'I need the key to the booze cupboard, Laura. There's no wine left in the fridge and I've got a photographer coming in later.'

Laura's head was bent over the fax machine. 'Hang on a minute, Claudia. I've just got to check this thing going through. I've nearly finished.'

'If you like I'll get it. Just tell me where it is.'

'In Charlotte's top left-hand drawer. There's a key-ring there. It's the one with the small red sticker on it.'

'OK.'

Claudia's sense of disquiet over Charlotte's absence had got deeper during the day. It was so unlike her. She'd kept trying her at home during the afternoon, but she obviously wasn't there. Nor had she phoned in to anyone. She pulled open the drawer, resolving to call her this evening. If Daniel was meeting her there, she'd be bound to be back by then.

The keys were hidden underneath a small polythene bag containing a white powder. She moved the bag aside and picked up the key-ring and then froze.

There was a tiny mirror lying next to a small black tube. She picked up the tube and examined it slowly. All the while she felt as if the carpet had just been pulled from under her feet. Her mind spun. There must be some mistake . . . But there was no doubting the evidence before her own eyes. She picked up the small bag and examined it warily. There were no more than a couple of teaspoonsful of the powder. She thought quickly and then picked up the bag, straw and mirror and stuffed them into her pocket, before Laura could come in and catch her. She carefully checked the drawer to see if there was anything else she should hide from prying eyes before deciding what to do, but there was not.

She breezed out as airily as she could. 'I'll drop the keys back in a minute, Laura.' She continued on her way to get the wine, all the while the kit in her pocket feeling as though it was burning a red hole through her thigh. She was streetwise enough to know just exactly what it was all about. But Charlotte . . . What the hell was she doing with coke? Years ago, way back in their youth, Claudia had done her stint of trying out dope and on rare occasions a line of coke. She'd even tripped on LSD once or twice – just to spite her father and to prove she was a true sophisticate. Only Charlotte had been bright enough to stay away from drugs. She had despised Claudia for it and had almost refused to have anything to do with her while she was 'experimenting'. She was a 'new age' woman long before her time. She had never smoked and her only vice, so far as Claudia knew, was booze. And that was always in moderation, barring the very occasional binge. But illegal drugs! It was inconceivable. Charlotte would not take those. It was impossible. There had to be some awful mistake.

Subconsciously she placed her hand over the contents of her pocket as she returned the keys to the drawer. She saw her photographer, and drank with him, but afterwards she didn't have the foggiest idea what they had discussed. She was in another world. One which had turned upside down.

Charlotte did not need drugs. She just didn't have that sort of personality. Even through the divorce she had held herself together. She didn't take sleeping pills; she hated tranquillizers and their effects. She moaned at Claudia all the time about her smoking. So what the hell was she doing with cocaine in her drawer? One thing was for sure: Claudia had to talk to her. As soon as she

371

possibly could, she left the office and headed straight over to Battersea.

She was relieved to see Charlie's little red Peugeot parked outside the house. She hammered on the door loudly. She waited a few moments for the sound of footsteps, but there was silence. She knocked louder this time. Maybe Charlie was in the bath, or the kitchen, or asleep.

After the fourth time of knocking Claudia decided to let herself in. Ever since their flat-sharing days they had always kept a key to each other's houses. It had meant that if either had had to go away suddenly the other could help attend to mundanities within the house. Or there were the rare occasions when keys were lost. Claudia would never have dreamed of marching straight into the house if Charlotte were at home. They were at an age now where privacy was of great value, and there were times when you didn't appreciate even close friends just barging in.

When Claudia turned the key in the lock and stepped into the hallway the house felt cold and unoccupied. She called out, just in case, but there was no answer. Then she checked the alarm system. It wasn't set. She went through into the kitchen but it showed no evidence of anyone having been there recently. The sink was clean; the draining board clear. She opened the fridge. It was almost empty save for a pint of milk, a couple of bottles of wine and a tub of margarine. The bin, too, was empty. Claudia's spirits felt lower and lower. The facts did not fit a woman who was expecting her lover to call around in an hour or two's time: a deserted house with an empty fridge. It was beginning to look more and more as if Charlotte had gone away. But if that were the case then what was her car doing outside?

Next Claudia went upstairs. Again the bed was neatly made and the room undisturbed. It was almost too tidy, as if it had been prepared for an absence. Claudia shivered uncomfortably. She had a very bad feeling about all this. She turned on a few lights as the dusk of the evening deepened and looked at her watch. It was 7.15 p.m. There was no point in going home yet; she'd better hang around to see if Daniel turned up, or indeed Charlotte herself.

She went into the sitting room and clicked on the television, and then another thought hit her. At first she pushed it away and tried to concentrate on watching the news. Then the more she tried not to think about it the more it kept coming back. 'Oh to hell with it,' she said aloud.

She stood up and started to search the room. She opened every drawer and every cupboard, sifting through papers, shuffling books around, moving bottles, until it became almost a frenzied attack on Charlotte's belongings. She wanted more evidence. She wanted to *know* that Charlotte took drugs. If she did, there would be some in the house. She turned all the rooms upside down, and was just putting them back together when the phone rang. Claudia nearly leapt out of her skin. Her heart started to pound and her breathing came heavier. God, she was jumpy. Jumpy and guilty. How could she snoop like this in her friend's house? At first she just looked at the phone, watching it ring, while she gathered herself together.

Finally she picked it up. 'Hello,' she said, trying to sound as normal as possible.

'Hi, darling . . . it's me. I've just landed. I can't wait to see you. Just think in about half an hour we'll be together. You'd better warm the bed right now. Grr . . . I can't wait, you sexy woman!'

'Ummm . . . er . . . Daniel,' Claudia stammered, 'it's not Charlotte, it's Claudia.'

'Oh.' There was an embarrassed silence while Daniel

collected himself. 'I see. Claudia. I . . . er . . . obviously thought you were Charlotte.'

She laughed nervously. 'I know. I'm sorry. Look, Daniel,' she went on quickly, 'can you get over here fast? I don't know where Charlotte is, and I think I may need your help. I'll tell you more when I see you.'

'What do you mean she's not there? We talked about this meeting daily for the past two weeks. Is this some sort of joke, Claudia?'

Claudia sighed. 'No, Daniel. It's not. Please . . .' the pleading in her voice was clear '. . . get over here.'

The phone clicked down. Claudia sank on to the chair. Her frown deepened. One of her last hopes had been that Charlie would, after all, be with Daniel. Something was desperately wrong. Whatever else she was doing, Claudia knew Charlie was crazy about Daniel. She wouldn't just stand him up unless something dreadful had happened.

She stared at the phone thoughtfully. Then her eyes drifted to where a small white card had been placed on the table. She picked it up and read it absently. Then she read it more carefully: 'The Sisters of Mercy Clinic, 14 rue St Honoré, Genève'. Then it listed the telephone number. She turned it over in her hand.

Impulsively, she picked up the telephone and punched out the numbers. She waited a few moments for the international connection. After what seemed like an age she heard a distant 'Allô . . .'

'Bonsoir. Est-ce que vous parlez anglais?' she asked in her best schoolgirl French.

There was a pause and then, 'Un moment, s'il vous plaît.'

Another woman came on the line. 'Can I help you?' she asked in heavily accented English.

'Hello, I'm looking for someone who I believe may be attending your clinic.'

'Are you a relative?'

'Yes,' Claudia said quickly. 'It's my sister. Charlotte Grange. She may be admitted under the name of Charlotte de Sallis. Can you please tell me if she's arrived yet?'

'Was she due here today?'

'Yes,' Claudia said, lying through her teeth.

'Just a moment.'

After a few seconds she was back. Claudia held her breath, hoping.

'I'm sorry, she is not here. We are not expecting anybody of that name.'

'Oh,' Claudia said, disappointment obvious in her voice. 'Tell me, Madame, what does your clinic do?'

'We specialize in dependencies. Alcohol . . . drugs . . . We try and help those with addictions.'

Claudia tried one more time. 'Are you sure she isn't there? You see she's disappeared and it's imperative I find her.'

'Madame,' the voice on the other end said quietly. 'You will understand I am sure that many of our patients wish to be . . . how do you say . . . discreet . . . when they come here. It is hard but sometimes they do not want their own families to know. We can only help you so far. Our first responsibility is to our patients. Every day we have new patients. I cannot say whether your sister is among them.'

'If I gave you a description . . .' Claudia said hopefully.

'I'm sorry I can't help you. Goodbye.'

Claudia swore at the dead phone. She knew damn well that if Charlotte had been admitted the woman would know. She was just doing her job and not giving it away.

If Charlotte had been planning to enter a drug addiction clinic then it was more than possible that she wouldn't want anyone to know she was there. But still the explanation didn't ring true. If she was an addict

375

they would have known about it. How could she have hidden the fact from them? Claudia, who knew her so well, would somehow have noticed a difference in her behaviour.

She thought back over the past few weeks. Charlotte's work seemed as consistently good as it had ever been. She'd been more than normal when she left for her holiday. Overtired and overworked, but that was easily explained. And that was precisely why they had bullied her into going. And since she had been back she had been OK. A bit down because Dan had been away. A little moody at times, but that was understandable.

Then she thought back to their last lunch. She remembered commenting on how Charlotte had lost weight. She had goaded her about her daydreaming. She had teased her about not eating properly . . . Not eating properly . . . Claudia frowned. No, that wasn't enough. Then she thought about her moods. Yes, she had been extremely snappy of late. Even Laura had commented on it. Hadn't Claudia herself called her premenstrual – and nearly got her head bitten off in the process. She shook her head. No, it wasn't true. Couldn't be. Then she pulled the small plastic bag, straw and mirror out of her pocket and put them down on the table in front of her and waited for Daniel.

He arrived minutes later. He gave Claudia a perfunctory peck on the cheek.

'Now, Claudia, where is Charlotte? What's been going on and why was I whispering sweet nothings to you on the telephone instead of to Charlie?'

'Sit down, Daniel. I'm going to get you a drink. I think you may need it.' Before he had a chance to say no, Claudia had left the room to collect the wine bottle she had already opened, and the glasses.

She handed him a glass. 'Here. Sit down. And I'll explain as much as I can.'

She began with the start of the day and how Charlotte

hadn't turned up for work. She could see his face get paler and paler. The man was clearly worried and she hadn't yet reached the bad bit.

'So, I looked in her drawer,' she continued, 'and I found this!' She pointed to the 'kit' on the table, which Daniel had not yet noticed. He looked at it curiously and then tasted the powder.

'Do you know what this is, Claudia?' he almost yelled.

She nodded. 'Of course I know what it is. It's cocaine. Together with all the paraphernalia necessary to snort it. But what's it doing in Charlotte's desk, Daniel? So,' she went on, 'I decided to come over here. The house is as you see it. Clearly deserted. Her car is outside. The fridge is empty. It looks as though she has gone on a trip. Then I find this card.' She handed it to him. He read it quickly, then he reached for the phone.

'Don't worry. I've already done it,' she stopped him. 'They say they haven't got anyone of her name in there. They're also quite cagey about the fact that some patients want to be anonymous. And what do you think the place does, Daniel?'

He shook his head. 'Go on, enlighten me.'

'It's a drug-dependence clinic. It's for treating addicts.'

'Jesus Christ,' he said quietly. 'No, Claudia. I can't believe it. I mean we've just spent a week together. She was no more on drugs than I was. She doesn't even smoke, for God's sake.'

'I know. She hates it. She used to get on at me for smoking dope in our youth. Charlotte's just not the type. She's too healthy. Unless she's flipped out completely and all of us have been too stupid to notice.'

'Do you think that's possible?' Daniel said incredulously.

'I've been going over everything in my mind. There are things, little things . . .'

'What things?' he demanded.

'Oh I don't know,' she said uncertainly. 'I feel as if I'm suddenly getting paranoid delusions.'

'Look, Claudia,' he said gently. 'If you've noticed anything strange in her behaviour I certainly think it's important we talk about it. Don't you?'

She shrugged. 'Well, I guess so, but I could have imagined it, you know.'

'Go on,' he urged.

'Well, she's lost weight to start with. Quite a bit of weight I'd say.'

'Well, how much?'

'Half a stone maybe.'

He nodded. 'Anything else?'

'Her appetite. We had lunch the other day and I think she ate one lettuce leaf. That's not like her, is it?'

'No. On Anguilla she was eating like a horse. Anything else?'

'Not really. It's just that she's been a bit . . . well . . . snappy. You know, bad-tempered. And she's not normally like that. And I'm not the only person to have noticed.'

Daniel looked sick. He drained his glass quickly. 'That doesn't sound very good, does it? Though hardly enough to convince me.' He began to look around the room. 'Claudia, have you . . . er . . . have you had a look around?'

'Do you mean have I searched the place?'

'Yes. That's exactly what I mean. Any more clues, as it were.'

'Nothing. Nothing at all. No drugs. No letters. No bills. Daniel,' Claudia said quietly, 'I'm scared for her. Where is she? I can't believe that even if she did have a problem she'd go off just like that. Something's very wrong. I can sense it.'

'I don't like it either. She hid her habit too well. Are you sure no one in the office knows where she is? What about her parents? She wouldn't have gone down there would she?'

'And not mentioned it? Especially when you were coming over. No way, Daniel. Charlotte just doesn't let people down.'

'What about the airlines? Have you checked them?'

'No point. They're not allowed to give out passenger lists. By the time we'd tried them all we could be here all night, and still get nowhere.'

'Then I'm going to Geneva.'

'I'll come with you.'

'Don't be daft, Claudia. There's no point both of us going. You'd better stay here in case she comes back. I'll call you as soon as I get to this place. I'll try and get a late flight tonight, even if I have to go via somewhere else. I'll take Charlie's car if the keys are here.'

'By the front door. I saw them as I came in.'

'I'll go now.' He looked at Claudia's ashen face. 'Don't worry. I'm sure she's OK. You stay here so that I know where you are and I'll call as soon as I've got a base, all right?'

'Take care, Daniel. And good luck.'

Claudia sat for a long time after he had gone, staring at the telephone, half-willing it to ring in case there was any news about Charlotte. The night closed in and she got up and drew the curtains. Eventually she went and lay on Charlotte's bed, taking off her shoes and jeans and rolling the quilt over her. She must have fallen asleep, for she was woken by the shrill tones of the telephone.

'Claudia?' It was Daniel.

'Yes,' she said sleepily. As she fought to clear her head she said, 'Where are you?'

'I've made it as far as Geneva. I'm sorry to wake you but I wanted to see if there was any news. You haven't heard anything, have you?'

'No. Not a thing. What's the time?'

'Six a.m. here. I'm going to the clinic soon. I'll call you later, about ten o'clock I should think.'

'Good luck,' Claudia said for the second time in twelve hours. She turned over, but she could not get back to sleep. What the hell were they going to do if she wasn't at the clinic? They were then back at square one with no Charlotte. They'd have to go to the police. And that would mean telling them she was on drugs. Or would it? Maybe they could omit that little bit of information. She was glad that she'd been the one to discover the stuff in Charlotte's drawer. Imagine if it had been Laura . . . Claudia would have to let Giles know that Charlotte wasn't around. Maybe she'd call in the morning and speak to Laura about it. Perhaps they could say she'd gone off to a conference. At least that would save lots of questions which they had no way of answering.

God, Charlotte, if you only knew the mess you were getting us into. I just hope you're all right, you old bag, thought Claudia.

Daniel was weary. He'd spent the best part of twenty-four hours travelling and his mind was not at its best. He filled his cup and drank his fourth strong black coffee, then rubbed the fatigue out of his eyes.

Nothing seemed to be straightforward where Charlotte was concerned. Just as he had begun to relax, believing their relationship had, after all these months, blossomed into something very special, this came up and knocked him flat. Drugs were an alien culture to him. He didn't 'do' them. He'd never had much time for people who did. Not that he didn't come across them – of course there were plenty in the agency life. Ten years ago coke had been the designer drug. You didn't get hooked on it, it was said, you just had a good time. Jesus, how wrong they had been. It only turned them eventually into a bunch of raving psychotics. It was just as addictive as heroin, or so he had heard, and there was so much hype over its derivative 'crack' and its devastating effects you'd have to be a mental defective to meddle in it.

Now Charlotte had behaved in some unpredictable ways in the past. But she was certainly never psychotic. Nor did she have any of the symptoms he could spot among several of his former colleagues: such as a permanent sniff from where the drug had damaged the delicate nasal membranes. Yet there was no other explanation for her disappearance. They hadn't rowed. He had no reason to doubt that she was looking forward to their reunion as much as he had been. He'd missed her terribly since they had last parted. When she'd left a piece of him had gone with her. He just knew she felt the same. But drugs . . .

He looked at his watch once more and decided it was time. He was already in the street opposite the Sisters of Mercy clinic. It was on the top two floors of a modern six-storey glass and steel monster of a building. Somehow, judging from its name, he'd expected a kind of tumbledown hospice. Not a bit of it.

He took the high-speed elevator up to the top floor and stepped out into a plush reception area. A woman in a sterile white overall dress looked up and spoke to him in French. He answered her in her own tongue. 'I am looking for this woman,' he said simply, holding out Charlotte's photograph. He had taken it himself while they were playing on the boat. It seemed a little incongruous that the healthy blonde beach girl, tanned and glowing, should ever need a place like this. He told the receptionist her name. She asked him to wait and he paced up and down the vast reception area, until she returned a few moments later.

'I am sorry, but she is not here.'

'She must be here.' Daniel had to resist the urge to shake the woman. 'I know she's here.'

She raised her eyebrows, clearly upset that he was accusing her of lying.

'I am sorry,' he said quickly, 'but do you have any other departments, or could she have come here and been transferred somewhere else?'

'I don't think so. We only have fourteen patients here at the moment. And they are all French or Swiss. Your friend is English, is she not?'

He nodded.

'She is not here.'

Daniel thanked her. He could do no more. He felt she was telling him the truth, not just protecting a patient's privacy. And somehow he had sensed she would not be here. It was not the kind of place Charlotte needed.

As soon as he left the building he called Claudia. She sounded as upset as he felt. 'Oh. Shit! What do we do now?'

'I don't know, Claudia. Do me a favour would you, and meet me back at my flat. I've left all my stuff at Charlotte's. If you could bring my case over I'll have a chance to change and we'll talk then. See if there's any news at the office . . .'

'I already have.'

'Oh. I'm getting a flight straight back. I should be with you in about four hours. Then maybe we should think about the police . . .'

Chapter Twenty-seven

❧❦❧

Detective Inspector Sims read through the reports in front of him once more. As usual, he wished he had more men out in the field. There just weren't enough of them to be in all the right places at the right time.

The files connected to Operation Amber littered the entire floor of his office. Hours and hours of meticulous investigation and correlation. Still, if everything went according to plan, the fieldwork should be over by the end of the week. *Amber* was due to be shipped from Holland in three days' time, and that meant that the heroin would be coming over too. Fifty kilos of it, to be precise, with a street value of £4 million. And Dick Sims knew exactly where it was coming from, and where it was going. He also knew who was behind it, who would buy it, and where they would sell it.

All in all they'd had a pretty successful operation. It had started with a tip-off that there was some pornography coming in via Holland, and that it was coming in as part of the *Amber* shipment. But when the customs lads had got their hands on the shipping crates at Felixstowe, not only had they found some particularly nasty 'adult' magazines, but also twenty kilos of heroin. That was when Operation Amber had started. The crates had been carefully packed up again, and the mega-task of surveying Giles Ferguson and his operation over here and in Holland had begun. It had involved a great deal of tact and diplomacy in getting his Dutch counterparts involved. At first Sims could not come to terms with their laissez faire attitude over the porn. It had been legal merchandise over there for such a long time, which was why such a lot of it originated there. But even they drew the line at some of the more gruesome activities portrayed.

The drugs were a different matter. People in possession of drugs for personal use tended to be dealt with leniently. Dealers on the other hand were scourged as much as elsewhere in Europe and the US. No city likes a drugs problem on the scale that heroin has achieved and Holland was one of the three main gateways from the poppy fields in Burma, Thailand, Pakistan and Afghanistan.

Dick Sims wanted Ferguson on British soil when the swoop was made. Extradition treaties were OK, but there was always the risk that the criminals could somehow slip through the net. He wanted to make damn sure that this one was well and truly hooked. He just wished that Giles Ferguson had not been quite so active in the last few days. Suddenly they were having to check up on new contacts. Whatever happened, they could not afford to let any of them get away. But they were running out of time as far as the investigation was concerned. The customs men at Dover planned to swap the heroin for bags of chalk, or flour or whatever. And that meant that the arrests had to be made before the stuff reached its destination. Dick did not want to feel responsible for a whole spate of gangland killings when the receivers realized they'd been duped.

All this time he'd assumed that the magazine staff were clean. None of the phone taps had picked up any contacts between them. He had deduced it really was a front, but that the front didn't know about the rear. Then suddenly, right out of the blue, Charlotte Grange had gone prancing round to Ferguson's house, and then gone off to Amsterdam with him.

Dick scratched his head once more. Just what was she to do with it? Maybe she was his girlfriend. He shrugged. Whatever happened, Ferguson had to come back with the shipment. He had done so the last time. He'd be impatient to get his side of the bargain. Once it was over here there was little point in him remaining in Holland.

Dick made his decision. Ms Grange would be arrested too. They couldn't afford to chance her running off and clearing bank accounts.

Now, Mark Foster. There was someone else who had appeared out of the blue. Their records showed very little about him, but they knew he'd been dealing in New York. That had been a real pain in the arse, sending two officers off to Ireland after him to see what he was up to. Still it had paid off. Van der Heim's general manager, it seemed, had entertained him for the night in his rather smart Georgian residence outside Cork. Then he had been chauffeured back to the airport this morning.

Dick had no doubt he was a courier. But he didn't want him picked up. Not yet. No moves were to be made by anyone. Not until the magazine had left Van der Heim, and that shipment was safely on its way. And until the fifty officers he had drafted in from the home counties to make the swoops, and including those in Holland, were given the go-ahead. Nothing was going to cock it up now.

Mark was sick and tired of hanging around the flat. At least he hadn't had to put up with Valentine being around. His stomach churned and he clutched his belly, doubling over with the cramps that kept hitting him. Come on, come on, he said to himself. How much longer was it going to take to work through his system. Even on the plane over, just three hours after he had swallowed the stuff, he had felt as if any minute he would have a gigantic shit. He'd gritted his teeth and ignored the cold sweat that broke out over his brow. All the way back in the taxi he'd hung on grimly to the safety bar, desperate for the privacy of the bathroom in the flat. And now nothing. For four hours he had paced up and down and all he had was stomach cramps.

If he'd guessed what they had intended to make him do, he might well have refused. It was a bit like playing Russian roulette, swallowing condoms full of heroin. You never knew when the 0.2 per cent failure rate would happen. And the bastard had certainly stuffed them full enough. Getting them down his gullet had been agony, but a mixture of oil and honey had done the trick. Each bag had been dipped into the slippery fluid and then he'd pushed it right to the back of his throat and swallowed. It felt like having the worst indigestion imaginable. And after that came the fear. All that poison inside his gut. All his stomach acids attacking it. And then the long journey through his bowel. If just one bag should burst then the contents would be quickly absorbed into his central nervous system and he'd die a particularly painful death. By the time the symptoms of poisoning showed, there was nothing anyone could do.

At least his journey from the tiny airport at Cork had been short. Even so it was a heavily guarded route. Thank God it was behind him. Next time Giles asked him to do a job, he'd say no. It was time to retire. He'd spent too long now working for these guys. And the money wasn't everything. He'd find some way of paying Eddy back and then he'd find something a little less stressful to do. He was getting too old for shit-sifting.

When he heard the flat door open he didn't take much notice. It was only Valentine. He hardly looked up when he saw the kitchen door open, he was too busy pushing down the Senokots. It was only when he heard the sickening click of a safety catch that he finally turned, just in time to look into the gun barrel before it blew his head off. The bullet travelled faster than his scream.

'I really think we ought to go to the police, Daniel. It's getting crazy. It's almost two days she's been gone. Drugs or not, she's in trouble. But if we tell them she's disappeared, do we need to tell them about the drugs?'

They were disturbed by the bell.

'I'm not expecting anyone.'

Claudia stood up too. 'Maybe . . .'

Daniel looked at her and quickly spoke into the intercom. 'Daniel!' The answering voice was breathless. It was impossible to tell who it belonged to.

'Charlotte?' he said, his voice rising in hope.

'No. It's me . . . Valentine!'

'Oh,' and then under his breath 'Shit. What's she doing here.' Then aloud: 'What do you want, Valentine?'

'Daniel,' he could tell that she was almost sobbing. 'Please let me in . . . please . . . You've got to help me. Oh God, Daniel, come on . . . ' She sounded completely desperate.

'You'd better come up then.' He turned to Claudia. 'Now what? As if we haven't got enough problems already.'

But when he saw the distressed state of Valentine, a few seconds later, he had to admit that whatever was wrong it had to be pretty catastrophic.

'What is it? Whatever's the matter?' he cried as she fell into his arms. She was shaking. He pushed her away from him so that he could see her face. She was ashen.

'Valentine! What's happened? Come on. Calm down, try and tell me.'

She looked at him and her mouth trembled as she fought to speak.

387

'Claudia! Get the brandy. It's over there, by the window.'

Claudia did as she was told and returned with a large tumblerful. 'Here . . .' she said.

Valentine took a hold of the glass and clutched it in both hands. 'It's Mark!'

Claudia looked at Daniel questioningly. He shrugged back at her.

'Mark . . . my brother. He's been murdered.'

Daniel took the glass from her and held it to her mouth. 'Come on, lovey, take a big drink and then start from the beginning if you can.'

'When I got home from work I went into the flat and there he was . . .'

'What happened to him?'

She put her face in her hands and shook her head. 'It was horrible,' she said between half-strangled sobs. 'I think he'd been shot. At first I wasn't sure it was him. You see, half of his head was missing.'

'Oh no,' Claudia cried, screwing her face up in horror. 'But why? Who would want to kill him?'

'I don't know. Well, I'm not sure . . . But there's more. You see, his stomach had been ripped open too. Oh no, I think I'm going to be sick again.'

She ran for the bathroom while Claudia and Daniel looked at each other in horror.

'Why me? Why us? Why did she have to choose to come to me . . . ?'

Daniel followed Valentine into the bathroom and waited patiently while she composed herself, handing her a large fluffy towel on which to wipe her face. 'Here, take another drink.'

She did as she was told. 'After that, while I was just standing . . . Well, to be honest I don't know what I was doing, I can't remember.'

'You're in shock – that's why.'

She nodded. 'Well, then the phone rang. It was

388

a man . . .' Again her hand started to tremble.

'Go on,' Daniel encouraged her, holding her arm gently. Claudia was standing behind Daniel's shoulder, trying to get to grips with the incredibility of the girl's story.

'And what did he say, Valentine?'

'He said that if I messed around in other people's business I'd end up the same way.'

She started to cry again and Daniel handed her a large Kleenex. 'Here. Come on, try and hold yourself together for a minute.'

She blew her nose loudly. 'Daniel, I didn't know what to do . . .'

'Have you told the police?'

'No. I was too scared. I just couldn't think. I suppose I wanted to get away . . . you know, in case they came back. And the only person I could think of coming to was you.'

'Terrific,' Daniel said under his breath.

'I'm sorry,' she said meekly. 'I didn't know who else I could trust.'

'And you thought you could trust me?'

She nodded and for the first time since he had known her he saw a very vulnerable and childlike Valentine. Her orange eyes were tinged with red. Her face was streaked with make-up and her nose glowed like a beacon.

He took a deep breath, sighing heavily. 'So have you any idea who did it?'

'None at all. I hardly knew Mark lately. You see he's been in America for a long time. Then he came back here last week, right out of the blue. For a meeting with . . . Oh my God!' She clapped her hand over her mouth. 'Oh shit!'

'What? You look even worse than you did just now, if that's possible.'

'I've just remembered something.'

'What?'

'Nothing. It doesn't matter.'

Daniel knew she was lying. The girl was terrified. But then why shouldn't she be? If you saw your own brother butchered on your kitchen floor, together with being given a threatening message, you had every right to be petrified.

'Look, Valentine, this is way out of my depth. You have to go to the police. There's been a murder! You have to tell them, and soon. If you're in danger they can help you more than I can.'

She nodded. 'Yes. Yes. You're right.'

'Who did he have the meeting with, Valentine? Do you think they're connected?'

She thought for a moment and then decided. 'Giles.'

'Shit!' Daniel said loudly. 'I knew that guy was bad news. How the fuck Charlotte could ever get herself involved with him. I told her . . . Look Valentine, Charlotte's gone missing. I'm . . . er . . . in the middle of trying to find her. I'll take you to the police, but I've got to find her. We think she may be in trouble.'

'What do you mean "gone missing"?'

'Look, it doesn't matter about the details. I just need to find her.'

'Then you should ask Giles.'

'Ask Giles? Why?' he snapped back at her.

She shrugged and looked at him carefully for a moment. 'Oh well. Why shouldn't I tell you? You might as well know.'

'Know what?'

'The other night, I borrowed something from Giles. A video.'

'What's that got to do with Charlotte?'

'It was a porno video, Daniel.'

He looked at her, a small sneer of distaste around his mouth. He waited silently.

Valentine studied the floor as she spoke. 'It was a video of Charlotte and Giles. They were screwing . . .'

'Don't be disgusting. That's a lie!'

390

'I've got a copy of it, Daniel. I swear to you it's no lie. It was fairly graphic . . .'

'Oh shut up, Valentine. You don't change, do you? Just more of your filthy lies!'

'Look Daniel, I've got no reason for lying. She's his girlfriend. You obviously don't know her!'

'Well, I do know her. I know she wouldn't do anything with Giles,' Claudia snapped. 'And as for making pornographic movies . . . that's just too ridiculous for words.'

'If you want to find Charlotte, ask Giles!'

Daniel stood and paced up and down the room. He shook his head. 'It's rubbish . . . nonsense.'

Claudia, too, stood up. She put her hand on his arm gently. 'Dan, I want a word with you, in private. Excuse us, Valentine.'

She led him through into the bedroom. She knew he was fighting to contain his anger. 'Daniel,' she said quietly. 'We don't know what Charlotte's got caught up in. First drugs, and now . . . well . . . this. Maybe you *should* try and find Giles. I think we should wait before going to the police. We might put her in even more danger . . .'

Daniel gazed back at her. His handsome features looked set in cold steel, his eyes held a fiery intensity. When he spoke it was with such vehemence it made her skin shiver. 'Whatever Ferguson's done with her I swear I'll kill him. Deal with Valentine. I've got work to do.'

Chapter Twenty-eight

Linda looked up from her magazine. She frowned at the heavy footsteps approaching the office. She wasn't expecting anyone. Then she grinned as she realized who it was that seemed in such a hurry.

'Tasty,' she thought to herself, and licked her lips voluptuously, putting her hand to her hair. She stood up and smoothed her dress down over her hips. Charlotte's boyfriend. Hmmm, well. She'd seen his picture often enough.

'Hello,' she said in her sexiest voice. 'Can I help you?' She could help him in lots of ways, she was sure . . .

'I'm looking for Giles.'

'He's not here.'

As she purred back at him, the alarm bells started to ring in her head. He wasn't looking for Giles. He was looking for his girlfriend.

Daniel stepped towards her menacingly. Instinctively she took a pace back. 'Maybe I can help?' she offered.

'When's he back?'

'I'm sorry, I don't know . . .'

Now he was leaning over her desk. 'I'm looking for Charlotte. I thought Giles might know where she is.'

'Why should he?' she said defensively.

'Why don't you tell me?' She had returned to her seat and now felt at a definite disadvantage. The man was towering over her.

'I don't know what you're talking about?'

'Oh don't you?' he snarled through gritted teeth. 'I'm

afraid, little Miss, that I don't believe that. Now, once again, where is Giles?'

'As I said,' she spoke quickly, 'he didn't tell me.'

'Then where's Charlotte?'

'I don't know what you mean. Why should I know where Charlotte is?'

He was leaning over her, she could see he was clenching his fists. She cowered away from him instinctively.

'I've just come back from Switzerland. I'm very tired . . . and impatient! I'm asking you nicely. For the last time, where?'

'Just because she's not at that clinic why should you expect me to know where she is?'

Daniel leaped forward and clutched both sides of the chair, pinning her down. 'I didn't tell you anything about a clinic.' He raised his hand and clenched it around her neck. He'd only ever hit a woman once before – and that had been Valentine. He could feel he was about to repeat the performance any minute. The little bitch knew, and he'd travelled all the way to Switzerland and back. And now she wasn't going to tell him.

When she looked into his eyes she felt real fear. He was like a hungry animal, ready for the kill. Nothing but sheer bloody murder stared back at her.

'You knew about that clinic. Nobody else knew. Now tell me. You'd better start talking now.' He smacked her across the face. She screamed out.

'Now, once more. Tell me!'

She sobbed. 'I can't.' Then she tried to bring her knee up to his groin but he sidestepped away. 'Oh no, you don't!' He held both her wrists in one hand and brought his hand down across her face once more. 'Believe me, I don't care for this, but until you tell me where your boss is I'm not going anywhere.'

'He's probably in Holland. I don't know where . . .'

Daniel raised his hand once more. 'Amsterdam, maybe,' she said weakly, 'or the studio.'

'Give me the addresses.' She nodded her head towards the Filofax on the desk. With his free hand he grabbed it. 'Where is it?'

'Look under Van der Heim,' she said dejectedly. Abruptly he let her go. She rubbed her sore wrists, and then almost under her breath she said: 'He'll kill me. If he knows I told you he'll kill me.'

'Well, just have the satisfaction of knowing that if you hadn't told me I'd have killed you. Now this had better be right. Is it?' he snarled.

She nodded meekly. 'Yes. But he may not be there. If he isn't then I don't know where he is.'

Daniel put the book in his pocket and left.

Twenty minutes later Linda Pointer hurried out of the magazine building into the busy Waterloo Road. She headed straight for the bank, being careful to hang on to the large carrier bag under her arm. She didn't notice the tall young man who followed her into the queue, and then watched her cash two cheques for a thousand pounds each.

When the cashier had finished counting the money she carefully zipped the money into her handbag and hailed a cab. The young man leaped into another taxi and in time-honoured fashion flashed his ID card and said to the driver: 'Follow that cab!' He took his radio out of his inside jacket pocket and pressed out the code. 'Blondie's moving. She's just been to the bank and she looks in a hurry.'

'Oh Christ. What's she up to?' came back the curt reply. 'Stick with her and keep me enlightened, would you, boyo?'

Robbo Evans had been tailing Linda Pointer for several weeks on and off. She was quite an interesting kind of girl. It seemed that she led one of those diverse lifestyles that encompassed executive secretarial, high-class whoring and international drugs smuggling. Quite a busy lady in fact. As they neared the crescent in Holland Park Robbo told the driver to slow down and stop across the road . . . He could see Linda jump out of her cab, but she didn't pay the driver. She went into the flat while the cab waited, double-parked outside the doorway.

'OK. What do you want now?'

'Just wait, thanks.'

Five minutes later she was back, a large suitcase in one hand. She shoved it into the cab and then climbed in after it.

As her cab pulled out, Robbo told his driver, 'OK. Let's go.'

They pulled out on to the Great West Road, up over Hammersmith Flyover and on to the M4 motorway. 'She's going to the fucking airport!' Robbo swore.

He picked up his radio. 'Chief. She's headed for Heathrow. What do you want to do? She could well be running.'

'How? What for? There's no way she'd have got wind of anything. Maybe she's off to Amsterdam.'

'Shall I stick with her?'

'Yeah, see where she checks in. Then let me know.'

Last-minute hiccups like this always happened, at the times when everyone's nerves were frayed to exploding point. Dick Sims was jumpy but he was buggered if he'd let it show. He was on his way down to the mortuary to take a look at Foster's body. Foster's sister and her friend were being held downstairs. He planned to have a little chat with them just as soon as he'd seen for himself what had happened. He intended to chivvy along the pathologist too. Twenty-four hours before a bust was not the time to be caught with your pants down. And they just about had been. They'd had a watch on Foster, but still they hadn't seen anyone enter or leave the flat. Apart from the sister. Yet they'd managed to miss a murderer. He shook his head in aggravation. Clever bastard. But they weren't dealing with the run of the mill crook. These were clever gangsters, with mafia-style tactics. They'd stuck an effective two-fingered gesture in their direction this afternoon all right.

The coldness of the mortuary hit him as soon as he went through the swing doors. One of the senior morticians met him and led him silently through to the place which always reminded Sims of an operating theatre. Except there was no oxygen ready.

'It's a bit gruesome I'm afraid.'

'Aren't they always?' Sims replied. After fifteen years of looking at bodies you got a bit blasé.

The corpse's head was half missing. The man had obviously been shot at close range with a pistol. A shotgun would have blown his head off completely. Sims frowned. 'What's this?' he said, pointing to the white-edged wound on the abdomen that showed the poor bugger's insides. 'A ritual killing?'

'No. More like a disembowelment.' The duty pathologist had arrived and looked over Sims's shoulder with detached professional interest. He was pulling on a pair of pale rubber gloves. They snapped into place and he bent over the fresh cadaver. 'Hmmm,' he said curiously. 'Looks like his lower bowel's been cut clean out.'

'That's nice,' Sims said. Even his cynical professionalism allowed for a touch of nausea. He turned away as Mr McEwen, or Mac the Knife as they secretly called him upstairs, delved further into the gaping wound.

'I'd say someone was looking for something. Could have been a courier maybe.'

'And they split him open like a baked-bean can to get at the goods, you mean?'

'Seems a little drastic, doesn't it? They could have waited for nature to take its course. Poor fellow.'

'Thanks, Jim. That ties in with what I thought. Do me a favour and see if you can do a rush job on this one. It's really important.'

'They always are . . .'

So. That explained why Foster had gone to Ireland. But it didn't explain why he'd been murdered. Sims wondered just how deeply involved his sister really was. She seemed pretty scared by it. Not just shocked. He had a strong feeling that something, or someone, had got to her. And whatever it was she didn't want to let on.

Before he went into the interview room Sims went back to his office. He wanted some time to think. The girl: Valentine. She'd been seen at Ferguson's flat. Her brother was now lying dead and had been carrying stuff for Ferguson. She was probably in on it and had obviously been threatened. Why had Foster been murdered? So far as Ferguson knew he'd done the run successfully. Unless someone else had got to him first.

Then there was the other girl. Claudia Williams who worked on *Amber*. And Charlotte Grange. She was in Holland with Ferguson. He'd have a word with the Williams girl about that. Maybe she was in on it too, and could throw some light on Grange's connection.

And there was one other connection that bothered him. Detective Sergeant Evans had seen Grange's boyfriend go into *Amber*'s office shortly before Pointer left. And Pointer had returned Charlotte Grange's car to Battersea after she'd been to Ferguson's.

There were too many loose ends for this stage in the game. And he had that bloody conference with the Super later on. He left the office and called to one of the WPCs: 'If Robbo comes back or calls in let me know immediately.'

*

Claudia was beginning to wish she'd never agreed to accompany Valentine to the police station. What had seemed like a straightforward act of support was turning into one of those nightmarish misunderstandings. They had been taken straight into an interview room with an accompanying officer who stayed with them the whole time. In two hours they had been offered just one cup of tea, and when Claudia had suggested she had to leave, she was told in no uncertain terms that she wasn't going anywhere.

Valentine seemed to be resigned to their fate for the moment, and had been numbly answering questions about her brother and how she found him. At least she hadn't started to blurt out information about videos as yet.

Claudia sighed impatiently and glowered at the young police officer. 'This is too much, really. I feel as if I'm a criminal and I've done nothing. Is this normal, holding someone in here indefinitely?'

The officer smiled back and said, 'In a murder inquiry it usually does take a long time. You see the more information we have at the beginning, the more chance there is of finding out who's responsible. You might have information that's useful without even knowing about it.'

'Well, I really don't see how I can help. I wasn't there. I keep telling you, Valentine's just someone I know. She wanted moral support.'

Detective Inspector Sims came into the room then and introduced himself. 'I'm sorry,' he said, his voice thick with charm and sincerity. 'I know this is inconvenient for you ladies.' He turned to Valentine. 'I'm very sorry about your brother. It's very shocking for you.'

She nodded weakly. 'Thanks,' she said quietly.

'Now, I've looked at your statements and I'd really like to ask you just a few questions if you don't mind.'

Claudia jumped in. 'Yes. I do mind. As I've just explained to this lady here I have nothing to do with this. I just happened to be there when Valentine turned up. I'd really like to go now. I've got things to do . . .'

He put his hand up and she broke off. 'I do understand, and we won't keep you much longer. Now, if I could just check a few things.' He ran through Valentine's statement, about the time she had discovered the body. Whether the door had been open, whether anything had appeared to be missing.

Valentine confirmed that what he said was true. She still hadn't told him about her phone call.

'So, now we get to the point where you met up with Miss Williams.' He turned to Claudia and looked her levelly in the eyes. 'Can you just tell me again where that was, please?'

'At a friend's flat. Daniel Cornwallis.'

'Near Tower Bridge, is that right?'

'Yes, in Acorn Court.'

'I see. And why did you go there first, Miss Foster, instead of coming to us?'

'I . . . er . . . don't know. I suppose I was shocked.'

'Right. And a bit frightened too, I expect.'

'Yes,' Valentine confirmed. 'I was frightened.'

'Now you went to see Daniel Cornwallis, who is also a friend of yours, Miss Foster?'

'Yes. He's an ex-boyfriend. I really didn't trust anyone else.'

The inspector raised his eyebrows as he scribbled away on his notepad but he said nothing. Then: 'Mr Cornwallis couldn't bring you in to the station.'

Valentine shook her head. 'No.'

'He was too busy,' Claudia added.

'It might be helpful if we knew where he is now.' They were interrupted by another police officer. The inspector left them alone for a few moments.

'Robbo's on the radio. She's headed for Spain. Her bags have been checked through.'

'Get them searched. Let me know what's in them. And when's the flight leave?'

'In a couple of hours.'

'OK, keep in touch.'

He returned to the ladies. 'Now where were we?' He grinned. 'Ah yes. Daniel Cornwallis. Where is he at the moment?'

'I don't know.'

Dick Sims watched Claudia's eyes. They flickered and her cheeks coloured slightly. So, she was lying. 'Maybe he had work to do at his office, hmmm?'

'Perhaps.'

'Or business to attend to at *Amber*?'

Claudia looked as if she'd been slapped across the face. She looked at the Inspector. 'What do you mean?'

'You work for Giles Ferguson, don't you, Miss Williams?'

'Yes.'

'In what capacity?'

'I beg your pardon?'

'What do you do? On the magazine I mean?'

'Oh. I'm fashion editor. Charlotte and I . . . that's Charlotte Grange . . . work together on it. She's the editor. Daniel's her boyfriend.'

'And you were with him?'

Claudia took exception to his insinuating tone. 'Only because we were looking for Charlotte,' she snapped.

'Oh. Have you lost her?'

Claudia's eyes narrowed. She could have bitten off

400

her tongue. She looked at the policeman and did not answer.

'Come come, Miss Williams. How can we help each other if you don't trust me? Is that where Daniel is now? Looking for her?'

Claudia nodded. 'Yes. She disappeared yesterday. She should have met Daniel last night, but she just disappeared. We've been looking for her since then.'

'But you didn't think to get in touch with us.'

'Not yet. We thought we'd try by ourselves first.'

'And where is Daniel Cornwallis now?'

Claudia shrugged. 'I've no idea. He didn't know himself where he was going. So I couldn't possibly tell you.'

Valentine interrupted. 'He was looking for Giles Ferguson. He thought Charlotte might be with him and he wasn't too happy about it.'

Claudia glared at Valentine. The stupid little bitch had really landed Charlotte in it now. Inspector Sims's lips tightened almost imperceptibly. 'I think we should talk some more about Mr Ferguson, ladies. I'll be back shortly. I hope you won't mind if I put you in separate interview rooms for the moment.'

'Fucking meddling imbeciles!' he cursed under his breath. So the jilted boyfriend was going after revenge. Grange had gone off with Ferguson and Daniel Cornwallis was going after them. Or so it seemed. In the process he was putting the whole of Operation Amber at risk.

Dick Sims had no doubt that that was probably why Linda Pointer was getting on a plane. Daniel had put the frighteners on her somehow. He had to be stopped before he got anywhere near Ferguson. For if Ferguson got wind that there was trouble it could jeopardize the whole shipment. Sims just couldn't afford to let that happen. Especially not over some stupid lovers' tiff.

He put out a notification to all ports. *Stop and Hold.* Then Robbo came back on the line. 'She's got a suitcase full of money. £50,000 to be exact. How the hell she thought she'd get it out of the country wedged between her underwear . . . What do you want me to do?'

Sims thought quickly. 'Bring her in! We can't afford to let her get away. If she gets in touch with Giles he'll smell a rat. Besides, there's a load of charges here waiting for her. Just make sure it's a quiet arrest to do with her luggage, etc. – Then bring her back here. Oh, and well done, Robbo.'

Chapter Twenty-nine

He watched the giant grey snake that was the River Thames wind out to sea beneath them. Out over the Isle of Dogs and the county of Essex, towards the Channel and Holland. The small jet was remarkably spacious, just eight seats and the pilot. It was less than an hour since he had left *Amber*'s offices, and within that time he had got to the City Airport, chartered a plane, filed the flight plan, and taken off. As easy as that. A gold card and no questions. The pilot had invited him to join him on the flight deck, but Daniel preferred his own company. He wanted time to assimilate all the events of the past two days.

Everything had suddenly gone wildly wrong. The woman he loved more than he had ever loved anyone, or anything, in his life was seemingly turning into some drug-crazed sex maniac. He had to find her. He had to discover just what was going on. He knew whatever had happened to Charlotte, Giles would be behind it. He must have tricked her or somehow brainwashed her into entering that seedy world, for Charlotte would not have done it voluntarily. Daniel just refused to believe that the glorious woman to whom he had surrendered his soul could turn out to be so depraved a creature.

It would take them about an hour to get to Amsterdam. His eyelids felt heavy and he finally gave in to the weariness that had been threatening to knock him out for the last forty-eight hours. His pants seemed to have been permanently glued to an airline seat, and the hum of the jet engines was becoming more familiar than the sound of his own car. His head dropped forward into sleep.

Charlotte screamed. It was a sound of gut-churning agony that echoed around the bare cell walls long after she had closed her mouth, a shrill, blood-chilling screech full of abandoned hope. She opened her eyes and saw Giles through the mist of her tears.

His face was expressionless. He handed the syringe back to Manfred. 'Give her the same amount in about twelve hours' time.' Manfred nodded his silent understanding. 'I'm going away for a while, Charlotte. Manfred will look after you while I'm gone, won't you Manfred?'

The monstrous mute laughed horribly and the sound replaced her faded scream, reverberating around the cold stone.

Charlotte looked back at Giles, but her eyes were empty, listless. The drug had already begun to take effect. 'What are you going to do with me, Giles? You can't keep me locked away here forever. Please . . .' Her voice was a thin whine. 'You've got to let me go.'

His lip curled into a sneer of distaste as he looked at her. 'You made your choice, Charlotte. Now, you should be grateful that you've got a free supply of heroin. Lots of people would kill for what you've got. You see, in another few days your body will start to need it. Then it really doesn't matter what I do with you. Who's going to listen to a heroin-addicted woman who's lowered herself to appearing in blue movies? You'll be just another psychotic addict, Charlotte. Given to delusions . . . That's if Manfred here doesn't accident-ally give you an overdose of course. We'll see.' He looked at his watch. 'Anyway, my dear. I can't stand here chatting. I've got a boat to catch. Do as Manfred tells you.'

The door slammed shut and she heard the heavy bolt being slid into place. She staggered over to the narrow bed and lay down on the thin, hard mattress, huddling her knees up to her chest, for warmth and comfort. She couldn't quite remember how many times they had come with the syringe. Four or five perhaps . . . It hurt like hell when they pinned her down and stuck the huge steel point into her arm, prodding away until they found a vein. Then it felt cold. Her whole arm tingled and then the drug took hold. Some of the time she slept. Some of the time her body seemed to have a will of its own, convulsing and twitching, or itching intolerably. It was hard to tell. She vomited and then laughed. Sometimes she felt at peace, almost happy. Time had no meaning. Not that she was aware whether it was night or day, where she was in the darkness. She just existed in a space beyond which there was nothing, and no one.

Detective Inspector Sims snapped at his colleague. 'What's happened on that APB? I want to know where that prick Cornwallis has got to. We must get hold of him before he reaches Ferguson. I've got a £2 million shipment of heroin coming over. And if it's fucked up now, after all the money and effort that's been put into it, just because some playboy takes a fancy to go after his flighty girlfriend, well . . .' he fought for words, 'our head will be on the block. Get on to Holland. Just in case he turns up there. Tell them to stop him if he comes in. Sea or air . . . just make sure they get him.'

Sims was already late for his meeting with the Super. He'd spent another hour with the two young ladies downstairs. His hunch that the Williams girl was not telling all she knew had eventually proved right. They'd been a very busy pair, chasing off to fancy Swiss drugs clinics looking for Charlotte Grange. He laughed wryly to himself. They should have come in earlier. He could have saved them the bother. He'd known where Grange was from the minute she'd gone to Ferguson's flat. He still wasn't certain just how deeply involved Claudia Williams was with Ferguson – she hadn't picked up any of the clues he'd dropped about his activities – unless she was a lot sharper than he thought.

Now that Valentine, she was a sly one. On the face of it she was more open than the other one. She didn't want to talk about Ferguson, that was for sure. Even allowing for the grief, she was jumpy. Whoever had put the frighteners on her had done a pretty good job. He wanted to find out just what it was she had done to earn a threat.

He knocked on Detective Superintendent Ian Hall's door, and pushed the door open. The man behind the desk smiled up at him. 'Dick. Come in.'

Dick sat down heavily opposite his superior officer. Even after two years working with him he still found it difficult to come to terms with the man's youth. He was one of the new breed of 'super officers', who joined the force as graduates and disjointed the noses of those officers who had worked their way up, slowly and steadily, from the age of sixteen. Even so, Ian Hall had earned his position well. He had come straight in from Cambridge, following a first-class degree in criminology. He was a real high flyer. Through shrewd hard detective work he had earned the respect and friendship of the team assigned to drug detection at the Yard. He had managed to cut through the bureaucracy that in the past had held up operations: ended petty interdepartmental battles over access to files; introduced slick central computerization which meant all departments could quickly and easily get to whatever information was available. He'd done a lot to open up a dialogue with the customs people too, who played an even more central role in the fight against drugs.

Hall could see that the strain was getting to his inspector. 'Tell me the update. Everyone should be on standby by now for tomorrow morning. Everything OK?'

Sims nodded. 'Yes. Here's my report on the latest . . . the Mark Foster murder.'

Hall read it quickly.

'I'm holding them here,' Sims added. 'I don't think we need them to go skipping round London just yet. Never know what they might try and get up to.'

'Good idea. Now what about this APB on Cornwallis? Any news yet?'

Sims shook his head. 'No,' he said firmly. 'Not yet. We're still waiting . . .'

They were interrupted by Murray Preece. He knocked as he poked his head round the door. 'Sorry . . . I was just coming in to join you and I thought you'd like to know. We've just heard from our Dutch friends. They spotted Daniel Cornwallis at Schiphol customs. They want to know what we want them to do with him. It seems they didn't think to pick him up.'

'Jesus Christ. What's going on over there? Bloody morons . . .' Sims snapped. 'Excuse me, sir, but I think we'd better get on to them PDQ.'

The Superintendent had already picked up the phone. 'Put me through to Pieter van Hool.'

Within a few moments he was talking to his Dutch counterpart. Sims could tell that he was finding it hard to control his patience as he explained the urgency and nature of the intercept. 'You see, Pieter,' he said quietly, 'if Cornwallis gets to Ferguson, the whole shipment could be stopped. Ferguson might disappear, and all our hard work over the past few months will come to nothing.' He raised his eyebrows across the desk at Sims and Preece.

They waited on the edge of their seats while Hall

listened to the telephone. 'I see. Well, why not a traffic offence? I don't know. You'll think of something. Only get him. Thanks, Pieter.' Fucking hell, he mouthed silently to his colleagues. 'Yes,' he added. 'Everything's ready here. Six o'clock tomorrow morning. Seven o'clock Dutch time. We go in. Providing the shipment's left and Giles comes back here. It's looking good at the moment.' He put the phone down.

'So. Let's hope they don't cock it up. We'll just have to wait and see what's happening. There should be some news on the freight soon. What time's the sailing?'

'Ten o'clock tonight.'

'And you're sure everyone's ready?'

'Sure. From ten o'clock everyone's in position. Fifty officers from outside London, who don't know it yet, are going to be sent to Chester Square, Dock-lands, Essex, Felixstowe, Oxford, Reading, London, Birmingham – all the distributors we know of – and they'll move in at six tomorrow morning. Then the real work starts.'

Ian Hall smiled back at the seasoned 'buster'. 'What do you mean?'

'Making sure the charges stick. We want confessions and very hard evidence. I'll be bloody glad when this is over, I tell you.' He took a cigarette out of his pocket and stuffed it in his mouth. 'Five years I gave up for . . .' He inhaled greedily and scowled at his superior.

'If I know you lot, you'll get those confessions,' Hall said darkly.

'That bastard Ferguson will be the slipperiest of the lot. We'll have to go by the phone taps and money laundering. The slimy bastard never goes near the drugs. What I wouldn't give to catch him with the stuff in his hands . . .'

'It's going to be a long night. Keep me informed, Dick.'

*

Even if Daniel had noticed the two men walking along the street towards his cab he would not have given them a second thought. He was too busy explaining to the cab driver that he wanted him to wait while he went into the Van der Heim building – the first address in Giles's secretary's black book.

So when he got out of the cab and they brushed against him he hardly looked up, but apologized as he stepped off the kerb. It was only when he felt a restraining hand on his arm that he looked up into the face of a tight-lipped young man. He looked at the hand on his arm and frowned. 'What . . . ?'

The second man was at his other side. He too clutched Daniel's arm. They pulled him back on to the pavement and then started to walk him back in the direction he had come from, and away from the Van der Heim building.

'What the hell's going on?' He started to struggle trying to shake his arms free, but they were too strong for him. A car appeared from nowhere. The door opened and before Daniel could resist they had bundled him into the back of it, sandwiched between the two men.

His first feeling was one of anger. 'What the fuck's going on? What do you think you're doing?'

Then one of them produced an ID card. Daniel glowered at it, still not understanding. 'Police? You've got the wrong man. My name's Daniel Cornwallis.'

The fairer of the two spoke. 'I know, Mr Cornwallis. We have instructions to take you into our headquarters.'

Daniel could not believe what he was hearing. He'd come halfway round the world, flown to Switzerland and back, and now to Holland, only to be picked up by a couple of imbecilic policemen. His voice was a tight rasp. 'You must be mad! Why, for fuck's sake?' He lurched across one of the men, pushing as hard as he could against his body, grabbing for the door handle. As

409

he did so the other man grasped his arm and pulled him back with a strength Daniel would not have judged he possessed. He leaned back into the seat.

'You'd better start explaining to me why, and fast – or I'll have you in court for wrongful arrest so fast your feet won't even touch the ground.' All three men stared straight ahead of them. 'I said what's this all about?' Still they did not answer him. He sighed, his anger so powerful he felt it could blow his head apart. With a supreme effort he tried to reason: 'There has to be some mistake. You can't just drag me off the street like this . . .'

'We're just following orders,' said the one on his left. 'We were told to bring you in.'

'On what charge?' he cried. The man did not answer him. 'I said on what charge, damn you!' His voice was rising along with his temper. 'If you don't stop this bloody car and let me out, I warn you there's going to be a lot of trouble.' Both men at his sides looked straight ahead, expressionless. It was no use.

He stared out of the rear window at the fast-disappearing site of the vast building. Then he saw the British-registered Mercedes cruise past them. 'Jesus Christ! – You've got to stop that car . . . Listen to me, for God's sake. That's him . . . Giles Ferguson. I've got to see him. Come on, you don't understand. Please . . . stop the car. You've got to stop the car, do you hear me . . . ?'

He leaned forward and shook the driver, but the two men at his sides pinned him back. 'You have to understand. My girlfriend's disappeared. I've come from London to find her. I've got to find out where she is. She may be in trouble. Look, whatever it is you think I've done . . . please stop that man. He knows something. He knows where she is.' His voice was desperate, pleading. In all his life he had never felt so completely helpless.

The Mercedes disappeared from sight. Daniel wanted to scream aloud. Instead his face set with brutal determination. He'd get to Giles eventually.

A few minutes later they arrived at the municipal police headquarters. Daniel was frogmarched into the building and then led into a small, artificially lit interview room. He paced up and down for several moments until an officer arrived. He spoke to Daniel in perfect English.

'Mr Cornwallis, I'm afraid that we have been asked to hold you by Scotland Yard. We don't have the details of why yet. I must ask you to give me your valuables. Your watch, passport and so on.'

'You must be out of your mind. I want you to tell me right now exactly why I'm here. I demand to see a lawyer immediately. I've done nothing.'

The other man shrugged. 'I'm sorry. For the moment there's nothing I can do. Now if you'll hand me your valuables, Mr Cornwallis.'

'Look. I'd like to explain why I'm in Holland. You see it's important. I've got some information that might be useful to you as well.'

'Yes . . .' the policeman said slowly.

'My girlfriend. She's . . . er . . . gone missing. I think she's with someone called Giles Ferguson.' The man's eyes flickered slightly. 'And I've just seen him driving through the city,' Daniel said quickly. 'I know he's a crook. I think he's a pornographer. Maybe he's involved in drugs too . . . and he runs his operation from a company called Van der Heim. They print a magazine called *Amber*. That's an English magazine. And Charlotte – that's my girlfriend – well, she's editor of the magazine. You see I think she may be in danger. I was supposed to meet her in London and she . . . just . . . well, disappeared. That's why I'm here. I need your help.' His words had tumbled out in a torrent, so desperate was his need to make this man understand.

411

'Come with me. Handcuff me. Whatever you like, only for God's sake help me find Charlotte.'

Pieter van Hool heard the note of desperation in Cornwallis's voice. He didn't doubt he was telling the truth. Trust London to get him involved with dragging innocents off the streets. He had every reason to mistrust Ferguson. Maybe Cornwallis's girlfriend was in trouble. It was out of his hands. The international operation was in motion. The drugs were already on the lorry on the way back to the Hook of Holland to be shipped. He'd just had confirmation of that. Now all they had to do was wait till the morning. Then Van der Heim, and the studio, would be overrun with police. After that Mr Cornwallis could be let out, but not before.

'I wouldn't know anything about that,' Van Hool said, almost coldly. 'Now unless you want some of my officers to come and assist you'd better hand over your stuff.'

Sims stuffed the last of the greasy chips into his mouth, and swilled them down with a mouthful of warm coke. Then he belched loudly. He looked at the clock impatiently. Only eleven o'clock, and the rest of the night to get through. His nerves, and his temper, were well frayed. He checked over the files again, making sure that everything was in order for the following day. He'd meant what he said when he'd told the Super that the real work started then. He had to get it right. If he didn't get statements and hard evidence against the suspects he'd have to let them go again. There had to be enough there to support the charges.

'Inspector, there's an urgent transcript for you from the chief suspect's phone.' One of the girls shoved the paper under his nose.

He scanned it quickly and swore softly under his

breath. 'That's it. That's what I've been waiting for. Bugger me . . .' Once again he looked at his watch. It didn't leave him much time. He reread the transcript.

Giles had returned to his flat in Chester Square. He'd made a call and it was obvious from the conversation just who that call was to. He specifically asked if Foster had been dealt with.

Sims could have danced around the office. If Foster had been dealt with . . . Oh, he'd been dealt with all right. Even now he'd be tucked up in his cold metal filing drawer of a coffin for the night. Sims's hunch had been right. Giles had had him murdered. And not only had he talked about dealing with Foster himself, he had also talked about the 'stuff'. Stupid bugger, Sims thought. Ferguson was getting clumsy. Much too clumsy. He should have known better than to have such incriminating calls on his own phone. He rubbed his hands together in satisfaction. This was the missing link. Indication of Ferguson's involvement. Now he was in it. Well and truly up to his slimy little eyes.

Giles's friend was going to do them all a huge favour and bring the stuff round to Chester Square at half past midnight. In precisely one and a half hours!

He picked up the paper and rang the Super. He was doing what any right-minded commanding officer would do, and that was getting some sleep, but he sounded very awake when he answered the phone. 'Sorry, sir, if I woke you,' Sims started off, 'but something very important's happened.' He quickly explained about the phone call. 'I want to bring the bust forward, to one o'clock – a.m. that is! We've got to move in on Ferguson while he's doing the handover. We can't afford to let this other bloke slip away. And I want to see him with those drugs. I believe they came from Foster's gut. But we're going to have to move bloody fast.'

413

'OK, Sims. Arrange for a car. Tell it I'll be downstairs in five minutes and I'll be on my way.'

'Thanks sir.'

By the time the Superintendent arrived Dick Sims had his action plan ready. He met Ian Hall out on the landing. 'Right, sir, I want marksmen to surround the flat. Out the back, where it backs on to the railway line, and round the front. I want twenty officers waiting in unmarked cars to move in as soon as the suspect enters Ferguson's flat. We'll give them two minutes then we go in.'

'You've got it. Just get it organized quickly. And I'll get on to Amsterdam. They'll have to bring their time forward too. We can't afford to have even an hour's delay between this end and that. All we need is one warning phone call for it to go wrong. What's happened with the customs lads?'

'It's on the boat. They checked it on at the Hook. The heroin is in with the magazines – and a load of porn too. They're ready to make the substitutions at this end.'

'What time's it get in?'

'Five o'clock. And it's not unloaded till seven.'

'Well, we can't afford to risk cocking up the Felix-stowe end. I want those little pricks caught with their pants down. Just one whiff of a bust up here and they'll run. We'd have our heroin but I bet no one'd come forward to claim it!'

'Yes, so do I, Chief, but we can't afford to let Ferguson get away with this meeting either. Do you want to bring it forward or not? We could carry on as before and let this go. We could bring the guy in when he leaves the flat – which gives us no hard evidence to charge him other than the phone tap; and that can't be used in court. Or we could move in on them both at one thirty and make sure Ferguson and he are nailed. We could take them both in and hold off the rest of the bust, as planned, and just hope nothing gets out.'

'Nail them, then, but be careful. We can't afford to cock up the other end. I want those dealers too. People are going to be waiting for that stuff. I want to catch them waiting. By the way, what's happened to our two ladies?'

Dick Sims looked sheepish. 'Still in custody I'm afraid.'

'Really. How d'you manage that?'

'Convinced them it was for their safety tonight. Valentine Foster, the sister, seemed more than happy to stay there. The other one took a bit more convincing. Never mind. We'll tell them both tomorrow that they were a major help in trapping a wicked drugs baron and they'll go home happy.'

'Don't you be so sure. We'd better not have writs slapped on us for wrongful arrest.'

'Ah, well, I haven't exactly arrested them. More like offered them protection. Their cells aren't actually locked . . .'

'You're a devious bugger, Sims.'

'I know, sir.'

Exactly one hour later, at twelve thirty, Dick Sims lit his fifteenth cigarette of the evening. He knew it was the fifteenth because he'd only bought the packet at six and there were only five left. 'Fucking Ferguson,' he swore aloud.

Robbo Evans looked at him. 'Fags. That's what. The bastard makes me smoke.' He offered one to Robbo.

'No, thanks.'

'Come on. Come on. Where is he? What's the time? He should be here.' For all his experience, Sims still felt his gut churning. The adrenalin was pumping through his system. He opened the car window slightly to let some fresh air in.

So far everything had gone smoothly. He took one more look around the square. Twenty armed officers were hidden between the cars, inside cars and in the small patch of green, fenced in in the middle of the square. They were all waiting for the signal, which would come from Preece and Davis. Then in. He was going to get a profound sense of satisfaction if all went according to plan. He liked nailing bastards like Ferguson. Drugs dealing on this scale would probably net him about fifteen years. Maybe less for good behaviour. But conspiracy to murder . . . Hiring the hitman . . . Sims wouldn't be happy until he got life. Twenty-five years would be too soon to let him out again.

The battered VW van was parked in its usual place. Sedge Davis and Murray Preece were swapping the watch at five-minute intervals so that they were at peak concentration. Everyone's nerves were running high. Preece was irritable, jumpy. 'I'll be fucking glad when tonight's over. All these months watching. We know so much about you, Ferguson, I'm looking forward to meeting you.' He laughed dryly.

Sedge was at the window. 'I think he's coming. Get the radio.'

Murray grabbed the radio and opened it up. 'Standby,' he said quietly. 'Suspect two in sight.' Then he joined Sedge at the window. 'Big bastard, isn't he?' he whispered to his colleague.

'A contract killer. You could stand next to him in the pub and never know.'

They watched him ring the bell and then quickly enter the flat. It was difficult to tell exactly what he looked like. Sedge did his best from the light that was available.

'Suspect two is six foot tall, wearing a black hip-length leather jacket, and dark trousers. Possibly a brown jumper. Mid-brown hair, curly.' He waited for the confirmation. The curtains in the front windows were closed and for once he was grateful. It meant that the marksmen could move into their positions without being spotted.

When two minutes had passed, the first five men approached the house. Within seconds they had managed quietly to open the front door. Silently, they ascended the stairs to the doorway of Giles's flat. Two of the men flattened themselves against the wall, guns poised, as a third threw a sledgehammer at the lock, choosing just the right spot for the wood to splinter and fracture. The door burst open and he dropped to the floor, allowing the two men nearest to tear through ahead of him, followed by two more behind them on the stairs.

'Stand still! Police!' they screamed.

Giles looked up in stunned silence. His mouth dropped open. 'What the fuck . . . ?'

He turned and fled into the bathroom, trying to slam the door, but a policeman was right behind him. Giles threw a handful of white sachets down the toilet and reached for the flush, but the policeman was too quick, throwing himself across the room so that the two of them landed with a sharp thud on the cold floor. Giles was heavily winded. His assailant lay on top of him, pressing his full body weight down, while he waited for assistance.

Giles's visitor had instinctively fled towards the rear of the flat, rushing into the kitchen at the first sound of the door breaking. He leapt up on to the stainless steel draining board and pushed open the heavy sash window. As he leaned across the open space and peered out into the night, he was blinded by floodlights. Even if he jumped, he couldn't see where he might land. And behind the floodlights were undoubtedly many more police marksmen. A pragmatist at heart, Harris recognized when the odds were against him. It was just part of the job. He raised his hands and waited for the inevitable handcuffs. He was pulled out into the hall and came face to face with Giles, who was also handcuffed.

Giles shook his head at the contract killer. 'Keep your mouth shut,' he threatened.

Dick Sims walked over slowly and poked Giles in the chest as he spoke. 'Whether he talks or not doesn't make any difference, Ferguson. We already know what a slimy murdering little cunt you are. You and your stinking little perversions. I've been watching you for months. Your friends in Holland too. You thought you were pretty fucking clever, didn't you?'

'Inspector, here . . .'

Sims turned and stepped into the bathroom where Robbo had been dipping into the toilet pan. Four small packets lay on the floor where Robbo had dropped them. Sims bent over them and looked carefully. Condoms. He turned to Giles and pursed his lips, nodding. 'Well, it doesn't take much guessing to know where these came from, does it, you fucking butcher? Take them away, boys.'

Chapter Thirty

At six o'clock that morning the first batch of cars slipped unobtrusively out of Amsterdam's police headquarters. Twelve officers were heading for Van der Heim, four officers to Kurt Wolfe's apartment, and another twenty to the old windmill.

Hoofdinspecteur Pieter van Hool rubbed at his unshaven chin, enjoying the harsh rasping sound his fingers made. He was on his way over to the windmill where the heroin was kept before being shipped off to England. After the arrests were made he'd have plenty of time to strip the place bare and get his forensic evidence. The best sniffer dogs would help him find out where the rest of the stuff was hidden.

His crack squad of undercover officers had already gone in. Storming an office block and an apartment block at seven in the morning would not pose too much of a problem. Getting ten gunmen up a deserted lane to an exposed pile of old buildings without being noticed did. They'd been lucky in that it had been a cloudy night with no moon. At four o'clock he'd received the confirmation that they had achieved their positions, and that the place was surrounded. Now they were waiting for orders to go in. Pieter was relying on their commander to surprise whoever was inside before entering with his own team.

It was 6.30 a.m. when his car pulled up at the end of the quiet little country lane. Three other cars drew in behind him and they waited silently. A few miles further on a helicopter was on standby, in case anyone unexpected was there. The best intelligence he had told him there was only the mute there. But the isolation of the place had made it more or less impossible to get a full-time surveillance in operation. A few porn 'stars' came and went at regular intervals, for this was the centre of Van der Heim's pornography business, as well as a drug clearing house. But they didn't stay over. As far as Pieter knew there was just the mute and the dogs. And by now the four rottweilers would be sleeping like babies.

At exactly 7 a.m. he radioed Kapitein Vate: 'Now.' And then once more he waited.

Manfred was just waking up. He checked the video screen. It was programmed to interchange between five cameras strategically positioned outside the building. Everything looked quiet. He stretched and pulled on his vest and trousers, shoving his feet into his sweat-starched socks, and then found the boots that he'd kicked off the night before. With a grunt he sat back on the bed and bent forward to tie the laces. His great gut made it hard for him to do it. Then he stood up and reached for his jacket. It was time to feed the dogs. He always made sure they were hungry before letting them out at night. That way they'd be more than ready to have a go at any intruders. He glanced at the video once more as he opened the door, and then stopped. He came back to the screen and pressed the 'freeze frame' button.

Intruders! At least four of them! He pulled his jacket on quickly and then reached for the inside pocket. He checked his gun. All six chambers of his Colt .45 were full. He opened a drawer at the side of his bed and pulled out a handful of bullets. The men were close to the main entrance of the barn. If he got a move on he could get up into the space at the top of the windmill, where the sail mechanism was housed, and pick them off.

He smiled happily to himself. It was time he had a bit of excitement in his life. This was better than administering to that piece of limp dishrag downstairs. When she'd first arrived he might have thought of giving her one, or two. Since she'd been pumped full of smack she didn't seem half so attractive.

He lumbered across the landing and down the stairs that led to the back entrance of the tower. He peered through the window and saw he was too late. There were now about ten men with guns at the ready outside. He tried blowing the whistle hung around his neck. Where were those fucking dogs? Those men should have been torn to pieces by now . . .

He looked around him, wondering which way he should go. Then, abruptly, he turned and headed for the cellars. He raced down the cold stone stairs to the door at the bottom. He put the gun back into his pocket and slid the two stiff bolts back so that he could swing the heavy door open.

Even his nose wrinkled at the stench from the bucket in the corner. The bedclothes were stained with vomit and the woman's hair was a tangled filthy mess. He slapped her to wake her. She shook her head from side to side. 'No . . .' she moaned. 'No . . . please . . .' She tried to curl up again and then she opened her eyes. It gave Manfred a sense of well-earned pride to see the terror in those bloodshot eyes. Her arms thrashed wildly at him and he grabbed them effortlessly, pulling them behind her. Her skin was a deathly white, which made the track marks in her arms appear even more red and angry.

He lifted her off the bed. There was a patch of dark red blood on the mattress which had seeped through her skirt. He pulled her to a standing position, but her legs buckled underneath her. He wrenched her arms again and pushed them forward into the small of her back, a silent warning to stand up.

She tried but she had no strength left. Instead she slumped forward, as if she had been broken in two, like a rag doll. He closed his arms around her front and half pushed, half-carried her out in front of him, back up the stairs – to come face to face with an automatic pistol. Manfred held the girl firmly in front of him, his own gun pointing back at the intruder. Then he turned the gun on Charlotte and held the barrel to her temple. The gunman frowned but kept his gun trained on Manfred. Manfred started walking backwards towards the rear door. The gunman called out: 'Don't shoot! He's got the girl with him!' as Manfred almost fell through the door and out into the courtyard.

He looked around him, quickly taking in the fact that there were now about twenty men, all with their guns trained on him. He looked over towards the car and dragged Charlotte with him until he reached the door of the vehicle. Charlotte was barely conscious. She was only dimly aware of what was going on. She just wanted him to let her go so that she could die quietly. She needed to lie down and let the exquisite blackness wash over her, so that she wouldn't have to feel any more.

Suddenly she retched, throwing up all over Manfred's arms, where he held her, spewing up the watery soup he had fed her the previous night. Manfred loosened his grip on her in revulsion, and she slipped down through his grasp and in that split second she heard a deafening crack, followed by two more. And then silence. She had fallen onto something soft and comfortable. She closed her eyes and slipped away into the dark, safe world of oblivion.

The girl was in a bad way. He looked at her limp arms and saw the fresh needle marks. She was filthy and she stank. Underneath all the dirt he could see she had once been a very pretty girl. At least she was breathing evenly. But when he saw the blood oozing out from between her legs he decided to get the helicopter. Drug addict or not, he did not want another death this morning.

Pieter van Hool sent the message back to headquarters. 'Let Daniel Cornwallis out and give him his stuff back. Tell him we're taking his girlfriend to the hospital. He can meet her there. Get someone to take him over.'

It took four of them to lift Manfred's huge bulk into the ambulance. There was no point in speeding anywhere with him.

The helicopter dropped down carefully and precisely on to the large pad on the roof of the hospital. Charlotte was brought out of the aircraft on a stretcher, transferred to a waiting bed and quickly wheeled inside the main building. A few moments later two doctors were busy checking her pulse and breathing. A nurse carefully peeled away her clothes.

A quick internal examination revealed what they had immediately suspected. She was miscarrying. The nurse was busy putting antiseptic dressings on to her arms and a sterile covering over her filthy hair. Then she inserted another syringe into Charlotte's arm, and withdrew some blood which she immediately rushed off for emergency analysis.

'Where is she?'

The whole reception area reverberated with the volume of Daniel's demand. He burst through the door with all the vigour that a night in jail had given him. He had been like a time bomb, just waiting to go off, building up a furious energy. The policeman who had brought him trotted ineffectually behind. 'Sir . . . Mr Cornwallis . . .'

Daniel charged over to the first person he saw.

'Where is Charlotte Grange? What's happened to her?'

The doctor looked at him nervously, wondering who this lunatic was who had just stormed the hospital. 'Please,' he began. 'You will disturb our patients.'

Daniel took a deep breath and tried to control his temper. He turned back to the policeman. 'If anything's happened to her I swear I'll make you pay for this.'

Just then another doctor appeared. He was accompanied by a rather tired-looking young man. He saw Daniel and walked over to him. 'Mr Cornwallis. I'm Inspecteur Munche. I've just brought your . . . er . . . friend in. This is Dr Pederson. He's just seen Charlotte.'

'What's happened to her?' Daniel barked. 'Is she all right?'

'Come . . .' the doctor took hold of Daniel's arm and led him along the corridor, away from the interested eavesdroppers. 'She has obviously been through quite an ordeal. The Inspector here has been telling me the circumstances before she arrived here.'

'Well, would someone please like to tell me . . .' Daniel interrupted.

'She is going to be all right. Unfortunately she is having a miscarriage . . .'

'Miscarriage? She was pregnant?'

'I'm sorry,' the doctor said gently. 'Yes. She was very early in her pregnancy but it seems that the shock of her ordeal, and the drugs . . . Well, she's haemorrhaging and we have to stop that. We would like to give her a transfusion immediately.'

Daniel had gone white. 'I don't understand. Charlotte was pregnant. I didn't know.' His voice tailed off. His head spinning once more with the implications of the doctor's words. 'And you said drugs. What drugs?'

'We are doing the blood test right now to find out

exactly what's in her system. But it seems that she has taken heroin. Quite a lot of it. She's still quite heavily drugged now.'

'Charlotte would never take heroin. You're lying.' He stepped towards the doctor.

Inspector Munche moved quickly between them. 'As soon as she's feeling able, we'll talk to her. Then hopefully she'll be able to tell us herself what's happened. It's probably best if you don't see her just yet. Doctor . . . ?'

'Definitely. She is very ill. I'm afraid it is best if you let us help her for the moment.'

'Can't I just go in and look at her. I won't speak to her. Just let me see her for a moment. Please . . .' All the fight seemed to have left him. The adrenalin that had carried him through the last forty-eight hours was now draining away. He felt weak and defeated. And now he just wanted to see her, to see for himself that she was at least alive. The two men looked at each other. The man's desperation was obvious.

'Then I will come with you,' said the doctor. 'Just for a minute. Come. Follow me.'

The curtains had been drawn in the small room and Daniel blinked at the tiny form tucked neatly into the bed. A drip bag containing clear fluid hung on a metal frame at the side of the bed, and a small tube fed it down into a catheter inserted in her arm. Her pale arms were covered in ugly purple bruises, and the veins showed an angry redness through her almost translucent skin. Her breathing was soft and even but her lips looked pale and lifeless.

Daniel stepped towards the bed, but the doctor restrained him. His voice was softly sympathetic. 'We want to find out just how much heroin is still in her bloodstream. Then we can give her something to stop the bleeding. Also, as soon as we know her blood group we can start the transfusion. In another twelve hours she should be awake and ready to talk. Why don't you get some rest until then.'

Daniel looked at him as if he were insane. At first he did not reply. He continued to stare at Charlotte's sleeping form. All he could think about was the last time he had seen her. Healthy and laughing. Loving and vital. The whole thing had turned into the most incredible nightmare. He should never have let her go back to Ferguson. And he had calmly watched her go back while he attended to his business in New York. God, he wanted to throw up. He'd put his stupid crass career before Charlotte. And now here she was. Drugged and bleeding. She had been pregnant. He choked back a sob. It had to have been their baby. For whatever had happened he knew in his heart that Charlotte would never willingly have been near Ferguson.

Finally he turned away, nodding his thanks to the doctor. As the door closed behind them he forced himself to ask the question he had been avoiding. 'Is she . . . will she be a . . .? Doctor, is she an addict?'

'Obviously at this stage it's impossible to tell,' he said gently. 'But I would say it's extremely unlikely. Let's just wait and see what she can tell us when she is able, shall we? Try not to worry about that at the moment.' He put his hand on Daniel's arm reassuringly.

'Doctor, if there's any change . . . anything at all . . . I'll be waiting here. Please let me know as soon as I can see her again.'

'Yes, yes, of course, Mr Cornwallis, of course.'

Someone was shaking him gently. His eyes leaped open, primed, ready to hit out. 'What the . . . ?'

'Daniel, it's me . . . '

His eyes cleared.

'It's me, Claudia.'

'My God, how did you get here? How did you know?'

'The police. In London. I kicked up such a stink that they told me where I'd find you, and Charlotte.'

His mind was still hazy. He'd spent several hours staring at the ceiling in the waiting room and must have dozed off. He flexed his shoulders; the muscles had set like concrete. 'How did they know?'

'It's a long story. Anyhow, where is she, and how is she? I couldn't really get the gist of what had happened except that she'd been locked up at some place of Giles's and was now in hospital. Whatever's happened? Can we see her?'

'Oh Claudia.' He put his head in his hands. 'I just can't forgive myself . . .'

'Come on, Daniel. You haven't done anything. Have you?' she said uncertainly.

'Yes. I let her come back to London to that bastard.'

'But you didn't know . . .'

'Oh yes I did. I found out about him shortly after you all started talking about the magazine. Just after the agency merger when Charlotte went off with Giles. You know, the night William was screwing Valentine. I started asking questions about Giles and learned that he was a crook. I did try and warn Charlotte but you know how headstrong she is.'

'Well, she never mentioned it.'

'No. Because she didn't believe it. And why should she? So far as she was concerned the important thing was running the magazine.'

'Well, that still doesn't make it your fault, Daniel. I don't believe you could have stopped Charlotte. You tried. And you couldn't.'

'I should have come back with her after the Caribbean. Instead of rushing back to New York. I should not have left her alone.'

'Oh for God's sake, Daniel, she's a grown woman. Just because this has happened you can't reproach yourself because you didn't nanny her. Now what happened?'

'I still don't know the full story. I came over, and as soon as I got close to Giles I was arrested.'

'Not you too! So was I. Valentine and I spent the night in "protective custody". They let me out at nine this morning. They invented some cock and bull story about how they wanted to keep us inside for our safety. It was impossible to leave. Then this morning just before the press conference, they announced to me that I had helped them trap Giles Ferguson, murderer and drugs baron. And I'm supposed to say "OK chaps, thanks awfully. Wonderful night in jail what?"

'It seems that Giles was responsible for murdering Valentine's brother, and that Valentine might have been involved with him too. I don't think she was, but they haven't let her out yet, as far as I know.

'Anyway they knew that Charlotte had left England with Giles and they assumed that she might be in on it, and as I worked with her on *Amber*, I might too. I have to admit, Daniel, that after hearing the stories about Charlie's cocaine, and the video, I was beginning to wonder. Giles was arrested late last night and the police operation started over here this morning.'

'So I gather,' Daniel interrupted. 'And they found Charlotte locked up in some cellar.'

'What?' Claudia gasped.

'Full of heroin.'

Claudia clapped her hand to her mouth. 'Oh my God. I didn't know. Nobody had told me. I thought maybe she was suffering from shock or something. What happened?'

'And she's having a miscarriage.'

'She was pregnant?' He heard the catch in Claudia's voice.

'Yes.'

'I had no idea.'

428

'Neither did I,' he said slowly. 'She was haemorrhaging when they found her. Somehow or other she was also full of heroin.' He was silent for a moment, trying to come to terms with it. 'We'll have to wait until she can talk to us before we find out what happened.'

'She wouldn't have taken it herself.'

'No,' he answered quietly. Despairingly.

'Dear Charlotte.' Claudia was silent for a few moments, staring thoughtfully at her feet. 'Can we see her? Have you seen her? How is she?'

'It's hard to say. She looks awful. She's got a glucose drip and they were going to give her a blood transfusion. It sounds unlikely she'll be addicted. If this is the first time she's taken it.'

'Well that's something I suppose. Daniel, why were you arrested?'

'I suppose they were worried I'd fuck up their operation. Same reason as you.'

'There was a big drugs shipment this morning. Giles was behind it.'

'The police thought that if I got near Giles I'd mess up their bust. They knew all the time what was going on.' Daniel narrowed his eyes. 'Seems they were prepared to sacrifice Charlotte.'

'I guess they didn't know she was innocent.'

'God. Now I know just what it feels like to be wrongfully convicted of something. You know, Claudia, for the first time in my life I couldn't do a thing to help. I was completely useless. Locked up and unable to make anyone believe me. It was the most terrifying experience. And all the while to know that Charlotte was in danger.'

'I know. In a funny kind of way I felt it too. The Detective Inspector was very careful to point out that I wasn't arrested. But I was. And they can be so devious. They twist things round so that you don't know what you're saying. I'm bloody glad to be out of there. At least they had the decency to let me know where you were and what had happened to Charlotte. When they'd got their precious bust out of the way, that is. Are you hungry?'

He shrugged. 'Not really.'

'When was the last time you ate, Daniel?'

'Haven't a clue. I think I had a sandwich at the police station this morning. I can't remember.'

'Come on. Let's go find the canteen. I'll tell the nurse where we are.'

'No, I can't. I have to stay here in case the doctor comes back.'

'Daniel, you'll be no good to Charlotte if you collapse from exhaustion. You look like death. They'll find us if Charlotte wakes up. I want to see her too, you know.'

He could see it was pointless to argue. 'OK, OK. But it had better be quick.'

She opened her eyes slowly and then closed them again. She had a thumping headache. She tried to raise her hand to her temple and then she realized there was something tight around her arm. Again she opened her eyes. She was in a small box-like room. Overhead was a large strip light, shielded by a plastic cover. She turned her head slowly. There were two drip stands at the side of the bed, one with a clear fluid and one with blood, both of which led to her left arm where a splint-like piece of plastic held the two tubes in place. She tried to sit up and immediately felt sick. She noticed the small cardboard bowl at the side of the bed just in time and retched into it. She took a sip of water from the glass at the side of the bowl and sank back exhausted.

As she lay there she became aware of a pad between her legs and a kind of shiny-sided plastic mat which felt squelchy under her bottom. She was wearing some kind of scratchy hospital gown and the pad, shoved between her legs, felt uncomfortably loose. She moved her knees and felt a warm stickiness ooze out on to the pad. She tried to sit up again and as she clenched her stomach muscles she once more felt the sickening wetness flowing from her womb.

The baby! In a flash she remembered. Her baby. Why was she bleeding? She was losing it. She looked behind her and pressed the bells and pulled on the cords. The lights came on, a buzzer buzzed. She waited. Afraid. Hurry, oh please hurry, she willed. Within seconds a nurse appeared.

She smiled brightly at Charlotte. 'Oh good, you're awake.' She spoke English, but she had a heavy accent. Charlotte was not in a fit state to wonder what it was.

'Please . . . I'm pregnant. And I'm bleeding. What's happening? What am I doing here?'

The young nurse flicked back the covers and looked at the pad between Charlotte's legs. She leant down, and pulled a sterile packet out of the drawer and removed the wrapping. She deftly swapped the pads over. Then she looked across and realized that Charlotte had been sick. She collected the bowl and then said: 'I'll tell the doctor you're awake. He'll be with you in a minute.'

Charlotte settled back and, bit by bit, awful dreamlike memories of the last couple of days filtered back. It was hard to separate the real from the imaginary. Then she saw the bruises on her arms. She searched for the tell-tale puncture marks. They were there. She could only see her right arm, for the left was strapped up with the drip.

The man with the needle. He had kept coming and sticking it into her. Putting her to sleep and making her feel as if she were going mad. There were great purple welts around the punctures where he had handled her so roughly.

Then she felt her hair. It itched like mad and when she put her hand through it it had the consistency of soggy baler twine. And it stank. She felt filthy. She wanted a bath, some fresh clean water to humanize her.

A man, clearly the doctor, entered the room. He smiled encouragingly. 'Hello, Charlotte. I'm Doctor Pederson. You've had a good long sleep since you've been here . . .'

'What's happened, Doctor? Why am I bleeding? Have I miscarried?'

He'd have to tell her sooner or later. 'Yes, I'm afraid you have. Your ordeal was obviously too much for the baby to stand. And when you arrived here this morning you were losing quite a lot of blood. As you can see, we've got you on a drip.'

'What about the drugs. They were giving me heroin, weren't they?'

'We certainly found heroin in your bloodstream, but you should be coming out of it now. At least you've had a nice long sleep. That's a good sign.'

Charlotte looked at him numbly. Nothing seemed to matter much now. Somewhere, way back in the corner of her mind, she vaguely remembered the bleeding. In some other consciousness she had been aware of it. And frightened by it. Now she knew why. She would kill Giles Ferguson. Her thoughts moved on. 'Will I be addicted . . . ?'

'I don't think so. Did you inject yourself?'

She laughed but it was a cold, bitter sound. 'Doctor, since I was a child I have had a pathological fear of needles. I could no more stick a needle in myself than fly to the moon. Someone else stuck it in for me. It's hard to remember exactly . . . I was locked up. They came every so often. All I can remember is the pain, and then the rest is just a haze.'

'That's enough for now. I want you to rest. You must

not get out of bed. If you need anything just use your buzzer. The nurse is right outside.' He walked towards the door. 'Oh, by the way, you have some visitors. Mr Cornwallis . . .'

'I don't want to see anybody. No one at all. OK?'

'That's fine. Wait until you're feeling a bit stronger.' He closed the door quietly behind him.

Charlotte turned her face into the pillow and wept.

Chapter Thirty-one

Claudia trotted along behind him. 'Daniel, I swear that's the fastest meal I've ever eaten in my life. Slow down . . . you're like a man possessed.' He had bolted down his omelette so quickly it hardly touched the sides, leaving Claudia halfway through her delicious-looking steak.

In the corridor they caught sight of the doctor. 'Dr Pederson . . .' Daniel called. 'Doctor, could I have a word with you?'

'Of course.' The man stopped and waited for Daniel to catch up with him.

'How is she, Doctor? Is she awake yet? Can I see her?'

'She is awake.'

Daniel had already turned in the direction of her room. 'Please, Mr Cornwallis. I have told her that you are here, but she doesn't want to see anybody. She is distressed, what with losing the baby on top of everything else. She's resting at the moment.' He frowned sympathetically at Daniel's crestfallen face. 'It's hard for you, I know. But really my advice is that you respect her wishes for the moment. I am sure that in a few hours she will be feeling much better.'

Daniel nodded dumbly. He heard the doctor's words as if from afar. He was still reeling from his own profoundly shocked state of mind. Try as he might, he could not stop his imagination conjuring up the dreadful torture she must have gone through. His own dear Charlotte. Kidnapped and locked up. Pumped full of drugs. Helpless. And now her frail, still form wired up to the drip . . .

The older man's voice was deeply earnest. 'My main recommendation is that as soon as she is well enough she should return to England. Physically I believe she is over the worst . . .'

'Thank God!' Daniel said quickly.

'But emotionally it will be very difficult for her. It would be better for her to be in more familiar surroundings, with her family and friends around her. This place carries all the associations of her terrible ordeal. She should be taken right away from it. She must have complete rest. It is absolutely vital that she has no more emotional distress. Her mind is very fragile at the moment. You must understand, Mr Cornwallis, that Charlotte has suffered the kind of nightmare that some never recover from. And on top of that, her grief for the baby . . .'

'I see,' Daniel said quietly.

'It is very sad about the baby. Yours I believe?'

'Yes.'

'The whole thing is really most unfortunate.'

'Doctor, when do you think I'll be able to see her?'

'Mr Cornwallis, I'm afraid that at the moment I must follow her instructions that she does not wish to see anybody. As I explained, hard as that may be for you, it is critical for her recovery that she gets as much rest as possible.'

'Yes, Dr Pederson. I understand completely.'

The kindly doctor reached out and touched Daniel's arm, reading the expression on his worn features. 'It must be very hard for you, I know. It's bad not being able to do anything. Just give her time. Once she is back in her own surroundings she may well feel more secure.'

'Let me arrange it. I'll have a private plane . . . nurses . . . Just tell me what she needs. How soon can she travel?'

'I think tomorrow, provided she has the proper support for her journey.'

'Fine, Doctor. Just leave it to me.'

The next day Charlotte, accompanied by two nurses, once more ascended to the hospital roof and was transferred by stretcher on to the waiting helicopter. She was taken to Schiphol airport from where a small private jet flew her to Heathrow. Then she was taken by ambulance to the luxurious Wellington Hospital in St John's Wood where Daniel had gathered together the best team of doctors available to care for her, including her own gynaecologist.

Bit by agonizing bit, the full extent of her ordeal was realized. She had been kept permanently drugged over a period of nearly seventy-two hours, locked in a cell, barely fed, and beaten. The bruises on her arms were beginning to turn a yellowish-green colour. The serious haemorrhaging had stopped before she left Holland, but she continued to bleed slightly for a few more days following the miscarriage.

Soon after Charlotte arrived the gynaecologist, Alison James, spent an hour with her, examining her and talking to her while Daniel paced up and down the plush corridor outside the room. Finally, when Alison came out, Daniel introduced himself.

Alison had a warm, motherly kind of face and regarded him sympathetically. 'It's very sad. Very sad indeed. I'm sorry . . .'

'Thanks . . .' he said weakly.

'It was yours, wasn't it? Losing a baby is always sad. But this is particularly tragic . . . I assume you knew her history?'

'What do you mean?'

'During her marriage . . . she's spent the last two years trying to conceive. She was desperate for a child. She thought she was barren . . .'

436

'Yes. We talked about it a long time ago.' That night when he had visited her in Richmond. He remembered it vividly. She had sobbed in his arms and then he had kissed her. That was before things went so wildly wrong.

'I knew she wasn't, of course,' Alison went on. 'She'd had every test which proved it conclusively. It was either a very deep psychological block or her husband's problem. He wouldn't have any tests so . . .'

'If it was psychological I suppose this might make things even worse?'

Alison James looked down at the carpet and shrugged slowly. 'Well, let's hope it isn't. And now she knows she's not sterile . . . It will take a while for the scars to heal . . . you know, the ones in her head. You'll have to treat her very gently.'

'She won't even see me at the moment.'

She heard the desperate note in his voice. 'Give her time. That's what she needs. You see she feels badly abused. Almost as if she's dirty. It's hard for people to understand what it must be like to be treated like that . . . just . . . well . . . worse than an animal.'

Daniel shuddered silently.

'She has to re-evaluate herself. Her sense of worth, her self-esteem . . . all that has to be rebuilt very carefully . . .'

'You sound like the psychiatrists and psychologists.'

'I've dealt with rape victims in the past. It's similar. The violation somehow makes the victim feel guilty. She has to deal with those feelings, Daniel. And if seeing you exacerbates them then you must respect her wishes.'

He nodded and turned away from her. He was going mad with despair. He needed to see her more than life itself but to see her could send her mad. He could not share with her the love he so wanted to give her. He wanted to hold her and kiss her and let her know that it was all right, that he would make everything all right.

He could share with her the grief over their lost child. Slowly he walked back along the corridor, feet dragging dejectedly over the plush brown carpet. Someone said something behind him, but he was too lost in thought to respond. Nothing much seemed to matter any more.

The next day Charlotte agreed to see Claudia. As Claudia bent over her friend and kissed her cheek, the pale skin felt cool and dry to her lips like thin parchment. 'Hello, you,' she said brightly.

Charlotte turned to her listlessly. 'Hi,' she said flatly. She watched Claudia fiddle with the pink tulips she had brought, plopping them into the vase the nurse had provided.

She smiled weakly. 'They're lovely.'

'How're you feeling?' Claudia pulled the low chair up to the bedside.

'Ghastly, thanks.'

'Oh. Which bit?'

'All bits.' Suddenly a great sob escaped her. The tears started to flow as if a huge dam had burst. She looked very small and lost; like a hurt child.

Claudia reached out and hugged her. 'It's all right, Charlotte. Cry as much as you like. You need to. Let it all out.'

For several minutes Charlotte cried and cried, with great racking sobs. Claudia cradled her gently and then passed her a tissue. She blew her nose loudly.

'Sorry, Claude,' she said. 'I don't mean to be pathetic.'

'You're not pathetic. You've had a terrible ordeal. You need to cry. You are doing marvellously, you know.'

She nodded. 'So they keep saying. But they keep asking me to talk about it. I can't . . . I won't.' Her voice started to rise. 'Claudia, every time I think about it I crack. I just fall to pieces. Look at me now. I

438

feel if I really let go I'll never stop. I can't. I just can't.'

'Maybe that's the point. Maybe they want you to crack. You have to do that before you can start to heal.'

She looked thoughtful. 'Like my mother. Remember after James died?'

'Yes, that's right. Look how she bottled it all up. Didn't you spend all your time asking her to let go?'

'Hmm,' she said noncommittally.

Claudia stood and walked over to the window. She stared out across the skyline. 'Charlotte,' she turned to face her once more, her voice almost a whisper, 'I'm very sorry about the baby . . . you never let on . . .'

'No. I had only just found out . . . And I wanted Daniel to be the first to know. I never got a chance to tell him. I hoped he'd be so thrilled.'

Claudia stared at her feet, uncertain of what to say next. She felt utterly inadequate. 'Well, I suppose it's nice to know you can have them, Charlie,' she said rather pathetically. 'Small consolation though, I suppose. I mean after those years of trying . . .' She broke off when she caught Charlotte's expression. She looked as though she would dissolve into tears once more any second.

'What if I can't have them after this? And let's face it. Who'd have me?'

'Now that really is ridiculous.'

'Claudia,' she said at last. 'How is Daniel? I mean, how does he seem? Is he OK?'

'Why don't you ask him yourself. He's here . . . he's been with you since you first got to hospital, Charlie. The poor man's going out of his mind because you won't see him. Really he's falling apart.'

Charlotte looked ashen. 'I can't . . .' Claudia could

439

barely hear her, her voice was so small. 'I just feel too ashamed. I can't face him yet.'

Alarm bells started to ring in Claudia's mind. She was afraid she might push her too far. 'OK,' she said quietly. 'When you're ready, Charlie. Just remember that man loves you. He needs you too.'

'I know,' Charlotte said quietly.

They were interrupted by a knock at the door. It opened slowly and Claudia exclaimed: 'Good God! What on earth are you doing here?'

Dick Sims looked embarrassed. He always hated having to intrude on the bedside scene, but his job necessitated boorish ways. 'Ah, Miss Williams,' he grinned sheepishly. 'How are you?'

'Oh terrific, thanks. Always feel better after a night in jail. Just like a health farm you know. Revitalizing and invigorating, ha ha ha,' she laughed falsely.

'I'm sorry about that. It was necessary. We had to catch Ferguson, and get the drugs, as you know. It's unfortunate that Miss Grange here had to be put through such a terrible ordeal.'

He turned to Charlotte and introduced himself and the woman police officer who followed him into the room. 'Miss Grange, I apologize for coming to see you like this, but I do have some rather important questions I must ask you relating to your . . . your . . .'

'Kidnapping?' Claudia offered.

'Yes. Thank you, Miss Williams. Now if you don't mind I would rather talk to Miss Grange in private . . .' Claudia started to protest.

'It's all right, Claudia. I'll be fine. You'd better do as the Inspector asks.'

'OK, darling,' she said softly and gave her friend a big warm hug. 'I'll come back and see you tomorrow.'

'Bye, Claudia, and thanks.'

Sims closed the door behind Claudia and came and sat by the bed. The WPC stood by the window, rather awkwardly. 'Do you mind if I call you Charlotte?'

'No.' She shook her head. There was something about his manner that suggested to Charlotte that underneath his tough cop exterior he was sympathetic.

'You've had a pretty rough time, haven't you?' he said gently.

She nodded.

'Well, you'll be pleased to know that we've got so much evidence against Giles Ferguson that he won't be out of prison for a long, long time.'

'Thank God,' she said fervently.

'Now, what I'd like you to do, in your own words, and in your own time, is tell me as much as you can about what happened. I understand you might find it a little distressing . . . Just tell me what you can.'

'I'll try. Where do you want me to start?'

'How about when he took you off to Holland? We know you went round to see him. You see, we had him under surveillance for a long time. But can you tell me why you went round there?'

Charlotte bit her lip and looked at him. The video. That meant she'd have to tell him about the video.

He saw what small amount of colour there had been drain from her face.

She couldn't lie to him. There seemed no point. After all she'd been through it was just one more piece of degradation to add to the rest. She swallowed hard, trying to find the right words.

'There was a video,' she began. 'Someone sent me a video . . .'

'Valentine Foster,' he interrupted her.

So he knew. But how could he? 'You know about her sending it to me?'

'Yes. You see we had her in for questioning too. Ferguson had her brother murdered. He'd also threatened her. Apparently because you told him

441

Valentine had got the video and had given it to you.'

'I see. Then you know what was on it.'

'I . . . er . . . understand it was a pornographic film.'

'Yes.' Her voice was barely audible. 'He raped me. He must have drugged me first. I didn't know anything about it. I didn't know that he'd done that to me. Not until I saw it myself that night. The night I went round to see him.'

The Inspector let her go on. He'd seen some of the video. But he wasn't about to let Charlotte know that.

'I was angry. I went round to sort him out. I was so stupid. I don't really know what I thought I could do. I just didn't think. But as soon as I got into his flat I realized how bloody stupid I'd been. He tied me up and drugged me. The rest is hazy. I can hardly remember. I suppose we must have travelled to Holland.'

She stopped and took a deep breath. The Inspector was afraid she might break down, but he let her talk on.

'After that I was locked up. He gave me heroin. I think he wanted to turn me into an addict and let everyone think I'd overdosed. That's all. You probably know more than I do . . .'

'Thank you. That's cleared up a few things anyway. You could press charges against him if you wanted.'

'What do you mean?'

'For rape. And assault. We've got the evidence we need. The videos and, of course, this . . . your ordeal. I'd like you to consider testifying against him.'

Charlotte thought for a few moments, scratching at the cotton sheet across her stomach. 'No. I'm sorry, Inspector, but no. I don't think I could bear to go through it all again. It would mean having to stand up in front of a courtroom full of people wouldn't it?'

442

'I'm afraid so.'

'I couldn't.'

'Without your testimony, Charlotte, we'd find it hard to press charges for the rape and kidnapping . . .'

'Inspector. If I agreed, I'd have to stand in front of a jury and talk about pornographic videos. People would have to see them. I couldn't bear the thought of my family and friends being subjected to that. I just couldn't bear it . . .'

'OK, OK,' he said gently. 'I understand.' He guessed as much. And in a way who could blame her? She'd been through enough without having to relive the whole thing several months into the future. With the size of the case they had to put together, it was going to take a long time to get it to trial stage. 'Think it over. Let me know. Here's my card if you want to talk to me.'

'Thanks.'

He was about to leave. She called after him. 'Inspector . . . those videos. Where are they? There were two copies, weren't there?'

'We've got them both. Valentine gave us one. The other was found in Ferguson's flat.'

'What's going to happen to them?'

'Well, for the moment we have to hold them as evidence. You see, they've been documented . . .'

'I want them destroyed.'

He nodded slowly. 'I can understand why.'

She flushed slightly. 'Can you do that? Destroy them, I mean?'

'I'll talk to the Superintendent about it. Under the circumstances I'm sure we could arrange something . . .'

'Inspector,' she pleaded, 'let me know. Soon. I don't want anyone to see those videos, ever. I just can't live with the thought that they even exist. You've got to get rid of them for me.'

'I'll do my very best for you.' And he meant it.

Claudia waved at the taxi, but just as it started towards her a black BMW appeared from nowhere and screeched to a halt in front of her. The passenger window slid open. She bent down and grinned at the driver. 'I might have known . . .'

Daniel smiled a little sheepishly. 'Can I give you a ride?'

She stood up again and shook her head apologetically at the taxi, now waiting behind, before getting into Daniel's car.

'Daniel, you're going to have to stop creeping up on me like this. Yesterday it was lunch . . . today you provide me with a taxi service. All to talk about Charlotte. I hope one day someone goes to as much trouble for me.'

'Where to?'

'The office, I suppose.' She looked across at his gaunt features. His eyes were sunk in their sockets and the hollows in his cheeks had deepened. In short, he looked bloody awful. 'Doesn't look as though you got much sleep last night.'

'No!' he grunted. 'Well . . . ?' he added, impatiently. They'd all come through too much together to bother about social niceties.

'She looked a bit better today. A bit more colour . . .'

'Good,' he sighed, relief softening his features for a moment. 'But did she say anything?' His voice carried an almost harsh note of desperation. Claudia's heart went out to him. She looked at him silently, trying to cushion the words that he least wanted to hear. As she answered him, she turned her face away, not wishing to witness his hurt.

'I tried, I really did.'

His fists tightened on the wheel, she sensed his body stiffen.

444

'She says she's too ashamed . . .'

'Ashamed! Jesus, how can she be ashamed? That's the last thing she should feel. Doesn't she know how much I love her? Why can't she just trust me . . . ? None of this was her doing. If only she knew how much . . .' He broke off and Claudia shifted in her seat, embarrassed at the rawness of his emotion. She too was helpless. She could see all too clearly that these two people should be together, and that only then could Charlotte really begin to mend properly. On top of everything else they should have time to grieve for the baby. They should not be isolated from one another, but safe and warm in the comfort of each other's arms.

'I asked her, Daniel. I pushed it as much as I could, but she said she wanted more time. Then that bloody policeman turned up.'

'Oh no! What now? Why can't they just leave her alone?' he shouted angrily.

'Quite! Anyway, I wasn't privy to what they talked about. I was asked to leave. Charlotte said she was OK so there wasn't anything I could do about it.'

'I thought the whole point was that she was to be kept in a stress-free environment?'

'I suppose they need their evidence.'

Again Claudia was silent. There was something else weighing heavily on her mind, hanging over her like a guilty secret she had no wish to be in on. Ever since Charlotte had told her, she had asked herself over and over whether she should tell Daniel. By doing so she would betray Charlotte, but it would help Daniel to understand her ordeal, and her frame of mind, a lot better if he did know.

'Daniel,' she said quickly. 'Let's go for a drink. I . . . er . . . don't have to be at the office yet, after all I'm only sorting out my desk really, clearing stuff out. Come on, I think we could both do with it.'

'OK,' he said. 'There's nothing else I've got planned. I

445

tried the office yesterday and all I did was move piles of paper round my desk and stare out of the window.'

She'd taken the plunge now, she had to tell him. But better over a stiff drink than a traffic jam. Thankfully Daniel didn't talk much either until they were seated at a table in the little wine bar off the Strand. Playing for time she lit a cigarette slowly while her mind tried to prepare the words.

'Daniel, there's something I must tell you . . . about Charlotte . . . and Giles . . . and that video.'

There. It was out. Daniel put his glass down on the table and looked at her bleakly, reading Claudia's extreme state of unease. 'What is it, Claudia? Come on, I might as well know the worst.'

'Remember the video, you know, the one that Valentine talked about.'

'Oh that. Yes, I remember,' he said slowly. Ever since his mercy dash around Europe Daniel had pushed Valentine's allegations aside, deep into his subconscious where they could lie forgotten. They were the kind of allegations best left to slip into a protective oblivion. Now here was Claudia bringing them up. He had to face it. He steeled himself.

'Well, it's true, it does exist – Charlotte told me. He raped her, Daniel, the night of the agency party. She didn't know anything about it because he'd drugged her. He made a video of it. I know it's true because Charlotte told me herself. I think that's why she feels so ashamed. In a way she feels dirty because of it . . . and violated. I think that's why she can't face you.'

Daniel's face crumpled. His mouth twisted and he made a strange strangulated growl deep in his throat. When words finally came his voice sounded strained and disjointed. 'I went round there that night . . .'

Claudia nodded. 'Yes . . . I know, you said.'

446

He was speaking almost to himself. 'I could have taken her away.' He groaned as if he'd been kicked in the gut. 'But instead I left her there with that . . . that monster. That murderer!'

For a moment Claudia was truly frightened. For she couldn't recall ever having seen anyone this angry in her entire life.

'It's lucky for him that he's behind bars because if I ever get my hands on him I swear I'll castrate the bastard.'

'Daniel,' Claudia's voice was urgent, 'you must not let her know. Remember she wasn't aware of it. You must swear to me that you mustn't tell her. One day maybe she might tell you herself . . . when she's ready, but until then you must not make her feel even more degradation.'

'I won't tell her,' he hissed through clenched teeth. 'I would just like to tear Ferguson apart. Claudia, would you mind . . . ? I have to be alone for a while.'

She watched him stagger out of the wine bar, resisting the impulse to chase after him. What she had just told him was almost too much for any man to bear. She just hoped she'd done the right thing and that by telling him he might understand Charlotte's state of mind a little better.

He drove, unseeing, through the London streets. He must have stopped at lights, for he was jerked back to consciousness by angry hoots behind him. The lights were now green. He shifted the car through its gears, not caring which route the black beast chose to follow. He had pushed his own autopilot button. The car sped smoothly through the city south-eastwards through Docklands and beyond. The sun beat down brazenly and the rest of the population revelled in its glorious warmth. To Daniel it was a blaze of torment, making him sweaty and uncomfortable and causing his head to throb. He had wound down all the electric windows but the breeze had no strength to cool him.

Soon he was leaving the suburbs behind him. The numbness of his mind and emotions lifted slightly. He yawned and his shoulders slumped. He felt exhausted.

The houses had given way to green and gold fields and the breeze, though still warm, had gathered the strength to nuzzle his hair. He was approaching a little pub that looked warm and friendly and above all, anonymous. He spun the car on to the gravelled forecourt and skidded to a halt, sending up a shower of stones. He got out and, without bothering to lock the car, stepped into the cool bar, blinking while his eyes adjusted to the dimness. He ordered himself a double whisky and retired to the furthest corner of the place, sliding down behind a mock oak table. Only then did he let himself think. To know what Giles had done was to carry the pain of a red-hot poker thrust deep into his chest.

Alison James's words came flooding back to him. 'She's like a rape victim . . .' she had said, 'feeling ashamed and abused . . .' Charlotte couldn't face him because she was ashamed. She had been tortured, humiliated and abused beyond human endurance and she was now too ashamed to face him. But he was the one who should be ashamed. For he had let her get tangled up with Ferguson. He should have dragged her from the bed that night. He should never have left after the fight in Richmond when he had warned her about Ferguson. He should have made her listen. And he should never have let her return from Anguilla without him. Reason told him that he could not have stopped what happened. But emotion told him he was single-handedly responsible.

Since the whole damn thing had happened he had only seen Charlotte twice. Once had been while she

448

slept in the hospital in Amsterdam, when her pale white skin matched the colour of the swathes around her head. But he had been forbidden either to touch her or to speak to her. She must not know he was there. Then, when he had flown her home from Schiphol airport, he had been in the cockpit all the time, while the doctor and nurse tended to her in the main cabin. Once during the flight she had drifted off to sleep, after the tranquillizers had done their job, and he had been allowed to climb through the little door and sit by her for a while. After half an hour, which to Daniel felt like no more than a minute, the nurse gently pushed him away and he returned, reluctantly, to his lonely seat next to the pilot.

He drained his glass. It was time to go. He knew what he had to do now. He returned to the car and slowly and deliberately headed back towards London and Charlotte. He was prepared to take the risk for them both. He knew what they needed.

His feet trod softly over the plush carpet of the reception hall where he had spent so many hours pacing up and down like an expectant father. The nurse looked up from her station and smiled at him. He headed straight for Charlotte's room but once outside the door he paused for a few moments, his heart hammering loudly in his chest. He stared at the smooth white surface of the door, with the demurely curtained window and the slip of paper with Charlotte's name printed on it. He had to follow his instinct and trust that he was right, but he was terrified it would all go wrong.

He pushed open the door. The room was full of the sight and scent of flowers. It was a mass of vivid colour, and most of them had come from him. Then slowly he looked over to the bed to where Charlotte lay, her hair spread across the pillow. Her cheeks had regained some of their usual pinkness and her breast rose and fell evenly in a deep, relaxed, healthy sleep. She looked beautiful.

In that moment, as he looked down at her, all the tension and uncertainty just seemed to melt away. 'Oh Charlotte . . .' her name fell from his lips in a great sob.

Her eyes flew open and she looked at him, stunned. She blinked and stared. 'Daniel . . . ?' she said softly, uncertainly.

'My love . . .' He rushed forward and very gently put his arms out towards her. She stretched out her hands and lifted her face to meet his as his mouth found hers. He kissed her desperately.

When he came up for air he spoke, his eyes misty with love and desire. 'I've missed you so . . . I've been so worried . . .' He covered her face with kisses and then pulled away once more, cradling her face in his hands. 'You've no idea how much I've wanted to see you. I just had to come, Charlotte.'

She clung on to his hands as tightly as if she were drowning. 'I need you too, Daniel. I'm glad you came. I wanted to see you, but I was scared . . . I felt so . . .'

'Ssssh . . .' he said. Then he put his mouth over hers once more and kissed her with all the love and tenderness too long denied.

Chapter Thirty-two

He'd wanted to whisk her off to Paris, or the south of France, or the Seychelles . . . anywhere she wanted. Just so that they could be quiet and have some time to heal their wounds and get to know each other again.

Charlotte had gently but firmly refused. She was grateful for the invitation, but the only place she wanted to be was home. Leaving again would have been like running away, and she might be afraid of returning. She had to learn to face life all over again. And now what she craved more than anything was some relative normality in her life.

She couldn't go back to work – it didn't exist any more. Now that the publisher was in jail, the business had been frozen. The magazine's assets could not be touched, pending the trial. All the staff had been suspended and were now trying to find new jobs. On top of everything else Charlotte had to deal with her feelings of guilt and responsibility for her staff. She could only console herself with the fact that they were all in the same boat together.

Physically she felt over the worst. Her bruises had faded and the score marks on her arms had entirely disappeared. She'd even started going back to the gym in order to get some tone back into her ill-used muscles. Her hair, which for weeks after the kidnapping had been lacklustre, was now shining with new health and body. On the surface she looked like the old Charlotte, or if anything, better than the old Charlotte. It was only when you looked deep into those misty green eyes that you caught a hint that something was amiss. There was a tiny, almost undetectable trace of hurt, of a deep wound that still oozed somewhere inside her. Her hands were not quite so steady as they had been before, and her nights were frequently broken by cruel night terrors in which she was barred in some stinking pit, alone and tortured, with a toothless monster prowling around on the other side of her prison door. Those nights she would wake up screaming, her bedclothes drenched in sweat and her body shaking in fear. On the few nights that she allowed Daniel to stay with her in her bed he would cradle her gently to him and whisper quietly in her ear, stroking her hair lightly, and soothing her with his caresses so that eventually she would drift back to sleep safe in the circle of his arms.

But in the six weeks since she had been let out of the hospital she had not let him love her in the way she knew he wanted to above all. She was petrified of making love. The first time he had tried was shortly after she had returned to the little house in Battersea. She had cooked for Daniel and they had got pleasantly tipsy on a bottle of Saint Emilion. He had kissed her and then tried to stroke her breast. At first she had pressed against him but then he felt her stiffen and withdraw.

'My love? Are you all right? What is it?'

'I don't know, Daniel, it's just that I don't think I'm ready yet . . .'

He had pulled away from her straight away. Not angrily, but gently and sympathetically. 'Of course, my darling. I understand. After what you've been through it's no wonder. You just wait, and whenever you're ready well I'll be here. We've got all the time in the world.'

Since then he had been a mother, father, brother and sister to her. He had made her laugh, taken her out, stayed in with her, talked her through her depressions and carried her through the nightmares. Their love had deepened and blossomed more than either of them thought possible, but still she felt she was not ready to meet his needs yet.

Early one gloriously sunny day, Daniel arrived carrying a huge hamper. 'Get your togs ready, we're going on an expedition. Today you and me are going in search of the great British beach.'

Dutifully she collected her swimsuit and tanning lotion and they set off in the car in search of sand and sea, Bruce Springsteen shouting at them from the stereo. Apart from when he had to change gear, Daniel held on to her hand firmly so that it rested comfortably against his bare thigh. Her hand felt cool and small inside his grasp. Clasped between his powerful but tender grip she felt wonderfully safe and cared for, as if all her security now nestled in the circle of his fingers. She wriggled her hand in further and his lips twitched into a small smile as he squeezed her fingers lightly in answer. She leaned back against the seat and breathed out slowly, feeling more relaxed and happy than she had done for many weeks, conscious only of the breeze through the open windows, and the delicious, dry heat of his hand.

Where her fingers rested, she felt she could discern a slight pulse, whether from her own fingers or his it was impossible to tell, but she was somehow reminded of his almost animal sexuality. She thought back to the first time she had met him when he had seemed like a restrained beast in his beautifully cut suit. Then she had felt threatened by him, now she felt protected by him. And that small pulse that throbbed between their fingertips brought back to her the pleasure his body had unleashed in her. Suddenly she was almost painfully conscious of his thigh, which before had been just a resting place for a trusting hand. Now it was a naked, hard, muscular limb that had pressed against her own languidly compliant body. She shuddered. The memory sent tiny tremors along her arms, down across her shoulders and through her tingling spine. She pushed down still harder with her hand, so that she could savour the feel of his skin.

She opened her lips slightly, for her breath had quickened and her breasts seemed to swell against the tight bodice of her cotton dress. Her whole body had started to tingle with this new-found awareness of him. She slowly gazed at his profile which had become so familiar to her. His eyes crinkled at the corners where he squinted at the sunlight, and the two lines of dark lashes met in an enticing little point. He too looked relaxed and happy. The hard set of his mouth, which had been present ever since he had visited her in hospital, now seemed to have melted away, taking the years with it.

She reached out and touched his mouth gently, brushing the very edge of his lips, in the crease where top and bottom met. The vague feelings that had been nudging her along were now becoming almost unbearable.

He turned to her briefly. 'Are you OK, my love?'

She nodded, afraid to speak for the lump in her throat. In any event, her eyes gave it all away. Her fingers itched to touch him all over, to feel his beautiful body against her hands. Tentatively, almost shyly, she stroked his thigh, letting the thick dark hairs tickle the tips of her fingers. Then she slid her palm more firmly and confidently along the inside of his leg, up towards his zip. She heard him draw in his breath and then almost hold it, as if he too were afraid.

'Charlotte . . . what's happening . . . ?'

Suddenly she wanted to laugh, to giggle. Her need for him was unbearable and delicious and paramount. It all seemed so easy now. The strangeness lay not in her behaviour, but in his question. What was happening between them should be the most natural thing in the world. She wanted to throw her head back and laugh out loud. 'I want you, Daniel,' she almost shrieked. 'I want to make love to you. I want to kiss you all over, every bit of you . . .' She reached over towards his zip and he caught a glimpse of something that looked remarkably like mischief in her eyes.

With her laugh the ice cracked. Until he heard that sound Daniel too had been shy. He had felt as though he must treat her with the kid-glove nurturing of the convalescent. He could not show her any passion, only tenderness. All his other feelings had been held severely in check. And with the passing of time, although their relationship was emotionally warm and loving and relaxed, a tension had built up around their sexuality. It was almost as if they had never been to bed together at all and the longer Charlotte had taken to lower her defences, physically, the more Daniel had built up a sense of reverence for her welfare. And that reverence was something of a barrier to cross in order to resume the idyllic love they had found on Anguilla.

Had she simply kissed him, and led him on through some kind of natural progression to their coupling, he would have felt self-conscious and timid with her. But that glint of mischief and healthy laughter showed him the old Charlotte. She was ready, and he too threw back his head and laughed.

His eyes never left the road ahead as she reached over with her other hand and very slowly and carefully unzipped his shorts and then reached down inside his pants to tenderly pull out his already swollen cock. Forming her hand into a light fist, she slid it up the length of the warm shaft and back again, feeling a delicious melting inside her gut as he moaned aloud and stretched his legs out as far as he could in the driving well. Still he did not look at her. Maybe, Charlotte thought, he might think it would stop if he broke the spell. He seemed to be almost holding his breath, anticipating what might happen next. Suddenly she wanted to show him that she wanted him more than anything.

She wanted to show him that she was all right, that she was ready to be his woman fully, that they could once more discover those parts of each other that had brought them to such peaks of ecstasy all those weeks ago. Undoing her seatbelt she bent her head over his lap and closed her lips over him, sliding him deep inside her mouth, savouring the delicious salty taste of him that brought her almost to the edge of her own orgasm. As she busied herself on him she realized that the car must have stopped, for Daniel was clutching at her hair and forcing his hips up towards her, driving himself deeper into her mouth. She knew he must be close to coming and still she worked her tongue around him, teasing and squeezing and licking in order to drive him crazy.

'Charlotte . . .' she heard him say, and he gently but firmly lifted her face to his. 'I want to make love to you, my darling.' His voice sounded gruff and throaty. He zipped his shorts up with difficulty and climbed out of the car. She got out too and he took her hand, leading her through the gateway where they had stopped and into a field of ripening grain. He flattened a space for them and lay down, pulling her down with him. He kissed her face desperately while she searched for his mouth with her own. Then he pulled away.

'Charlotte . . . are you sure?'

She nodded silently and returned his kisses as passionately. He stroked her face and hair and laid light butterfly touches on her eyelids, then very slowly he slid his hand up her skirt and slipped his fingers under her knickers, finding her soft and warm and wet and

456

ready for him. This time it was she who sensed he was holding back, as if he were afraid.

She deftly slipped her pants off and pulled him over on top of her, feeling the agonizingly beautiful sensation as he slipped into her. With every thrust of his, she rose to meet him, bracing herself hard against him, matching his desperation with her own. The sweat broke out on their bodies and their legs slipped together as if they had been bathed in warm oil. She craned herself upwards into him, so that she could feel his hard chest against her breasts, and she clutched him so tightly she felt she might hurt him. She had no thought for the hard straw on her back, or the uneven soil beneath that. Nor did she mind the tiny flies that tickled her arms. Both Daniel and Charlotte could have been trampled upon by an angry farmer for all they cared, for they were lost in their own private paradise, oblivious to everything except their own two bodies, now exploding together in shattering orgasm, crying out in their ecstasy.

They lay there for a long time, silently, just revelling in the feel of their bodies, full of joy for what they had rediscovered. Eventually Daniel was the first to move. Charlotte rearranged herself and was sitting up demurely when he returned from the car. He carried the picnic hamper over to her, and then spread out the rug.

'We could have done with this just now,' he laughed.

'I didn't notice,' she said softly, grinning back at him.

'Hungry?'

'Like I haven't been in weeks,' she said, gleefully lifting the wicker lid and peeping inside to see what goodies he had seen fit to bring. One by one he unpacked mouthwatering slices of smoked salmon, delicious asparagus rolls, fine French cheeses, boiled

quails' eggs and crisp salads; followed by fresh strawberries and passion fruit.

'Daniel . . .' she sighed, utter happiness oozing out of
every pore, 'how on earth did you manage to put all this
lot together?'

'I just made a telephone call yesterday. Messrs
Fortnum and Mason did the rest.'

'Mmmmm,' she sighed. 'What a perfect day. But what
about the seaside?'

'Well, quite honestly, my love, after what's happened
today I think missing the seaside is probably one of the
best things to have ever happened to me. This little field
here is the only place I want to be right now, next to
you. Here, have some more champagne.'

She held out her glass and laughed. 'My God, the
decadence of it. Champagne and screwing in the straw.'

'Tumbling, my love, not "screwing", we're in the
country now. I'd like to tumble you again too . . .'

He lurched towards her and she sprang out of the
way. 'Later, you animal. Maybe after lunch. I suppose
you're going to be insatiable, now your enforced
celibacy's over.'

He laughed and disappeared off to the car again,
leaving her to finish the plump strawberries. When he
returned he sat down next to her and then lay down on
his side, his back turned towards her, leaning his head
on his crooked arm. He seemed intent on studying
something.

She leaned over to see. He was reading a magazine.

She felt abandoned. They had just shared the most
wonderful lovemaking and he had now withdrawn
from her to read. It was as cold a move as if he had
turned over in the bed and gone off to sleep. Here she
was still warm and loving and he chose to read a bloody
magazine. She pouted at his shoulders. Then she could
contain herself no more.

'Daniel, what are you doing?' she said coldly.

'Hmmm, what did you say, darling?' He half turned towards her but still held the pages open, as if he would immediately turn back to it, having dealt with her.

'What are you doing? It looks as though you're reading.'

'Oh yes,' he smiled innocently, 'I am. You don't mind, do you?'

'Yes, as a matter of fact I do! What we just did may mean nothing to you, but to me it meant a hell of a lot, and now all you're interested in is reading some magazine.'

'Well, actually I bought it for *you*.' He stressed the last word. Then he closed the magazine up and handed it to her. 'Here . . . it's yours.' She looked at it. It was the last copy of *Amber* to be published.

She looked up at him, hurt and anxiety crossing her features. 'Daniel, if that's a joke it's not very funny.' Her voice rose indignantly.

'Why don't you open it!'

She glowered at him, but did as he bid her. She opened the cover and there, clipped on to the inside page, was a contract. She read it quickly, and then read it again, still not understanding. 'But what does it mean, Daniel? It seems to be some kind of share contract.'

'One hundred shares of *Amber* to be exact.'

She shook her head. 'I still don't understand. What does it mean?' she repeated.

'It means, my darling Charlotte, that you own *Amber* . . . Here . . .' He pointed to the line. '"Editor in Chief and Publisher, Charlotte Grange".'

'But how can I possibly? I mean it's frozen, isn't it? Pending the trial. That's why everyone lost their jobs!'

'Oh, that *Amber* is. This is a different *Amber*,' he said in a voice which implied that he was stating the obvious. 'This is the new one . . . yours, my darling. The new one with the old editor . . . and the old staff if you want

459

them. But you've got new premises, . . . and new printers,' he added quickly.

'What have you done?'

'I told you, I've bought you a magazine. Let's just call it an early wedding present, shall we?'

'But you haven't even asked.'

'I just did.'

She pulled a little moue. 'And if I say no?'

He bent and grabbed at the copy of *Amber* clutched between her hands which she quickly snatched out of his grasp. 'Well, I'll have to take it back and find it another home.'

She clutched the magazine tightly to her. 'Oh no. I'm afraid you'll have to take us both.'

He knelt down beside her and pulled her into his arms. 'I couldn't have lived with it any other way.' He leaned his head forward and pressed his mouth to hers, until her arms reached out for him, casting the copy of *Amber* aside, burying herself inside his embrace, the only place on earth she ever wanted to be.

Fontana Fiction

Fontana is a leading paperback publisher of fiction. Below are some recent titles.

- ☐ KRYSALIS John Trenhaile £3.99
- ☐ PRINCES OF SANDASTRE Antony Swithin £2.99
- ☐ NIGHT WATCH Alastair MacNeill £3.50
- ☐ THE MINOTAUR Stephen Coonts £4.50
- ☐ THE QUEEN'S SECRET Jean Plaidy £3.99
- ☐ THE LEMON TREE Helen Forrester £3.99
- ☐ THE THIRTEEN-GUN SALUTE Patrick O'Brian £3.50
- ☐ STONE CITY Mitchell Smith £4.50
- ☐ ONLY YESTERDAY Syrell Leahy £2.99
- ☐ SHARPE'S WATERLOO Bernard Cornwell £3.50
- ☐ BLOOD BROTHER Brian Morrison £3.50
- ☐ THE BROW OF THE GALLOWGATE Doris Davidson £3.50

You can buy Fontana paperbacks at your local bookshop or newsagent. Or you can order them from Fontana, Cash Sales Department, Box 29, Douglas, Isle of Man. Please send a cheque, postal or money order (not currency) worth the purchase price plus 22p per book for postage (maximum postage required is £3.00 for orders within the UK).

NAME (Block letters)_____

ADDRESS_____

_____